D0374795

Mother India

MOTHER INDIA

A Novel

Tova Reich

SYRACUSE UNIVERSITY PRESS

A section of this novel was written at the Radcliffe Institute for Advanced Study at Harvard University.

Syracuse University Press
Syracuse, New York 13244-5290

First Edition 2018
18 19 20 21 22 23   6 5 4 3 2 1

∞ The paper used in this publication meets the minimum requirements of the American National Standard for Information Sciences—Permanence of Paper for Printed Library Materials, ANSI Z39.48-1992.

For a listing of books published and distributed by Syracuse University Press, visit www.SyracuseUniversityPress.syr.edu.

ISBN: 978-0-8156-1106-6 (hardcover)   978-0-8156-5454-4 (e-book)

Library of Congress Cataloging-in-Publication Data
Names: Reich, Tova, author.
Title: Mother India : a novel / Tova Reich.
Description: First edition. | Syracuse, New York : Syracuse University Press, 2018.
Identifiers: LCCN 2018024320 (print) | LCCN 2018025396 (ebook) |
    ISBN 9780815654544 (E-book) | ISBN 9780815611066 (Hardback)
Subjects: LCSH: Jews—United States—Fiction. | Jewish fiction. | Satire.
Classification: LCC PS3568.E4763 (ebook) | LCC PS3568.E4763 M68 2018 (print) |
    DDC 813/.54—dc23
LC record available at https://lccn.loc.gov/2018024320

Manufactured in the United States of America

To the memory of my father,
MOSHE WEISS

Contents

Ma

THE HOLY MAN SAID, "Whosoever dies in Varanasi will achieve liberation, even a cockroach."

It was the boldface pullout quote in a magazine my mother opened at random during chemotherapy at her local medical center in Brooklyn. Lounging on the salmon-colored leatherette recliner as the toxic infusion dripped into her veins, Ma read every single word of the article. She had been looking forward to death as liberation was how she justified it to me later—so what was this business now of having to schlep all the way to Varanasi, India, nearly eight thousand miles away on the backside of the earth?

But as she continued to reflect on it, she recognized that liberation was actually not in the cards in the Jewish death deal. Where you landed in the next world, heaven or hell, *Gan Eden* or *Gehinnom*, depended on your docket in this one, you were never truly liberated from the fallout from this life. And this was also true in the over-crowded Hindu cosmos, with its thirty-six million idols and *getchkes*. Depending on your performance evaluation on this earth, you were reborn in another form, as a starlet or a slug, to plod all over again. Only if you died in Varanasi were you guaranteed moksha regardless of your record, the holy man declared, only by dying in Varanasi in the lap of Mother Ganga would you achieve true release from the wheel of life, liberation from the grinding cycle of death and rebirth. The afterlife was this life, the one she had been living. This was a truth Ma now grasped. She had suspected it all along, it explained everything. She had been stuck in the punishment of her afterlife all these years. She had no interest in another sequel.

It was not an accident that Ma's hand had fallen upon that maga-zine and that it had opened itself up like an exhaled breath to that page. It was her karma, she told me with the wicked grin of an initiate. The holy man was speaking directly to her; he was sending her a message, special delivery. It was then and there, as she spun it to me afterward, in that chemo parlor with its décor the color of viscera that she was swept up by her inspiration. She would stop all her treatments and go to Varanasi to die.

Anyone who had ever laid eyes on my mother or scanned a few bullet points of her résumé (if she ever had a résumé, which certainly she did not) would find it absurdly farfetched to believe she could be capable of gestating such a heretical desire, much less summon up the energy and nerve to actually carry it to term. We're talking here about an ultra–Orthodox Jewish woman closing in on the finish line of her eighth decade in a lifespan traditionally calculated at three score and ten, hanging on past the statute of limitations, living on borrowed time—the wife of a rabbi, a rebbetzin, mother of nine, grandmother to many. How many? Don't ask. That's a question she would have never answered. Jews do not count their own; God does not take kindly to that, it can be fatal. On top of that, she was stricken with stage four breast cancer, an Ashkenazi Jewish specialty like gefilte fish; it had occupied all her territory, though you might never have guessed it by eyeballing her. As a proper religious matron, she had always worn a wig, well before she lost all her hair from the chemo, and she still weighed in at close to 250 pounds. "Finally, a diet that would do the trick," Ma said, recalling an inappropriate thought that had shot through her brain when she had gotten her diagnosis—a secondary benefit of illness. "But nothing doing." And she waved a hand in resignation down over the mass of her stubborn flesh.

The other deviant thought that had flashed with the news of her death sentence, Ma admitted to me later, was that now, finally, she had been given permission to make her exit, following, of course, the ritual sadistic formalities for the sake of family, of pretending to fight for her life, pulling out all the stops, pushing to the limit of cutting-edge medical technology no matter how agonizing or pitiful or futile or costly, no matter how much everyone in her orbit secretly wanted to close her file. A longtime fan of obituaries, Ma's first thought as she pored over those case-closed mug shots every morning was invariably, It's over, Lucky you, No one will bother you anymore, Don't worry, you're not missing a thing. Still, suicide, it goes without saying, was not an option. First of all, it's a sin. Second, it's hard, it's messy, it requires a lot of initiative and motivation; you need to be a self-starter. But above all, it is not considerate, it would inflict too much pain and guilt on your loved ones, not to mention how boiling mad they would be at her for doing this to them, how unforgiving and lacking in understanding or sympathy.

But the truth was, she was tired of forever being pressured to hold out. She had been looking forward to the liberation of death, it would finally make her breathe easier, as it were. And now this woman, my mother, who always did what was expected of her, who had never openly rebelled in her life, whose axis of influence was a lopsided tri-angle with three fixed retro-shtetl points, Brooklyn, Miami, Jerusalem, suddenly gets the news that it ain't over 'til the fat lady sings. A grand finale was still required of her. She still had to rise from her bed and muster whatever remaining shreds of vitality she possessed to drag her 250 diseased pounds to the faraway rotting stage of Varanasi, packed with filthy bit players and reeking scenery to belt out her final full-throated aria if she wanted to achieve true liberation. A casual bystander might find it incredible that such a woman would heed such a casting call, but to my mind, it was inevitable, it made total sense.

Needless to say, I don't want this story to be about me, but as it happens, the notion of India was not all that alien to my mother despite her super-conventional stereotypical lifestyle (viewed, of course, in the context of the overall bizarreness of rigidly observant Jewish practice). For that, I am obliged to admit, I deserve the credit, or whatever. And so it is necessary for me to make what I hope will be limited to a cameo appearance in what is, let us never forget this for a minute, my mother's end-of-life story.

The fact is, I'm an old India hand, a Hin-Jew, a Jewbude, how-ever you want to process it. My fascination with India began in my earliest years, thanks to my mother as it happened, who at that time knew nothing at all about the place except that its starving children were feverish to get their hands on the slabs of schnitzel that my twin brother, Shmelke, and I were taking so for granted, dragging them listlessly around our plates, swirling them like finger paint through pools of ketchup instead of eating them. The problem was enormous, insoluble. How could I get the schnitzel to the starving children of India in time to save them? It was beyond my powers, I was flooded with guilt. That was my introduction to India, a faraway land swarming with kids dying for my schnitzel.

Then, when Shmelke and I were maybe five years old, before we were torn apart yet again and sentenced to separate bedrooms, I happened to find in a garbage pail set out for pickup on the curb of our Brooklyn street a picture book sodden with coffee grinds and potato peels, about Hindu gods and goddesses, an object I instinctively assumed to have been confiscated from some kid in our neighborhood who had gone off the rails, God alone knows at what station she ended up. Shmelke and I read this contraband every night, not including the Sabbath, under the covers with a flashlight, we knew all the stories by heart—by heart! I was particularly blown away by the tale of the twin brother and sister, Yama and Yami, the first mortals on earth. Like Yami, I begged my Yama, my twin brother, Shmelke, to marry me. Why not? Why should this not be possible? How could there be closeness tighter than that of twins, so spiritually conjoined? Only an arrogant fool would presume to insert himself between two so bound up together even from the womb and attempt to split them apart. Hadn't Cain and Abel, according to legend, married their twin sisters—for how else other than through the implicit existence of twin sisters could all that begetting have gotten its kick start, since no mention needless to say is made of female births in the first family? Yet Shmelke turned me down, a rejection that still throbs in memory to this day, like a savagely amputated limb. It was against the laws of the Torah, he pronounced sagely: The nakedness of your sister you may not uncover, Leviticus chapter eighteen verse nine. Already he was a prodigy, an *ilui*, a category applied only to boys, with a royal career mapped out before him by our father and his hand-picked team of tutors and groomers.

I don't want to dwell on this, but the gist is, with regard to India, having suffered rejection by the one whom naked I had embraced for nine months in the womb and all that preceded this and followed from the moment we emerged from between our mother's legs into the night, I basically went native. My former wife, Geeta, is Indian, a stunning blue-eyed, mocha-skinned Kashmiri of the Brahmin caste, which makes her also, in a sense, for what it's worth, a rabbi's daughter. Together we ran a travel business in Mumbai, known in those days as M&G (Meena—that's me, formerly Mina—and Geeta) Sati Trips. In Sanskrit *sati* means good wife, but it's also the word for the outlawed (like dueling, yet also not without its legendary satisfactions) Hindu practice of the widow immolating herself in the flames of her husband's funeral pyre. For our primarily female clientele, however, we repackaged this intrinsically sexist concept in an intriguing new light with the prompt of our slogan: India Is Hot. Jump In. The message resonated phenomenally with our women seekers, predominantly from North America and Israel, who flocked to my call to ashrams and meditation sites, yoga retreats and Ayurveda healing centers in India—in Kerala and Tamil Nadu in the south, or, depending on the season, the good old reliables, Dharamsala and Rishikesh in the north—for periods of about two weeks.

It was a travel-intensive enterprise. Too often, I admit, I was flying madly here and there, stroking clients, dealing with our far-flung agents, fine-tuning tour schedules, handling emergencies physical and spiritual from Delhi belly to Dharma syndrome, managing drug flipouts, the whole deal, forced by all of these pressures to delegate my daily responsibilities as a single mom for my daughter, Maya. Thank God I'd mostly been able to find decent childcare (with some painful exceptions), especially since Geeta, Maya's adoptive mother no less and a lady with an enviably flexible schedule to say the least, proved maddeningly unreliable even in her finest hour, and Maya's semen donor, my stab at a husband, Shmiel the schlemiel Shapiro, was out of commission, a willing exile in Jerusalem where he was known as the Holy Beggar, self-appointed caretaker of the gravesite of the celebrated Hasidic minstrel Reb Shlomo Carlebach.

Strumming out of tune the only three chords in a minor key that he managed to halfway master, Shmiel could be found every day except the Sabbath up at the Har haMenukhot cemetery, parked under a marquee emblazoned with the epitaph, "*Mamesh a Gevalt* the Sweetest of the Sweet," his cardboard guitar case open at his feet filling up with coins and bills deposited by the stream of pilgrims and lost souls and borderline cases trudging up the mountain to join the sing-along, to weep and spill out their hearts like water at the holy grave. The good news was, for the first time in his life my loser ex was making a halfway decent living. Far be it for me to have begrudged him, yet it might be worth noting the obvious here, of which I am perfectly aware, if only to justify why against my nature I ever hooked up with a man in the first place other than to fulfill the predestined birth of Maya. His name is one of the diminutives for Shmuel, Samuel, like the name of my brother, Shmelke. All my life I have been searching for my lost inner Sam, the holy man might have said.

With regard to my mother, though, the main point is, that thanks to me, not only India, but also the possibility of rebellion was not so foreign to her, not in the heavens but on the near horizon, close at hand. Ma had me as a model, my lifelong career as a free radical, its early onset in my adolescent acting out—black hair wild to the waist, diamond stud in the cleft of my nostril, lotus tattoo like a locket at the base of my throat, the full original presentation of my identity politics—and these were just some of the external manifestations that she and my father the rabbi and the entire neighborhood and the whole congregation of Israel could actually witness and testify to.

He pretended as much as possible to be oblivious to all of it, my father the rabbi—that was his defensive stance; he wouldn't see it so it wasn't there. (Like God who is also invisible? I challenged him.) He also dismissed my fixation with India, refusing to take seriously any religion reputed to be nonviolent (however mistakenly), such as Hinduism or Buddhism: not major players, harmless, pareve, neither meat nor dairy. My worship was benign, nothing that required emergency excision, certainly not in the same league as a religion with muscle, a hard-core apostasy like converting to Christianity, God forbid. So when I brought Geeta to them as my true intended, my destined one, my *bashert'e*, he at first made a big provincial joke out of it, claiming Geeta as one of ours, insisting that she was really just another nice Jewish girl, a Marrano, a member of the lost tribe of Menashe, she looked like such a proper *balabatische Yiddish'e maidel*, and wasn't her name Geeta after all, such a respectable Yiddish name, Gitel, it means good, he had an aunt named Gitel, *Tante Gitel'e*, murdered in the gas chambers by the Nazi killers, may their name and memory be blotted out from the face of the earth.

But I would not back down, I refused to allow him to patronize my reality or the reality of my bride. Sorry Pop, no way Geeta is Jewish, Geeta is purebred Indian, 100 percent, top caste. It was then that my father spat into our shared air space the word "*Indyk!*" which means not only Indian in Yiddish but also turkey. Good, at least he's mad now, I thought, at least it has registered finally that I'm not kidding around. *Halleluah!* I cried. And digging even deeper into the praise-God book of Psalms for further ammunition, I added jubilantly, *Hodu laShem Ki Tov*—Give Thanks to God for He is Good—because *Hodu* means not only thanksgiving, it is also Hebrew for India. Therefore, as I pointed out to my father the rabbi and scholar but no gentle-man (what for a gentleman?), it can also be interpreted as "India is to God for it is good"—and within the godly goodness of India, I embraced my divine Geeta, my wife. The old man barked out a sharp little laugh, rejecting the seriousness of this new development as well. Such relations between women were meaningless. The Torah does not even condescend to mention them for the sake of forbidding them because they produce nothing, they're ridiculous, the mechanics were beyond his imagination.

Still, I would not let him dismiss me. I insisted on due defer-ence to my choice, a full-scale wedding, never mind that I was already an independent operator at an advanced age. It was a father's responsibility to give his daughter a proper wedding, not like the slapped-together, under-the-radar shotgun affair that had made it official between me and Shmiel. This time I was going to collect all the celebratory shards of broken plates and glasses I deserved—the dancing chairs, the complete smorgasbord including the ice sculpture in the shape of a swan, every last crumb of daughterly entitlement. "So you want a Jewish wedding?" Ma remarked after a prolonged thoughtful pause when I was done with my pitch. "Nu, so okay. But just in case you don't happen to know this, the custom is, the bride's family pays for everything except FLOPS—flowers, liquor, orchestra, photography, and sheitel (that's the matron's wig). So since it's a question of money, what I need to know right now is—are we the parents of the bride or the groom?"

Privately, not long afterward, Ma recapped for me something she had read, also in a magazine—that it had been scientifically proven that certain women prefer women because they find men too powerful and threatening. And then she confided an odd bit of personal trivia—that she herself, ever since she had been a young girl, would play this little trick in her mind, turn a man into a woman whenever she experienced him as too uncontrollable and dominant, a practice she occasionally indulged in even to that day. "How?" I inquired. "By imagining him in a dress, of course, silly. Even your father sometimes. It's very becoming." My mother—she was such a bandit, or, as she would have pronounced it, ban*dit*. God, I miss her and her rapier wit.

Well, enough already about me. Bottom line—India was heavily punctuated on my mother's radar screen. When it became clear that Ma was not budging, that she was firm in her determination to finish up in Varanasi in order to achieve liberation as the holy man had guaranteed, she let my father know her intention, framing it as her last wish. What could he do? How could he deny her? Would anyone with a heart turn down a dying child's final request for a trip to Disneyland? The same principle applied in Ma's case. I proceeded, not only as a good daughter but also as a travel specialist, to make all the arrangements and booked Ma's passage to India. Toward the end of December, around Christmastime by the calendar of the goyim, we flew Turkish Air business class to New Delhi, with a brief stopover in Istanbul, and then Kingfisher from Delhi to Varanasi. *Hodu laShem Ki Tov.*

The apartment I had leased in advance for my mother was located on the ground floor of the building in which the Chabad mission was housed, not far from Assi Ghat, the southernmost of the eighty-plus ghats stretching along the sacred bank of the Ganges River in Varanasi. My strategy was to settle Ma in a place where there would at least be some familiar markers, even if it were nothing more than the smell of chicken soup simmering on Friday afternoons wafting on the wings of malaria flies. The emissaries who ran this outpost, the *shlukhim* Rabbi Assi (yes, of Assi Ghat, an auspicious coincidence—short for Assaf) and his rebbetzin Dassi (Hadas), had in fact been very helpful to me in nailing down and setting up the apartment, and though we never came to a formal agreement, it was understood that they would not only be aware of Ma's presence, they would also check on her regularly to make sure she was still breathing and had everything she needed, they would be my point team on the ground and serve as my contacts in case of an emergency. This was a mitzvah, the chance to perform a *hessed*, an act of loving-kindness for another human being; it was an opportunity that had fallen into their laps, as if from the heavens, they considered themselves fortunate and blessed.

I feel obliged to note here, with no intention whatsoever of diminishing the generosity of Assi and Dassi but for the purpose of complete transparency, that they also were acutely aware that this old lady they would be babysitting was none other than the mother of Reb Breslov Tabor, as my twin brother, Shmelke, was known by then—notorious, hunted, the fiercely controversial leader of a rival sect, but still, indisputably, one of the *gedolim*, one of the greats of the generation before whom all must rise when he enters your airspace. It was bottom-line nothing less than an honor, and so they conceived of it, to be of some service in her final hours to the holy mother who bore this genius. And after all, Ma was a seeker, too, not so very different from all the other

Jewish seekers who passed through this polluted idolatrous city whom they were charged with rescuing, mostly young Israeli post-army kids crashing after all the stress of their mandatory stint in wretched holes like Gaza and Jenin, ravenously into drugs, sex, and music—only my mother was into death at the other end of the age spectrum.

They were not ageists, Rabbi Assi and his rebbetzin Dassi, they were inclusive, they didn't discriminate when it came to saving Jews. They too had come to Varanasi from Israel, from secular families, he from the development town of Dimona in the South, home to the Black Hebrews who are not Hebrew and the nuclear reactor that doesn't exist, she from the grim city of Afula in the north, otherwise known as the anus of the world, famous throughout the Middle East for the balls of falafel it excreted. They made their way to Varanasi in search of enlightenment directly after their rite-of-passage military service, and, like all the other deluded Israelis, sank to the lowest depths in this idol-worshipping underworld, they would spare me all the ugly details, until the true path revealed itself to them, as if a veil had lifted to illuminate what had always been there, their birthright, their legacy, right there in front of their eyes—It was like a vision, the rebbetzin recalled, We were as if dreaming. They would look after Ma, they assured me. The holy Rebbe Himself had sent them to this heathen place precisely to reach out to such wandering Jews, even to such endangered species as my mother no matter how little life remained in them yet. And soon, soon, God willing, the holy Rebbe Himself, our Master, our Teacher, our Rabbi, will rise from conceal-ment in His true form as the Messiah the King to rescue the living and to raise the dead.

Well, he'd better hurry up, I was about to say but held my tongue. The other day Ma dropped a reference to cremation. Does the Mes-siah do ashes?

What I need to report here, though, is how irrationally, regres-sively thrilled I felt when my mother approved of nearly every detail of my arrangements. Not only that, but for the first time in God alone knows how many years she even gave me a compliment on my appear-ance—she admired my long black braid. "So shiny, like a shampoo ad in a magazine." She pressed her finger tenderly on the red tikka on my forehead as if she were suctioning up the last moist cake crumb from the table—my third eye, the sign that I am a married woman.

As for the apartment, she was unambivalently enraptured by it—it was perfect. She had never had even a room of her own, much less an entire dwelling place. She appreciated the mezuzot that Rabbi Assi had affixed to the doorposts. She was pleased with the simple but adequate furniture, the clean bed, the soft couch, the sturdy kitchen table and two solid chairs, the dishes and cutlery and pots and pans all clearly marked in big, bright letters for clouded eyes—blue for milk, red for meat. She acknowledged my thoughtful considerateness in choosing an apartment on the ground floor with no steps for her to negotiate. She was grateful for the uniformed guard at the door of the building in the wake of the bloody slaughter by terrorists at Nariman House, the Chabad headquarters in my own city of Mumbai. She especially enjoyed the drop-in visits of the two oldest of Rabbi Assi and Dassi's seven children, the fraternal twins (precious evocations of Shmelke and me no doubt), Menachem Mendel and Chaya Mushka, age six. There was always a supply of unhealthy treats stocked for them, such as bags of Bissli and Bamba imported from Israel, in a special drawer they flew to directly.

But above all she was delighted with the small terrace situated off the living room with its white molded plastic porch furniture. During her first weeks in Varanasi, her period of adjustment, she would sit there almost every day for as long as there was light with a can of diet soda on the table beside her or an unglazed clay cup of lemon tea, which she sipped to its dregs through a sugar cube wedged between her dentures, then thrillingly threw on the stone-tiled floor smashing it to pieces, ecologically recycling it back to the dust whence it had come. With her edematous feet propped up on a stool, she took in the uproar, the perpetual frenzy of the swarming street as if on stage before her, streaked with color, pulsing with sound—ox carts, bicycle rickshaws, autorickshaws rumbling by, horns bleating in desperation nonstop, children running wild, weaving through the throngs, picking pockets, squatting to defecate on the ground with one arm extended for alms, naked sadhus smeared in white ash with matted hair, beggars with missing limbs, women pounding on car windows, opening and closing their mouths like marionettes to mimic hunger, deformed children harnessed to mutilated babies, goats, cows, water buffalos, stray dogs, monkeys, now and then a boar, once an elephant, several times a day a dead body covered in saffron-colored cloth, bedecked with garlands of orange and yellow marigolds, borne through the streets on a bamboo stretcher followed by chanting mourners on the way to the cremation ghats of Harishchandra or Manikarnika along the banks of the Ganges.

When things quieted down, toward evening, she would continue to sit there leafing through magazines, talking on the cell phone I had given her, feeding pieces of challah and matzah to the silver-gray monkey that had befriended her whom she called Fetter Feivish, since he reminded her both in expression and the habit of casually manipulating his privates of her long-dead Uncle Feivel, or simply leaning back with her head resting against a cushion and her eyes closed, her face turned up to receive the last rays of the sun.

The weather was still warm and comfortable when I settled my mother into her Varanasi apartment. The crushing heat had not yet arrived to stupefy the brain and bring on the annual epidemic of sluggishness and madness. The monsoon season was still months away with its drenching rains that would flood holy Mother Ganga and send her waters choked with the ashes and bones and unburned body parts of the dead and the rotting carcasses of lepers and pregnant women, children and cattle rising up the steps of the ghats and lapping like a prehistoric monster through the streets of the city.

The apartment also came equipped with a servant who was sitting on her haunches in a corner of the kitchen in a kind of copse composed of the squeegee, the stunted straw broom, the mop, the dustpan, and other assorted forlorn cleaning implements as Dassi was showing us around, so that we did not at first notice her during the tour. Only when the rebbetzin announced that she was also throwing in her helper as part of Ma's package, and called out, "Manika?" did she come into focus, a tiny creature, black and shriveled like a prune. She flashed a bashful toothless smile, and automatically twitched the loose end of her green-and-orange print cotton sari forward over her head like a monk's cowl. The rebbetzin said, "Manika means jewel in their language, and I'm telling you, she is like her name. She's my gem."

Ma objected ardently, it was the only feature she disliked in the entire setup. She had been looking forward to living on her own, she valued her privacy, she didn't want or need a maid, but the rebbetzin insisted. "She's a present, you can't refuse a present, a very good girl, from the sweeper and toilet cleaner caste, we don't hold by that but it's the lowest of the low, she'll lick the cow caca off your feet for two paisa, that's their mentality, she'll do anything you ask, you won't even know she's there, like a fly."

For my part, although I found the rebbetzin's patronizing, even racist language deeply offensive, I pleaded with Ma to accept, if only for my sake, for my peace of mind, so that I could feel reassured that she would not be alone after I left. What if you slip in the tub? What if your food goes down the wrong pipe? What if something happens? My mother shook her head—she didn't want this *alter cocker* around, it made her feel like an old lady. "She's probably younger than I am, Ma," I said, but still my mother wouldn't yield. It was only after I reminded Ma of the courageous loyalty of the Indian nanny who had rescued the baby Moshe'le during the Mumbai massacre, an event as Ma well knew that had seriously impacted my life also, and of how this blessed Sandra ayah had gone on to become a heroine of the State of Israel and deservedly so, that my mother softened and finally relented, in patriotic solidarity, to hold out an incentive to other budding righteous gentiles no matter what caste, no matter where situated on the great chain of being, to do the right thing and save a Jew.

And in the end, she was happy for the company, even though, or maybe in part because they had no common language between them to communicate with. Nevertheless, they understood each other in their bones, like mother and daughter. She especially loved the long head and foot massages Manika administered, and her unfailing cheerfulness, which given her circumstances was a mystery Ma sought to unravel in the hope of gaining some spiritual insight, she told me. This was during a telephone conversation after I had already left Varanasi and returned home to Geeta and Maya, and to my office in Mumbai. Ma then went on to inform me with the superior air of an old India hand that the name Manika fit her even better than the rebbetzin could imagine—not only because she's the rebbebtzin's so-called gem, but also because of the way she would creep into Ma's bedroom at night to steal a piece of jewelry. (Ma believed in jewelry, especially gold, you could never have too much; in this as in so many other ways, I might point out, Indians and Jews are more alike than you would ever have dreamed of in your philosophy.) "She thinks I'm sleeping while she's poking around in my jewelry box, but the whole time I'm awake and I'm thinking—C'mon, hurry up, take what you want from in there and get out. Just finish your business already and let me sleep. Same like I used to think in the old days, with your father, when he used to bother me."

There was also an unforeseen advantage in setting Ma up with a servant, which I regard as priceless and treasure to this day. It emerged very soon after my departure, when I began to receive photos taken by Manika on the cell phone I had left with my mother, a reasonably high-tech mobile toy that gleamed like an onyx gemstone, which this illiterate little woman from a village without running water or sewage system or electricity promptly mastered thoroughly. These pictures form a kind of visual archive of Ma's time in Varanasi, charting her sojourn there. At first, they tended to be taken against the background of her apartment, generally on the terrace where the light must have been best. It seems my mother did not object despite the traditional strictures she had abided by all her life against allowing herself to be photographed for reasons of modesty (and also, to be completely frank, because she always thought she looked too fat). Here in Varanasi she was mellow, laid back, zen, going with the graven-image flow, easing into liberation.

The pictures that stand out from that period focused on her evolving look. In one, Ma is wearing the long tunic and ballooning pants of a *salwar kameez*, to my eyes, on my mother a costume utterly shocking, completely mind-blowing. When I mentioned it during our daily telephone conversation (yes, I called my mother every day, religiously, I'm such a good girl) adding that all of us—not only I but also her daughter-in-law Geeta and her granddaughter Maya—thought she looked absolutely gorgeous, that it suited her perfectly, Ma reflected that she had never worn pants in her life, not counting her underpants, she had never thought she would live to see the day when she would be wearing pants publicly on the outside, she should say a *She'hekhiyanu* that she had been kept alive and sustained to reach this season. The only pants she had ever expected to wear other than her personal oversized pink bloomers, her long turn-off granny *gatkes*, she went on to make a point of informing me, were the breeches that would form a part of her white linen gender-neutral burial shroud, which of course she would not be alive to see, no one would see them other than the pious ladies of the holy society who washed and purified and dressed her body for the grave, and the worms and maggots who devoured her.

In another photo from this period, Ma's head is tightly bound in a glossy magenta kerchief streaked with gold tinsel. She's sitting on her porch with Fetter Feivish, her fancy Sabbath wig plopped askew on his head. With tweezered fingers, the monkey seems to be picking nits out of her everyday wig, which is perched atop the egg-shaped Styrofoam wig stand propped on the table. "Yes, darling," Ma said, automatically slipping into her role as reinforcer of my self-esteem by complimenting me on my keen powers of observation, "that's what he's doing, Fetter. He loves lice, they're for him a delicacy, like for us chopped liver."

This was my mother, the same woman who had passed on to me her fear of animals, which still resides in me on a subliminal level but which on the surface I manage to give the appearance of having overcome, a Jewish mother who true to the boilerplate would do anything for her children, turn herself into a doormat and beg them to tread upon her, but at best could only bring herself to satisfy our entreaties for a pet by offering a doomed goldfish swimming in deep depression in a plastic bag, which she had won in a synagogue raffle—and now her best friend was a beast, a monkey, this son of Hanuman. As for her wig, I never saw it on her again. She kept her head covered with a succession of brilliant silk scarves wrapped like a turban over the downy white fuzz of her hair, which was beginning to sprout back like a tender lawn. And I never again saw her dressed in the long skirt and loose long-sleeved blouse or sweater or jacket that is the Orthodox ladies' official uniform for public appearances or the housecoat for at-home leisure wear, but always either in a salwar kameez or on special occasions, a Benares silk sari, and of course, topping it all, a shawl. Even with her mass of natural built-in padding and insulation, even before she had been consumed by malignancy, Ma was always cold. Our task as children had always been to run and fetch her a sweater or a blanket. When we would reach up for her hand, we always found a tissue there, crumpled for warmth, as if enclosing an ember rescued from the flames.

Ma is wearing a deep-green silk sari embroidered with gold thread and embedded with mirror chips and a pale pashmina dupatta, in one of the first of the series of pictures showing her venturing out of her Varanasi apartment, seated in the carriage of a rickshaw, the driver, malnourished, his brown face cratered by a childhood disease he could not have recovered from too long before, half-straddling his beat-up bicycle, beaming jubilantly. "That's Bulbul, my personal chauffeur," Ma explained. "Don't worry so much, Meena'le. He maybe looks like a ninety-pound weakling, but he's strong like an ox, he can pedal like nobody's business. He calls me Mama and tells me I'm light like smoke, the little *tukhes* licker, even though my own personal *tukhes* is hanging the whole time over the bench from the rickshaw because it's a bench not made for zaftig old ladies like me, it's made for Indians with no meat on their behinds. But I'll tell you something, Meena'le, I love that boy, I turn my pocketbook upside down and shake it out in his hands, all my rupees I give to that little no-goodnik, my last red cent." Another image in that series shows Ma enthroned in the rickshaw carriage with Manika tucked in beside her, like a tiny doll from which most of the stuffing had leaked out, a favorite, beloved doll the child refuses to leave home without. Bulbul must have shot that one.

There then follow a series of photographs in which, in addition to her personal staff consisting of Manika and Bulbul, Ma is also shown accompanied by a strikingly glamorous woman young enough to be her daughter, on the wrong side of forty-five by my estimate, though others less experienced in sizing up women would have pegged her as much younger. This newcomer on the scene is always impeccably groomed and made up, dazzling white teeth showcasing dentistry at its most state of the art, nose job, face-lift, silky platinum hair, trendy bling, tight tank top, studded leather jacket, designer jeans, stiletto-heeled boots, the works, a masterpiece of maintenance—Zehava, Ma said, my life coach. She pronounced it *koi'akh*, like the Yiddish for strength. In her former life, Zehava had been a stratospherically high placed minister in the Israeli government, with a portfolio in finance or the military, not something soft and womanish such as health or education, a paragon of feminist achievement—a big shot, according to my mother, a very important hoo-ha in the kitchen cabinet of the Knesset. Her name used to be Golda in those days, and she really did in her previous incarnation look uncannily like the legendary Golda Meir. But then she quit everything and changed her life—had an extreme makeover and turned into the Zehava, who, it seemed, had adopted my mother as her pet project.

Zehava's transformation was breathtaking. Manika sent me links to before-and-after photos of Golda/Zehava from an overpriced internet café meant for mommy-and-daddy-subsidized Lonely Planet travelers in the Assi Ghat area, the proprietor's threadbare sleeping mat glimpsed on the floor through the half-drawn curtain in the rear. Before her metamorphosis, you truly might have taken her for Golda Meir's twin sister, Golda's reincarnation, Golda's gilgul, Golda's avatar—chunky build, stocky like a babushka, no-nonsense boxy clothing down to her super-sensible shoes, grizzled graying hair pulled back into a severe low knot to expose a well-scrubbed, coarse-skinned face aggressively stripped of any artifice, small shrewd eyes, bulbous nose laced with a cobweb of red vessels, dark mustache, cigarette plugged between thin dry lips. Now, in her new emanation, she was like the flawless marble statue that had been buried inside the rough stone, liberated by the sculptor, like the scullery maid transformed into the princess by the touch of the godmother's wand. A YouTube video that Manika also sent to me features Zehava decked out in an iridescent leotard snug as a second skin and shimmering split tulle skirt, gliding smoothly in glass slippers across a polished floor with a devastatingly charming partner at least half her age twirling her to show off her tight satiny panties as the music pounds in a clip from the television show, *Dancing with the Stars*. Zehava is the star.

Nobody comes to India and is not in some way changed. That is the truism behind Zehava's radical transformation. She had written a book about it, *Transfiguration: The Seeker's Path to the True You*, which was a best seller in Israel, Moldova, the Upper West Side of New York City, and South Korea (where it was translated as *True Jew*, to tap into the vast Korean market of Talmud readers mining for the secret of alleged Jewish academic genius and financial wizardry). Now, as an exercise, Zehava had taken on my mother as her ultimate challenge. The secret of Zehava's success was India—more precisely, Hinduism, even more to the point, the linga, the symbol of the great god Shiva, destroyer and transformer. By visiting the temples of Lord Shiva, draping an offering of flowers around the erect linga, sprinkling some holy water, and worshipping there through immersion in a state of profound meditative self-obliteration, the supplicant is in effect destroyed and then transformed. The promise of transformation—of restored youth and health and desirability—is exponentially increased the more Shiva lingas you visit. Varanasi is Shiva's city, his stomping ground. In Varanasi, there are said to be over one hundred thousand Shiva lingas of every variety. In Varanasi, it is said, there is not a piece of ground the size of a sunflower seed that is not capable of bringing forth its own linga. The pictures that Manika sent to me from this period show Ma and Zehava smiling broadly on either side of flower-draped lingas in an astonishing range of sizes and materials and colors, thick and thin, tall and short, mud and marble, granite and gold, cream and crimson, one in particular I remember standing out for the glowing light bulb at its tip. Of course Ma knew what a linga means to people with dirty minds, she responded when I inquired tentatively. I could feel her blushing at the other end of the phone. She had had nine children after all, although it is true she had preferred not to look. "I'm sitting Shiva," Ma commented with a dry laugh. "Why not? Why not give it a shot? What can it hurt?"

That to me was the bitterest revelation of all. I had not realized until then how much comfort I had taken from Ma's insistence that she not only wanted to die, she was looking forward to death and the liberation it would bring with every remaining metastasized cell. It had been on the basis of that assertion that I had supported her in her Varanasi adventure, made all the arrangements, carried out all her wishes. I was giving my mother what she wanted, honoring her living will, I was her enabler, I was helping her to die with dignity. That she had declared with so much conviction that she wanted nothing better than to die made everything so much easier for me, banished any qualms and reservations. And now here she was turning the tables on me, trying to wheedle a reprieve, choosing life, putting herself on life support, placing her trust in this operator, this hustler Zehava, in a last desperate plea bargain for an extension. Had I been in Varanasi at that time, I would have pushed Zehava in all her high-maintenance glory into the foul waters of the Ganges alongside the slimy bathers and the sweating launderers and the idol worshippers doing their puja not only for the sin of raising false hopes, but for the crime of betraying the entire feminist agenda, for choosing her inner Zehava over her Golda, which is completely unforgivable.

How to understand Ma's weird fixation with Zehava and her preposterous Shiva linga weight loss and transformation program? In the end I concluded that the only reasonable explanation was that she figured it might turn into a boon for India's tourism, which could translate into more business for me. Ma was always looking out for her kids' welfare. If she noticed someone talking to himself in the street, for example, she would hand him one of the cards she had had made up to publicize the powers of my twin brother, Shmelke. Go see my son, Reb Breslov Tabor, in Jerusalem, a miracle worker, a healer, he will make you normal, much cheaper than a psychiatrist, even with the airfare. But hey, bottom line, whatever Ma's good intentions might have been on my behalf, however much she might have had my interests at heart by cultivating this con artist at the expense of her true desire for moksha, Zehava was messing with my mother's head, it was a nonstarter. And not long after, Zehava was out of the picture—literally, the ones Manika was sending to me. No matter how many Shiva lingas Ma had stroked, she had not lost a single ounce, nothing at all had been transformed or transfigured. In a routine update email, the rebbetzin Dassi speculated that the cancer seemed to have dug its claws into my mother's spine with a vengeance; it was becoming more and more painful for Ma to get around, though she still had her appetite, and her mood was still positive.

The final set of photographs sent to me by Manika opened ominously, like dead birds strewn in the sand on the way to the sea. The first few pictures in this series did not even include my mother, but rather images of what she saw as she was carted by Bulbul in the bicycle rickshaw around Varanasi, and what for reasons it was left to me to decipher she had instructed Manika to photograph and pass on to me. There was a single theme to all of these pictures. They all showed stones upon which the image of a married couple was carved in relief, posed side by side united in devotion, monuments placed as a shrine near the spot where the good wife had set herself aflame on her husband's funeral pyre. Ma was drawing nearer to the fires—that was the obvious message. So it did not surprise me at all that when next I saw my mother come into virtual focus it was at the burning ghat, the great cremation ground of Manikarnika.

Manikarnika means jewel earring, Ma explained to me—Same like my girl, Manika. It has to do with some *bubbe meise* of theirs, one of their gods losing an earring there or some sort of *narishkeit* like that. Ma, of course, didn't hold with such nonsense, but she was drawn by the idea of likening death to a lost earring. She had once read, in a magazine geared to ultra-Orthodox women, that a holy Jewish sage and mystic had said that if you find sixty-nine earrings you had lost, you would achieve redemption. One loss after another—that was life in a nutshell—you lose everything until you have nothing.

She was conveyed to Manikarnika Ghat sometime in the morning and sat there all day, often into the night. The fires burned twenty-four hours, never stopping, for my information. She arrived in the bicycle rickshaw with Manika squeezed in beside her in the carriage and Bulbul pedaling furiously. He would pull up as close as possible to the top of the steps. Four eunuchs awaited her; she had won their hearts weeks before when they passed her terrace begging in their hormonally deep belligerent voices, which she softened and soothed by feeding them *rugalekhs* and strudel while stroking their arms. The eunuchs greeted the arriving rickshaw with bowed heads and palms pressed together in a namaste. They approached, bearing an ancient palanquin with a flaking gilt cabin and shredded upholstery, which they had appropriated from the decaying museum in the crumbling palace and fort of the Maharaja of Benares on the other side of the river where the dead souls go. Each of these eunuchs was a formidable giant, unusually large for an Indian man, thick layers of makeup masking their stubble, false eyelashes, long dangling earrings jingling as they moved sinuously, parodying an idea of woman, lustrous saris in silk and chiffon synthetics. Effortlessly they lifted Ma's 250 pounds from the carriage of the rickshaw and transferred her to the seat of the litter. With the poles resting on their broad shoulders, they bore her halfway down the steps to a platform in the middle of the cremation ghat, the best seat in the house, the ideal position for viewing. Manika followed closely in their perfumed wake, carrying a folding lounge chair and a pile of cushions, and set it all down on the designated spot. Gently, as if positioning a rare artifact, the eunuchs moved Ma from the palanquin to the chair and parked her there.

This is where my mother sat all day for three weeks, eighteen days in total not including the Sabbath when it is forbidden to drive, and on Fridays she was delivered back to her apartment early, in time to light candles and welcome the Sabbath queen. The weather was still mild. If it grew cool as evening descended, Manika would spread a blanket across my mother's lap, though the flames rising from the dead burning day and night were like a monstrous furnace perpetually heating this last earthly station.

On each one of those eighteen days I was sent a single picture. The central figure was always my mother in her chair on Manikarnika in a white sari with a blue stripe, like a grotesquely inflated Mother Teresa, the end draped over her head, which is tightly wrapped in a white kerchief threaded with gold, and over her shoulders a wool paisley scarf. Her eyes are blacked out by an oversized pair of sunglasses, a celebrity guarding against being recognized and mobbed by her fans.

Each photo presented another variation to ponder, like impressionistic studies by an artist in changing lights. What was not visible to me was what Ma herself was seeing, what it was that drew her to this inferno again and again; her dark glasses guarded her thoughts against betrayal, reflected nothing, nor was she forthcoming when we talked at night about what was unfolding before her day after day. In a single phone conversation only, after I had pleaded with her, in pity she opened up slightly, as I remember it, to liken the scene she was witnessing to an end-of-days landscape of altars, human sacrifices laid on top of them, burning, roasting, pluming in smoke, flaking into ash. Your body that matters so much to you in your lifetime, that is such a big deal to you, this body is basically the same like everyone else's, Ma said, with everything in the same place more or less. You think you're different but you're nothing special, you start with the head, you end with the feet, arms, legs, *kishkes*, bowels, your shriveled and dried-up little unmentionables that give you so much aggravation and *tzores* in your life—who needs it? You take up so much and so much space on this earth, sometimes a little more, sometimes a little less, but always, give or take, the length and width of an altar, that's what you see at Marnikarnika. Most of the bodies brought here for cremation are small—very small—Ma observed, Not like my body, but it's all the same basic model. These are so small though, most of the time you can't tell if it's a man or a lady stretched out there on the altar wrapped in a sheet with the face bagged like for an execution. You think they're all women they're so small, but they could also be shrunken old men, in death the differences are wiped out. It's just so relaxing to sit there so warm and toasty and watch, Ma said, it's just such a relief to finally stop fighting, to just sit back and surrender yourself to the facts of death.

The photograph of the day, on the other hand, communicated far more information. And, I should note, it was a testament to how my mother came to be regarded that these pictures even existed in the first place. As every tourist is forewarned, it is forbidden to take pictures at the cremation ghats, out of respect for this most personal of religious rituals, never mind that it is so transparently enacted in public, and in deference to the mourners, who in any event, seem strangely detached and almost indifferent, like the dead themselves, they do not scream and yell openly, to wail and tear your hair is considered bad form, inauspicious for the dead poised in this delicate space of transition. Self-appointed guardians of the faith prowling the burning ghat on the lookout for any violators of the no-photos rule will pounce on alleged flouters, but not one of them ever dared to mess with my mother or her support staff. She was protected by her eunuchs, their long red lacquered fingernails curled like talons to rip them to pieces, lurid lipstick-smeared mouths quivering in readiness to open and let out a hideous harpy shriek.

In the first of these eighteen pictures, Ma is captured with her eunuchs robed in luminescent saris in shades of red, two eunuchs on each side, all leaning in toward my mother enthroned in her chair shrouded in widow white, flanking her with crimson lips pursed into a Cupid's bow and heads fetchingly posed in a flirtatious tilt. In another of these earlier pictures Ma is not even making eye contact with the camera. She is engrossed in sharing her lunch with her gray monkey, Fetter Feivish; Ma is eating a banana, Fetter is sipping from a can of diet soda through a straw. There are a few more photos of Ma with other snacking animals in this open-air death processing factory— one surrounded by seven emaciated black cows, dung caked all over their flanks and tails, grazing on the discarded marigold wreaths that had decorated the litters of the dead, another with a goat, the upper portion of its body clad in a torn striped polo shirt, to whom Ma is feeding a piece of saffron-colored cloth laced with silver ribbon that had been used to cover a corpse, another showing Ma with two wild dogs in front of her gnawing on a human foot.

But most of the images by far are of my mother adorned with heaps of flower garlands, gold, red, orange, circling her neck, draped over her head, spilling out of her lap. At her feet are rows of small baskets fashioned out of leaves filled with flower petals, sprouting bouquets of incense sticks. On cloths spread out on either side of her are piles of coins and rupees, and offerings of sweets in vibrant colors and textures. "Oh no, I would never touch that stuff," Ma said when I inquired. "What are you talking about? It's not even kosher. It doesn't have even an *OU*, not even a *K*, I'm not even talking glatt. Besides, it's very fattening. There's nothing I can do about it. *Hutz-klutz*, all of a sudden they decide I'm some kind of saint, or *nokh besser*, it shouldn't happen to a dog, a god—Mamadevi, the latest goddess. As if they didn't have enough already—now they have thirty-six million and one. Ma Kali, they call me. At first I thought they were saying Ma Kallah—you know, like a bride? Mother of the bride, ha ha—but no, wrong again. It seems they really have this dolly named Kali, she's one of their big shot goddesses, mother superior, they tell me, and also she likes to hang around the cremation grounds, like me. I even saw a picture of her, on an old calendar in Bulbul's rickshaw. Black face, long red tongue sticking out of her mouth like a very bad girl, her hair a mess, bloodshot eyes, cut off heads everywhere spritzing blood, crazy lady breaking all the rules and nobody can stop her, out of control. But thank God, at least she's skinny. Maybe even too skinny, if such a thing is possible. So, okay, so now I'm Ma Kali—I accept, why not? Every day they come and bring me presents. I try to tell them they're making a very big mistake—but who ever listens to a crazy old lady?"

Lurking in a corner of almost all of these pictures is the figure of a small, slight man, baldheaded, bare chested, with leather *chappals* on his feet, a white dhoti around his waist, round wire-rimmed glasses. In the eighteenth picture he takes center stage. "That's my end-of-life guru," Ma said when I ventured to ask. "I call him the angel of death. Every day he comes up to me, he points to the burning fires, and he whispers in my ear, 'It's the end of life, Mama. How do you feel about that?'"

"How *do* you feel about it, Ma?"

"I'm not worried, mama'le. Guru-shmuru. What does he know? He knows from nothing." Silence fell, long enough to trigger the fear that I had lost the connection when, suddenly, Ma's voice resurfaced. "My mama, may she rest in peace—she would never let anything bad happen to me."

· 2 ·

THE NEXT DAY the rebbetzin Dassi called. Ma had taken an unmistakable turn for the worse. I should come at once.

I was in Jerusalem when I received the call, putting the final touches on the schedule for a two-week retreat at a meditation center in Dharamsala for some of the veteran members of Women in Black who, for over two decades, had been holding vigil in their black kerchiefs every Friday afternoon before the Sabbath at France Square (which they had renamed Hagar Square), not far from the official residence of the prime minister of Israel, against war and violence in general, and against the occupation of the so-called West Bank in particular. I am ideologically very sympathetic to this noble cause and was working especially hard to reward these obviously extremely well-deserving heroines with an amazing experience. Even so, I immediately dropped everything and handed over the entire dossier of their itinerary to one of my agents on the ground, in our branch office in an old Templar building in German Colony. I took the first flight out of Tel Aviv that I could get—price in this emergency was of course not an issue—and landed in Mumbai in the early hours of the morning. From there I connected via SpiceJet to Varanasi, arriving at my mother's apartment in the late afternoon.

The rebbetzin Dassi was in the kitchen, cradling an infant in one arm who was nursing at her breast, a toddler dragging down on her skirt. With her free hand she was stirring a pot of rice and lentils on the stove for her other children, who were climbing like monkeys all over the sofa in the living room, the cushions piled up to form the ramparts and turrets, the chambers and hidden recesses of a fort. Dassi nodded a somber greeting and jerked her head toward the closed door of my mother's bedroom. Ma was in bed, with Manika's face poking out from under the covers beside her. I kissed my mother's dry forehead, like old parchment under my lips. "Ma," I let out. "What took you so long?" she said. "I was waiting. I have to talk to you. I didn't know if I could hold out much more." Her voice was feeble, practically inaudible.

Manika rose from the bed and left the room in obedience to a wordless signal from my mother. Ma indicated to me to draw nearer and bring my ear close to her mouth. "If you love me," Ma spoke, "put your hand under my thigh and do me a favor. Do not bury me in America or Israel, or in the ground anywhere. But when I am dead, carry my body along the ghats, from Assi to Manikarnika. Cremate me there and throw my ashes into the river."

With my hand under my mother's thigh I argued fiercely—her last wish, so beyond recall, such an unfair burden to lay on the back of your own child—but she would not listen to reason no matter how intensely I struggled, even when I resorted to an appeal to her lifelong religious convictions and observance, which was truly ironic since personally and publicly I had rejected all that. It's a sin, a violation of our faith, and so on and so forth, I argued. The Torah says, Dust you are and to dust you return. We Jews bury our dead, that's why we were given the land of Israel as our eternal estate—our resting place, in other words, our graveyard, our cemetery. Ma shook her head. She had already taken up too much space above ground. She could not bear to be weighed down under the earth with generations stomping on top of her, lying on her back in her grave looking up between their legs, the idea alone gave her a headache, suffocated her. She could not accept being plunged into the darkness, a plague so thick you could touch it. She could not abide the rain falling on her grave, the frost, the snow, the cold, she suffered at the very thought. She could not give herself over to be consumed by worms and beetles, recycled in the food chain, processed and excreted. She'd rather go up in smoke and be removed from the system.

The family will scream bloody murder, they will disown you, I said. Ma's lips tightened. Let them compare her to scattered dust, then. For scattered dust, you are not required to sit shiva, you are excused from saying Kaddish.

You would have no grave or marker, I said, there would be no place you would be on this planet, I would have no place to come to if I need you.

Ma looked at me as at a stranger. She could no longer be at her post forever, faithfully waiting for me in case I needed her.

When the Messiah comes at the end of days, I cried in desperation, you would have no remains, you would have no body to resurrect, you would be reduced to ashes.

She closed her eyes sanctimoniously. She would be in good company then, with the six million.

Throughout this ordeal, my hand was under my mother's thigh. I could feel the weight and heat of her body in which she had lived her life, through which she had experienced her reality, I could feel what it was like to be her, the constriction of her fears, the insistence of her desires, my hand was very close to the womb that was the source of my own being. This is a very ancient form of oath taking, the hand under the thigh, biblical. It was what the patriarch Jacob required of his son Joseph when he too was on his deathbed, under the thigh, grazing the testicles, through this most intimate contact transmitting the full urgency of his final wish with regard to his own funeral arrangements, to be conveyed back to the land of Canaan to lie with his fathers in Hebron rather than to be buried in Egypt, a wish Joseph granted with an extravagant royal spectacle of mourning, though first he could not resist embalming the old man in accordance with Egyptian rites albeit in breach of Jewish ritual, probably a good idea after all, to forestall the inevitable rot and stink on the long trek through the scorching wilderness to the final destination. Jacob's thigh under which Joseph's hand was pressed had been wounded when he had wrestled with the angel of God until the break of day in Mahana'im. My hand under my mother's thigh, I could feel how grievously she too had been wounded, how damaged she was.

"I'll do it, Ma," I said.

She startled me by opening her eyes. "Promise me."

I promised.

Satisfied, Ma signaled to me to leave the room. She needed a few minutes of privacy, to gather herself. I am myself a great believer in respecting other people's right to privacy as I would hope they would respect mine. After what I had just been through, and the great burden of the promise to my mother that I had just taken upon myself, I practically lurched out of Ma's bedroom in search of my own space. The only place to go for some solitude in that apartment raucous with children was the bathroom. I staggered in, locked the door, sat down on the toilet slumped with my elbows on my knees and my head in my hands, like Rodin's *Thinker*. What I was thinking was, Why is my mother doing this to me? How had I failed her that she was demanding this last extreme act of devotion from me? Was she creating this scenario so that I would leap into the flames of her funeral pyre? Was that why she had sent me all those pictures of the inscribed sati stones? I believe I must have drifted off into another dimension, lost touch with my reality for a brief spell on that toilet, depleted by my travels, emptied by the devastating scene I had just enacted with my mother, voided by the promise I had committed myself to that would, so to speak, put the final nail in the coffin of my alienation from my origins. I woke up shivering, agitated by a memory from my childhood—Ma always cold, piling on sweaters and shawls and scarves, blankets and quilts. She hated the cold—the cold, cold ground. It clamped her with terror. She held with those who favored fire. She must have tasted of desire, as the poet says, and I never gave her credit.

When I opened my eyes, the last mysterious light of the waning day was filtering in. It was only then that I noticed I was not alone. Manika was at the other end of the bathroom, bent over, pushing a broom, its bundle of straw wrapped in wet rags. The walls and ceiling and floor of the bathroom I now saw were covered with undulating gray insects, strange feathery otherworldly bugs, like waves of silver gossamer, like a gauzy veil, like ash. Soundlessly, with her muted broom, Manika was pushing these ghostly creatures down the drain in the center of the cement floor. Our eyes met. I rose at once, flushed the toilet, and left.

Dying is a very private human act, like going to the toilet, like sex. One of the more embarrassing aspects of the punishment of those who are condemned to be executed is to die in public. They wet and soil their trousers, their sexual members are aroused. Even animals that are mortally wounded are given the grace to be allowed to slouch off into a secluded corner to die with dignity. Ma was no longer there when I reentered her room, she had been eliminated and effaced. A stranger had taken her place in the bed, waxen, bloated, rigid, swollen blue hands and feet, a figure that in no way resembled my mother. I would not have been able to identify this suspect in a police lineup. I do not believe in the soul or the anima or the ch'i or the vital spirit, not even in the *neshama*, literally, the breath of life, the Jewish soul train, or any of that mystical junk, but that creature in that bed was not my mother. It was a husk, a hollow shell, a carapace, such as a locust casts off. My real mother had taken advantage of the privacy I had granted her to escape through the window.

What followed then was like the worst kind of dream—the dream that paralyzes you with horror and won't let you go so that you can never wake yourself out of it into the relief that it was only a dream. From the moment I returned to that room until we disposed of the remains, I did not leave the side of Ma's impersonator for a minute. I had already paid a terrible price for my brief absence, which my mother had exploited so cruelly by snatching her death when no one was looking and running with it, stealing away forever. Now I resolved to remain fixed in my place, partly, yes, in homage to the Jewish exhortation to guard the dead until properly settled, which I count among the more humane and enlightened mandates of my lost faith, but above all in my determination to show my mother that I was capable of honoring the promise I had made to her.

I could feel Ma's unquiet presence vibrating there in the room, watching me as I watched over her, challenging me, testing me, loitering there to see if I possessed the spirit and life to follow through and keep my word. Already there were forces converging to obstruct me. Within the hour after Ma split, the pale gray flies that Manika had been sweeping down the drain in the bathroom started migrating into the room, forming a frothy canopy of filaments and streamers over the corpse, which had begun to emit the stench of decay, sending it forth in putrid shafts that seemed almost to glow. The rebbetzin Dassi opened the door slightly, pressing her bundled infant up against her nose. She glanced into the room, took in the situation, automatically muttered the obligatory phrase of acceptance and fatalism, Blessed is the True Judge, shoved the door closed with her shoulder, collected her brood, and rushed out of the apartment with Manika following swiftly after, as if on assignment.

Within minutes, Rabbi Assi himself showed up, striding into my mother's bedroom without knocking or announcing himself in any way, with the entitlement of a doctor on rounds in a hospital. I was at that instant still focusing inward on how to carry out the incredibly complex and loaded task before me in strict compliance with the highly transgressive promise my mother had extracted, so I did not fully apprehend his approaching heavy tread. There was no question in my mind that I would do everything in my power to realize Ma's last wish. She had already broken so many taboos and taken so many risks and sacrificed so much in her quest for liberation, she had rid herself of all desire in her surrender to death other than that single final request, I could not fail her now at the finish line. I was immersed in the immediate problem of how to deal with my father and siblings on the issue of cremation, which without doubt they would find irredeemably abhorrent and repugnant, when the rabbi burst into the room. I had just come to the decision to proceed with the rite as soon as possible exactly as Ma had requested and to hit the family with the news of her passing and the manner in which the remains had been disposed of after the fact—after nothing was left but some clumps of fibrous black ashes in the dark womb of Mother Ganga. There would be nothing they could have done to prevent it thanks to the gift of ignorance I will have bestowed upon them, so they would in no way be liable. I alone, already dead in their eyes, a branded defiled spirit, would be guilty.

Rabbi Assi muttered the requisite verse of consolation and resignation, *Barukh Dayan haEmet*. With his fingers stroking his nose up and down in what he fancied was a discreet gesture in no way connected to the rank smell suffusing the space, and pinching his nostrils together so that his words were partially muffled, he instructed me with full pastoral authority that Jewish law requires that the funeral take place immediately, optimally on the very same day if feasible. That was fine with me, I replied; as night was already descending, I was in any event planning it for the first thing next morning. His eyes opened wide in bafflement. But where was I going to bury my holy mother, peace be upon her, in this idolatrous place? He went on to advise me that he had the infrastructure at hand for the purification and preparation of the body by a holy society of righteous women in strict observance of Jewish tradition, and for its shipment to Israel or America, or whatever hallowed ground I chose, for a proper burial; he was offering me a full deluxe funeral and interment package free of charge purely out of his love and respect for my holy mother, a true seeker, may her memory be for a blessing. It then fell to me to let him know that my holy mother the seeker of blessed memory had requested to be cremated. "I promised her, Assi," I said. With my right hand under her thigh, like Joseph at the deathbed of Father Jacob in that famous scene from the Torah. If I forget my promise, may my right hand forget its cunning.

Calmly at first, Rabbi Assi instructed me that my promise was null and void. My holy mother, may her soul be bound up in the bond of eternal life, was now in another place, a place of wisdom and enlightenment, where she now sees her error and recognizes the truth. She now prefers a proper Jewish burial, he assured me. Therefore, my under-the-thigh oath to my mother, may the memory of the righteous be for a blessing, is canceled, void, invalid, without force or standing or power, completely vaporized as if with the full clout of the Kol Nidre prayer intoned on the eve of Yom Kippur, annulling all the year's oaths. I was not only permitted to break my vow, I was obligated to do so as it had been superseded by what my holy mother, peace be upon her, actually wants now at this very moment as she stands at the gate of heaven. What she wants now, Rabbi Assi advised me with complete certainty, is to return to the earth from which she had come. I merely shook my head. Nice try, Assi, good *khop*, but no cigar. It was Ma's living will to be cremated. Unless she shows up now to tell me right here in person that she has changed her mind and signs a release waiver, I'm moving ahead as scheduled, all systems go.

I continued to shake my head like a pendulum back and forth as Assi poured out a string of objections mostly pertaining to the reasons for the prohibitions against the mutilation of the body, dead or alive, from tattoos to autopsies to cremation—sacred vessel, God's image, on loan from God, the whole predictable banal drill. When finally it sank in that I was battening down the hatches and not budging, he drew out his last and best card. "Very soon now, very quickly in our time, the holy Rebbe Himself, our Master, our Teacher, our Rabbi, will rise up from concealment in His true form as the Messiah the King to rescue the living and to raise the dead. If you go ahead with this atrocity, your holy mother, peace be upon her, will have no body to resurrect. On that great day she will be forced to come back to life in a different body and no one will recognize her and no one will greet her." "That's okay, Assi," I said, for some reason oddly serene maybe in reaction to his foaming agitation, "Ma never liked her own body very much anyhow. Next time around, I think she'd prefer thin." "*Vantz!*" the rabbi spat out. He turned furiously, sparing himself the indignity of a total public meltdown, and darted out of the room. Frankly, I was stunned that Assi knew some Yiddish, even if it was limited to a few common curse words. He was dark skinned, I had taken him for an Oriental Jew stemming from the Levant or North Africa, Sephardi, though of course some Yiddish must have been part of his purebred Ashkenazi Chabad curriculum. And I wasn't sure if by *vantz*, which translates as bedbug and is not exactly meant as a compliment, he was referring to me or with his pidgin Yiddish to the swarm of insects hovering over my mother's double in that bed, like the gray cloud over the Israelites in the wilderness. Tomorrow, it would be replaced by the pillar of fire. Now I was even more unshakable.

It was not the last I would see of the rabbi, of that I was sure the second he stomped out in such a rage. I needed to remain exceedingly vigilant and alert. And just as I had predicted, he was back within the hour, this time accompanied by four of his toughest Hasidim, elite ex-paratroopers by the looks of them, lugging a heavy-duty stretcher. It was obvious that they intended to seize the body by force, to kidnap it in order to save it from the abomination of being consigned to the cremation pit. From the rabbi's perspective, there are times when it is permissible, in the name of heaven, to commit even an act explicitly forbidden in the written law, such as kidnapping, an act, moreover, for which the death penalty is mandated (though some might argue that this same severity does not apply if the kidnapping involves a corpse, especially one slated for the fires). It was entirely correct in this emergency, according to the rabbi, during the small window of opportunity still open to them, to use any means necessary to rescue the dead from an impending sacrilege, including brute force and vio-lence. Clearly my mother had been in a deluded state when she had made her final request. Assi was acting in her interest, for the sake of her salvation in the world to come.

Shortly before the rabbi and his gang of four showed up, however, Manika had returned with our quartet of eunuchs. They were hang-ing out with me at the bedside keeping the corpse company, the ends of their saris drawn in a discreet ladylike flip across the lower portion of their faces due to the intensifying stink of decomposition, when the rabbi and his forces charged into the room, pushing the door open so savagely with the metal corner of the stretcher. Our four mighty eunuchs rose at once, positioned themselves silently in a phalanx for-mation along the bedside facing the invaders, the first line of resis-tance, their lipstick-stained teeth bared, their arms raised with clawed hands like tigers set to pounce, displaying the long red-lacquered dag-gers of their fingernails.

The unanticipated presence of the eunuchs along with their menacing maneuver brought the rabbi and his troops to a sudden halt, plunging them into a heated argument, to which, on our side, I alone was privy as it was conducted in Hebrew. The rabbi's boys were indeed all Israelis, hardened veterans of the Israel Defense Forces morphed into stoned and sexed-out seekers in India, and now, seized by the influence and inspiration of Rabbi Assi himself, newly minted penitents, returnees to the faith. The crux of their debate was whether or not it was permissible for them to engage in battle with an enemy of questionable gender. Were their opponents women or men? If the former, were the laws of *negiah* applicable, prohibiting the physical contact that would inevitably ensue from hand-to-hand combat? If the latter, would not one be rendered impure simply by touching the perversion of the garb of a woman on the body of a man? And what if parts of their bodies had been altered by surgery or implants or hormones or some other repulsive engineering to resemble the female form? And whether they were male or female, what about the danger of inadvertently being brought to a state of physical arousal by wrestling with these freaks?

Of course they were men, Rabbi Assi contended with exasperation, urging his warriors on, no different from an enemy who confronts you in camouflage or in the disguise of a burqa or chador. It is your duty to fight them, just as it is your duty to rescue a drowning woman regardless of your male status, the prohibition against touching the female does not pertain in such a case involving a threat to life, which trumps even the holy Sabbath. The drowning woman here is the dead body on the bed about to be sunk to the depths of the river in the form of ashes, and the life that is threatened is her afterlife.

In any other circumstance, all of this pilpul and Talmudic disputation displayed by his students, not to mention the laudatory manifestation of the desire to adhere to the law to the strictest hairsplitting letter, would have been a source of extreme pride to Rabbi Assi, confirmation that all of his teachings had penetrated and taken root in the minds and hearts of his flock. But now he was growing increasingly impatient, their momentum was slipping away. And then their situation turned utterly hopeless. A pack of gray monkeys led by Fetter Feivish leaped into the bedroom, invading the premises through the door that the rabbi and his men had carelessly left open. The monkeys seemed to know who the enemy was, I believe by a sign from Manika who understood how to communicate with them, and began to harass them mercilessly, swatting them with their tails, climbing up their legs and onto their shoulders, nipping at their fingers, tugging their side-curls, pulling off their black flying saucer hats and putting them on their own heads, like in the children's story about the caps for sale once so beloved by my daughter Maya, so that in the end the rabbi had no choice but to turn and abandon the battlefield, shouting at me as he and his raiders made their exit that he washed his hands of all of it, it was now all on my head, I would pay a very heavy price for it if not in this life then in the next, I might be the daughter but in this situation I was tantamount to the son, the rebellious and wayward son, condemned to death by stoning.

At this juncture I feel it is necessary and appropriate to pause for a moment in my narrative of these traumatic events to acknowledge my debt to Manika. There is no doubt in my mind that without Manika, I would not have been able to honor my mother by carrying out her last wishes exactly as she had mandated them to me, I would not have been able to pull it off on my own. It was during the period between Ma's disappearance and the immolation of the shell she had left behind that Manika's extraordinary administrative and managerial powers and her fierce loyalty came to the fore—attributes that continued to enrich my life, for she remained at my side for many years after. After it was all over, I presented her with a thank-you gift of a perfect new set of teeth made to order, brought her to Mumbai with me where she served as my daughter Maya's ayah, and, as an extra bonus, engaged a private tutor to teach her how to read. But during those terrible dark hours, when I was confined like a captive to the bedside on guard duty, it was Manika who took care of everything and made all the arrangements, operating on her own initiative, without requiring instructions or even a list, which she would not at that time have been able to read in any event. She knew exactly what had to be done, she did not have to be told, she stored it all in her head and made everything happen. Truly, she is my gem, to quote the rebbetzin, the jewel in my crown.

Manika not only had the foresight to summon the eunuchs and mobilize the monkeys, anticipating the looming threat from the rabbi and his cohorts, but after that incident she made sure I was never again alone. There was not a moment subsequently when I was not surrounded by defenders and comforters—our four eunuchs and many of their fellow travelers just being there for me, spending quality time, spraying fine mists of patchouli into the air with atomizers they pulled out of their purses, Fetter Feivish and the mischievous members of his simian tribe tearing open bags of Bamba and Bissli meant for the rabbi's kids, Bulbul and the delegation of bicycle rickshaw wallahs coming and going, and other assorted visitors. We sat around with our dupattas or the ends of our saris stretched demurely across the lower half of our faces because despite all the perfumes and joss sticks in the world, we could not deny the percolating smell of rot diffused by the microbes and bacteria released at last to gorge inside the carcass. With exemplary reverence and refinement, Manika knotted a kerchief like a pulley tightly around the still-uncovered face of the deceased as if it had a toothache, in order to close its mouth, which had been hanging down slack, wide open, revealing gray gums, an obscene dangling uvula, a swollen tongue, and all the secrets of my childhood.

It was Manika who made all the advance arrangements at the cremation ghat—paying double the fee in anticipation of what would be the extraordinary nature of our cortege, which would include the essential participation of the eunuchs in full regalia, hiring the services of a willing priest at double the price, purchasing double the amount, due to the unusual size of the body, of the best sandalwood for the pyre, the best ghee for fuel, the best incense for fragrance, and so on, price was not an object. Manika was the one who went out with two of our eunuchs as her fashion consultants on an errand to buy the shroud, as well as the lustrous saffron-colored and gold-ribboned coverings, garlands of flowers in abundance, an extra-sturdy reinforced bamboo bier on which to carry the corpse in the processional along the ghats, cords to tie it down securely, and all the other supplies. With a wall of eunuchs screening the bed for privacy, Manika washed the body and swaddled it in the thin sheet of the shroud, shooing away the flies and moths as she labored, this tiny woman performing all the heavy lifting on her own without an audible sigh or groan. And shortly before we all set out, because of the prohibition against the participation of women in the cremation rites due to the well-documented female tendency toward hysteria and the possibility that a lady overcome with grief might lunge headlong into the flames, which is now illegal, it was Manika who transformed me into the eldest son, into my male twin, into Shmelke, by draping me within the concealing folds of a pure white robe, and she shaved my head entirely, leaving only a small tuft in back, a little below the crown.

We set out while it was still dark, our four noble eunuchs honored with the first round of bearing aloft the bamboo stretcher on which the shrouded body had been laid out, blanketed with vivid cloths for warmth, heaped with garlands of flowers for beauty, firmly anchored with strong bands to prevent shifting or slippage or any unseemly accident along the way, God forbid. As the eldest son and mourner in chief, renamed Mani for the occasion, I walked directly behind. At my side was the hijra guru himself, the eunuch chief in all his splendor, conferring upon Ma the distinction of his presence and the blessings of good luck in his power to grant it as she embarked on her journey toward liberation. Then followed an escort composed of additional initiates in the exclusive society of eunuchs as well as members of the fraternity of bicycle rickshaw wallahs led by Bulbul, all of them eager for the honor of taking their turn carrying the effigy of my holy mother. Making up the rear, at a respectful distance, came the woman and the animal, Manika and Fetter Feivish, accompanied by several of his colleagues. This was the core group, the nucleus around which many other spiritually attuned seekers would amass as we made our way from Ma's apartment chanting, *Rama nama satya hai*, the familiar verse intoned over and over again every day by funeral processions wending through the lanes and alleys of Varanasi—the refrain that reverberated in your ears day and night and could never be fully unplugged, *Rama nama satya hai*, God's name is truth.

In faithful compliance with Ma's extraordinary request to be transported to her final destination not by the traditional route through the constricted streets of the city itself but rather along the wide promenade at the top of the broad concrete steps of the ghats, we progressed from the apartment through some twisting roads and alleys, then down the clay slope to our first station, the great Shiva linga under the pipal tree at Assi Ghat. The darkness was still intense, an hour at least remained until the sun would begin to rise over the eastern shore of Mother Ganga, there were no electric lamps or other lights to guide our way as the power had failed as usual, yet already there were bathers and pilgrims at Assi Ghat performing their daily salutations, rising wet from the holy river as if reborn, their clothing clinging to their bodies and rendered translucent, climbing up the slippery incline. By the light of candles affixed with their own melting wax around the base of the linga, I instantly recognized among the Shiva devotees Ma's girlfriend Zehava, despite the helmet she had on to protect her hairdo. I did not hesitate to approach and introduce myself. Addressing her in Hebrew, I informed her whose remains we were now carrying, and invited her to show her respect to the dear departed by joining our cortege.

She declined on two grounds. First, she was at that very moment engaged in an emergency political action to counteract a string of outrages perpetrated by a radical group that provocatively called itself SS, which stood for Safe Sex, and, to add insult to injury, used the Indian Aryan backward swastika as its symbol. As a Jew she simply could not countenance such Nazi references however much she might be in agreement with this organization's program to stem the population explosion that dumped more poor people in India than in any other country on the face of the earth, and however deeply she was in accord with its agenda to stop the rampant spread of sexually transmitted diseases and especially AIDS by truck drivers on gouged-out Indian roads whose throbbing vehicles so agitated their groins and sex organs that they had no choice but to seek release with infected prostitutes at rest stops and then bring the disease back home as a present to their own wives in their villages. Moreover, she absolutely could not tolerate the repellent tactics of this group, including its most recent particularly offensive campaign to promote the virtue of protected sex in a startling act of desecration that would make everyone sit up and pay attention—swathing every Shiva linga they could get their hands on, no matter how small or large, with a condom. Just before our arrival, as it happened, she along with a few other Shivaniks, had peeled off an extra-jumbo plus-sized rubberlike condom from this very impressive linga under this pipal tree right here at Assi Ghat. Clearly, it was more vital that she devote her energies to this immediate crisis. A threat to the living always took precedence over attending to the final rites for the departed, who were anyway already no longer players and past caring.

That was the first reason Zehava gave for not being available on such short notice to join our procession. Her second reason, which she stated succinctly since it required no explanation, was that as a matter of principle she boycotted Hindu funerals since they excluded women for sexist reasons. Hysterics, all of us—and she telegraphed a sisterly smile, taking it for granted I was on her wavelength. That was her inner Golda talking, and I told her so. No, it was her outer Zehava, she corrected, the highest articulation of feminism, the most powerful manifestation of liberation—women's liberation in the full expression of the lived reality of her femaleness. "Your wise mother, may she rest in peace, she understood this. She told me you'd never get it—and she was right."

So, Ma had talked about me to this vulgar stranger, and in such a negative light. It required all my self-control to keep from bursting into tears at this betrayal, sobbing wretchedly like a little girl again until I was panting and could no longer catch my breath, falling down crying right there at the foot of the Shiva linga at Assi Ghat, and beating the ground with my fists in a tantrum like your stereotypical female hysteric—but it was necessary to maintain the decorum of the occasion. Lips pumping fishlike, throat constricted as if an umbilical cord had again been twisted around my neck by Shmelke my twin, I nevertheless had to carry myself with adult male dignity and move on. Already our forces were advancing, the bamboo litter at the head with the cadaver like a beached whale dredged up from the sea strapped down to it carted by the next shift of four eunuchs. I took my rightful place directly behind, followed by the founding core escort, our ranks swelling with bystanders and gawkers as we processed along the way—sadhus and holy men, yogis and ascetics, beggars, boatmen, launderers, pushers, touts, dreadlocked kids stoned on hashish, strumming their sitars, banging their tablas, seekers, tourists, the jet-lagged and the insomniac and the homeless, dogs, goats, monkeys, cows. The mood was celebratory and festive, and not discordantly so. Death held no terror here even in the darkness of night. This was Kashi, the city of light where death was bound up in the fabric of life, accepted like any other bodily function, taken in, passed through, and eliminated.

We made our way chanting along the promenade rising above the holy river Ganges, past Tulsi Ghat, and the Jain Ghat, and onward, with the hope of reaching Harishchandra Ghat as our next station, to switch bearers, change horses as it were, when an unforeseen event occurred at the ghat named for the great god himself, destroyer and transformer, Shivala Ghat. This is the ghat favored by cows and water buffalos, herded here from the cramped teeming interior of the city and marched down the steps into the waters of the river to bathe and cool off, leaving in their wake great wet mounds of waste matter, sloppy heaps of dung. On the bright side, when our bearers stumbled and slipped on the muck, they managed to stop their slide after rolling down only about four or five steps and were spared crashing down the entire flight. Most importantly, the body on the stretcher thank God remained securely in place and did not suffer the humiliation of plummeting with a horrifying thud. Still, it did not emerge unscathed. It was smeared with shit as if it had been rolled like dough in sugar, the eunuchs were shrieking, their saris and makeup were ruined, we were obliged to stop and wait while they descended into the water with the stretcher and submerged entirely to clean off as best they could. When they came up out of Mother Ganga there was no time for drying, no warmth from the sun, which had not yet risen, our schedule had been disrupted, it was imperative to move on. Ten fresh eunuchs, four on each side in file, plus one at the head and one at the feet, were now required to ferry the waterlogged body, weighed down even more by the coverings soaked through and through. Alluding to the excrement that had in such a ghastly spectacle toppled the guest of honor and her bearers, the hijra guru said, "It is the filth of Shiva and therefore pure, all opposites are illusion." We took whatever comfort we could from this wisdom as we continued on our way.

Because of this unexpected pit stop at Shivala, we now moved ahead at a purposeful clip in our legions, chanting our *Rama nama satya hai*, hoping to pass Harishchandra Ghat without stopping there to pay our respects as we had originally intended. This, however, was not to be, and perhaps in hindsight it was correct that we pause for some moments of silence at this holy site, since it is the more ancient of the two cremation ghats and regarded by many of the Kashi old-timers as the more sacred and therefore the preferred access route to moksha. What prevented us from pushing ahead directly was the small mob of children who slept in Harishchandra in the shadow of the electric crematorium, and in the pavilion, and on the benches, and along the retaining wall, and in any sheltered nook they could curl up in the fetal position to stick their thumbs into their mouths even among the open-air pyres, burning continuously. The boisterous parade of our throng passing in the night jolted them into wakefulness. Illuminated by the fresh and smoldering flames of burning bodies, the urchins descended on us like tiny demons, the whites of their eyes and teeth gleaming in the darkness of that underworld as they penetrated our ranks, circling our legs, squeezing in very close, groping, clawing, grasping, begging, stealing.

Still, even as they clung to us and hung from our necks and arms, we barely slowed our pace, plowing ahead, shooing them off like mosquitos, the eunuchs letting out terrifying cries and howls from the monster abyss of prebirth dreams, startling the imps into flight. We thought we had succeeded in shaking them off entirely, but a small hardcore contingent had regrouped ahead of us. In a straight row barring our way, they were squatting bare-bottomed and defecating, staking out their territory like dogs, looking up at us defiantly, sniffing and grinning triumphantly. It stopped us in our tracks, their pathetic barricade. We stood there gazing far too long, overcome by the realization that this was their only line of defense, there was nothing we could do to save them. So we simply circled around and went on. I wanted to call out to my mother, Ma, wherever you are (certainly not in that obscene blob we were hauling), these are the poor starving children of India you were always reminding me about when I refused to finish all the food on my plate—take a look, Ma. Ma, why did you have to fixate on Manikarnika for your cremation? You're too heavy, Ma. You love little children, Ma, you could have chosen Harishchandra. Then we would already have arrived.

We advanced past Kedar Ghat, churning onward, lugging our load through ghat after ghat, past the launderers slapping saris against the stone and stretching them out to dry as the sky began to lighten and we came to Dashashwamedha, the busiest of all the ghats. To the east, at our right, Mother Ganga was already crowded with bathers and pilgrims performing their daily puja. The silvery dark water was strewn with flower petals and flickering with candles floating in banana leaf baskets, gifts to the gods. Boats packed with tourists and guides plied up and down, stopping to bob on the water to allow the passengers to gape at the quaint rites. Along the ghat itself in front of us and to our left, streams of devotees were descending to the river to carry out their ablutions, washing their bodies with the murky water, brushing their teeth with neem twigs, gargling and spitting. Hawkers peddling snacks and souvenirs, boatmen and masseurs, drug dealers and flower sellers and silk merchants and guides already were hustling for clients—it was business as usual at dawn on the main ghat, the only remarkable intrusion was our procession of dropouts transporting physical remains of extraordinary proportions through this sacred territory rather than through the streets of the city, chanting in one voice our praises to the truth of Rama. Now our ranks already swollen by the mixed mob collected along the way grew even greater in number, increased by the curious and the sensation seekers pressing in for a good vantage point as we stopped at one of the pandit stations shaded by a bamboo umbrella, and I climbed onto the wooden platform to say a few words in memory of my mother.

This eulogy was the only feature of the familiar Western ceremony that I retained. My mother never mentioned it, so she never explicitly forbade it. I wanted to have an opportunity to say something and I knew it would not be possible to betray my woman's naked voice when we arrived at the cremation ghat, Manikarnika. With the ancient priest sitting cross-legged on the platform under his bamboo umbrella looking up at me tolerantly through steel-framed glasses, oddly familiar like Bapu on all those rupee notes, I spoke my requiem in English, hoping it would be incomprehensible to the more fanatic members of the audience so that no one would take offense at the irregular nature of our congregation and observance, and deem it all some kind of mockery.

The truth is, in recalling the words of my eulogy, I'm not sure if what I am now reporting is what I actually said or what I wish I had said or even if I dared to speak at all, I was so wiped out physically and so emotionally drained by all the events of the past days. But assuming I did speak, I believe this, more or less, was the content. I believe I went on for a bit, addressing Ma directly, assuring her that I was carrying out her wishes to the letter, exactly as she had communicated them to me when she had trapped my hand under the weight of her thigh so near to the opening of the birth canal through which I, followed by my twin brother, Shmelke, had made our entry into this world of woe, hoping, I guess, that she would find some way to express her approval and gratitude from the other side in the presence of these onlookers, a simple thank-you, some small token of appreciation and recognition, it was the least she could do. The rest of my eulogy, as best I can remember, was focused on speculation as to why Ma had wanted to be processed in this particular way, so alien to someone of her background and lifestyle. If she was thinking along environmentally friendly, ecological recycling lines (which I doubted), I might have speculated that it would have been more sustainable for her to have requested to be laid out on a mountaintop like carrion in the Parsee way and devoured by vultures; I would have done whatever she asked, she could have counted on me. In any event, in choosing between burial and cremation, clearly she preferred to leave a greater carbon footprint than to take up extra space on this already overcrowded planet. Finally, in conclusion, I played with the idea that Ma had chosen to avoid a traditional rite because at all costs she did not want to be called a Woman of Valor, an *Aishet Hayil*, which is how every respectable dead religious Jewish woman is summed up and characterized in the eulogy at her funeral and on her gravestone regardless of how she may or may not have conducted her life. Charm is false, beauty is vanity, a God-fearing woman, she will be praised, and so on—this is the *Aishet Hayil*, the grunt in the army of husband and sons, laughing all the way to the end of time. Ma wanted no part of that—that was my hypothesis. She'd rather go up in smoke. I turned to the great corpse at my feet, supported by the eunuchs as it was partially propped up against the platform on which I was standing, and addressed it directly. "So Ma, I just want you to know that you have made your point. Rest assured, you are no *Aishet fucking Hayil*."

The priest attending cross-legged uncoiled like a cobra and levitated unexpectedly. "Ah, it is Mama-ji," he said. "I knew I recognized her. So the end of life has arrived for her. Yes, she is gone, but she has not yet come. She is poised now in a very dangerous place. It is a very delicate moment." He raised his index finger significantly and placed a red tikka on my forehead. "Go at once, the gate to moksha is soon closing."

We sped northward in a blur through the remaining ghats—Man Mandir, Meer, and so on. The sun rose on the eastern flank of Mother Ganga, and we arrived at Manikarnika.

There's something about ritual, especially death ritual that sucks you in like a sealed train and carries you along to the end of the line, you need to accept that you're in it for the ride. Not that I went like a sheep to the slaughter, not that I didn't in some measure resist. It took so long for that great mass, allegedly my mother, to burn completely, that at a certain point, well beyond the three hours allotted for the incineration of an average body, the Doms began to hassle me to conclude the ceremony and vacate the cremation grounds. No way I was going to just follow orders, and not out of any personal elitism either—certainly not because the Doms are untouchables, predestined to sink their hands into the pollution of death—I trust that by now you know me well enough to give me more credit than that. No, it was because I knew they intended to wrap up Ma's case the minute I turned my back and left—sweep up the ashes along with the big chunks of meat and body parts that had not yet been deconstructed, and toss the whole lot into the river to be ravaged by the dogs, ogled by tourists in their boats, pounded by oars like a schnitzel, devoured by snapping turtles and strange sea monsters. The assembly line had to be kept rolling, and Ma was clogging up the works. The Doms may belong to a defiled caste but they are also reputed to have prospered garishly. Death is big business, Varanasi, the mother lode.

So it was an exceedingly long day—from dawn when we arrived at Manikarnika chanting, *Rama nama satya hai* and marched purposefully down the bank of the ghat directly to the ritual bath mikvah of the Ganges to give Ma her final dunk, until dark when Ma combusted to the last crisp, and I performed the ultimate filial rite required of me, following which I was free at last to go my way. And yet, though I know the day streamed into the night until it blurred into a day that was neither day nor night, and though my memory when I revisit it takes the form of frames unfolding in slow motion, like video replays of a sports event that bestow an aura of gravity and consequence on the smallest details—despite all that, while I lived through it, it seemed to race by, like a fleeting dream.

Throughout, I felt Ma's hovering presence, as if she were checking out the scene from wherever she was, doubtless horrified at the attention garnered by the remains attributed to her, especially at the terminus of Manikarnika. The sequined and spangled spectacle of her eunuch bearers had been enough to turn all heads during the processional, but at the cremation ghat itself, the sacred space where nothing is sacred, where all pretension and artifice are stripped away, and everything is transparent and on view, the action truly stopped at the sight of the massive husk itself that my mother had shed. The Dom Sonderkommandos standing knee-deep in the sooty water sifting with sieves of mesh and screening for gold teeth and jewels that might have been deposited with the ashes, froze in their labors to stare at the body as it was lowered for its last dip. The emaciated haulers in ragged lungis and shredded T-shirts unloading the boats, trudging up the hill to add to the great woodpiles stacked behind the ghat, paused with the burden of logs pressing down on their heads at the landing platform where Ma's double had been laid out to dry, gaping with dropped jaws and blackened toothless gums. The regulars and hangers-on and loafers and prowlers speculated and bantered at the novelty of this imposing specimen. It couldn't be an elephant as it was forbidden to cremate a beast on this holy ground, so it could only be a man of enormous wealth, a maharajah or a prince, an eminent personage who, though he could doubtless afford the purest ghee to fuel his own cremation, might even derive some perverse postmortem satisfaction from saving a few rupees by recycling all that built-in fat.

Converging from all sides, they formed a merry parade behind the main attraction as it was moved on its bamboo stretcher from its drying rack to its next station at the ghat, and set down on the ground beside the capacious altar of sandalwood constructed for it by the Doms. Cows and goats squeezed through the crowd in anticipation of a grand feast as the cords were untied and the appetizers and salads of beribboned cloth and flower garlands cast off; dogs pressed in to sniff out the territory, chewing on bones dredged from the scummy water. With a great communal intake of breath and a deep grunt, the Doms joined hands to heave the body wrapped in the thin sack of its shroud onto the bed of the pyre, which partially sank under its weight, collapsing the lattice-like gaps between the pieces of wood expertly arranged for the flow of oxygen to feed the flames. There it rested on top of the altar, served up, its pathetic mortal shape fully on view for all to see. The staggering mound of its torso rose behind its feet, which were pointed in the general direction of Mother Ganga as if about to soon set out. The Doms went to work piling the sandalwood on the peak of the belly, the logs sliding down its slope one after another, to the jolly amusement of the bystanders, until at last an artful meshing was devised, and the body was entirely encased in kindling, leaving only the knob of the hooded head exposed at the other end of its soaring bell curve.

The little priest, who had stationed himself at my side so close I could hear his neurons synapsing, rummaged deep inside his dhoti, then pulled out a cell phone. There had been no ring, he must have set it on vibrate. With the phone pressed to his ear he was nodding emphatically, but since no sound came out of his mouth, my eyes followed the arc of his gaze, which was focused intensely up the slope of the ghat to the very top, where Manika was positioned talking animatedly into her cell phone, gesturing furiously. Manika was directing the show from above, she was the power behind the throne, pulling all the strings. It was an exquisitely complex and above all sensitive operation to bring together, not least because each of its elements was in violation of the faith, from its leading lady, the Hebrew corpse herself in all her splendor, to its supporting cast of bearers and mourners of ambiguous gender. But this little sweeper and excrement wiper Manika was on top of every detail. She was wielding the clout of money. The priest too was on retainer and was being lavishly rewarded.

Orders received, he shoved the phone back down into the folds of his dhoti, dragged me along to the boss Dom assigned to the job, and pointed severely to a significant stash of untouched ghee. The crooks had been caught in the act, attempting to pirate these blocks of soft gold to sell a second time, figuring Ma could stew in her own juices, but Manika was having none of that. We stood there grimly, alert and unblinking as more and more cakes of ghee were inserted into strategic pockets of the pyre, leaving just enough in reserve to add as needed once the entire bed had been set alight. Fistfuls of incense that had also been hoarded were now generously sprinkled on top and scattered within. The priest handed me a flaming sheaf of twigs, ignited from the eternal fire that the Doms are said to maintain, and instructed me as the eldest son and chief mourner to walk around the altar, like a bride circling her bridegroom under the canopy at a Jewish wedding, only counterclockwise, because in death time unravels and leaks back into chaos and formlessness. When my bridal bouquet of burning twigs became too hot to hold I gave up running in circles like a rat in a maze, shoved it deep into the heart of the sandalwood cage, and set my mother on fire.

The netting of logs spun by the Doms in which the victim was caught collapsed almost instantly, sizzling and frying the great hump of the belly until it simply deflated, liquefied, and then seemed to vaporize. Her right leg flexed suddenly, startling me, as if she were unfolding in an effort to settle into a more comfortable position. A bare foot kicked out, the horned yellow toenails shockingly flecked with chipped polish, cherry red—and I had always thought I knew my own mother. The thin muslin in which she was swaddled clung to her skin, blistered, melted into translucence, outlining precisely each delicate seashell whorl and crevice and cavity of her ears. Dom boys stoked the fire with long wooden poles, throwing in more incense, adding ghee and sandalwood to keep it going.

She burned for more than twelve hours, through the day and into the night. In the darkness stray dogs gathered around and stretched out on the ground to sleep, warming themselves by the hearth. What I would not have given to lie down beside them and rest, just another dog among the dogs. But I never moved from my place, never turned my eyes away, I kept faithful vigil into the night since that was my duty. One by one our entire mixed multitude, including our inner core of eunuchs and Bulbul and Fetter Fluvioh, crept away. Manika, alone at her post overlooking the inferno, and I, in the ninth circle in the pit down below, were left standing in the dark, my little Virgil priest still joined to me at the hip, paid by the hour.

The body laid out on top of the altar had been reduced to pulverized white bone dust and ash that the Doms would collect and dump into the river. Only the skull remained, resting with unseeing eyes in its place as on a pillow. In accordance with my duty as mourner in chief and eldest son, I accepted the bamboo stick from the hands of the priest in order to perform the last rite. I smashed it down on the skull, cracking it open and liberating the soul.

Ma, Ma, she sobbed.

But I scuttled away and never looked back.

Maya

O MY DAUGHTER, Maya, my daughter, my daughter, Maya—twice you fell in love, at twelve and at thirteen, both times in Bombay under the lashing rains of the monsoon, most dangerous of seasons, the nighttime of the gods. The gods of the East understood the demonic power of the rains to seed wild growth and release passion and calamity. That is why the gods go to sleep during the monsoon, and holy men are forbidden to travel. But you Maya, child of water and illusion, you went out.

Geeta hated my gods-of-the-East, holy-men mantras in all their boring, predictable variations, as she never held back from reminding me. This was one of the running themes in our arguments, which reached a crescendo that scorching May she left us, as the dark clouds gathered for the monsoon season. Forgive me, Maya, I know how much you suffered from our fights, the screaming in the night, the crying, the doors slamming. Geeta loathed my romanticization of India, as she characterized it over and over again in case it had slipped my mind. How could I be so softheaded on India when I was so ruthlessly sharp and unforgiving about my own lost Jewish faith? That's what she wanted to know. India was nothing but a filthy, backward, pitiless sewer, she informed me with all the condescension of a born insider enlightening a clueless alien—a ticking time bomb with a moronic religion, vulgar god dolls, infantile superstitious worship practices, nutcases parading around in diapers muttering drivel. So deep, wow! Nothing but a holy scam, a con job, I should have known better, born into the business as I was, a rabbi's daughter. (Don't go there, I would caution myself when she would plunge into these rants, control yourself. Above all do not bring up now her sweet little Ganesha shrine in the corner of our bedroom illuminated at night by the flat-screen TV, her personal four-armed potbellied elephant god comforting her all her years like a beloved stuffed animal, big Dumbo ears, long swinging linga of a trunk. I was the mouse at the foot of the elephant watching her perform her puja. To me it was all so dear, so dear.)

And don't get me started on the caste system, Geeta would push on, an obscenity perpetrated by the rich and powerful to justify their entitlement, to squelch every charitable instinct since it follows that however wretched your life, you deserved what you got based on your conduct in your previous incarnation. Even more cynically, if you hoped to improve your status in your future birth, your suffering in this life was mandatory; any effort by misguided do-gooders to relieve your misery was counterproductive. The starving children of India were monsters in their past lives. Don't even bother feeling sorry for them, much less finishing all the food on your plate.

She would know. Because when she finally got it together to leave us in the middle of that sweltering June, on your first day back at school after your two-month summer break, her billionaire father dispatched a black Mercedes down from Delhi with a driver in livery followed by a fleet of gleaming white Tata vans, her dear old ayah coming along as part of the entourage to wipe her nose and hold her hand through the separation anxiety. Thank God you were spared this sight, it was sickening, but you remember surely that she was in a wheelchair then, from having burned her feet firewalking. She had been threatening to leave, nothing new, but this time unlike all the others she had actually taken the extreme measure of doing the groundwork, flying up to Delhi to line up a job as vice president in charge of human relations for an NGO chain of orphanages for abused girls. In case you've ever wondered, her declared human relations specialty was the culture of bullying, so harmful to a young girl's self-esteem. Well excuse me, but in the context of rape, so-called honor killings, mutilations, child marriages, forced sex enslavement, trafficking, beatings, acid burnings, starvation, and shitting in the street, to mention just the short list, a focus on bullying, to put it mildly, is quite an indulgence. Of course, thanks to her family's influence, landing the job was a foregone conclusion. Still, there was one point on which that slimy nonprofit with its eye on the prize (Nobel, Peace) could not budge if it had any hope of maintaining a good working relationship with the Hindu cosmos, earthly and divine: the rite of passage hazing to propitiate the combustible female principle as manifested in the savagely powerful mother goddess, Kali—the requirement that each new top management recruit walk on a bed of burning coals, like a stupefied fakir, levitating above it all. Holy men say there's a method to carrying this off without suffering any collateral damage, but the divine mother Kali, creator and punisher, engorged with all that hot female energy, would not be deceived. The pink soles of our poor Geeta's aristocratic feet that I had so often taken into my mouth and adored were tandooried, turned scarlet like a baboon's behind, ulcerated and blistered, the skin hanging in shreds.

Sitting with her thumb in her mouth in her fat ayah's lap in the state-of-the-art wheelchair her father had also sent along, she was steered by a turbaned retainer to the limo after the vans were loaded with the eight new jumbo-sized suitcases packed to bursting, not to mention furniture, paintings, books, linens, carpets, china, silver, kitchenware, and so on—any detachable object of value that she could claim and fit into the transport. She ransacked the place, took everything she could take from the penthouse condo that was our home in those days on Malabar Hill with its magical view of the sea. You remember how we would stand there at the great floor-to-ceiling expanse of windows, Maya, you and I, and imagine we could see over the waters into the houses of other little girls just like you in all those countries far away with names also beginning in the letter *I*—Iceland, Ireland, Italy, Iran, Israel.

But no way would I have let her take you from me, Maya, not that she tried, I'm sorry if it hurts you to hear. She seemed to have lost interest in you over the last year or so, and truth be told, in me as well. This may be too personal a disclosure between mother and daughter, but I'm telling it to you because I believe it will bolster your self-esteem, reassure you that it was not your fault, if you knew that our sex life, Geeta's and mine, was virtually over. It was a classic case of lesbian bed death, which usually hits around the five-year marker (not too different, by the way, from sex apathy in the heterosexual single-partner bedchamber), though for us it struck between the third and fourth year, still within the statistical range if that's any comfort. But coming back to you—knowing Geeta, there's no doubt she emotionally disconnected because you had blossomed into such a mature, beautiful young woman, and if there was one thing her royal highness did not appreciate, it was competition; like Snow White's wicked stepmother, this queen too had to be the fairest of them all. Still, had she tried to stake a claim, I would have fought like a tigress to keep you, like a desperate wild woman I would have fought even from my disadvantaged position with regard to power, influence, money, and, let's face it, my hopeless situation as a stranger in a strange land far from my home turf, condemned to a life sentence as an outsider with no reprieve, no matter how hard I might struggle to fit in. Still, I would never have let them have you, Maya, I would have stretched myself out under the wheels of their rolling motorcade rather than give you up. You were the one thing in our joint household, Geeta's and mine, that was nailed to the floor. You were not a movable feast. Even now I cannot bear the terrible thought of how things might have turned out had I let you go.

So thank you Shiv Sena and Bal Thackery and the whole right-wing, fascistic, cretinous gang of Hindu thugs and goondas, I gratefully acknowledge you at this point. At least you were there for me when I needed you. There was no chance that Geeta's daddy-ji, even with all the resources and connections at his command, would ever go public with our case given the affront to Hindu culture and religion that our sexual preference and lifestyle represented to the xenophobic zealots. No chance that he would ever take the risk, personal and financial, of fighting in open court for custody, never mind that he is your own grandpa (adoptive, admittedly, but even so—behold the limits of his commitment and take heed). No chance that he would ever have allowed the sordid details to be laid out for the entire hungry population of one billion plus to gawk at and gorge upon and regurgitate in an invigorating after-dinner riot. Two women copulating, two women consecrating, two women cohabiting, two women co-parenting—explain that to the Sena boys. Such abominations do not happen in Hindustan, they never were and never have been and never will be. In no way would your grandfather have risked discharging all of these delectable family secrets into the Indian mosh pit—too much information, extremely bad for property and personal health. I pause here to note, Maya, that as soon as Geeta left us for good, I took pains to go through the official bureaucratic channels to change our company's name to M&M Sati Trips. For you, Maya, you and me, melted together, like the candy, our two *M*'s conjoined forever by the stigmata of the ampersand, inseparable.

It was a bitter end. We had been together almost five years, Geeta and I, not including the extended lapses and separations, in my case for business travel and to oversee the end-of-life managed care and remains disposal of my late mother, may her memory be for a blessing, in Geeta's case, I can now no longer afford the indulgence of deluding myself, to perpetrate her treacheries and betrayals. But there were precious moments of intense closeness, and yes commitment, especially in the early stages of our relationship, which you may not remember, of course, you were so young and oblivious, like a spirit hovering, a holy waif, before you blossomed into such a ravishing young woman and were scarred by our battles. There was even a time we were considering having a child together, as near to our own biological offspring as possible, with my fraternal twin brother Shmelke, by then butterflied into a leading rabbi and guru, serving as the donor, either in a series of personal appointments with Geeta until he succeeded in performing the mitzvah in the time-honored way, or with a rack of test tubes sloshing with his sacred sperm. Shmelke, with whom I had for nine months shared a womb of our own, was the other free radical in our sibling brood. As our mother used to say, If you ask me to count how many children the One Above blessed me with, I can only answer that there are not seven, plus the twins, Min'ke and Shmelke. Growing up, we looked disturbingly alike; apart from the strictly gender-specific clothing we wore and the hairstyles (until the age of three, his in long ringlets, mine hacked short), most people could not tell which one of us was the boy and which the girl. And in fact, the deal was almost consummated when the whole project fell apart, and with one thing and another, never taken up again—just one sorry side effect of Shmelke's forced flight from his longtime headquarters in Jerusalem, ending up finally after long and arduous travail in Kolkata, where he could continue to pursue in a warm and accepting environment his mind-blowing spiritual teachings, offering so much healing and consolation.

Since her departure, though, we have not seen each other, Geeta and I, not once. She disrespected me grievously by refusing to grant me the pittance of a private audience even when I dragged myself over seven hundred miles up to Delhi to petition in your behalf, Maya. She never bothered to come down to visit you; set that as a seal upon your heart. She left us flat, not only you, but our union, hers and mine. Remember, we were married not once, but twice, rabbi and pandit, two traditional weddings with all the trimmings—a Jewish ceremony followed by a dark meat roast chicken reception in Bensonhurst, Brooklyn, courtesy albeit grudging of my biological sponsors, the rabbi and rebbetzen, in a gilded mirrored catering hall owned by the mafia under the elevated tracks with the D and N trains rumbling overhead, a Hindu ceremony paid for by her clan in a mirrored gilded private room at the Taj Mahal Hotel (where else?) featuring mostly her pals from the Mumbai Bollywood scene thanks to the movies her father bankrolled and her bit parts in the dancing chorus when she was in the mood for a workout, a spectacular party.

God, she was beautiful that night at the Taj, your adoptive mother, in her blood-red silk Benares sari and gold bangles, the henna filigree intricately stained on her palms rising up along her arms like the most elegant lace evening gloves, like creeping disease, the heavy diamonds clasping her throat and suspended from her ears, her headpiece sewn with lustrous white pearls setting off her oiled black, black hair. She was playing the bride in a Bollywood film, another over-the-top Indian fantasy wedding production. Still, we were an astonishing couple in India, a two-mom household insisting on recognition, legitimization, but truth to tell, at bottom no different from any other nuclear family unit with a beloved child at the center of its solar system, interpreting your every sign like astrologers, poring over you, obsessed, like weathermen watching the skies day and night, utterly powerless to talk about anything other than you whatever the season. I did not have a family fortune like Geeta, but I had you. I gave her the ultimate gift of motherhood. You were the greatest treasure in my trove. I shared you without reservation, I gave you. I bought off your father, convinced him to give up any and all claims. I lured him away from the Singing Rabbi's gravesite in Jerusalem with the promise of spiritual nirvana, an all-expenses-paid private deluxe tour of every ashram in India, north and south. As far as we know then, he had never returned. The last reported sighting of the yacht we had hired for him in which he had set sail over the horizon deeper and deeper into the mysterious east after he had put his signature on the official papers—Shmiel the Holy Beggar Shapiro hereby gives up all property rights to the female Maya and so on—was coming up upon the coast of the Andaman Islands. For six years I believed he had been eaten. I erased his *Shapiro* from your book, Maya, and slung a hyphen like a lifeline between Geeta's *Devi* and my *Tabor* to attach them to you. Maya Devi-Tabor. In you, East met West. Despite the postcolonialist mindset, in you the twain met. Devi-Tabor—our goddess with drums and tambourines, and all the women coming out dancing behind you.

Everything—I gave her everything. There was nothing I held back. Who can fault me then, when a month after she dumped us I trekked up to Delhi and stationed myself a barefoot supplicant outside the gate of her family's compound under the eyes of the uniformed guards swinging their lathis, the monkeys screeching and baring their teeth on top of the stone walls. My demand was not negotiable: child support, full throated and open handed, or no-holds-barred disclosure in all the media of the scandalous, shameful decadence of the tiny elite of the indecently rich and sinful in this seething land of unspeakable need and injustice—enough to ignite mayhem between the factions of resentment that would have recast the memory of the riots between Hindus and Muslims of the last decade of the millennium into a trance party. Reparations—she owed me, she owed you. Yes, for you Maya I debased myself, and it paid off. They paid us off—coldly, impersonally, mechanically, but they paid, like good Germans. There was nothing to do but set pride aside and shame, and to take it. The checks arrived like clockwork. You would never be hungry, you would never squat in the gutter, a beggar's bowl raised between your palms, you would continue to live with all the comforts and opportunities that were your entitlement. This was Geeta's buyout from us at no personal cost to her, no penalty other than payout for what she had done to me, to you. She never had to face me and see the rapid rise and fall of my chest and the ripple of the quiver I struggled to suppress in the unnaturally wide-open eyes of she who had been slapped.

Within half a year after our separation, when you were already at boarding school in the US, she married again without having the decency to even pretend to go through the motions of filing for divorce. Face it, girl, I tell myself, she never really took our marriage seriously. It was not real, it had no binding meaning, it was nothing but liberal slumming, sexual experimentation, she could afford it. The minute she wanted out, all her same-sex hoo-ha turned into vapor. She could move on as if what had been formalized between us were disposable—no truth, no consequences, no need for a legal mop-up. For sure that was the counsel she had been given by her family's top lawyer, Samson Elijah, the man she left me for—You don't have to bother going through the hassle of a divorce, baby, that marriage was a joke, not even a starter marriage, just two little girls playing house, you be the daddy I'll be the mommy. Whatever small comfort I could derive from seeing her stuck with a Jew again for her sins was hollow. Something about us must turn her on, some baseless myth or idea, something primitive but powerful enough to overcome her Aryan Brahmin alarm sensor against untouchables, the flipside of whatever dangerous and incendiary delusions about us Jews that have turned others off over the centuries, with such catastrophic consequences.

He was from an old Bombay Bene Israel family, low-caste untouchable oil pressers swollen to moguls in the spice business. But what truly set him apart from most of the other youth of his tribe was that after full-body exposure to the bounty of America at Harvard College and

Harvard Law School, preparation H all the way down, he did not glee-
fully jump into the marching ranks of the international Indian diaspora conspiracy but packed his bags and came home to the tinderbox
of India, an occurrence noteworthy for its rarity. The intoxicating rot
of Jewishness smothered in all the perfumes of Harvard—for Geeta,
what could be sexier? I ask you. It is common knowledge that her
father acquired him for a stratospheric sum. The old gangster made
him a partner in the business, that's on the record, invited him to join
the noble enterprise of polluting the subcontinent from the Arabian
Sea to the Bay of Bengal, from the Himalayas to the Indian Ocean,
with shopping centers rising like mushroom clouds on leveled slums,
an offer, by the way, that he had never seen fit to extend to me, not
that I would have done anything other than stand on principle and
refuse. Samson was the man she was with that cosmically auspicious
night I met her. I recognize now that she had been cheating on me all
along with Samson Elijah with his gelled black ringlets almost shoulder length, his wet-look hair scrunched on either side of a too-wide
middle part, coifed to hide something suspiciously male patterned.
With this prize specimen and who knows what other hijra of indeter
minate gender she had been deceiving me, discounting me those years
of our doomed marriage in which she had never for a minute believed.

I was alone as usual the night I met her, in my spot on the balcony
of the Leopold Café overlooking the scene below, my pitcher of beer
in front of me placed on the table by Pasha the waiter as soon as I sat
down, without any superfluous exchange between us other than the
coded nod of recognition. It was a Wednesday in late November. In
the US, it was the eve of Thanksgiving, and as I brooded over my beer
that night I was clutched by the pangs of exile. You were too young
to comfort me, or to ease my loneliness at the time, Maya, only eight
years old, born at an apocalyptic hour in the land of Armageddon at
the turn of the millennium. Thank God, you were safe at home that
night, guarded by your ayah, Varda, in the apartment we were renting
during that stage of our journey after I unloaded your father the Holy
Beggar and we moved our spiritual epicenter from Israel the land of

the Messiah syndrome, to India the land of the swami syndrome, to the buzzing corrupt super-metropolis of Mumbai sinking under the weight of its overpopulation on its soggy landfill, to set up a sister branch of my tour operation business, known in those days as Seekers International.

Do you remember Varda Aunty? To give credit where it's due, despite all her shortcomings, her deceitfulness, her deviousness, and so on, had it not been for Varda coming so fortuitously into our life at that time, I would not have been relieved enough of childcare burdens to carry on full steam with my business, put food on the table for you and a roof over our heads, fork up the scandalous baksheesh required to get you into Cathedral, not to mention the tuition and all the essential extras for that most posh of feeder schools to the world's most elite universities so crucial for your future, or, for that matter, to treat myself to a few hours at the Leopold a couple of nights a week to ruminate over a pitcher of beer for some necessary restorative inner peace. All in all, I still maintain that in retrospect we were incredibly lucky to have come upon her on the very first day we moved into our building on Hormusji Street in Colaba, down the narrow teeming lane from the Mumbai Chabad center, and best of all, a short stroll from the Leopold. Clad only in her bra and panties with her varicose veins pulsing and bulging like one of those light-up tourist street maps, she was standing on her head on the landing outside her door when we arrived, going native like all those Indians carrying out their most private personal maintenance activities in public spaces, out of sight of their core inner world whose opinion matters, but under the eyes of millions of strangers who are meaningless to them and don't know who they are. We took each other's measure immediately, she scrutinizing upward, I down, recognizing at once a fellow member of the tribe, the Israeli oldies floating on the airwaves from her flat, triggering nostalgic synapses unnecessary for identification purposes but serving as gratifying confirmation, sealing our instant relatedness.

She had come to India to find her son Golan who had, in her opinion, dropped out too long in Manali in the North on his post-traumatic post-army rite of passage travel flip-out. Within a week of running into his mother as he was closing a deal on some stash with the local Hebrew-speaking Indian hashish wallah, the boy turned around and headed straight back to Israel, morphing in due time into a life insurance salesman, an amusing anomaly in the land of Gog and Magog teetering on the brink of extermination. Varda, meanwhile, settled in Mumbai where she went native, trading her senior citizen hair dye from Israeli burgundy to Indian henna orange. My second thought after laying eyes on her perpetrating her daily exercise routine in our faces, after classifying her intuitively and definitively as a fellow wandering Jew, was, Bingo! Maya's *metapelet*. For someone messed up in my particular way, a Jewish mother is a known quantity, ideal nanny material. I could handle the damage control, no problem.

Sitting in the balcony of the Leopold gazing at the action below, breathing in the secondhand heat of bodies pressing against the bar running along the wall behind me, I was prostrated again by the renewed awareness of how alone I was. When did it happen? Swirling in the ripeness of the semidarkness all around were couples and groups, muscle, hair, mouths, teeth, bodies that to my eyes were nothing but vessels evolved to house sexual organs packaged at all levels and degrees of attractiveness desperate for pleasure, mindlessly driven to breed and then self-destruct. No one saw me, I was invisible, my time had passed. Now and then some odd soul would take the risk, slide into the empty chair opposite me and venture the opening moves only to be wished away, a mortal presence too sad to absorb. Better to be alone. Too much weakness and neediness already coming into focus, in the end it would all trail off into familiar squalor and meanness. But supposing I wanted a part in it—how was it done, how did you play this game? I had forgotten the rules, I no longer knew the steps to this dance. All of those living units agitating frenziedly around me, in squads of twos, tens, were closed off from me, sealed up unto themselves, with a private history and a present known only to themselves, an intimate smell unique to themselves, a sound frequency only they could discern, out of my range. They were the insiders, I was on the outside, excluded. Who among them would ever notice or care about me enough to bother to sponsor me, as it were, take my hand, lead me into the inner circle of light? How would it profit them? What did I need to do to penetrate the walls they put up to shut me out, what did I need to do to belong?

From my solitary perch on the balcony I watched her enter at the usual time with her retinue, giving off star power glow that emanated from within her and shot out like rays from her skin, hair, stride, her flashing style, or perhaps it came from the light that instantly flicked on in me and beamed on her the minute she appeared. I had viewed her many times before and was always waiting, waiting without quite realizing it on my nights at the Leopold for her descent, a goddess from the heights. My eyes followed her every step as she was ushered in with her tight little clique, plucked by the establishment's powers ahead of the queue of kids and tourists, expats and locals, hoodlums and hangers-on crushed against the wide unshuttered entrance and led straight to the prime table down on the main floor directly in my line of fire.

The group was unusually relaxed on this night, I noticed, ironically unwired for a change, infused it seemed with a more solid assurance of well-being, eerily calm. One of the women, someone I had not seen before, had a baby in a sling carrier that she nursed at the table while sipping her beer; when she was done, she let her breast remain casually out and ready for the next feeding, exposed in the most natural and charming way, poking from the nest like a curious little bird eager to check out the scene. They laughed, chatted, flirted, but without the shrillness and preening and desperation I had noted on other evenings, serenely nursing their beers and absently extending their paws to scoop up some crisp munchies. Geeta and Samson were depositing bits of spicy prawn chili into each other's mouths, crossing their arms on the tabletop like hand wrestlers to pat away each other's grease with a napkin. I watched as if through a window, it was a party to which I had not been invited. They were native specimens in a glass case, command performing their tricks in a private audience for me, exclusively for my entertainment. For as long as I looked at them they existed, I told myself; when I turned my eyes away they would cease to exist. I got up to pay my bill. It was already around nine o'clock, late, time to snuff them out and head home to real life—to supervise your homework and bath, Maya, the sacred hour of your bedtime. I slung my bag over my shoulder, waved farewell to Pasha the waiter whom I would never again see in this life (when I look back now at my actions that indelible night, the one thing I regret is not having left him a bigger tip), and headed down the stairs, approaching the periphery of their aura and breathing it in, though they took no notice of me, no different from a fly.

The moment I waited for on those nights, the cherished antici-pated moment when I would pass within a foot of her and inhale her voraciously on my way out to the street, the greatest intimacy I could ever imagine myself aspiring to with her—that was the moment of the first explosion. Smoke plumed up almost immediately, and after that the screaming, wailing, panic. I ran and grabbed her, pushed her under the table, and like her majesty's secret service exploiting the only window of opportunity for physical contact between common folk and royalty, I dared to throw myself on top of her for her own good less than a minute before the second grenade was thrown, sput-tering out like a cautionary warning very close by. Then came the stac-cato of the machine gun firing rapidly, nonstop, seemingly at random. It was as if I were dreaming. It was as if we were extras captured in yet another battle scene in the endless cycle of Mumbai's gang wars, this time being fought out on the atmospheric turf of the Leopold Café, like a stage show to draw tourists into this noir hotspot. It flashed through my mind that maybe Samson was the guy the Indian mafia had fingered this time and come here looking for; it might after all be in everyone's best interest to end this drama simply by identifying him and handing him over.

Cautiously I lifted an edge of the skirt of the tablecloth that was our sole screen of defense, and poked my head out a fraction in an effort to locate where Samson might be cowering, praying not to dis-lodge the sheet of glass I knew was flattened over the splayed menus on top and send it crashing. One of the assassins was only two feet away from me, spasmodically jerking out his AK-47, shooting frantically, indiscriminately, even into bodies seemingly already dead. Small and scrawny and intense, greasy black hair, cheeks so pathetically smooth over which a razor had never passed, the feathery dark down of a mustache, milk-white teeth, a rucksack on his back filled with ammunition like any other third-world tourist who could handle an automatic rifle and a satellite phone but didn't know how to use a flush toilet—this was just a kid, sixteen or seventeen years old maybe, the gang lords had sunk to a shameful new low in the recruitment of their hit boys. Later, of course, I along with the whole tuned-in world was notified that it wasn't a gang war this time around but a full-blown terrorist attack, and these poor primitive suckers doing the dirty work were *shahid* wannabes, suicide martyr material plucked from the most miserable holes in Pakistan and sent over the waters to turn civilization into carnage on their blood-red carpeted road to paradise. But while it was unfolding it seemed so unreal, so unbelievable, like a scene from a Bollywood movie. I was waiting for the villains to sling their AK-47s over their shoulders and break out in rousing song and dance, and I was not afraid.

In the space between the dying down of the shooting and the dawning absorption of all that was happening, I dragged her out from under the table. She was trembling audibly. It was all I could do to hold back from scooping her up in the cradle of my arms and carrying her away to a safe zone if one still remained on this planet. Grasping each other's hands, like two little girls fleeing a boogeyman lumbering behind them down a dark alley, we ran across the war zone restaurant, past bodies huddled on the bloodstained floor, wounded or struck down forever or simply shocked out, overturned tables and chairs, shattered glass, smashed crockery, bullet-pocked walls and doors and windows, the metallic smell of firepower, the rust smell of blood charging the atmosphere. I cast my eye for a sign of Samson but could not find him. Later she filled me in that he had escaped at the first all clear with the bare-breasted woman and her suckling, commandeering one of the taxis that were by then already being requisitioned to ferry the victims and survivors to hospitals, and rerouting it to the sanctuary of his lair in Bandra. So she had been in touch with him, I should have made a mental note, but she related this information with dripping revulsion, and she chose to stay with me. By the time we reached a side door of the café, the ghostly end-of-the-world silence in which everything had been frozen, rendered all the more silent by the punctuation of the shrill insistent ringing of unanswered cell phones in the pockets of the dead and dying—that silence now cracked open never to be recovered. The crying and screaming was terrible as we ran out into the darkness to escape it down a narrow lane toward the sea.

Our flight came to its terminus at a seawall outcropping, and we collapsed on the rocks. The Taj Mahal Hotel in all its opulent grandeur loomed darkly above us nearby, and beyond that rose the great basalt stones of the Gateway arch on the waterfront. Welcome to Mother India. A weighty silence engulfed us from which every living heartbeat had been bled. We could hear the lapping of the tide in the distance. The plaza was hauntingly deserted, even by police and criminals. The world had come to an end. We lowered our heads into our hands and wept. I did not forget you, Maya. The airwaves gave off no signal from you, the smooth black cell phone in my pocket was a miniature tombstone. Everything had been blown up and swept away, nothing was left. We were alone.

We wept for all the noble reasons, for having survived, for the massacre that would define us now forever, for the meaninglessness and absurdity of human suffering and striving. The long manicured finger of her left hand, the one not for eating but for washing after using the toilet, pressed into the corner of my eye and tenderly traced the path of a tear down my cheek. I yanked the elastic out of my hair and shook it loose. Her eating hand slipped coolly under my kurta against the skin of my belly, then down to the cord that held up my homespun cotton khadi Gandhi trousers, liquefying me. The world had come to an end, the possibilities were endless. I could go on, Maya, but as you know, I don't consider this an appropriate subject for a mother to share with her daughter, so I'll stop here. Let me just say, as I've told you many times, men have their practical uses, but when it comes to loving a woman, they don't know what they're doing. The conclusion is obvious. All I will add here for the sake of closure is that on that night of all nights what we enacted on the rocks, she and I, was the natural consummation of our destined union born in the shadow of mortality under the table on the bloodstained floor of the Leopold Café. Later, afterward—ah, such rich signifiers!—entwined in each other's arms, we fell asleep in a cleft of the rocks.

To this day I don't know what woke us up, the sound or the light. There was a series of thunderous blasts and the sky lit up, illuminating a hidden universe of lovers tucked in the niches and crannies of the rocks, their eyes startled open and fluttering wildly. Spears of flame were shooting up from the Taj. Its magnificent dome seemed to be burning. There was a brilliant otherworldly light, neither day nor night. What time was it? I foraged in my bag for my cell phone, and it was only then, Maya, that I realized that the reason I had not heard from you was that time had stopped for me at the Leopold when I turned off my device to prevent a ring from jolting the killers and drawing their hyper-jittery attention to our huddled mass under the table. It was now nearly midnight, I saw, and there were six messages, five from you, text and voice, all identical, Mommy, come home *now*! The sixth was from Varda Aunty: Terrorist Attack Chabad House Saving Maya-Baby.

Black smoke canopied the Taj. I turned to her and said, Go home, it has nothing to do with you, it's all about the Jews again, but she shook her head. Under no circumstances would she leave me at this time. The child was in danger. Nothing is more precious than a child. One little Jewish girl. Ten little Indian boys. It is the lesson of the Holocaust. A Jewish life is worth fifty non-Jews. A fine thought. The wisdom of the terrorist handlers recounted in the aftermath, final instructions but flipped: one dead Jew is worth fifty dead non-Jews. Everything was deconstructing all around us, but we were armed with our newly hatched love and we set forth to rescue you.

The sea was black to our left as we ran clutching each other's hands, knees bent, stooped perpendicular, like enemy targets in all those war movies, locust scuttling from trench to trench. Hunched over in this way, we wove unimpeded through the web of darkened alleys and lanes, arriving too soon at our besieged backstreet, swept clean of its night crawlers and regulars, and muffled as if under an executioner's hood. Police in khakis and soldiers in jungle camouflage with helmets weirdly festooned with twigs squatted against the buildings, pistols and rifles cocked at Nariman House, the Chabad center, lit up like a stage with its fourth wall gouged out to expose the furiously ravaged interior cavities of its set. From its blown-out windows intermittent bursts of gunfire sputtered down, a bullet-sieved white flag waving like a mockery of surrender—the rabbi's ritual garment, fringes flying.

The *paan* wallah proprietor of the stall across the road hauled us in as we hugged the walls of his tin-roofed shack sidling past, scolding lunatics (meaning us, me and Geeta, eyeing Geeta greedily, what was this luxury item doing here in our savage bazaar?)—we were the lunatics, not the villains center stage in the show now being broadcast live direct from the Chabad house across the pit. Two locals had already been shot, he was telling us this for our own good, maybe they were already in Hindu heaven by now. Some old guy fleeing from the house trying to pass himself off as yet another Jewish victim had been lynched by community watchdogs, taken for a terrorist, his bones broken into pieces, it will require hundreds of thousands of dollars in mental health therapy to get him to venture out again to peddle his diamonds. The Israeli army was expected to make a surprise appearance any minute, its legendary, ruthless, crack, elite commando force of superheroes slated to swoop down in the darkness of night to drop their nuclear payload right here in a spectacular display of fireworks, right here on Hormusji Street, according to the most top-notch reliable sources, which is why the street is being evacuated—hadn't we noticed? Bad girls, you deserve to be spanked—what are you doing out on such a night as this?

Don't worry, Geeta said to me. We will find her.

She took my hand and led me away to you. It was such a blessing, to be enclosed within those brackets of reprieve from the weight of always being in charge to which I had been sentenced for life. I let myself go, let myself be taken by Geeta, I put myself in her hands, though she could not possibly have had any idea in which of the buildings in this war zone you were crouching terrified, or from which you might have been spirited away by the lords of evacuation. She was sublime that night, Geeta, pure essence of mother animal in the wild, she picked up your scent as it had translated itself through me and brought us straight to our building, straight to our floor, our door, which she opened with the key she plucked neatly from my purse.

Inside, darkness and void, nothing, nothing, you were not there. No sign of life—those words bore down on me, *sign of life*, none, not even a note from Varda, the least she could have done was to leave a note to quiet my pounding heart. So we were located within the minefield after all, it was as I had always suspected. You had been evacuated, cleared away, ethnically cleansed for your own good. Where had they taken you? To what detention camp, what *umschlagplatz*, what collection point awaiting deportation? We ran out into the hallway and vented our four fists in wasted rage on Varda's door, rattling the tchotchkes inside, the brass elephants, the laughing Buddhas, the incense burners, sending the mauve Post-it note with the smiley face she had affixed to that door twirling slow-motion downward to the floor. *Gaga*, she had written in her loopy Hebrew with her signature violet felt marker, and beside it an arrow, pointing upward.

Up on the roof the party was already full blown. The residents of the building had all spumed upward and out with their dogs and cats and birds and goats, their numbers strengthened by friends and neighbors also escorted by their pets expelled from the restricted zone, all variety of spongers and oglers including news media types, camera wielders, journalists, bloggers, along with politicians carping the diem, as well as army sharpshooters and snipers who had identified the prize view from our rooftop. We had been declared to be just at the outer fringe of the officially designated off-limits strip, as it turned out, safe, if such a concept can be said to exist on this planet. It was past one, Thursday a.m., predawn, Thanksgiving Day. Everyone was settling in on that rooftop for the grand finale however long it would drag on, staking out a space, spreading blankets and camping gear, laying out food and toothbrushes and water and other supplies, setting up computers and assorted electronic hookups to supplement whatever might not be detectable to the naked eye with a running minute-by-minute authoritative stream of what was unfolding on the ground. The Chabad center glowed in the dark across the divide suspended in the black hole of an alternate universe, silent, a mass of hot gas about to combust.

We searched for you everywhere on that rooftop, Maya, we searched for you but could not find you. Daughters of Jerusalem, if you see the one my soul loves what will you say to her? Tell her I am sick with love for her, sick. A group of Israelis sitting cross-legged in a circle on the floor around a centerpiece of six burning memorial candles was strumming guitars and belting out defiantly "Am Yisrael Hai," the rousing Carlebach tune that brought back to me involuntarily so many memories of my *kumsitz* days with your father, Shmiel. There among them in that campfire circle, eyes closed fervently, was your nanny, Varda, singing along. Okay, Varda, we get it, the Nation of Israel still lives, still yet, as we used to say in Brooklyn—but where is Maya? As if in answer, a gunshot rang out from the Chabad house below, floodlit in the crater, then a scream such as never was and never had been created, a woman's scream, followed by sobbing, sobbing, and Geeta cried, There she is, and yes, there you were so young and tender in your pajamas, your mouth open and no sound coming out.

You were such a sensitive, delicate child, Maya—what could Varda have possibly been thinking by bringing you up to this rooftop and allowing you to witness such X-rated abominations? Still, there was no point in confronting her at that moment, high as she was in the orbit of her Jewish persecution and survival support group, and besides, her responses would have been predictable: The child needs to know, she needs to see with her own eyes how they hate us and always will hate us, in every generation they will rise up against us to destroy us, she's got to be taught, and so on and so forth. I made a mental note to myself: Later, later when all this is over, deal with Varda.

We carried you down to the apartment, Geeta and I, and laid you our baby on the bed between the hovering warmth of our two bodies, murmuring to you, stroking you until at last your face rigid with horror, your mouth frozen in the zero degrees of a scream thawed to life again and the voice you had lost was restored to you. The voice in that scream was the voice of the rabbi's wife, distorted, but you had recognized it, you knew her voice when she had a voice, she was our neighbor, your friend. What had they done to her to wring out such a scream? What sight had they flashed across the screen of her eyelids before she might have closed them forever? What was the last thing she saw in this life?

We had met her and the rabbi her husband nearly three years earlier, not long after we arrived in Mumbai and settled into our apartment. It was a Thursday too, I remember. We were returning home from your admissions interview at Cathedral, which went very well, I'm proud to say, and he was lugging home over his shoulder like Santa Claus a canvas sack stuffed with a dozen bleeding chickens he had just freshly slaughtered for the Sabbath. He decoded us instantly by our surface DNA and invited us to his table. The chickens were roasted, she supervised her dark-skinned menials in all the preparations, she blessed the candles and fed the hungry—the Lonely Planet gang, the dutiful tourists sweating from the rounds of Jewish heritage sites, the diamond traders from Ramat Gan and Antwerp and Forty-Seventh Street in Manhattan, the Israeli post-army dropouts, the spiritual seekers, the useless kosher eaters, wandering Jews, eternal seekers, passing through on the road to the messianic age, a cast of millions in multiples of six. When it came my turn to introduce myself around the table our first time there, I said, "I used to be a rabbi's daughter when I was a little boy." The rabbi coughed up a sharp laugh, bunched his wiry red beard in the shaft of his fist and adjusted the black velvet yarmulke on his head. "Ah, a rebel!" he declared. "Like your brother, the famous Reb Breslov Tabor. But still yet we love you. The Rebbe says it's a mitzvah to love all Jews, irregardless." Already he knew everything worth knowing about me.

The rebbetzin in her long sleek Sabbath wig sat down next to me, took my hand, and confided that she was pregnant. It was her third pregnancy; her first two babies had not survived, cut down by a hereditary Jewish disease. "Jewish hereditary diseases are so unfair," I commented, "considering that just being born Jewish is a hereditary disease." What drove me to regress like that, to act up like such an adolescent? Why was it so vital for me to signal that once I had been an insider, I knew their territory, but I had seen the light and now was proudly out? To this day I still cringe with shame when I remember that first night. Even so, she embraced us, Maya. She smoothed your cheek and said, "Such a sweet little girl, the sweetest of the sweet, may no evil eye befall you. When my baby is born, God willing in a good hour and in good health, I hope you will be friends. I hope you will come to visit every day."

You visited so often in your uniform on your way home from school I suppose I should have set limits. They could have brainwashed you, reeled you in, another stray Jew; I was familiar with their mission and their tactics, I knew their power. But you insisted on going, and swept over by personal nostalgia and my conviction that the familiar, however harmful, was at least manageable, I let it happen. Almost every afternoon you stopped by for a short playdate with little Moshe while Varda waited for you outside their building smoking bidis with the security guard. (And where was *he* on that day the monsters rose up out of the wine-dark sea and cut a straight path to this Jewish hostel?) Intentionally, she did not remain inside to consort with Moshe's ayah Sandra, in order to show the entire world so wildly attentive to her every move that she was not a common nanny in the same category as this little peasant from Nepal, she was really an astrophysicist slumming as a childcare provider; as for the guard, he was actually a chemical engineer between jobs, she informed me. "Moshe'le is my favorite baby in the world," you would say. "His mama lets me hold him and carry him around."

The night little Moshe's mother let out that scream you lost your voice, Maya. For hours you did not speak a word there on our bed lying between Geeta and me, until dawn when released at last from the evil spell that gripped you, you turned to Geeta and said, "What will happen to Moshe'le?" "He will be saved," she replied with an assurance no one would dare contradict as you sank into sleep, and over your fragrant head our lips met like the wings of the cherubim over the holy ark.

As we slept in our apartment the constant pounding on the roof directly above us did not abate. Up and down the stairs there was stomping and thudding all through the night constricting my throat and chest with a deep grinding-bass pulse. I knew I must wake up for the sake of my family, to protect you from a threat I sensed very close by, but a great weight was pressing down on me, and I could not move, as if I were paralyzed. Mama! you cried out to me, but you were too far away for me to reach you. I summoned up every remaining shred of my strength to rip the coils holding me down in which I was trussed and drag you from the window where you stood staring into the cockpit of a helicopter, the pilot's dark eyes smiling on Geeta, shaking his helmeted head side to side in a movement the rest of the world translates as *no*, but in the official Indo-Aryan and Dravidian body language of the subcontinent it is *yes*—yes yes yes.

We waved as his helicopter brushed our window so close, dipping down low then lifting and whirling away, no longer ours as it joined the flock of choppers suspended under the clouds. From the windows of buildings all around faces popped out, citizens were spilling out onto the balconies, the street so strangely deserted last night was coming back to life, filling with humans panting with curiosity and excitement at a calamity not strictly their own, stray dogs, goats, the whole teeming mob, all pressing toward the poisonous blot of Nariman House. A large white van had drawn up there, maybe an ambulance, maybe a hearse, the airwaves were buzzing, something was happening. Still creased by sleep we ran barefoot up to the roof. With Geeta carving out our pathway we shoved to the head of one of the packs gathered in front of a screen. "It's Moshe'le," you cried, pointing to the baby on the screen. "He wants his mama."

Ima, Ima, baby Moshe was sobbing on the screen, the bullet-pelted facade of the Chabad house in the backdrop behind him, sobbing in the arms of his ayah Sandra, blinking in the dusty late-morning daylight of the street. He would not stop crying despite all her tricks to calm him, nothing could stop him from calling, Ima. His body stiffened, arching desperately in the direction of the place that contained his heart's only desire, as if he would launch himself from the street back inside there whatever the consequences. A clump of fuzzy black microphone spider-heads was thrust at Sandra's face as she was being lifted into the white van struggling to hold on to the baby. She had been hiding in a closet when she heard him crying, she paused to recollect. She didn't think, she said, she just ran and grabbed the baby. She found him wandering dazed in circles around his mother and father lying there so still on the floor—but alive, Sandra insisted, still alive. "My rabbi and his lady, they were so still—I should have carried the baby out, then run back inside to save them. I will never forgive myself." The door of the van sealed behind her like breath expiring, like a spaceship, just as a grenade tossed out of one of the windows of the Chabad center exploded nearby killing a scapegoat, and the crowd ran for cover.

Varda materialized beside me. "Ha, super-ayah Sandra! How much do you think they paid her, those guys in there, for that little public relations stunt? Muslim freedom fighters release Indian nanny with her Jewish charge in a compassionate gesture. We love all little children. It is the Zionist entity we must uproot. Tell me something—who arranged for that van to show up just at the right minute? Such a big hero, Sandra! Say bye-bye to your ima, Moshe'le. You will never see her again." Tears were streaming down her face.

Everyone was weeping on that rooftop as they milled in front of the screens watching the baby crying inconsolably for his mother. It was a communal cry-in, incredibly cathartic, an emotional enema, the deeply satisfying pleasure shared by an audience in a packed movie theater viewing a tearjerker together, absorbing the same stimuli and responding as one. But this was not just discreet sniffling and dabbing at the corners of the eyes with a tissue. It was racking sobs, loud and heaving, wailing. I stood there among them taking it all in, struggling to suppress the lump rising in my own throat, fighting to keep my voice from breaking out in howls and losing itself in chorus with theirs. There's nothing like the cry *Mother* to turn on the waterworks even in the most base and hardened human specimen. I had had a mother too, gone up in smoke. With all my willpower I resisted being manipulated like a Pavlovian dog by this universal trigger, it took every ounce of my inner strength to keep my emotions from churning up and flowing over. Those weeping most openly and lustily, I marveled, were the mighty special commando saviors who now dominated the scene on the rooftop, armed with submachine guns and gleaming knives with sawtooth shark blades. They were the ones who had been stomping up the stairs all through the night I realized to take up their positions on the roof. Now they stood there sobbing helplessly in their black jumpsuits as the baby on the screen bawled, Ima, and would not be comforted. Tears poured out unrestrained from the catlike eyeholes of their black balaclavas.

The commando who materialized as the leader of the unit assigned to our rooftop wept his fill, then dried his eyes, gave his nose a good blow, and turned to peer into his scope pointed at Nariman House. In a deliberate public display of professional diligence, he took his time surveying the scene, communicating coordinates and other data to underlings. Only when he had thoroughly satisfied himself that his duties had been properly dispatched did he acknowledge the reporter and cameraman agitating his airspace. "The mission is Shoot and Scoot," he declared. "My boys are the cream of the cream, tried-and-true veterans of the Gujarat riots, class of 2002. We know how to deal with these loonies. The Israelis are breathing down our necks. There's nothing they'd like better than to jump in and take all the credit. I don't give a damn if it's Jews in there, or Israelis or Disraelis or Queen Victoria's pet monkey. I have one word to say to you Israelis, so listen up: This one is our baby! This is Mother India, a sovereign nation. You stay out of it!"

Not too far away on the rooftop, a politician in jacket and tie was discoursing expansively, aiming his remarks at the entire subcontinent and the movers and shakers beyond, sucking microphones like lollipops poked forward by media enablers. He was pleased to announce that the situation was now under control at the Taj Mahal

Hotel. Based on a classified intergovernment update he had just now received, all he was in a position now to disclose was that guests still inside the Taj were safe, they had taken refuge in the Chambers, the posh members-only lounge, where they were enjoying free drinks and tasty hors d'oeuvres, settling in comfortably for the duration until the crisis is fully resolved by our brave first responders. The terrorists have no clue where they are hiding and will never find them.

Even Varda had found a reporter and cameraman team settling for her insights during this lull in the siege, while commandos and snipers stood around sipping chai from unglazed earthenware mugs then hurling them against the stone parapet or like missiles down into the empty street. She identified herself as a proud Zionist, an Israeli, and a Jew in that order, who unfortunately had already had far too much experience with situations like this, she wouldn't wish it on her worst enemies. If there's someone out there who imagines for one second that the Jews are not the main target of this little exercise and the designated victims as per usual, she was here now in the fabled land of enlightenment to enlighten them. She reached into the pocket of the vest over her *kameez*, drew out a crumpled sheet of paper, and held it out in front of the camera lens. "This is the terrorists' top handler who is now pulling the strings from Pakistan," Varda declared, bobbing the photo annoyingly to rivet the audience's attention to the image. It was a blowup of a headshot of a man, balding, ponytailed. He reminded me of someone—someone I associated with group-spirit dining, maybe at the Leopold Café. At first I thought it might be the celebrated writer of a doorstop novel about the Bombay underworld—what was his name?—a former murderer and hoodlum who had reportedly escaped from life imprisonment in Australia to become a bestselling author with a cult following and whom I would spot now and then holding court at his reserved table at the Leopold with his consort at his side, an Indian princess, stunning even through her veil. But then it came to me, and I remembered where I had seen this guy. It was at the Chabad center, at the Sabbath table. He had been wearing a yarmulke. I had filed him away then as just another hung-up Jewish male on the road, indulging a midlife identity crisis.

For two weeks at least he had lived at Nariman House, Varda briefed the press, a Muslim fanatic disguised as a religious Jew, scoping out the place, Varda could now authoritatively assert, stashing ammunition, planting bombs, turning it into the terrorist base in anticipation of the attack. She, Varda, had sat right next to him at the Sabbath table. She shuddered at the memory. Between the chicken soup with matzah balls and the schnitzel he had dared to reach out his hand and touch the tip of her chin, urging her never to pluck out her bristles; he found them very sexy. She would never forget his face, she went on. It was the face of the devil. His eyes were two different colors. One eye was green, the other, brown.

Varda's voice breaking this news reached us when Geeta and I were already back down in my apartment. We were lying naked in bed making love with the television blaring to keep the sounds of our intimacy from assaulting your innocent ears, Maya. We stared mesmerized at the screen. OMG, did Varda really say that about the bristles? On TV? Did she actually think that what she was sending out over the airwaves about a terrorist mole at the Chabad house was good for the Jews? And how could this guy have hauled all those supplies and ammunition into Nariman as she claimed without anyone inside wising up to what was going on right under their roof? Was this an inside job? Maybe the guy with the ponytail was really a Jew after all. Maybe he was a Mossad agent setting up the operation to incite even greater hatred of Muslims in the hearts of over a billion mother-loving Indians, to stir up riots and ethnic cleansings and partitions such as the world had never seen.

Geeta turned to me and nuzzled my face with her lips. "I just love the goat hairs on your chinny-chin-chin," she whispered. "Never tweeze them—okay?" A laugh squirted out of me, I thought she was spoofing, but she placed her long slender hand softly like a stopper over my mouth and said, "No, really—I'm serious. Promise."

We were living those days of the siege in a bubble, abdicating the responsibility for our survival to the protectors entrusted to watch over us. Mumbai was paralyzed, schools and businesses shut down, its masses huddling in high-rises and slums and chawls as the beasts ran wild through the streets. It was an enforced vacation from daily life, from all the schedules and stresses that constricted us, and though we knew that outside our sealed door catastrophic events were unfolding, it was, I admit, a restful break for us, a time-limited reprieve, an interlude, and we let ourselves sink into it. What else could we do? We had no choice, it was out of our control. You spent the time playing quietly in your room with your same-sex parents' paper dolls. Geeta and I passed the day in bed not even bothering to get dressed.

Toward evening we put on robes and gathered at the kitchen table for a simple vegan Thanksgiving meal of dal that Geeta shaped into a rooster of India, *tarnegol hodu* as they have it in the holy tongue, a *tuki*, decorating it with a wattle made of sweet mango pickles and setting it on a bed of basmati rice. You gave thanks for mommies, the more mommies the merrier, and you added a little prayer for baby Moshe's mommy, may he see her again soon, amen. Geeta gave thanks for the terrorists for bringing us together, but for nothing else, thank you. I lifted my third bottle of Kingfisher and drank to that too but added, Yes, there is one more thing to thank them for: empowering me to do what every self-help guru and spiritual mentor so strongly advises but which only today, thanks to the enforced confinement imposed by the terrorists, I've succeeded at accomplishing—living in the moment. And mindfully.

We slept deeply through the night, having by then already been conditioned to the sporadic bursts of gunfire and explosions, the tramping on the roof, the stampeding up and down the stairs, until sometime in the morning when a series of blasts such as had not been in the repertoire until then jerked us to alertness. We threw on some clothing and headed out of the apartment. The door to your bedroom was still closed as we had left it the night before. Why trouble you? Let the child go on dreaming in her purity and innocence.

From our rooftop we had an unobstructed view of commandos rappelling down on ropes dangling from a helicopter onto the roof of Nariman House. At street level, a commando brigade stormed the building through the front door. The fighting raged through the afternoon into the evening, so prolonged and intense for a battle between such a reputedly crack battalion of well-armed warriors and by most accounts such a small band of unseasoned guerrilla amateurs that I was almost leaning toward giving some serious credence to Varda's paranoid conspiracy theory about enemy infiltrators and ammunition stockpiling. Rocket fire boomed from Chabad house, windows shattered, black smoke and tear gas poured out, walls crumbled exposing the bullet-riddled wasted interior, soot smeared walls, furniture broken in pieces illuminated like a postapocalyptic movie set by floodlights aimed from surrounding rooftops. Toward night what sounded like a bomb exploded, set off by the gunmen according to sources, rocking buildings up and down Colaba Causeway to the Sassoon Docks, sending everyone diving for cover.

When darkness descended the fighting finally waned for the first time that day. For a brief otherworldly moment, we were encased in the unaccustomed texture of silence. Then great cheers burst out from the throng of onlookers now packing the streets and alleyways, celebrating on surrounding rooftops and balconies. The commando heroes were filing out the door of the war zone of Nariman House grinning jubilantly and waving their arms, flashing thumbs up signals and *V*'s for victory, graciously bending down to accept kisses of gratitude from exquisite little girls, in training as sex slaves. The siege was over, the insurgents were dead. So thorough had been our commandoes' sweep that not one perpetrator had escaped alive to terrorize ever again, the populace was assured.

The young rabbi and his wife and the other Jewish hostages did not come out to take their bows in that triumphant curtain call. Maybe it was simply a tactful gesture of deference to the heroes of the hour lest the victims steal the limelight. Maybe they had been whisked out a back door, maybe even on stretchers in a condition not suitable for public consumption. Was there a back door? We were dying, dying to know what happened to them, there were all kinds of speculation. They were alive when the Indian forces entered but were killed in the crossfire. They were already dead by the time the showdown began, murdered by the terrorists. They had been spirited away to Israel by the Mossad in Elijah's chariot for a joyous reunion with little baby Moshe in his reed basket fished out of the Indian Ocean. There were rumors of barbarism and torture. The bodies had been mutilated, what looked like a fetus had been ripped from her belly, his member had been hacked off and stuffed in his mouth, two women guests at the house were bound together with wire, raped and slashed, the eyeball of a male hostage was resting on his cheek, Torah scrolls were smeared with excrement and torn in shreds, stray dogs and feral cats were roaming, licking the blood-soaked floor, it was a pogrom. The fate of the hostages was the main topic on all the screens on our rooftop in the aftermath of the final battle—along with postmortem wrap-up interviews with the commando heroes. "We went in, we did our job, and we got the hell out of there," a beaming commando laid it out for the interviewer. "I'm not going into details. I don't need those crazy human-rights wallahs breathing down my neck." I turned to Geeta as one does to one's closest dearly beloved to share the moment, but she was no longer at my side.

She was not in the apartment either. I ran down the stairs outside and there you were, Maya, in front of our building, whimpering and drooping as if you had been drugged, so small and slight in Varda's arms. A restless mini-crowd of street regulars already bored with the main event, searching for new action in other places, menaced around you as a runt reporter who seemed to have lost his way in life, wearing a badge affiliating him with an outfit called the Hindu Orphans Press, stood there videoing Varda with his mobile phone. "I had to save the child right away," Varda was declaiming. "There was not one minute to waste. She was no longer safe in her own home. It had been taken over by depraved criminals. She was in grave danger. I did not stop for one minute to think about myself. I grabbed her and ran." This was one sick lady it now struck me, your soon-to-be-former nanny, Varda. How could I ever have left you alone with her? Forgive me, Maya. Her grandiose delusions were pathological. Among nannies, she was deserving of the most honor, more honor even than the great Sandra, innocent babes she snatched from the jaws of death. Her paranoid delusions were off the charts. Not a single sanctuary remained on this planet that had not been infiltrated by alien invaders. She was the savior, celebrated and feted.

There was a great roar nearby and your eyes darted open, but then as if losing interest you turned and stared at Varda, cocking your head with such sweet curiosity, trying to make sense of her bizarre utterances. Varda cupped the back of your warm shapely head in the palm of her hand and sought to draw you close to her breast almost smothering you, but you wriggled desperately out of her clutches, squirming down barefoot to the filthy road paved with shit crying, Mama, Mama, and with both arms spread out wide you ran toward me as I squatted down in the filth opening my arms in turn so wide to receive you, and the motorcycle gunning behind me now roared in front of me slowing down just enough for Geeta to lean over and scoop you up and set you down between her and the rider in his leather goggles and Luftwaffe cap with a frill of black hair peeking out on the edges, and Geeta sang out, Let's go for a ride, Maya, and you weren't even wearing a helmet.

· 2 ·

THE NANNY WHO SAVED YOU WAS MANIKA. True, she no longer was technically your nanny by the time Geeta dumped us; you were twelve, a woman. Had it been your fate to be born in a village somewhere in India, you would already have been squatting in your mother-in-law's hovel picking the worms from her dal, wiping her grandson's behind with your left hand while her son, your husband, followed his bliss building a career poking wires into tourists' ears to trowel out the wax. But at first, when I brought Manika home from Varanasi as my mother's legacy, she was your faithful ayah. When you no longer needed an ayah, she simply was grandmothered in as a member of our household, your companion, your duenna. She fed you with her own hands when she came to us as your nanny, you were so ethereal, so slight—Such a bad eater, my mother would have lamented. Manika shadowed you with spicy snack mixes to pique your thirst, relieved by chasers of warm cardamom milk and rich mango lassis. She never left you alone, she was your personal secret service attachment, she moved within your breath cloud. When Cathedral barred her from entering your classroom along with the other privileged little scholars, she staked a position in the schoolyard. When it banned her from the yard after she attempted to scratch out the eyes of a kid she suspected of looking at you funny, she took up her station across the road in the public domain. There she stood every day from drop-off to pick-up, her eyes burning through the stones of the fortress in which you were imprisoned lest anyone dare harm you. It made the children laugh and play to see faithful little black Manika at school —but tell me, Maya, how many of us in this life have been the repositories of such love? I said to myself, Someday you will understand and appreciate, it will become a song, a poem, a ditty, you will no longer be ashamed.

We were dogs with our tongues hanging out, panting from the heat when Geeta left us. The air pressed down upon us, and behind it the weight of the monsoon, but still the rains would not come. The ground was parched, the breasts of beggar women suckling in the street were dried up and shriveled. We pushed our way out against the heat wall in daylight hours to do what was necessary, hunting, gathering, then staggered home and collapsed on our beds, Manika shuttling between us. I was grieving over my loss, entering the second stage. All that futile stage-one denial had gotten me nowhere, I moved on to anger, fury at her for abandoning me, reviewing obsessively all of the humiliations and betrayals and deceptions that now were so obvious, how could I have missed them, I must have been blind. I could not swallow it, I could not swallow anything Manika brought to me, I sucked lemons and spit out bitter seeds.

You at least ate, I was relieved for Manika's sake. No matter how prostrate you were with the lethargy of the season, you ate. Your bed was gravelly with salt crumbs, slick with oil stains, sticky with sweet drinks. Your nymphet days were well past by then. More than a year earlier, Geeta had summoned me to observe you as you slept, your covers kicked off, thighs pulpy and succulent. When had you morphed into such a morsel? At breakfast next morning, as you were shoveling rose petal jam straight from the jar into your mouth, Geeta asked, Do you really need that, Maya?—and snatched the spoon out of your hand, a highly counterproductive tactic as I happen to know exceedingly well from the experience of having grown up with a fat mother. Nevertheless, I switched loyalties, siding with Geeta against you, I admit it—I chose her over you as we held you there captive at that table counseling you as a team for your own good about the importance of diet, exercise, not wearing horizontal stripes, and other weight-control and fat-concealing tips, especially now that you had been initiated into the sisterhood of blood, sweetening our message by reminding you of what a pretty face you had. More and more you were coming to resemble your grandmother, Manika noted with so much pride—my mother who had gone to such lengths across the planet to remove herself almost without a trace from the system that had insulted her so profoundly, who had trekked so far at such cost to achieve moksha, to unstrap herself from the torturous wheel of life, achieve liberation from the cycle of death and rebirth, and here she was nevertheless, reincarnated in you. Rosy plump cheeks for pinching, breasts like cream for licking, hips like a basket for filling, you who had once been such a dark-eyed heartbreaking waif, ethereal with two thick braids down your back that I plaited every morning standing behind you as you picked at your breakfast—you had been recycled into my mother. Manika, how did you do it? And where would we find the rabbi to take you off our hands and marry you?

The windows of the heavens crashed open at last, the rains came slashing violently down, flooding and clogging the vessels of the city, heaving up in great spasms the foundation of sewage and garbage it rested upon, coating its millions with a mossy fuzz. We were extras in a Bollywood horror movie, topiary animations lumbering about ponderously as if risen from underground. For weeks we did not see the sun. We dwelt in dampness, confined by the monsoon within our four walls for hours of gray daylight, battered by darkness.

Manika believed you were sad because Geeta had left us. It is I who am sad because Geeta has left me, I corrected. I've lost not only Geeta but my best shot at India, now I belong to nobody, nowhere. Maybe there was a time once when Geeta had paid attention to you, Maya, willingly looking after you when I was forced to travel for business, even bringing you along some nights like her pet lapdog to exclusive clubs and restaurants when there was no school the next day, or taking you on long holidays and adventures to spas and exotic settings where white tigers stalked and peacocks strutted, treating Manika too, buying fancy gifts for both of you, trendy clothing, designer saris, diamond studs, gold bangles, ruby slippers, every hightech device update, but that was history, all that had ended more than a year ago. For a year at least Geeta had lost all interest in you, she scarcely noticed you. When she left us she was not thinking about you; when she left me she wanted the hand-held luxury ergonomic bidet, she didn't want you. No, I explained to Manika, the child is not sad because Geeta split, she is sad as in SAD, Seasonal Affective Disorder, presenting with depression, hopelessness, apathy, carb craving, and so forth due to the leadenness of the monsoon, the absence of sunlight. I went out in the gloom to buy a light-therapy box to reset your circadian rhythm, and ordered Manika to park you in front of it for as many hours as you would tolerate it, supplementing with St. John's Wort, and Dr. Bach's Rescue, and mustard flower remedies, reinforced with yoga and meditation.

The light-therapy lamp could also be beneficial for your acne, you decided, like those aluminum foil reflectors offering up to the healing rays of the sun gods the mottled fruit faces of your grandmothers, or the tanning beds upon which your mothers were stretched and tortured, and since in any case you were already lying around inert, paralyzed, there would be no extra exertion required in letting it shine upon you. One Friday in June with the weekend looming, in the bleak afternoon teatime hours of the day, too early for dinner or bed, you were soaking up the beams of simulated sunlight to impregnate you with joy when suddenly the permanent battleship gray of the monsoon season engulfing us deepened to pitch black, and there was an explosive boom. The power grid of the entire subcontinent had collapsed. Light was drained from all of India, everything came to a halt throughout the land—traffic, railways, airports, waterworks, the complete slapped-together inadequate improvised substandard electrical infrastructure gave up with a groan, including your light-therapy lamp. It crackled in an otherworldly golden red zigzag as if God were calling you from the burning bush—Maya, Maya, put your shoes *on* your feet—and then it went out.

You bolted up from your bed as if recharged. Cloaked in darkness you groped your way to the table where Manika, so spiritually tuned in at that time, had already set out the two brass candlesticks that her beloved mistress, your grandmother, would light every Friday when the sun went down in Varanasi even as she was plotting to set herself on fire like a pagan in this polytheistic land and incinerate herself to ash. With gestures as if programmed, you blessed the candles and brought back the light. You opened both arms in a welcoming circle to greet the Sabbath queen and drew them back toward yourself three times like a swimmer treading water to save her life, as if to say, come in, come in. You covered your eyes with the flattened palms of your hands and recited the blessing over the candles, taking on with this ritual the burden of the daughters of Eve down through the generations to restore light to the world, in perpetual atonement for the first woman's original sin of falling for the seductions of the snake and plunging her descendants into darkness.

By the light of the Sabbath candles, Manika showed us a printout of the email she had received. It was from the replacement Chabad rabbi, Mendy, and his rebbetzin, Mindy. They were inviting all of Mumbai's nannies and their guests to a special Friday night dinner that very evening in honor of the heroic nanny Sandra who had saved baby Moshe from the hands of the murderers who rise up against us in every generation, may their names and memory be blotted out. Manika had already RSVP'd for three.

We clothed ourselves in our Sabbath best, and over that we draped our rain ponchos. We pulled up our green rubber Wellington galoshes over plastic grocery bags to slosh through the streets streaming with putrid brown rainwater. Manika packed our dress shoes in my company's tote, a personalized gift bag stuffed with a stash of goodies and essentials that I presented at orientation to each embarking spiritual seeker. This one had been intended for my dear friend and repeat client, the staggeringly rich Washington, DC, heiress and hostess, Charlotte Harlow, but fortunately just in the nick of time I noticed the typo imprinted on it; some joker had replaced the *w* of her surname with a *t*, so I decided to keep it—why waste a perfectly good bag?— and put in a rush order for a replacement. Manika was the only non-Jew among the three of us, which meant that by strict religious law she was permitted to carry objects beyond the home boundaries on the Sabbath. It was not that I wanted to give to the new Chabad emissaries a false impression with regard to the level of my observance or piety. It was simply an irresistible need to send the message that they were dealing with a seasoned insider, albeit lapsed, a former member of the club, an initiate who knew the ropes and saw through their agenda, a warning to them in effect not to try any funny business, especially with you.

With you our precious jewel bezeled between us, Manika in front gripping one of your hands leading the way, I the rearguard clutching your other hand, we set out single file into the perilous darkness illuminated here and there by yellow lights powered by emergency generators. In our hooded rain ponchos, we were silhouetted like medieval pilgrims fleeing the apocalyptic devastation of water and plague through the deserted streets of Colaba and the Fort District, trusting our survival to Manika our guide. Not far from the porpoise atop Flora Fountain, in front of a massive edifice, weighty and indestructible in the mighty Victorian Gothic style bequeathed to Bombay by the British occupiers, a tank with a rotating gun was stationed in the brilliant glare of the headlights of a cordon of army jeeps.

This was where Manika halted. A sizable military battalion, uniformed and fully equipped, was encamped there, the troops smoking and checking their cell phones, carrying out official duties. Manika immediately drew out the invitation and handed it to the officer in command. She opened the sack and dumped our shoes into a designated bin, took off her boots and plastic bags and poncho and indicated to us to do the same. Two pitiless attack dogs on leashes were brought forward to sniff us. A female officer approached and without a word began the pat-down, frisking us one after the other right out there in the public space since this was India where nothing is private, her hands exploring the entire topography of our bodies, over and up and in between, nothing was sacred, nothing was new or unique or special, we were all endowed with the same stuff, simply variations on a theme. Ah, to be touched by a woman again, it was good, how I missed it, though I did not appreciate at all being forced to witness the same treatment administered by this low-level type to my child. Watch it kiddo, I was tempted to blurt out, that's my innocent daughter you're violating, but Manika telegraphed a cautionary glance and I restrained myself. Clearly, she had been here before, she knew the drill.

We were subjected to full-body radiation exposure in an X-ray booth, then waved through to what looked like a bank vault but was in fact a private elevator manned by two guards armed with submachine guns, which whisked us up to a floor that had no number and let us out in front of a retractable steel grille. Four more officers were stationed here, and the entire security procedure was replayed in quick time—documents, body check, metal detection, interrogation, and so on. At last the steel grille was drawn back to reveal a thick door padded in black leather and studded with brass nails, which was opened, and beyond that another door, mahogany, elegantly wrought and richly lacquered such as befitted this luxury apartment building. Nailed to the doorpost was a large ornate silver mezuzah, which out of perversity I kissed as Rabbi Mendy himself opened the door.

Standing over six feet tall with bulging biceps taut under the sleeves of his black suit jacket and a scar that snaked down the side of his face, starting somewhere under the brim of his black fedora hat and ending somewhere in the thickets of his black beard, he resembled a bouncer at the entrance of an exclusive private Jewish club. The outline of a holster was traceable at his belt, not to be mistaken for a cell phone pouch, for only a weapon would trump the Sabbath in a situation where there is potential danger to life. He had been a decorated hero of the most elite combat unit of the Israeli Defense Forces, hailed throughout the land as the number-one Krav Maga champion wrestler, a celebrity raptly spotlighted for his beautiful women, hard partying, underworld pals. A terrorist would think twice before messing with this guy. With a broad pugilist smile that showcased a wide gap, the space of a missing tooth top center, he welcomed us into a grand salon brightly lit by a private generator and flickering Sabbath candles on a long banquet table covered with a white linen cloth, weighed down by gleaming silver and china and crystal goblets and golden braided challah loaves yet unblessed.

"Eh, just in time," he greeted us in heavy Israeli guttural, seasoned by Brooklynese, acquired during his return-to-faith apprenticeship years in the Chabad universe of Eastern Parkway, Crown Heights, following his sensational penance voraciously detailed in all the Israeli media. "A *guten Shabbes* to the ladies from the family of the *heiligen* Rabbi Tabor, may he live on for many good and long years."

So he had been briefed on our personal data. "Are you referring to Rabbi Tabor senior or junior?" I inquired coyly.

"Eh, you mean Shmelke, your brother. The Holy One Blessed Be He never makes a mistake. There is also a reason for Jews like Shmelke Tabor, though we might not be blessed with the divine wisdom to understand it."

Just as I was about to correct his reference to my brother by pointedly adding the title Rabbi, the rebbetzin Mindy came forward to take over host duties, as all three of us new arrivals were female and therefore her responsibility in the division of labor department. Her bitumen-black Sabbath wig streamed down her back in thick straight tresses, certified kosher imported from China due to the rabbinical ban on locally grown Indian hair from the heads of idolaters. "Sorry about all the security hassles, ladies," she immediately said, "but you know the situation. The Indians don't want another embarrassment like at Nariman House—need I say more? Anyways, you can never be too careful." Her accent I could GPS exactly—the heart of Crown Heights, specifically President Street between Brooklyn and Kingston Avenues, there was more than a fifty-fifty chance that she was Chabad royalty, matched up in heaven with this rising star from the Holy Land. "Good Shabbes, Manika darling," she exclaimed, as if just noticing the presence of the background support staff. "Thank God for our little nannies—am I right or am I right?" Leaning over as we stood there observing her, she gave Manika a warm hug. "Go and sit down by your girlfriends, Manika darling, *fress* to your heart's content." She indicated the section of the table where the nannies were clustered, already dipping their fingers into the serving bowls of hummus and potato salad even before the chanting of the blessing over the wine.

Malkie, the eldest daughter, now approached, carrying a baby brother not yet three with his long golden ringlets and bib stained orange from mashed carrots or squash. You remember Malkie, of course. She was the second of the rebbetzin's eleven children, seventeen years old at the time, flashing a large emerald-cut diamond ring, three carats minimum. She had just been engaged to a Crown Heights boy of excellent pedigree, first-class *yikhus*, but was obliged to wait to be married until a suitable bride could be found for her brother Shmuly, older by one year, who was much too fussy for his own good, according to reliable sources. A good daughter who still listened to her mother, Malkie took you in hand, escorted you to the corner of the table where the teenage girls were quarantined for everyone's sake, introduced you, brought you in, performing the mitzvah of Jewish outreach by drawing you closer, which bottom line was the family business—Jewish missionaries snagging the souls of wandering Jews who had wandered too far.

I tried to pick up your frequencies at the table, to check on you to make sure you were at ease, but you were too distant on the women's side, and with the din of platters coming and going, choreographed by the squad of Indian servants, men in livery all of them armed, and the clatter of cutlery and the buzz of conversation soaring into the singing by the men at the top of their lungs of the Sabbath *zmirot*, pounding their fists rhythmically on the tabletop, you were lost to me on the airwaves. I had been directed by the rebbetzin Mindy to a place close to the head of the table for some reason, perhaps my perceived distinguished paternal lineage I figured at first, where Rabbi Mendy sat in state. To his right on the women's side, beside me on my left, was a wizened old woman from what I could see of her. Her head bound up in a tight babushka that defined the slope and cavities of her skull was lowered over the open prayer book on her plate as an indication that no food should be placed there, as if sanctified words alone would be her portion, like those proper ladies in novels who placed their handkerchiefs in their wineglass in a genteel refusal of wine and all gross spirits; someone's mother, I presumed. On my other side sat an Israeli woman from the consulate, sunk in turgid Hebrew chatter with the woman to her right. It was such an awkward position for me to be in—to be so prominently situated yet so publicly ignored and excluded, I hoped you at your end were faring better socially. Maybe that was why Shmuly, the rabbi's son and heir apparent seated with the men almost directly across from me to his father's left took pity and leaned forward to draw me into conversation by asking me if it was true that my brother, Shmelke, believed that a woman who submits to the desires of a holy man can prevent another Holocaust. The old lady to my left lifted her face, black as if charred in a furnace. "Ah, you don't remember me," she whispered.

Tall and dark like his father, but wiry, not yet muscle bound, with a thick fringe of black eyelashes that almost brushed the lenses of his glasses and a flushed complexion still only lightly matted with pale down, Shmuly resembled his sister, Malkie, consigned to the other end of the table with you and the other girls, almost as disturbingly as I resembled my twin brother, Shmelke. In compliance with the admonition of the sages that partaking in a meal without talking Torah is like making offerings to the dead, and in his role as the promising son of a leading Chabad emissary being groomed to take over in his turn one of the most influential posts, a critical hotspot, Shmuly now rose to offer a few words of Torah. First, though, he took a moment to welcome the guests at his family's table, singling us out for a special distinction award, you and me, Maya, "Close friends of the Mumbai martyrs, peace be unto them," he proclaimed, zooming in on you especially. "Little baby Moshe'le best playmate," he called you. "Maya here had the z'khus, the high privilege, of playing with Moshe'le every day, she knew little Moshe'le, my friends, she knew him, she was like the best big sister to him."

So that was the explanation for my seat of honor, I reflected—mother of Maya. Manika had talked us up, laid out the main selling points, Manika was our public relations advance team. Then he plunged into his Torah talk, focusing on the death of Miriam in the Wilderness of Zin, read in that week's Bible portion, hailing Miriam as one of the first great recorded nannies. She saved the life of her little brother Moshe by babysitting from a distance when he was set afloat on the Nile in a reed basket to escape Pharaoh's death sentence against all the Hebrew male newborns—just like our beloved nanny Sandra saved the life of our own little Moshe here in Mumbai from the hands of the wicked Pharaohs and their henchmen who rise up to destroy us in every generation, and in our time too, Shmuly declared.

He beamed an irresistible smile of gratitude at the little flock of nannies fluttering at the table and gestured with both hands for them to stand up and take a bow. All the assembled then rose in ovation and began clapping and singing and dancing in a circle, the men with the men around the table, stomping with their hands on each other's shoulders, the women more sprightly in a modest corner apart with the nannies seated in the center, whom some of the bigger girls raised up in their chairs, they were all so small, so slight, two lifters per nanny were more than enough to bear the weight securely.

Aloft on her chair, Manika flashed a joyous grin, black gummed from a lifetime chewing paan. She drew off from around her neck the rose silk dupatta that Geeta had given her and grasping it at one end she fluttered it toward you, Maya, and you caught the other end of the scarf in your hand, and there you were dancing like Miriam the prophetess after the splitting of the sea, that night I saw you dancing, I will not forget it, and all the women and girls coming out after you with song and dance.

Miriam is all about water, Shmuly went on once the dancing subsided and all the guests staggered back to their seats and slumped down again, submitting to their fate of sitting through the speech. Her name means bitter sea, *maryam*—a mixed message, like our monsoon, flood and darkness, but also cleansing, cooling, growth. In Miriam's merit the Israelites were provided with water in the desert, our sages tell us. She dies and is buried, and the next thing you know the water system shuts down, just like our electricity shut down tonight. Right away the Israelites start complaining to Moshe. Where's our water, Moshe? So what else is new? From time immemorial we *Yid'n* have always been big complainers. And God says to Moshe, Take your staff and go talk to the rock before the eyes of the people and water will come out. You have to wonder—why does Moshe need a stick to talk to the rock? Is this the first case of, Speak softly and carry a big stick? And why does Moshe hit the rock when God says to him loud and clear, Talk? He was a prophet, he could see the future; he knew what would happen if he didn't listen. Oh yes my friends, he was a prophet—but even a prophet is human. Moshe was mad, boiling mad. Moshe had a temper, a holy temper, he exploded only in God's name. Like when he came down from the mountain and saw the people worshipping the golden calf, and he threw down those two stone tablets in such a rage and smashed them to pieces. He had knocked himself out for these people for so many years, and now here they are belly-aching about the water. How could they hassle him at such a time like this, when he had just lost his beloved sister, his faithful nanny? Didn't they have any consideration? He was in mourning, it shouldn't happen to us. He would have liked to whack them, he would have liked to give them such a good *zetz*, but instead he takes his stick and whacks the rock—two times yet! I think there's a word for that in mental health lingo. You can check it out with Rabbi Dr. Freud. Transference? Displacement? Channeling? Whatever. So Moshe, he gives it to the rock, two good clops. And what is his punishment for disobeying God? Shut out of the land. Sorry Moshe, you're not going anywhere. You're staying right here in the desert. No Promised Land for you.

My friends, the Holy One Blessed Be He who knows all, past, present, and future, ordered Moshe to take the staff because he knew he would hit instead of talk. He knew Moshe needed to act out, to vent. He knew Moshe had to get it out of his system. And the Holy One Blessed Be He who is merciful above all also knew and understood that at that moment Moshe in his heart of hearts no longer wanted to enter the Promised Land. Why? Because his beloved sister and nanny would not be coming too. The One Above understood that Moshe's greatest desire at that moment was to stay in the desert, in exile, in the diaspora, close to his beloved sister-nanny, Miriam, until the arrival of our Master, our Teacher, our Rebbe, the Messiah the King, may it be quickly in our time.

"My friends"—Shmuly was wrapping up—"the Talmud talks about *yisurim*, pain and suffering. It talks about the yisurim of love. I won't go into what the rabbis mean by love here, but in my opinion Moshe was suffering from love, from the agony of lost love when his sister, his Miriam, was taken away from him. It also talks about the yisurim necessary to acquire the land of Israel. Nothing worthwhile in this life is gained without yisurim. That also applies to a delicious meal such as we are all enjoying here tonight. To earn it you have to suffer a little, say a few prayers before and after, sit in your place now after eating your fill when maybe you'd rather go home already and loosen your belt but instead you're stuck here and forced to listen to me yakking and blabbering on and on." He flicked me a reproachful glance, then cast his eye to the far end of the table where you were sitting, and remained sternly riveted on you. "So my friends, here's the deal. Come back tomorrow for a delicious lunch, you're all invited to come and continue our celebration in honor of our awesome nanny heroines. But please—before you give yourself the reward of eating, you should also be ready to undergo some yisurim, it's only right. First go to shul and pray, do a little necessary suffering, it's not too much to ask. Tomorrow morning before treating yourself to another delicious meal, go to shul. Spend a few hours sitting in shul talking to the Rock."

Next morning, following orders at your insistence, the three of us were the first females to show up at the blue Sassoon synagogue, Knesset Eliyahoo, and make our way up to the ladies' balcony. It was so early that below us, in the main sanctuary, a full quorum of ten adult males had not yet arrived to launch the significant prayers. "No minyan yet," Rabbi Mendy sang out. "Only eight people." Okay, I thought, maybe Manika doesn't count in the category of people because she's not Jewish, I'll even grant that for argument's sake, but by my calculation, when you're talking people, with you and me up in the peanut gallery sharing the oxygen supply, the sum total is ten—so let's get the show on the road, Rabbi.

Very soon after, though, three glistening well-fed Baghdadi males appeared and took their places with showy entitlement at their personal pews affixed with their names engraved onto polished brass plates. The service proceeded with Rabbi Mendy at the helm, his prayer shawl drawn over his head, tucked behind each ear to keep it in place, reciting the liturgy expertly and with dispatch, but in a voice so creatively out of tune, it was a revelation, offering new insight into the text. A klatch of Baghdadi wives came chattering up to the balcony, steeping it with the scent of their toiletries and perfumes. Just before Shmuly rose to chant the week's Torah portion, the rebbetzin Mindy processed in with her entourage headed by Malkie, the bride-to-be, and her pride of younger daughters all in their Sabbath finery, accompanied also by the skeletal dowager beside whom I had been seated the evening before at the Sabbath table. They took their reserved places on the balcony bench almost directly across from us, nodding to us in greeting over the chasm of the male sanctuary below that we Jewish princesses could penetrate only by diving down head-first and breaking our crowns.

Shmuly's voice, in contrast to his father's, was high pitched and extraterrestrially sweet, as if the hormonal shakedown had not quite taken. You leaned forward with your elbows planted on the balcony railing, your palms joined together as in a namaste, your brow resting against the steeple of your fingers pointed heavenward as he melodically cantillated the tropes he had so perceptively deconstructed the night before—I'm quoting from your wildly enthusiastic recap of his little talk that you articulated with such polish, thanks to your high-priced college-prep education, during our walk home in the night. Death and drought, rebellion and retribution, archetypal motifs. From the front row bench on the balcony where we were sitting you looked down over the railing upon the top of his head in his black velvet yarmulke bent over the open scroll, you did not take your eyes off of him for one minute. Your mouth hung open so soft, your temple vein pulsed blue, your breathing was visible.

Listen to me, you dreamer, I wanted to cry out, Do you think you can squeeze even one drop out of this stone? Do not believe it, my daughter. It will not happen. Neither by rod nor by word.

Once again now you were stopping off at the Chabad center every afternoon on your way home from school. I should have put the kibosh on it. It was on every level a danger zone, however fortified and security-padded a cell it might appear to be to the undiscerning eye. I of all people should have known it could only lead to disaster.

But Manika was with you every minute, I told myself, your chaperone, she would save you. She stationed herself a step behind you, self-erasing like a page-turner for a pianist on the concert stage; you would never lose your place, you would never get lost. Manika was a fixture in the room with you the entire time, present in the moment, unlike Varda when you used to visit baby Moshe'le in Colaba, demonstrably setting herself apart, depositing herself outside to schmooze with the terrorist disguised as the guard. O, protect us from our protectors, I say.

But as for Manika, even if in her heart of hearts it had been her desire to loiter with the security contingent stationed at the entrance leaning against the tank chewing her paan, it was not an option. There was no room in that huddle under the tent, she would have been drenched. The windows of the heavens had been cast wide open, the rains burst down in furious sheets, soaking the earth and heaving up all the filth only just below the surface. You and Manika sloshed through pools of brown sludge, kicking up excrement of all varieties and rot every step of the way on the road to your life-altering vision at Chabad, and soon the guards posted there under their sagging tarps no longer troubled themselves to poke their necks out into the deluge to stop and frisk. They waved you through without even raising their heads from their snakes and ladders. You were defanged, profiled, certified members of the inner circle, family.

So what did you do today at the Chabadniks? I would ask at the dinner table, attempting conversation. Your answer was always the same: Nothing. That was also the answer you gave to my regular daily interrogations: What did you do in school today? Nothing. Whom did you hang out with? Nobody. Manika squatting on the floor would bring her face down even lower into the bowl from which she was feeding with her fingers. I could not induce her to sit at the table after serving us no matter how much I cajoled. It was truly embarrassing, I prayed no one would walk in to witness this abject scene and make unwarranted assumptions about me. On the wall behind her against which she was propped a great water stain had bloomed, mildew rimmed and blistered at its heart, even in Geeta's luxury flat on

Malabar Hill where we were still holding out, even that proud princess was not insulated from the seepage, the monsoon's revelations of
what lies beneath, just below the paint job.

Later, after the light no longer leaked out from under your sealed
door, Manika would slip into my room to tell me everything. Her
English had evolved thanks above all to the call center videos she
watched obsessively on the internet (her two favorite phrases were,
I can definitely help you get that sorted, and, I do apologize for any
inconvenience). Her ambition now was to enter the outsourcing stage
of her life after the completion of the nanny stage the moment you
flew the nest, on her path to stage four, the fatal stage, total final
renunciation, *sannyasa*.

The rebbetzin Mindy with her brood was equipped to provide
a matching personal playmate for children of all ages, but you chose
to spend your face time at Chabad with Malkie, Manika informed
me, who accepted you even though she was five years your senior, in
her bridal season. Malkie possessed an enviable collection of paper
dolls, which she stored in labeled shoeboxes on the top shelves of her
wardrobe, with a specialization in weddings, Jewish weddings. She
seized the opportunity of your eager presence, a younger girl with
whom she could play with these dolls for hours in an orgy of delicious uninhibited regression. She altered the dolls' costumes—raising necklines, lowering hemlines, lengthening sleeves, rendering the
transparent opaque, the form-fitting draped—and she also designed
fashions of her own private label for the bride and groom and the
entire wedding party along with the ritual accessories, emphasizing
modesty, what she called *zni'us*. As you sat with Malkie on her girl-
hood bed, Manika reported, dressing and undressing the dolls, she
instructed you as your elder and mentor on the importance of zni'us.
Bottom line: no part of the body may be uncovered in the presence
of men and boys other than your two essential woman-of-valor hands
below the wrist to plunge into the suds and crud. Your absorption of
these strictures was a new fact on the ground I was beginning to glom
on to after you began your playdates at Chabad, when the Cathedral
office called to inform me that you were refusing to put on shorts for

physical education class. I do apologize, Maya, but I thought at first it had something to do with body image issues related to your thighs.

Manika went on to report how the two of you would sit there on that bed enacting with the paper dolls the series of events leading up to a wedding as Malkie ticked them off, from the first matchmaker-arranged meeting of the couple possibly destined for one another in a public space such as a hotel lobby, to the engagement, the formal introduction of the parents in order to hammer out financial and other essential arrangements, and the betrothal party just a few weeks later. "For verification purposes," Manika intoned, this was as far as Malkie herself had personally experienced. Nevertheless, Malkie strode boldly into the future using the paper dolls in the outfits she had created for them as visual aids to walk you through frame after frame of the fantasy wedding itself, an event every young Jewish maiden could look forward to as the high point of her life, one Malkie knew intimately from having danced at so many, including even a hazy description of the bride's prenuptial immersion in the ritual bath for which the two of you stripped a paper doll down to her bra and panties, as far as you could decently go, dunking her until she was limp and useless in a cyst of stagnant rainwater speckled with dead flies that had collected on the windowsill. But beyond the wedding itself Malkie never went, she just didn't go there, that was where the story always ended, in the mist of happily ever after. She had been put on hold while her brother Shmuly checked with his supervisor, Manika said, in search of perfect wife material.

You did not notice him right away the first time he came into his sister's bedroom. You were swaying on your toes on top of a wobbly folding chair, arched precariously forward, your face thrust into the blackness of the open wardrobe, reaching for a shoebox of paper doll accessories labeled, Head Coverings: Snoods, etc. "I hope I'm not interrupting your girl talk," Shmuly said—and it was only then that you realized he was there, gazing at you from behind freely and unobstructed, and so you fell from on top of your camel, my child, like Mother Rebecca when she first laid eyes on Father Isaac, you came crashing down on the floor. "I'm sorry, I'm sorry," you were whimpering in mortification on the carpet as Manika scurried to check you for any visible damage, and then to gather up the contents of the box that had scattered everywhere murmuring, "I'm here to assist you in any way I can"—and Malkie stepped forward to discreetly draw down the hem of the skirt of your school uniform which had ridden up immodestly over your knees as Shmuly stood there with his hand over his mouth to cover up a spasm of wicked laughter—other people falling is always so funny, the stuff of slapstick. His blank gaze was fixed doggedly on the night window against which the rain thrummed, as it is forbidden to look upon a female in disarray, much less touch one not related to you, even a girl of twelve like you, still so pure and innocent—untouchable, like Manika.

You came home earlier than usual that day, but only after first sitting there on that bed sticking it out a little longer for a respectable time span out of pride, your head lowered, your eyes cast down as he recapped for his sister the *shiddukh* setup date he had just returned from in the lobby of the Taj. In response to one of the questions he routinely asked a prospective bridal candidate—what is the thing about yourself that you would most like to improve?—instead of answering my soul (four points), or my heart (three) or even my mind (two) or my brain (one), she replied, My legs (minus four). "Can you believe it?" Shmuly asked, addressing Malkie. "A grown girl, sixteen and a half, on the marriage market already? Maybe from a twelve year old still with the chubby ankles and baby fat *pulkes* you would expect such a brilliant answer," he said, turning at last from Malkie to acknowledge you with a warm smile. "Especially when she goes to the fanciest *goyische* school money can buy and has such nice pretty eyes."

That happened on a Thursday. The next night, Friday, Sabbath eve, you fell again. We were in the Sassoon synagogue where we had gone to earn our meal ticket for the Sabbath table at the Chabad house, which was the correct protocol as Shmuly the young rabbi in training had so diplomatically clarified. It was just the two of us that night. I had agreed that Manika should remain at home working on her online outsourcing course, though it was in my opinion an utter waste of time, her English accent was hopeless, the lilt of her speech screamed Indian, she was way too old, no way would she ever be hired. But I appreciated having some alone time with you, quality time, and so we headed out into the downpour, you and I, mother and daughter.

Shmuly was standing with a few of his brothers and his father, Rabbi Mendy, after the closing of the Friday night services to welcome the Sabbath queen at the bottom of the stairs leading up to the women's balcony, the steps slick with the rain and mud that had been dragged in. "Good Shabbes, Masha," he greeted you as you descended the staircase fully clothed, including your rain slicker with the hood already drawn up. "My name is Maya," you snapped back, and went tumbling down the rest of the flight, thank God only five or six steps I counted more or less as I scrambled in desperate maternal angst after you. "I'm sorry, I'm sorry," you couldn't stop chanting to the small klatch of women in attendance that evening who had clustered around you wringing their hands and quieting their hearts as the men stood back paralyzed, trying not to gape. Why were you apologizing like that? What had you done wrong? I would have given anything to scoop you up in my arms at that moment and carry you away to a safe zone childproof against falling and other life hazards, but it was impossible, you were already such a big girl, my darling.

"Don't touch me!" you hissed the minute the door to the ladies room sucked shut behind us. Your tights were in shreds at the knees, but thanks to the long skirts you had taken to wearing, not much was really noticeable. There were bruises here and there which would spread into black-and-blue pools under the skin over the next few days I knew—we Tabor women bruised so easily, my mother, you, I—but otherwise there was no discernible serious damage at least to the outer shell. We had been spared, it was a miracle, a bit of cosmetic touch-up and you would be presentable again. You insisted on carrying on with our plans, making our appearance at the Shabbat dinner as if nothing had happened. You were a trouper, my brave little warrior daughter, I was overcome with such admiration and respect.

The next day, at Sabbath lunch I watched in horror as you fell again. You and Malkie and a few other proper young ladies were strutting your domestic creds by helping with the serving, you were carrying out from the kitchen a tray piled high with small appetizer plates of chopped liver and gefilte fish, each mound-shaped dropping topped with a decorative swag of raw carrot. "Don't fall, Masha," Shmuly sang out to you. Instantly, as if he had just injected you with a brilliant idea, as if he had pressed a button to a hidden trapdoor, down you went. "I'm sorry I called you Masha," he said, standing over you sprawled in the middle of that mess of first course on the floor that looked now before it had been consumed suspiciously like how one might imagine it would look after it had made its way through the system and come out the other end. "It's just that when I see you, I also see Moshe, little baby Moshe'le, because you knew him personally—such a privilege! People are saying he is a miracle boy, that he is destined to come back to Mumbai on a white donkey one day to take over the Chabad house again and avenge the murder of his holy mother and father. Moshe, Masha—you can do worse than to be mixed up with that holy child, I didn't mean to push you down the stairs, God forbid."

On Sunday you rested, at least from falling, as far as I knew. School was closed; there would be no Chabad pit stop on your homeward route. I had given Manika the day off to visit a friend from her village who had just arrived to the Dharavi slum to work in the construction business clearing rocks, so there was no chaperone on call that day to escort you. Manika had offered to take you along to watch the slum potters squeezing their clay, she even invited me to join for "quality assurance," but there was no way I would allow you to be exposed to such filth and pollution, and especially now while you were going through this bizarre pubescent hormonal falling stage, I didn't even want to begin to imagine what you might sink into should you happen to take it into your head to fall in that slum with its open lakes of raw sewage and waste where the children played. We would have a nice quiet Sunday, you and I, it would be a treat. During the wet season my tour business typically slowed down almost to a standstill, and though in the past I had used the time to visit my branch offices in Jerusalem and New York for networking purposes and to catch up with administrative details, this monsoon I was obliged to stay put in Mumbai because as you know I had no responsible adult to leave you with, Geeta had abandoned us. Now I realized it was a blessing in disguise. Our Sundays would unfold slow and easy, an unforeseen gift of time to work on our relationship, focus on some mother-daughter bonding.

The door to your room remained shut the entire day. If you stepped out to use the toilet, I must have missed it. I knocked to summon you to meals, but you informed me from within you were not hungry. I left a tray on the floor outside your door, although I knew you kept a stash of sweet and salty snacks in the back of your closet, you would not starve. I set that tray down anyway simply to preempt you from concluding that I considered it just as well you were not eating, it wouldn't kill you to lose a few pounds. From inside your room I could hear the familiar prayers from my childhood. You were listening on your laptop to cantorial videos, sometimes singing softly along, learning the words and tunes.

When you emerged at last I was already in bed for the night. You knocked and came into my room in your nightgown, which had become your sleepwear of choice since you had given up pajamas as well as pants and all articles of clothing that could by any inference be regarded as male apparel and therefore forbidden. "Didn't you get dressed at all today?" I asked as you stood there just inside the entryway. You shook your head. "My mother, your grandmother, may she rest in peace, used to say, 'if you don't get dressed, the day didn't happen.'"

You were silent for a respectful span to absorb this deep ancient wisdom, then you proceeded to deliver a little speech, as if you had rehearsed it; clearly it was for this purpose that you had come to my room. "I want to apologize for how I behaved today, Mommy. It was a sin. The Torah commands us to honor our mother and father. I should have listened when you called me to come out, to eat or whatever. I'm sorry. I know you're worried about my falling all the time. If it makes you feel any better, I just want you to know that I'm never happier than when I fall, it's the most amazing feeling in the world. The whole time I'm thinking—I'm going to fall, I can't stop myself, here I go, I'm falling, falling—and then I fall, as if my knees, my legs, my limbs, my entire body from head to toe, has melted, it's like I'm flooded with warmth and light. Malkie says that it's like what happens to the chosen ones in the Torah, when God calls them and they fall upon their faces, and they answer, Here I am. She's right, that's exactly what it's like—like I'm in God's presence. I just wanted to tell you, so you wouldn't worry."

The punishing rains continued to pound down into July, the fountains of the deep split open pushing upward the soggy landfill of our amphibious city only newly emerged from the sea, still conflicted between wet and dry. You took upon yourself to rise earlier to say your morning prayers before heading off to school with Manika sloshing in your wake waving down a cab. You declared yourself 100 percent strictly kosher now, refusing to partake of the hot school lunches I had prepaid in full with no refund forthcoming, packing a bunch of bananas in your rucksack instead to sustain you through the day. At home, since we were confirmed vegans, you agreed to share some of our foodstuffs but only after I bought a new set of personal tin *thali* bowls and utensils for you at the local bazaar, which you hauled to the Chabad ritual bath and immersed before using, reciting the designated blessing. "I'm twelve years old," you announced, as if this would be news to me. "I'm a woman now, I'm responsible for my own sins. Until I turned twelve, my sins were on your head, Mommy, sorry about that."

How had such ideas seeped into your brainpan? This was precisely the kind of mindset, defined by sin, that I had struggled so hard to escape, this was why I had come to India as a seeker of true meaning and spirituality and union with the divine, to shield you from such destructive guilt trips and to purge myself as well from the authoritarianism of the original Abrahamic faith that had messed so negatively with my head. Later, when Manika came into my room for our nightly wrap-up, she corroborated that what I was hearing was yet another example of Malkie's brainwashing, as I had of course surmised. What sins could such a blameless child like you possibly have committed before you turned twelve that were likely to fall on my head? I demanded to know from Manika, not that I wasn't ready, willing, and able to take on any and all of your sins at any time of your life. Manika looked down at her feet. I'm sorry this has happened to you, she was mumbling. What can we do to make it right?

One thing we couldn't do for sure at this point, I knew, was to put a stop to your visits to the Chabad house, or forbid you from consorting with such a bad influence as Malkie. You and Malkie were tighter than ever, inseparable. In the synagogue you circulated holding hands, calling yourselves soul sisters. Only the previous Sabbath as we were walking together toward the Chabad house for lunch, dodging the violent traffic as we sought an opening to cross Mahatma Gandhi Road in the Fort District after morning prayers, Malkie said to me, "I just want you to know that I love Maya with all my heart and soul. She is like a sister to me. I wish she could be my true sister. I wish she could marry Shmuly. Then we'd be real sisters. Too bad she's only twelve, I just can't wait that long." And she held up her hand, the one clasped to yours, the one with the dazzling rock on its fourth finger, she held it up toward the heavens, turning it this way and that in an effort to catch a glint of sunlight as Rabbi Mendy strode briskly past in intense conversation with Shmuly, but the clouds were low and dark, there was not a glimmer of light present to land on the facets of the stone and set them aglow, the toe of your boot as she pulled your arm upward to show off her bling snagged on an irregularity in the pavement and in the slow-motion seconds before I could reach out to save you, your sister wannabe Malkie let go of your hand and down you flew onto the sodden concrete, hitting bottom, crying, Sorry, sorry, sorry.

The all-consuming discussion between Shmuly and his father as they swept past us when you fell in the street raged on in feverish whispers throughout the Sabbath lunch in the pauses between the ritual requirements, so that they scarcely fulfilled their mandate to reach out to their guests, including me in my usual place at the table so near to them, the spectral old woman as always shedding ash from the other world to my left. Following the Grace After the Meal, when everyone had escaped to process the digestive overload, you approached hand in hand with Malkie to ask permission to stay through the afternoon until three stars would be visible in the night sky, not very likely in the monsoon season, and the Sabbath queen would regretfully be ushered out. As I was rising to work out the logistics with Manika in the kitchen where she typically hung out, socializing with her fellow low-caste colleagues, Rabbi Mendy made a downward gesture with his hand indicating that I remain in my seat, Shmuly turned to you and said, "I hope you don't mind, just a few questions, then we'll let you go and you can play with the dollies," and the rebbetzin Mindy slipped into the empty chair to my right—all of them pouncing on us in a single pincer movement in what seemed like a preplanned coordinated three-pronged action.

The matter at hand that had been preoccupying the rabbi and his heir apparent concerned Moshe, little baby Moshe, a matter of great urgency for their future in Mumbai and beyond in the inner power circle of the Chabad elite. Aside from Moshe'le's nanny, Sandra, with whom they were banned from communicating by the boy's family and who would not talk to them in any case, you and I, they advised us, and you especially, are likely to be the only ones still around now who knew baby Moshe intimately during the first two crucially formative years of his life, when everything is determined. Was he a normal child, in both the negative and positive sense? The public had a right to know. Some said he had been irreparably damaged psychologically as a result of witnessing the butchering of his parents. Others said he possessed special powers like Moses our Teacher even as a baby—that he was born circumcised and came out of the womb talking Torah to his mother and father, and that now he continues to communicate with them every day morning and night, earth to heaven.

"Tell us everything you know," Shmuly said in his most ominous, still soft voice, his eyes fixed on you in a concentrated focus perhaps for the first time, boring into you as if to flush out your lifeblood until your face drained white, you looked as if you might swoon. It struck me that I ought to put a stop to this inquisition at once. Why was I just sitting there paralyzed, letting them torture you like this?

"He was not even two," you said finally, "and I was only eight."

"Old enough to remember."

"He used to stick his hand into the flames of his mother's Sabbath candles," you offered at last after a long silence. "Then he would put it in his mouth. He burned his hand and his mouth." This was a graphic image I didn't remember ever having myself observed, a disturbing sight you had witnessed more than once apparently but never shared with me. A daughter is supposed to confide in her mother. How had I gone wrong?

"Eh, like Moshe our Teacher when he was a little baby, when the Egyptian wise guys decided he was destined to grab away the throne from Pharaoh the king," Rabbi Mendy interpreted. "So they put down in front of him a piece of gold the same like the crown and also a burning hot coal. Any normal kid would go for the gold—right? But the angel Gabriel, he takes little Moshe's little hand and plops it down on the burning coal, and Moshe picks up the coal and puts it into his mouth—kids put everything in their mouths. That's the reason for why Moshe Rabbenu was 'heavy of speech and heavy of tongue,' like the Torah says, why he couldn't talk so good—because he burned out his mouth. So, did baby Moshe also have a stutter like big Moshe?" the rabbi asked you.

"I don't know, I don't remember, he wasn't even two, he couldn't really talk yet."

"Something's definitely not right here," the rebbetzin said, pushing hard, baring her fangs like a tigress sensing danger to her cubs. "Why didn't they stop him from sticking his hand in the fire? It's criminally irresponsible. What kind of parents would do such a thing? They could have lit the Shabbes candles in a high place where he couldn't reach. They should have been reported to the child protective services if you ask me."

"The answer is right in front of our noses," Shmuly said. "They were grooming him to take over the world for their own gain and profit, trying to clone him into Moshe Rabbenu, turning him into a

Moshe Rabbenu celebrity starting with that public relations bit about the hand and mouth burning, like those Indian firewalkers, whatever they're called—the fakers—excuse me, fakirs."

Before my inner eye Geeta with the charred soles of her feet rolled off into the sunset in her wheelchair, never to return. The old woman next to me brought her mouth up to my face. Her breath was stale, her lips bubbling with white foam, like fat on the fire. "Pay attention," she sprayed into my ear, "the child is in danger."

She was referring of course to her grandson Shmuly, eighteen years old, from her perspective still a child. He had been reared with all the entitlement of Chabad royalty. Now he was being dethroned by an upstart little kid. The brilliant future they had all envisioned for him at the center of the innermost Chabad court, a major player sought out by presidents and prime ministers and kings on anything related to the Jewish question, with all the collateral benefits flowing to them as a family in terms of power, prestige, prosperity—all that was now on the endangered list. According to the rebbetzin, the overreaching, the sheer heresy in the circles surrounding baby Moshe was mindboggling. She sat there spuming as if a valve under pressure had been released. There was talk that baby Moshe was saved from the slaughter by a miracle, an angel from God in the form of the little Nepalese peasant Sandra; that he had been set apart, chosen for a special destiny, there were even some who called him a Holy Child. Excuse me, but the last time I heard Holy Child it was in reference to you-know-who, Yoshke Pandrek, JC, I'm not even allowed to say his name, a very goyisch idea to put it mildly, plain old *apikorsus*. Then there are the other heretics, the ones who say that baby Moshe is the Rebbe's gilgul—like the Rebbe's reincarnation? As far as I'm concerned, this is not one iota different than the fairy-tale garbage they believe right here in this cesspool of idol worshippers—Vishnu-Pishnu, Krishna-Pishna. Please! How can the Rebbe have a gilgul? You can only have a gilgul if you're dead already. Everyone knows that the Rebbe is not dead. Any day now he will come out from that grave where he's taking a short rest and rise up again as the Messiah our King.

The talk at that table was intolerable, there was nothing I wanted more at that moment than to extricate myself, go home and take a shower, and with luck, drag you out with me. I could have forced the issue by citing the fifth commandment now that you had become so pious in your observance, which would oblige you to honor your mother, but you wanted so badly to stay on with your "soul sister," Malkie. I understood the pull of your desire to be close to that other girl. I didn't have the heart to cause you more pain especially at that moment, after they had put you through such an ordeal. My only consolation was that Manika would remain to look after you and keep you from harm.

As I stood at the door wrapping myself in my rain gear, the rebbetzin came up to administer her mandatory hug that every female guest was required to endure going and coming, and by the way, to also invite us, you and me, for an exclusive VIP preview tour of Nariman House now in the process of being restored into the new Chabad center—The best revenge, let them see that they couldn't destroy us, the people of Israel live. The renovations were still underway, she advised me, but you could already see the finished product taking shape—a synagogue, a study hall, a kosher restaurant, a hostel for travelers, an internet café, a resource library, offices, a museum in memory of the slain martyrs, fabulous, fabulous, no expense is being spared, everything top of the line, everything high end, one look at it even at this stage and you would see in a flash where all the money went, all those donations, you would see immediately how ridiculous, how slanderous, how just plain ugly they are, those accusations of embezzlement.

I spent the remainder of that Sabbath day at home stationed at my computer scouring the internet for the goods until I blew the electrical circuits throughout the subcontinent, tripped the power of my building's backup generator, ran my battery dry. Where had I been? I must have been napping. It was by then already old news. Mumbai Moshe'le was a gold mine. Undisclosed millions reportedly had been harvested at fundraising events held across the globe after the terror attack. What happened to all that loot apart from the well-publicized trust fund set aside for the orphan? There were cries of theft, fraud, falsification of accounts—a squalid unseemly feud tearing apart the innermost circles of the organization. The heartrending banner of little baby Moshe'le crying, Ima, Ima, had been unfurled throughout the civilized world and milked for all it was worth. There had been an avalanche of sympathy, the megarich had opened wide their purses, but already I understood that nothing I could possibly see during our private exclusive VIP tour of the restoration of Nariman House, only just begun four years after the event, could match the sums that must have been amassed and stashed under God alone knew whose mattress. She might not have possessed the subtlety to realize it, but the rebbetzin had just confessed as much, she had alerted me. I could read the subtext. Finally, my eyes were opened and everything was revealed.

On the appointed Sunday in the middle of July, we pulled up in our black-and-yellow taxi, you and I, behind two black Mercedes limousines already double-parked in front of Nariman House alongside the caravan of police trucks that had evolved over the years since the terrorist attack into a fixture on that dysfunctionally narrow street, objects of resentment and hostility by merchants and residents alike. A pack of urchins was buzzing around the limos, darting in to press their noses against the tinted windows and snatch a glimpse of the drivers in the splendor of their uniforms and the luxuriously plush interiors, then scampering away, shooed by armed guards and police in khaki uniforms languorously stroking their lathis up and down. Manika had not accompanied us; she was attending a one-day women's self-empowerment seminar offered by an NGO in a slum near the airport. I had given her the time off and had even sprung for the fees.

An Indian worker in a hard hat was posted behind the security wall at Nariman House's newly installed steel door, straining against its weight to keep it partially open for us. We were late, it had taken forever to get you moving. You lay curled up on the sofa muttering something about Malkie having forewarned you that our VIP tour group would include a major donor and his daughter, that she had been tasked with looking after the daughter and making sure she had a good time, that there was really very little chance Malkie could spend any time with you during the visit—so what was the point of going? It was only after I clamped down, an indulgence I seldom permitted myself when it came to you, insisting that I, your mother whom the Torah charges you to honor, had been investigating the backstory of the Nariman House restoration project and it was really important for me to seize this opportunity to get behind the scenes to follow the money and check out with my own eyes what's going on there. Only after I had made that case for myself did you get it together to overcome your resistance and start moving, in compliance with the fifth commandment and its promised reward of length of days—a long life, an outcome that no one could possibly have wished for you more than I, my Maya. It was essential therefore that you obey me.

Despite our lateness, we nevertheless lingered for a while in the street in front of Nariman House, knee deep in water, rancid and brown like old tea essence filmed with scum, afloat with objects large and small, dead rats, dead dogs, live lizards, to gaze nostalgically up and down the street—Hormusji Street, our street. Nearby, a building had collapsed, struck down perhaps only yesterday by one of the wild storms of this very monsoon season; there were still some electrical wires and strips of metal that the scavengers had not yet ripped out. Down the lane we could see that the roof of our own building had caved in, the same roof on which we had all gathered during those first rapturous nights of my passion for Geeta to watch the unfolding of the terror attack on the Chabad center as if it were an apocalyptic blockbuster on a giant screen. The roof, too, might have been a casualty of the attack; the wear and tear from that very night could have compromised it structurally. Whenever it came crashing down, though, I felt confident that Varda had not been under it, she was still operational somewhere on the planet, doing her harm, I had no doubt about that. I had not seen her in years, not since we moved into Geeta's flat on Malabar Hill very soon after the terrorist incident, but I had heard from someone that she had been spotted with several other women in a Tel Aviv storefront window, all of them clad in so-called intimate wear, with a prominent price tag hanging from each of their necks as if they were being offered for sale as part of an in-your-face protest action against sex trafficking of women including very young girls in Israel and throughout the civilized world, which was, it seems, Varda's latest cause.

The roof of Nariman House itself was covered with a heavy blue tarpaulin to protect it from the lashing rains that could mow down far more solid structures. The building was now completely caged in the orthodontia of scaffolding from which, here and there we spotted such festive decorative touches as tassels dangling from bars, garlands of flowers, clusters of coconuts, streamers and ribbons, shimmering gold, magenta, turquoise, like trucks on the Grand Trunk Road hurtling to an early death in Lahore. Within the scaffolding, the Nariman House facade was even more dilapidated and undistinguished than I remembered it, looking as if it could disintegrate in an instant, blotched and blackened with fungus and pollution, with the added punctuation now of the ellipses of bullet holes not yet deleted. The hard hat posted at the entrance waited smiling and uncomplaining, keeping the door sufficiently open to signal unqualified welcome as the heavily armed security personnel in the temporary porta-guardhouse, the sturdiest structure on the block, took their time checking our identification documents against the names and numbers that had been provided in advance, gravely examining the papers we had handed over to them, then riveting their eyes upon us again and again, their heads bobbing up and down to verify that the photos and our faces matched and were one and the same, nodding finally in a signal that looked like *no* but on the subcontinent actually means *yes*—yes, come in, welcome to the slaughterhouse.

The orders were to take us directly up to the fifth floor where the living quarters of the martyred rabbi and his rebbetzin had been located. The VIP delegation was already up there now on its tour under the expert guidance of the museum's chief designer plucked from the most cutting-edge upscale New York firm. We were very late, we had almost missed the whole show and were in danger of not being seated, the hard hat reminded us with a rueful smile, making a not altogether successful effort to avoid a tone of reproach. I felt aggrieved for your sake. The good news, though, he added, is that the tour itinerary had skipped over the fourth floor with the intention of returning to it on the way down and making it the last stop since that was the highlight, the grand finale of the fireworks; after the fourth floor it was all downhill, anticlimax. That was where the madam and the sahib were executed. He put a finger up to each of his temples to illustrate—bang bang.

As we made our ascent he kept cautioning us to take care, ladies, I implore you, I am responsible. The staircase seemed to be wobbling under us as in a nightmare, there were black holes, missing risers, gaps along the banister. I grasped your hand and placed my other arm around your waist to steady and steer you, to guide where you set down your feet, anxiously conscious of the falling stage you were going through at this time in your development. The walls of every floor we passed were brutally cracked and cratered, as after an earthquake. The place seemed to be a hopeless ruin, a wreck. What was the point of trying to salvage it? Better to tear it down and start all over again from the beginning. Yet on every floor as we continued our climb we could see busy workers, building materials and tools piled in the corners, an upbeat atmosphere of industry sending out positive vibes, signs of purpose, though to what end and at what price were beyond me. What a mess! The words popped out of my mouth. "Yes ladies, today a mess, tomorrow a holy Jewish temple, covered in Kevlar—our Hebrew National in a bulletproof sheath top to bottom, protection to the maximum."

We arrived on the fifth floor, the former residence that we, and you above all, knew so well, which, I had heard, would eventually showcase a replica of the holy family's living quarters, including a kitchen with a talking fridge that when opened would expound on kosher laws as part of the outreach mandate to educate unsuspecting visitors. Voices were coming from the direction of little Moshe's room, drawing us in. It was such an overwhelming experience to stand once again in that doorway surveying that familiar space now with the full knowledge of what had transpired that almost immediately you threw yourself down prostrate on the floor overcome as if on sacred ground, just as you had described it to me, as if seized by a supernatural force. Malkie and a petite girl standing opposite holding hands let out a joint gasp, then brought their free hands simultaneously up to their mouths in horror. The rebbetzin made a sharp move forward as if to stoop to your aid, but Shmuly raised his hand like a traffic cop on duty to stop her. "Don't try to pick her up, she's too heavy for you. Anyways, she's okay. She's used to it, she's a faller," he added unforgivably with a little laugh. I glared at him as I was helping you to your feet. "It is a spiritual moment for Maya, like a divine visitation. Places have their power." That was all I said. It was stunning to me that someone like Shmuly so saturated in the Hasidic tradition of uplift was still so incapable of recognizing ecstasy when it lay stretched out on the floor at his feet.

We stood against the wall, you leaning into me as if to keep yourself from falling, leaning into me as you used to do when you were a small child in a strange place, as if it were just the two of us against the whole world, and we listened as the top museum designer described the plans for this space. He was an American, a secular Jew or maybe not even Jewish at all to judge by the yarmulke rising to a peak on his head, made in China of a glossy gold synthetic and stamped with the logo Bar Mitzvah of Elvis Goldberg. He had donned this headgear out of respect for the holy site upon which we were treading and in deference to the two significant players in his audience whose goodwill was essential, Rabbi Mendy and another man, bearded, robed in a black, heavy, silk kaftan richly tailored, stretched open into a keyhole in the vicinity of his navel area across a rajah's paunch—without doubt, the major donor.

Except for some necessary structural and cosmetic touchups, the museum designer was expatiating, the room would be restored to its original form, as it had been when baby Moshe'le had occupied it: the ornamental frieze of brightly colored Hebrew alphabet letters, the cheerful markers charting Moshe's growth, even the furniture and toys, all of that would be recreated—"Everything the same for when baby Moshe comes back to replace his father," Rabbi Mendy chimed in, turning to the major donor, who flipped a nod of approval.

Was this his idea of a joke? His buying into Moshe's return was astounding, a public betrayal of the aspirations of his own son and the family's ambitions for Shmuly as they had expressed them to us with such agitation so recently, soliciting our input and support. Besides, what if Moshe never wanted to return to Mumbai, a perfectly understandable post-traumatic reaction? Had anyone even considered that possibility? What if Moshe'le didn't want to be a rabbi after all when he grew up? What if he wanted to be a dentist or a rock star? What if he had a sex change and became a female rabbi? What if he came back and didn't want to play with his old toys? "Something fishy is going on here," I said in your ear. You recoiled from my breath as if I were an alien species with a contagious terminal disease, pulling away from me and curling into your shell, and made no response. I must have unintentionally embarrassed you, speaking too loudly and too freely. You always claimed that I was missing the whispering gene and the appropriateness gene, maybe both on the same chromosome.

We took our place at the rump of the group as it exited baby Moshe's past and future quarters, following docilely behind the museum designer and the rest of the flock lumbering down the precarious steps to the main exhibition space on the fourth floor. The sections of wall and ceiling that had been ravaged by shelling and grenade blasts and spectacularly pocked with bursts of bullet holes were already protected behind glass like precious artifacts bearing testimony. "We will leave it as we found it," our guide informed us with suitable solemnity. The spot where the rabbi and his wife were murdered will be marked with a plaque engraved with the traditional phrase, May God Avenge Their Blood—which should not be interpreted to imply any negative Islamophobia, our guide hastened to caution. What it means is, the business of vengeance is left to God; that's not our department. The main installation will be seven glass plinths representing the seven *Noahide* ethical laws incumbent on all humankind. Through the prisms of these seven plinths the sunlight will be refracted, casting a rainbowlike arc in the room, like the rainbow after the greatest of all monsoons in history that wiped out every living being on the face of the earth in the time of Noah, the rainbow that symbolized the Lord's promise never again to destroy what He had created—Never Again! The main point, the designer elaborated, is that this museum is not only about the six Jews who were murdered here, or about Jews in general in any configuration of six, six million or whatever, or even about the 166 men and women of all faiths who were mowed down in Mumbai in this attack and whose names will be inscribed on the terrace of honor right here in this museum. This is a museum about the rainbow coalition, all of humanity in all of its diversity, in all of its victimhood, survivorship, and trauma, including Hindus, Christians, Muslims, even the terrorists themselves, if I may be so bold. The overarching message, like a rainbow, is humanistic, inclusive, universal—global morality.

"Beautiful, beautiful," the major donor said.

"I agree with you 100 percent, Reb Meylekh," Rabbi Mendy said. "The Rebbe himself was all the time saying to us shlukhim that just like it's our job to reach out to all Jews to obey the 613 commandments, it is also our job to reach out to the goyim to obey the Seven Laws of the Sons of Noah—don't kill, don't steal, don't fool around with your sister—stuff like that, the basics. Why? Because it's good for the Jews."

"Seven laws, seven plints, beautiful, beautiful, a good investment, vort' every penny." The major donor, whose good name we now possessed, Meylekh, Hebrew for *king* with a Yiddish inflection confirmed by his accent—Yiddish with some other garnish, maybe a pinch of German, plus a soupcon of French—tightened his silk *gartel* rope belt around his belly and paused to ask a question. "So nu, apropos, I vas vundering—vhat's a plint'?" Without waiting for an answer, he turned and headed toward the exit. He had heard enough.

He was from Antwerp, we learned on the drive home. Exiting Nariman House, the rebbetzin Mindy graciously invited us to join her along with Malkie and Reb Meylekh's daughter Ella in the ladies' limousine, the smaller and older model of the two. Four of us squeezed into the back seat, while you, still a growing girl, sat in comfort buckled up in front alongside the driver. Malkie notified us that Ella had just completed her secondary studies at an exclusive finishing school for ultra–Orthodox Jewish girls in Switzerland. With my practiced eye for female stock I took her in as she sat there wedged demurely between Malkie and me in her designer suit perfectly tailored to her trim size-zero figure, her coordinating heels, works of art worthy of being mounted on a plinth. She had majored in shopping. I probed gently. What were her plans? "Selling gay engagement rings—for same sex marriages. It's a huge new market. Business is business." She offered me a charming, suspiciously intimate smile. Her accent was European, refined. The rebbetzin leaned over toward me across the two girls. "I hope you see now from our visit that it's all aboveboard. Embezzlement? Please! Everything 100 percent kosher. End of story." I nodded, stroking the exquisite softness of the limousine's leather interior with true appreciation. Every cent well spent, I could not have agreed more.

You made no gesture to join me in the back after the rebbetzin got out with the two girls alongside the tank at the fortress they called home, and with a pointed smile in my direction sealing our collusion, ordered the chauffeur to deliver us to our door on Malabar Hill. We were not invited to dinner. "I'm never going back to Chabad again in my life," you announced from the front seat as soon as the driver put the engine in gear, the first words you uttered since we had entered baby Moshe'le's room. You were facing forward like a stone in the passenger seat, not deigning to turn around.

In spite of your stated resolve, however, Chabad came to us. Its latest bulletins continued to prance along the internet; I at least had not unsubscribed. Three weeks after our visit to the museum concept in progress, the online Chabad personals prominently featured the announcement of the engagement of the young man, Mr. Shmuly Schlissel, may his candle shed light, of Mumbai, India, to the chosen one of his heart, the bride, the virgin, Miss Ella Goldwasser, may she live, of Antwerp, Belgium. The entire Jewish community of Mumbai was invited to the gala *vort*, to be celebrated in the grand ballroom of the Taj. The wedding itself would take place at the end of August in Antwerp, where the young couple would reside, and where, I learned later, Malkie would also be settling after her marriage, so inseparable had she become from her future sister-in-law. Shmuly would be joining his future father-in-law's diamond business, with Malkie's husband as his chief of staff. No young man was better prepared than Shmuly to lead the campaign against the main threat to the survival of the ancient and venerable Antwerp Jewish diamond establishment—the rogue Indian diamond traders descending in their hordes with their goats and monkeys and painted idols, the international Indian conspiracy. Shmuly straddled both worlds. The silk road to heaven where this match was made was paved with diamonds.

The rains began to subside around the time you cut loose from Chabad. Still the ground was saturated, everything that once was hidden had been heaved up and exposed on the surface. Pigeons perched on our windowsill bearing tampon applicators in their bills. We came out of the dark blinking and went back to planting our vineyards full time. I prepared for our move to a flat I had found back in Colaba and focused intensely now on the coming tourist season, which due to personal circumstances I had seriously neglected—excusable maybe, but still, the workload had piled up, I was swamped, the stress level was intense. You set off to school every morning with Manika trotting behind you, chanting, Enjoy the rest of your day. In the evening you came straight home, no longer stopping for your spiritual fix at Chabad. You ate your meal, went into your room and closed the door. You were remote, into yourself, normal for an adolescent, but overall you seemed calm, at peace. The good news was you had stopped falling. I gave you your space.

The day Shmuly's engagement was announced, I did not mention it at the dinner table. You gave no sign that you were aware of it. That night as I was lying in my bed in the dark with my eyes open, weeping as I remembered Geeta, you came into my room to comfort me. You curled up beside me, burrowing into me as you had done so often when you were a small child before Geeta had invaded our lives. It seemed the most natural thing in the world. You buried your face in my neck, the passage of years shrank to nothing. I placed an arm around your shoulder drawing you even closer. You babbled into my body. It was not your fault, Malkie had told you, you were only a child, it was the fault of others, adults. It was not something you had done, it was something that had been done to you, against your will. Still, even though you were innocent, you were required to do *teshuvah*, Malkie had said, though even the most severe repentance could never fully erase the damage and renew you, it would never be possible for a boy like her brother to marry a girl like you at any age because you are spoiled.

You were zoning in and out of sleep—shuddering from the static of your sobs. I put my face into your hair to breathe in the scent of freshness that had always moved me with such tenderness, but tonight your smell was humid, gamy—female. What do you mean spoiled? I never spoiled you. Who said you were spoiled? It was a childish crush, nothing more. Your innocent heart had been ensnared by a snake who seduced you for your baby Moshe'le connection, then dumped you for blood diamonds. You are blameless, pure. What is this spoiled garbage? Time to move on. Get past it, Maya. Tomorrow the rains will end. Even with my schedule so overloaded I was nearly choking, I made the decision then and there that for your sake, tomorrow we would set out to Kerala, to Amritapuri, to visit our guru, the divine mother Amma, and receive her darshan. It has been too long that we have not seen her. Amma will look at you and instantly understand everything, I said as your breathing grew calmer and you rested at last. Amma devi will give you her healing hug and set you firmly back on course.

· 3 ·

WORKING WITH AMMA'S TEAM was always a pleasure. I had been dealing with her outfit over the years in connection with my tour business, providing a steady stream of clients for shorter and longer stays at her ashram, some of them serious potential major donor material, many morphing in time into significant supporters and contributors, all of them committed shoppers, snatching up Amma dolls and jewelry and rose-scented soap and bits of cloth that Amma had sat upon with her buttocks comfortably splayed and other assorted Amma tchotchkes and holy relics. At a certain point we had even embarked on preliminary discussions revolving around setting up an Amma satellite ashram in Israel in the desert on the brink of the great Ramon crater, not far from the maximum security prison where Yigal Amir, the assassin of the sainted Prime Minister Yitzhak Rabin was being held for life, within shooting distance of the cell in which his conjugal visits with his mad Russian took place as the press massed outside, straining to hear their post-coital whispers as they lay spent side by side in his prison bed sharing their grand dreams for the fledgling messiah she would bear from his wild seed.

These plans fizzled out eventually, but this did not in any way diminish my faith in the incredible efficiency of Amma's operation, which was borne out in every interaction directly connected with my business. This unparalleled competence and responsiveness was due to the fact that their guru, Mata Amritanandamayi Devi, known as Amma, was above all the ultimate mother figure. When your mother tells you to do something, you'd better listen if you know what's good for you.

As a mother in India, Amma was a far more formidable figure than Indira-mama ever was, to take just one example, because unlike the lady prime minister and all mothers by definition with the purported exception of the Virgin Mary, Amma had never been forced to undergo the indignity of being literally fucked to the best of anyone's knowledge, slander to the contrary about wild orgies with her cutest swamis notwithstanding, and she never had to deal with the day-to-day of actual children. All of humanity were her children, a much more manageable situation. Mrs. Gandhi could declare a state of emergency, but whatever its duration, it inevitably would have a beginning and end. Amma's state of emergency was a built-in permanent fact of life, giving her unlimited authority forever, which she would never abuse in a tyrannical or dictatorial way because she was Mother, and Mother is good. While governments stalled, twisted up like pretzels, hopelessly incapable of getting their acts together, totally inept in the heat of such crises as tsunamis and earthquakes, Amma waded waist-deep through the foul water and floating turds on her own two bare thick-ankled peasant feet at the head of her army of devotees and got the job done, rescuing thousands, putting up shelters, homes, hospitals, universities, pouring crores of rupees into the relief operation. Amma gave the orders, she made things happen. She was not content like so many others, the pope, imams, rabbis, and sundry similar type *makhers* to just stand there grinning smugly for the cameras mouthing platitudes about the worldwide blight of human trafficking and slavery, to take just one of her causes. No, that was not Amma's way. She said, Let all my little children who have been violated and exploited and discarded come to me—and she opened her arms wide and rushed them into her orphanages and schools that had sprung up overnight at her command.

Truly, despite unsubstantiated reports of temper tantrums, slappings, scratchings, bitings for even the smallest mistakes especially in the public relations department, as far as I was concerned, Amma was perfection. Every encounter I had with her or her staff was an unalloyed positive experience, but though I believed with full faith in Amma's gift of spiritual energy and insight, and though whatever she might have demanded of me I would have obeyed without hesitation, between us it had always remained strictly business. Whenever I came into her presence anew, I bowed down to the ground to touch her feet giving the homage due a mother who sits for twenty-two hours straight without a toilet break (wearing adult diapers, according to her detractors, Huggies of course), hugging one stranger after another, making eye contact that seemed to bore right down into the very depths of an afflicted soul as if to pump in an infusion of love, offering comfort and solace, breaking the Guinness world record for total number of body hugs dished out with feeling.

For me, though, it was a personal point of honor never to allow myself to be pushed by the saint's facilitators against her ample breasts to become the beneficiary of what by all accounts was a mind-blowing transformative maternal embrace. I had a mother of my own, thank you very much; dead or alive, one mother was as much as I could handle. Through her interpreter I struggled to explain that my reluctance to join the legions of hugged did not signify anything personal about Amma. For example, it had nothing to do with whatever might have rubbed off on her white sari or hefty arms or plump face in the way of deadly bacteria, say, or human body odors, or other dreck and schmutz and contagion and disease from her hours of hugging the unwashed masses, including lepers whose sores she licked, according to apocryphal lore. It was simply that I was allergic to hugs from either the giving or receiving end. I attributed this aversion to PTSD stemming from the discrimination and suffering endured by my twin brother, Shmelke, the Jewish guru, who was famous for hugging every living creature who crossed his path regardless of status or phenotype. He was an equal opportunity hugger—and what was his reward? Driven out of the Holy Land with his followers, ejected from one place after another in search of a resting place for the soles of his feet. It seemed that when it came to hug therapy, female providers benefitted from affirmative action in their favor because bottom line, they were judged harmless, the hug was not an opening move, it was the climax, punitive measures therefore were never taken against them. That's just the way it was, there was no point fighting the inherent sexism in it. Amma listened to my explanation regarding my hug phobia; it's hard to know how much she took in, it involved such a Western mindset and concepts. When I was through with my spiel, she waggled her finger at me, and with a sly gleam in her eyes declared in Malayalam through her translator, "On the day you come for my hug to save your life, I will be sitting here waiting for you." I chose to accept this as a blessing.

You, on the other hand, at those times I was compelled to take you along with a group to Amritapuri, typically when Geeta finked out on her parenting responsibilities and I had no one to oversee your care, would climb joyfully into Ammachi's lap for your hug. There you would curl up, your beautiful lithe young girl's body going limp and relaxed as Amma hugged you to herself with all her might, tickling you playfully, stroking your back clucking, MaMaMa, bringing her face down into your silken hair to breathe in your heavenly fragrance, holding on to you far longer than was practical for the continuous efficient flow of the conveyor belt of the masses of aspiring huggees awaiting their assigned turn, to the unconcealed agitation of her inner circle of enforcers conferring tensely on the stage in their bright orange robes. Yet not a single one of her closest attendants would ever have presumed to interrupt this prolonged communion no matter how seriously it disrupted the schedule because it was believed that you were among the rare souls with the power to inspire Amma to reveal her true identity as the incarnation of the goddess. This conviction grew out of an astonishing event that occurred during one of your early hug encounters, when, pressed against Amma's bosom, you told her through a translator that you had just been to the Kali temple on the ashram grounds. "Kali is very scary," you confided to Amma—not an unreasonable reaction. With her garland of skulls and girdle of severed arms and earrings of dead fetuses, her tongue sticking out of her mouth lolling down like an obscene red flap on her blue-black face with its eyes crazed with bloodlust, a detached head dripping blood held up by the hair in one of her four arms, her warlike stance, foot stamped down on the body of lord Shiva her husband, who seemed to be either dead or just relaxing and enjoying himself, Kali was a child's nightmare. Amma rocked you like a baby who had woken up in the dark screaming. "Do not be afraid of Mother Kali, my child. Do not be deceived by her terrible exterior. Kali is the warrior-mother, destroyer and creator, punisher and rewarder, nothing can stop her from doing her will, she is the force, she is Mother Nature, she is the greatest of all mothers, love her, respect her, obey her—or else!"

Instantaneously transformed, Amma pushed you away from her with such force as if she were ejecting you from inside her own body, fortunately into the arms of one of her handlers who caught you like a seasoned midwife. She rose from her cushioned throne on the low dais, stuck out her tongue for all to see, and with her face contorted into a ferocious mask, her arms flailing wildly so that they seemed to multiply into four arms, she raged in an otherworldly voice, "I am Kali Ma, warrior-mother, goddess–rock star"—throwing everyone present in that hall, veterans and visitors alike, prostrate onto the ground, overcome by this vision, this manifestation of the divine, many of them writhing and weeping, some fainting and struggling for breath so that they had to be spirited away on stretchers by medical emergency crews from Amma's Ayurveda clinic and her world-class hospital across the river. I alone was left standing, caught up in a fit of hilarity with Amma when our glances collided and our thoughts clicked. Amma's laughter was later featured on her website as a precious glimpse of divine bliss, the highest maternal wisdom, according to the hermeneutics spin. She had a highly developed website from which you could purchase ashram gifts and elixirs, and even virtual hugs in an emergency, when you were in crisis far away, in desperate need of Mother. The site was managed by a devotee who twenty years earlier, at age eighteen, had sold his internet startup for an undisclosed stratospheric sum to dedicate the remainder of his life to Mother.

When you came to my bed that night, babbling gibberish about being spoiled, ruined, your self-esteem in tatters, and I proposed a healing visit to Amma, I wasn't even sure if the guru was at her ashram, she traveled so frequently to personally deliver her actual hands-on hugs. On top of that, I certainly could not guarantee that after your deep dive into the Chabad ritual bath, you would be willing to set foot on soil polluted by idol worship. You promptly agreed to come along, however, one of your first overt expressions of rebellion against the indoctrination you had been put through, for me a truly reassuring sign that the process of mental and emotional healing was underway. I was so proud of you.

A quick call to my contacts at the ashram even in the early hours of dawn confirmed that Amma was in residence, as was often the case in August and September as the monsoon season waned, barring an unforeseen world crisis or other major humanitarian emergency during which every afflicted soul inevitably cries out for Mother. Amma always heard their cry, dropped everything and came running. She was, and I insert this here with a heart bursting with admiration for this amazing lady, addicted to the camera, a shameless self promoter, not for personal aggrandizement, I hasten to add in her defense, but solely as a tool to manipulate the media on whom she depended to spread her message. Her staff was expected to function on all cylinders at very short notice, so when I called it was totally set up to handle my request. I was assured that arrangements would be made at once for our visit—unfortunately too brief, I informed Amma's personnel with regret, a day at most, due to intense work pressures. I proceeded to book a flight for the next morning on IndiGo air from Mumbai to Cochin for the two of us and for Manika as well as a special treat—she had never been hugged by Amma and had never flown in her life, for Manika it would all be a delightful first.

A driver from the ashram, a devotee called Krishnapuri, who in his former life when he was known as Chris had been a pilot on Air Force One before giving it all up during the Clinton administration and coming to Amritapuri to perform *seva* selfless service for Mother, was waiting for us at Cochin International holding up a sign with our name inscribed on it. He took over our luggage, heavy with the requisite offerings to Amma, including my mother's candlesticks, her silk saris, and whatever jewelry remained that Manika had not filched with Ma's full laissez-faire awareness, plus decorative and household artifacts that Geeta and her goondas had missed while ransacking the Malabar Hill flat, which all in all was a good thing as there would be less junk and fewer painful reminders for me to transfer to our new digs in Colaba. We were led to the ashram car parked in a VIP spot for the three-hour drive along the Arabian Sea through the backwaters lush with tropical greenery to Amritapuri, rising like a vision as if out of nowhere into the night sky, its lofty pink buildings brilliant with the only lights on the subcontinent that never failed, Amma would never have tolerated that.

From the window of our room on the fifteenth floor in the hotel's top-class wing, I could see the light pouring out of the main hall where Amma sat and dispensed public darshan. It looked as if Amma were pulling one of her all-nighter marathon hugging sessions, an athletic display of extraordinary stamina for which she was so justly renowned. Thanks to my longstanding business relationship with the Amma operation and the well-endowed clients I brought in, we were assigned a room in the luxury category. I could not help but be aware, though, that there was a higher level of accommodation one floor up that had not been allocated to us this time; we had not been offered the upgrade. In Amritapuri, nothing happened by accident, without Amma's direct input. Like all great mothers, Amma was 100 percent hands on. Our room assignment could only mean that an exceptionally important guest was visiting. It crossed my mind that it could be the famous movie actress Sharon Stone, who had been running around at that time cheerleading and boosting for Amma devi, the angel, the hugging saint. I could only hope that if Sharon was not scheduled to be given a private audience, such as is sometimes granted by the pope and by other distinguished personages in the papal league like Amma to special friends of influence, when her turn came during public darshan to assume the position in preparation for being launched by a staff member for her hug in the bosom of Amma, she would be a good girl and remember to wear her knickers.

Standing at that window looking out beyond the world of Mother, if such a world truly exists or matters, it crossed my mind that we could simply run down to the main hall now where Amma was sitting, you and Manika could grab in your hugs, we could then check out at dawn or even directly after the darshan and talk Captain Krishnapuri into earning a few extra seva points by transporting us back to the airport, maybe even hijacking a plane and flying us home in presidential style, returning to Mumbai by early afternoon at the latest. Things might have turned out so differently had we seized that moment and gone for it. But you were already phasing into sleep patterns in your bed under a huge portrait of Amma, her moon face shining benevolently down upon you and Manika, who was cocooned in a blanket on the floor at your feet. After the spiritual hazing you had been put through in Chabadland, you had taken to sleeping as much as possible, a common teenager syndrome, I had read in a magazine somewhere. Teens required almost as much sleep as newborns and babies, according to the experts, due to an accelerated stage in the growth and development of their unstable nervous systems.

Now, with Amma smiling down upon you, it was as if you were recharging your batteries for the next morning when, before queuing up for your hug, you planned to revisit the original cowshed shrine in which Amma had experienced her first ecstatic visions when she was a young girl of about your age, swept up by compassion and love for all suffering creatures, moved to spread her arms wide and comfort with her embrace all the wretched of the earth, human and animal, including the family cows whom she kissed like Mrs. Murphy, their faces and flanks and tails smeared with dung. From what you had personally shared with me regarding the ecstatic nature of your falling stage, I recognized that you too counted yourself as an initiate in the rarified ranks of soul sisters seduced by the spirit while still legally underage, young girls who refuse all offers of marriage and survive by eating feces and shards of glass, as Amma was said to have done, who are shunned by family and tied to trees, beaten by their fathers for giving away the family treasures. I recognized that it was essential to give you the space you needed to work through this dangerously delusional stage without sabotaging your future, so that you would come out on the other side back on track. I counted on Amma to support me in this, which is why I let you sleep, and resigned myself to waiting for the morning.

Amma's active energy source was love, and the idea of Mother is love without limit. That's why she never dried up like a battery or blacked out like the chronically failing electrical grid of Mother India. She was the ultimate Mother, powered eternally by love juice. The first person we met almost immediately after we stepped out onto the ashram campus the next morning, as if he had been posted there to wait for us, informed us rhapsodically that Amma was still hugging away in the main hall, she was on a roll, unstoppable—gods do not need sleep like spiritually challenged mortals or neurologically temperamental teenagers. We had better rush to get our hug tokens if we wanted a good number for our turn in line.

The air was pendulous with the sense of a rare holy hour. Amma was very on, in tune with an exceptionally high spiritual chord not discernible to the rest of us. Banners, flags, posters, and giant portraits everywhere with Amma's face blown up, smiling so beatifically, beaming such sweet unconditional mother love and acceptance, seemed to be glowing especially brilliantly that morning, as if backlit by a heavenly radiance, like stained glass windows. Devotees were chanting the three hundred names of Amma, singing *bhajans*, meditating, crawling on the ground and picking up litter with their teeth, a singularly mystical form of seva. In the cowshed temple, worshippers were enacting a fire ritual and doing their puja, but as it turned out the cowshed was not your final destination after all, as I had assumed you had intended. Instead, you cast a bored glance at the scene there, then walked away and led us directly to the food court area, choosing the Western-style cafe where you ordered everything on the menu including a large pizza with tomato sauce (Let them eat pizza, Amma had ruled, when confronted with the hungry Western mobs at her gate), pasta with pesto, a grilled cheese sandwich, mashed potatoes, a cheese omelet, muffins and pastries, washed down with milkshakes from the juice stall. Amritapuri was strictly vegetarian, gliding toward a full commitment to veganism blocked only by a nourishing mother's concern for the needs of her Western children. Already its food service was certified organic, local, composted, recycled, solar powered, sustainable.

You consumed every carb molecule and fat globule spread out in front of you slowly and silently, with no sign of feeling pressured about securing a good spot in the queue for your hug and no sense of embarrassment, a proud fat girl flaunting her human right to eat. Amma wanted you to eat. Amma said you may not be excused from the table until you cleaned your plate. Amma was feeding you. Mothers feed their children. Feeding her children is right up there at the top of a mother's job description.

The main hall was packed when we arrived, not only with transient seekers and tourists, but also it seemed with the entire population of ashram residents, filling every space on the floor and vying nonviolently for precious spots on the stage directly in Amma's force field, praying, chanting, meditating in anticipation of a rumored stunning revelation. After we removed our shoes as was required and set them on the rack outside the entrance, divested ourselves of all carry-ons, passed through the security gauntlet of metal detectors and X-ray scanners, you and Manika were each handed your token with a number indicating your place in the hugging queue. Despite the masses that had poured in that morning, the numbers you were given were not a long way off from the ones already flashing up on the board, like at a train station with its row of ticket booths, alerting you that your turn is coming up, you're next, prepare yourself—know where you are going. From previous visits, I was aware that a stash of tokens was kept in reserve for visitors of status flagged for special treatment, media types and celebrities, politicians, major donor material, and also the chosen people with nothing obvious to recommend them, set apart for reasons known only to Amma herself in her divine maternal wisdom.

A volunteer named Shosh, a former attack-dog trainer in the Israel Defense Forces, a white shawl draped over her hair, ushered us to our seats in the front very near to the stage, removed the reserved signs stuck there, and with a blunt hand gesture, indicated to us to take our places. All of this was entirely in accord with the professionalism of the Amma operation as I had come to know it over the years. Holding a number of premium seats in reserve is always good policy in any people-moving performance-oriented enterprise; distance from the stage always needed to be factored in to optimize human traffic flow and keep the assembly line moving smoothly. We would not have a long wait. Our presence had been anticipated, we had not been forgotten even in this moment of intense spiritual excitement. Flexibility was built into Amma's shop, to accommodate among other contingencies, sudden visits from persons of interest, among whom we felt ourselves privileged to be counted.

The stage directly in front of us was a great hive with the queen bee at its center surrounded by her attendants, monks and nuns, every cell filled with devotees sunk as in honey into a personalized form of sitting meditation practice, from catatonic obliviousness to heads thrown back rotating wildly, dreadlocks flying. The music blared nonstop filling the hall, pouring from the speakers, band after band replacing each other in shifts. It was a coveted honor to play for Amma during a sacred hugging session, and especially one such as this, so spiritually high.

The band on stage just then was an all-female group called Lakshmi and the Survivors, consisting of women and girls of all ages, some as young as five or six by my estimation, all costumed in crisp white linen. The leader, on clarinet or oboe (I could never tell the difference between those two but it was for sure a mouth instrument of some sort), was a clone or exact double or the twin sister of Monica Lewinsky, if not the great Monica herself. But it was only when my eyes took in the star singer, a senior citizen in her late sixties, that I realized who had gotten the best room at the ashram hotel, the one denied to us. It was Charlotte Harlow, my repeat client. I was the one who had introduced Charlotte to Amma during her first tour with me. She had subsequently become an ardent Amma supporter and devotee, taking the spiritual name Lakshmi, for the goddess of prosperity—money.

I recalled now that I had heard that Amma had tasked Charlotte with the care of rescued girls, abused through the sex trade, the ones who, based on the wisdom of the guru, would not thrive in her shelters in India, but would benefit most from being sent out of the country to live in Charlotte's mansion on Foxhall Road in Washington, DC, under the care of professional PTSD therapists, be educated in one of the two most prestigious local girls' schools of which Charlotte served on the board, either National Cathedral or Holton-Arms, and be given the full entitlement of private instruction, from tae kwan do to music training at the famous Levine conservatory, which Charlotte also endowed. The fruit of these music lessons was now on display in the band right before us—violins, flutes, and also voice training to provide the backup for Lakshmi/Charlotte clutching the microphone, singing in her aged, tobacco-ruined, upper-crust New Orleans–accented voice, "The House of the Rising Sun," the Joan Baez version. "It's been the ruin of many a poor girl, and me, oh Lord, I'm one," she crooned huskily over and over again like a mantra. This was the only number performed by Lakshmi and the Survivors but nobody seemed to mind. It was after all just soundtrack, and it was in the nature of soundtracks to repeat themselves. It was background music—the kind of music that is played over and over again while you are kept on hold to reassure you that you are still in the queue, you have not been forgotten.

We were on hold as the main show unfolded in the foreground. That was where the star attraction, Amma herself, sat on her low mother-soft settee like pouf throne, all eyes upon her. The packed line of hug seekers inched along slowly and steadily toward her, flanked by seasoned crowd-control enforcers. As they approached the godhead, each supplicant was relieved of eyeglasses and any other facial obstructions or hazards, including nose, lip, eyebrow, and other rings in unexpected places that might rub against Mother's ethereal personal surface area. Faces and other exposed body parts were sanitized with a baby wipe. The entire prepped package was then collapsed down to its knees at Amma's feet, in readiness for the gentle tilt into her bountiful chest to receive a public hug of extraordinary intimacy lasting twenty seconds on average but sometimes as long as two minutes at Amma's divine discretion. She signaled its conclusion by offering from her own hands a *prasad* that had been passed to her by a devotee performing one of the most desirable forms of seva—handing Amma the prasad for the freshly hugged, a gift of candy in a packet of sacred ash. Clutching this precious prasad, the drained human specimen from whom so much emotional and spiritual pus had just been squeezed out, was lifted up by the armpits, cut off from the maternal source as if reborn, removed and replaced by the next in line.

I could see all this unfold very clearly from where I was sitting alongside you and Manika, but the entire ritual, enacted over and over again, was also projected on a giant screen at the back of the stage, frame after frame visible to the ends of the hall of Amma's mighty embrace, Amma rubbing a back, stroking a cheek, looking deeply into eyes and getting it, understanding exactly what was needed—planting a kiss, smiling, laughing, tickling, cooing baby talk, Amamama, loving unconditionally, comforting the suffering souls buried in her cushiony breast aching for the mother that is every human being's inalienable right, handing to each of her children a piece of candy as the immortal rabbi of Chabad had once not quite handed to me a crisp new dollar bill but rather set it down on the table for me to pick up when I was a teenager and my mother had arranged an audience for me at his main headquarters at 770 Eastern Parkway in Brooklyn, New York, in the hope that his blessing would straighten me out; I was such a difficult kid, Ma said, headed for no good. For me the institutional choice between a gift of sweets or cash spoke spiritual volumes, which went a long way, I felt, to explaining why I left Brooklyn for Bombay. Where was there another guru like Amma who gave of herself so personally in this way, who allowed herself to be felt up in public by her needy, deprived children? The rabbi of Chabad would not even touch me, he would not touch a strange unrelated female of any age, he would not even hold one end of the dollar bill for me to grasp the other end, but dropped it on the table between us instead like a bone dropped for a dog. And now here I was observing Amma's full body hugs in large-scale format stretched out across the screen, Amma's children whispering their most private secrets into her ear, weeping, sobbing, fainting, falling into a trance in her arms so that they had to be peeled off by a volunteer like a limp rag to keep the show rolling.

On the giant screen all the assembled to the far ends of the hall could witness Amma's unparalleled gift of empathy in full blockbuster display, and not less impressive, they could also observe her administrative genius, they could watch with awe her brilliance as a multitasker. They could see with their own eyes how Amma could hug so full heartedly and mindfully, and, at the same time, give orders to her staff, how she could hug the next seeker in line while finishing a conversation with the one who had just been extricated, how she could carry on with her hugging without skipping a beat while talking or texting on her smartphone or checking her email, which was perhaps the most uplifting and affirming sight of all, the one-armed hug showcasing the promise of technology deployed in the service of humankind. Nobody protested or objected. Everyone knew that it was essential for a mother to be a multitasker, and Amma was mother supreme.

Amma continued to text on her mobile as Manika knelt before her, holding up as an offering a huge red carrot that she pulled out of the knot in her sari. The texting went on as Manika, so tiny and compact, curled up in the shallow saucer of Amma's lap, resting her head against Amma's breasts, lost in their fullness, as if pumped up with mother's milk, talking with the intensity of one who feared any minute she might be interrupted and silenced, crying so hard the bones of her entire little body rattled and shuddered as if she might break apart in pieces. I had never seen Manika talk so much, or with such fervor, as if she were telling something she had never dared tell anyone before, dredging it all up painfully, pounding her hollow chest with both fists, and I had never seen her cry, not once, not even as she watched my mother burn.

Amma absorbed it all, this heavy word flow, she nodded and murmured, wiped away Manika's tears, stroked her hair and cheeks, caressed her shoulders with her left hand, while she continued to text on her smartphone with her right. She held Manika locked in her embrace for five minutes at least, prioritizing a first-timer, some said, which was her policy, but it was a radically long stretch, and even after she released her and you were settled in Manika's place against Amma's breasts nestled within the secure loving circle of Amma's arm, Manika went on telling her story standing there at Amma's right as Amma texted while rocking you in the crook of her left arm, purring, My daughter, my daughter, and softly singing lullabies to you so that very soon your eyelids grew heavy and drooped, and then you were asleep.

I admit that as I witnessed all this, I could not suppress the feeling that it was one thing to multitask while hugging Manika, but when it came to my daughter, I expected Amma to give you her full, undivided attention. She owed me. I was not a connection to be slighted. I had brought Amma many valuable contacts, including Charlotte/Lakshmi Harlow croaking away up there, warning her baby sister to never do as she had done. The vibes of annoyance I must have been giving off were picked up by Shosh, the former IDF attack-dog trainer, who looked me in the eye and commanded: Sit. Down. Stay. That was when I noticed that Amma too had fallen asleep cradling you, like an exhausted mother who had been rocking her baby for ages, and now at last the baby was finally asleep. The hall was hushed. Lakshmi and the Survivors were on pause. Movement was frozen, as if a spell had been cast in a fairy-tale castle. All eyes were gripped by the holy pietà vision of Amma sleeping, with you asleep in her arms.

Suddenly Amma's eyes shot open. She stood up, holding you in her arms extended like an offering. Her long red tongue came out, lolling down unfurled. She lifted you with ease. She was strong; as a young girl toiling in the family cowshed she was known to carry a sick cow for miles. Manika approached from the right, Monica Lewinsky from the left, little Manika and big Monica, sisters, joined by some of Amma's closest attendants in their orange robes, as if the ritual had been rehearsed. They lifted you off the altar of Amma's arms and stood you up wobbly on your legs, supporting you from all sides. They walked you over to the band. Charlotte herself came forward to welcome you into the circle of Lakshmi and the Survivors, drawing a white linen shift over your head as if preparing a human sacrifice. The band no longer was doing "Rising Sun," but providing backup instead for Amma, center stage, now fully transformed into the goddess Kali your mother-protector, singing your mantra over and over again—Om Kali Kali Kali, Om Kali Kali, Ma Ma Maya, Ya Ya Maya, Ma Ya Ya Ya—swaying from side to side faster and faster, clapping her hands over her head, stamping her feet, rising higher and higher into a place of spiritual exaltation, taking along with her the entire assembly, everyone soaring, shedding their earthly mass, joyously accepting the darkness and light, creation and destruction embodied in Mother Amma Kali, leaving me behind, motherless, childless, alone, an earthbound speck with no gift for spiritual abandon, and no gift for happiness.

The kiss of the godmother. Instantly her kitchen cabinet swung into action. That very night, you were shipped off with Charlotte and her band back to the USA, no problem, no special interventions required. You always carried your American passport. I was meticulous about making sure that as the daughter of a US citizen born and bred sojourning in dangerous lands you had this precious, essential document, and moreover kept it in your possession at all times, insurance against the inevitability of another Holocaust.

It all happened so fast, there was nothing I could do to prevent it. It was as if a boulder had been slammed down on my head. I was knocked out. The boss called me into her private office behind the former cowshed, a rare insider invitation. Multitasking as always, astride a stool with her legs spread, bare calloused feet stoutly planted on a floor carpeted with straw and manure, thick hands tugging at the teats of a cow so fat it almost entirely concealed the bilingual aide behind it so that it seemed as if the cow with her ruminating mouth was doing the translating, Amma laid out the facts on the ground. Manika would remain at the ashram, emptying the toilet compost pails, a form of penance for a sin committed most likely in a previous life from what I could surmise, a caste thing, her karma. You would depart that evening with Charlotte and her troupe on a direct flight first-class to Washington, DC, where you would be given every advantage, including a tip-top education at an elite girls' school with the very same name as it happened as the one you were now attending, Cathedral, so hardly any adjustment would be necessary. There in the capital of the free world, looked after by a five-star team of mental health professionals, you would heal. If all went well as planned, you might be able to return home for your summer vacation—when the rains came again, in our monsoon floods. As for me, in ten minutes I would be starting my journey back to Mumbai, Amma informed me. My suitcase had already been packed courtesy of the staff and stowed in the trunk of the car. Krishnapuri was idling at the wheel right behind the cowshed. At Cochin Airport he would exchange his chauffeur's cap for a pilot's helmet and fly me home in Amma's private jet.

The former milkmaid who for relaxation and nostalgic reasons it seemed still liked to keep a hand in, passed her full bucket to an aide without the faintest splatter, and wiped her palms on her white sari. Capisce? Yes, I understood. I appreciated her concern for your welfare, I said. It was probably true that you were suffering from a mild form of depression, I was ready to concede that. You had been traumatized. The last four years had been hard, bookended by your Chabad encounters, the psychological insults dealt you first by the terrorists and then through Shmuly by the double whammy of first love and betrayal, not to mention your cruel abandonment by your adoptive mother Geeta and the death and difficult disposal of my mother, your grandmother, resulting in the erosion of your self-esteem, precipitating, then exacerbated by, your unfortunate weight gain. Did I get it all right? Amma nodded her head up and down. I took that to be *yes* in Western terms, though side to side in India also meant *yes*. Maybe the Indians just didn't know how to say no. Maybe that was their problem. Maybe that's why there were so many of them.

I accepted it all without protest. To this day I cannot explain the extreme passivity that overcame me, as if I had been drugged. Later on, it was suggested to me by my brother, Shmelke, an ordained guru just like Amma, that the explanation for my strange failure to resist in any way, in manifest contradiction with my sense of myself as a proactive mother, was related to an instinctive healthy recognition of my own desperate need at that time for some relief, for a private space of my own in order to undergo my personal healing process for all the losses I too had suffered. I needed you to go away, for my sake and yours—that was Shmelke's original interpretation, his brilliant new *hidush*. I needed to be alone, being alone was a delicious illicit pleasure

I craved, I needed a break from you and all the burdens and worries that came with the blockage in my life that was you, my own daughter. A preposterous, horrifying notion, I said to Shmelke—I rejected it completely. What did he know of women, of the maternal instinct? I am mother. That is my main identity, the justification ultimately for my existence, my link on the great chain of being. Nothing could be more terrible for a mother than to have her child taken away from her, it is the primal fear.

As the plan for this seemingly unnatural separation was being laid out before me, I had reassured myself that it was after all coming from none other than Amma herself, the paradigmatic archetypal mother. Amma was the generative force behind it, the mother who was making it happen. It was a mother's idea, which by definition can only be for the good of the child. I remember how this thought seeped like a painkiller through my veins as I stood—yes, stood—there in that shed undergoing your amputation from me, listening as Amma unpacked the intricate logistics of the plot through what seemed like the chewing organ of a talking cow. If Amma is proposing this, then it must be right, I told myself. Save the child, that was the bottom line. The child was at risk—accident prone, susceptible to all kinds of harmful influences, in danger of being seriously derailed, and now here was super-mom Amma swooping down to perform a classic rescue—transporting the kid to an exclusive boarding school to keep her on track, a solution, I had to admit to myself, that was essentially in tune with my own child-rearing philosophy, especially as it applied to preteens and teenagers, with their hormonal big bangs. Granted, the kid is going through a stage, and you as the mother must allow it to play itself out for the sake of her mental health, her growth and adjustment, but you must also do everything in your power to prevent her from destroying herself in the process. The exclusive prep-school education that Amma was prescribing along with all the other perks was the obvious way to keep you with the program—that was my thought even then as I was losing you on the floor of that cowshed. No matter how badly you screwed yourself up during this admittedly normal, age-appropriate stage that supposedly would pass—it would pass as all life cycle disruptions pass—the entitlements that would become your portion would still land you in some prestigious fortress of higher education, you would be wearing protection, you would be kept on course with no significant long-term damage or fallout, everything would be okay.

In less than ten minutes I was going to be carted away. I would not even be granted a moment to say goodbye to you, to give you an embrace that would keep an ember of mother's warmth stored within you through the winter of our separation. A fast break—that was deemed to be the wisest course, always the least painful option in a situation universally acknowledged to be right up there at the top of the human suffering charts—the ripping of a mother from her child. In any case, Amma assured me you were doing fine, I could see for myself. She whipped out her phone from among the folds of her nine-yard sari and swiftly accessed the app for the video camera streaming in a room presumably somewhere in the ashram where I could observe you surrounded by Charlotte's band of survivors, unwrapping presents, one high-tech toy after another. You were laughing uninhibitedly, with childish carefree abandon as I had not seen you laugh for ages.

Were there cameras everywhere in the ashram? I must have spurted that question aloud, without full consciousness. Amma barked a seasoned laugh. "Amma does not need cameras," she said through the grinding lips of the talking cow. "Amma sees all with her third eye." She pointed to the bindi on her forehead above her eyebrows, the white circle of purity with the red kumkum dot inside it signifying the sixth chakra center, the zone of insight, rich with the deepest wisdom—so so deep, the deepest of the deep, as your ex-father Shmiel the Holy Beggar used to intone. I recognized then that what was now happening had all been determined, as if from above. This is how it would be and not otherwise. I was helpless.

"Maya, Maya—when will I ever see you again?" I cried out.

You stopped playing with your devices and turned around sharply as if you had heard me, staring directly at me with unseeing eyes, without registering. There you were facing me as if from a planet far away on the screen of Amma's smartphone. It was a setup that reminded me of the baby monitor I had once installed to keep you in my sights, but vastly updated, with no material barriers in the ether. But now in this new age I could not only see you and hear you, I could even talk to you and sing to you from my end from wherever I was in the world, no matter how far away. I should have seized the moment to sing "Die Gedanken sind frei" the Pete Seeger version, your favorite lullaby, to remind you of your basic human rights—who you are and where you came from—but convulsed with grief, I was levitated off the ground by two Amma controllers and borne away to the waiting Black Maria.

I wept through the entire flight from Cochin back to Mumbai. I'm telling you this Maya not to make you feel guilty but just to let you know how I ached for you, my forehead pressed against the window seeing nothing outside, only a black hole of sorrow sucking everything in. My sole consolation was that you would be wired head to toe, I had seen your loot. We could communicate online, I was assured before I left the ashram, once you were settled into your posh new quarters and habituated to your new life and the mental health dominatrices gave the green light for the resumption of our normal mother-daughter intercourse.

And we did communicate during that time of separation—by Skype, in chat rooms, instant messaging, texting, email, Facebook, and so on, but only you were allowed to initiate, that was one of the ground rules. The other rule was, you would not allow yourself to be seen. Those were your wishes. I needed to respect your wishes, I was advised.

I accepted it all. I was on call full time, perpetually psyched to receive your summons no matter how else I might at that moment have been otherwise occupied, and I also resigned myself to the blocking of the camera, to the banning of your image on my screen. Even when I was in Washington, DC, on business in cherry-blossom April around the time of your thirteenth birthday, the despots decreed it would be in your best interest if we did not actually meet face to face. I was half a block away from you, having coffee with Charlotte Harlow, your keeper. You and I touched base by phone.

I described to Charlotte how I pictured you possessed of your former heartbreaking beauty once again. You wanted to surprise me with your metamorphosis when we were finally reunited, I said—in that way I comforted myself for your allegedly self-imposed purdah. I imagined you shedding all that baby fat inside of which you were hiding, and emerging in dazzling glory like a butterfly ready to be seen. You were on the school lacrosse team, Charlotte informed me, you were involved in other fitness activities too; you were doing well in your studies, you were in the top group in math; you were participating in extracurriculars, you had played the black witch Tituba in the school production of *The Crucible*, raising the dead and going mad in a jail cell in Salem, Massachusetts; you led a healthy social life, you were close to Charlotte's other survivors and had made some new friends in school, an anorexic and a recovering bulimic, or maybe it was a recovering bully, you even had a boyfriend, a Princeton-bound senior at St. Albans, Charlotte mentioned his name but it slips my mind—it ended in junior, or maybe with a roman numeral III. Charlotte was my source. An investigator must stroke the source, make nice to the source in order to keep the line open, and especially in this case, because you were so reticent in our conversations, so unforthcoming and private, though always properly polite, waiting for me to pull the plug and sign off. But at least you were doing everything right from what I could ferret out. You were squarely on track, exactly as I had hoped.

· 4 ·

AND JUST AS I HAD HOPED, when the heavens caved in and the monsoon rains came crashing down at the end of June and I went to meet you at Shivaji International, I almost did not recognize you, you had slimmed down so radically. You were a stunning young woman ready to step out for all to gaze upon, any mother would have trembled with terrifying pride.

You had come to Mumbai for your summer vacation to do volunteer work in the Dharavi slum within shooting distance of the airport in which we greeted each other. Your plane had just flown low over the *basti* as it came in for landing, raising a mini-tsunami in the open brown sewage lakes, drowning out the sound on all the satellite TVs, the only source of light in every hovel. Dharavi had the distinction of being one of the largest slums on the planet. Community service in Dharavi was a highly coveted internship for prep school students with Ivy aspirations. There were summer camps for super-rich kids that for a fee exceeding the lifetime earnings of many slum dwellers put together offered two weeks in Dharavi sorting through the mountains of garbage scavenging for recyclables. But you were the real thing, any good admissions official could spot that in an instant. You had competed through the regular channels for the internship offered by a local nonprofit called Slum Power, you had no legacy, no affirmative action, no special *protectzia*, and you were chosen. It would look really great on your college application in three or four years' time.

The next morning before eight, two strangers showed up at our door wearing jeans and bright orange T-shirts inscribed with the words, *Slum Power, NGO¡*—the exclamation point upside down, blooming into a raised clenched fist like a mushroom cloud. The subtext of this early-morning visit was that jetlag is an indulgence of the rich and pampered, the starving children of India can't wait. They had come to fetch you, to take you to Dharavi for your first day—"To orient you," as the young man explained, "since we are in the Orient," he added in excellent English with an appealing smile that showed off a keyboard of strong white teeth in his dark handsome face. His name was Samir, Samir Khan, a Muslim, "But you can call me Sammy, mama," he offered obligingly. His silent partner was Sita, a Hindu; Sammy was the designated talker at this party, it seemed. Slum Power was committed to diversity, Sammy said with a nod to Sita who was also smiling in such a professionally friendly way. "Multi-culti, yes?" he elaborated, shaking his head in that endearing Indian way from side to side. Yes, I agreed, and now they would be diversifying even further with you, I reflected, their token Jewess.

Sammy and Sita were codirectors of Slum Power's internship program, he told me. They were in their early twenties by my estimation. They had come to show you how to travel safely and efficiently by train to Dharavi through the Churchgate station, always a treacherous trip in any weather but especially so now in the monsoon downpours and wetlands. Sita would accompany you to the ladies' compartment of the train, necessary to avoid the occupational hazard of being groped and so on, and instruct you further on how to protect yourself from being pushed by the ruthless commuter mobs, not excluding women, out of the open doors of the car onto the track and crushed like a bug. His role would be general escort, as is proper since in truth women should not be permitted to go out into the street unaccompanied by a male relative, he observed with an ironic smile to signal that he was in politically correct disagreement with his own words coming out of his own mouth—he was only kidding. I could consider him my daughter's big brother, he reassured me.

All of this special treatment was happening at Charlotte's behest, I recognized that. Charlotte was a major donor to Slum Power, acting in turn in zombie obedience to top-down orders from Amma. Special favors, kickbacks, payouts, corruption—this was the grease that fueled everything in India, and especially Mumbai, so-called nonprofits and charities not excluded. I gave no indication that I understood the unsavory inner workings of the system, however; it would not have been in your best interest to show off how clever I was, however much I was tempted. I went to your room to inflict against my will the necessary blow under the circumstances of waking you up after the long ordeal of your journey and the stupefaction of your circadian rhythms. "What are they wearing?" was your only question, mumbled in hoarse grogginess. "Jeans—and this." I handed you the oversized orange Slum Power T-shirt uniform they had given to me for you to put on.

While you were showering and dressing, I eased their wait by offering some chai and biscuits, and sat down myself with them at the table to socialize. I understood that even though you had agreed to live with me in our Colaba flat during your internship rather than be housed in some one-room shack with no toilet or running water in Dharavi itself with a multigenerational family of ten minimum in order to enjoy the full-body slum experience, the likelihood was minimal at this stage in your life that you would reveal anything of importance to me about your activities or anything else, in typical teenager mode. Now at least with these two as my short-term hostages, there was a chance to tap the politeness obligation in order to get some inside poop.

They were actually only sixteen, Sammy and Sita, I learned to my mild surprise, extraordinarily poised and mature for their years; I should have guessed—slum kids age fast and die soon. They had grown up in Dharavi, which was really a mini-city within the maxi-city of Mumbai, as Samir who was monopolizing the talking described it, with all the infrastructure of a city in the form of what some might characterize as a cautionary tale. They had acquired their English by watching American films on TV. Every basti family owned a television set, he informed me, even if they owned nothing else, it was a vital connection to the possibilities of the outside world, it was the only thing that made life tolerable. Because of how well they had taken to English, and also what was regarded to be their personable and congenial natures, Sammy admitted with a modest dip of his head, they had been selected to lead Slum Power's internship program, which catered primarily to North American kids, most of whom were paying top dollar for the privilege of shoveling waste matter out of the open sewage dumps. Slum Power also sponsored a recycling plant, a *papadum* bakery for women, a pottery factory, a fair-trade crafts workshop, and other small businesses in Dharavi. After expenses, including worker's wages, every paisa was plowed right back into these startups and other essentials—so much was needed: electricity, water, sewage, toilets, roads, the list went on and on. The nonprofit survived on contributions. The donation form could be found on its website, all types of payments accepted, including credit cards and PayPal. Sammy took out a pen and scribbled the URL on a napkin, pushing it toward me across the table and remarking, "In general, I disapprove of paper napkins for environmental reasons—but sometimes they come in handy." He flashed his ingratiating smile.

"So Maya's going to spend her internship baking papadums?" Finally, I was moving the conversation in the direction I wanted it to go. The two of them paused to stare at each other, then as if programmed, simultaneously coughed up an amiable laugh. Sammy turned to me and sandwiched my hand between both of his, gazing into my eyes with practiced empathy like a doctor about to give vital test results. "Mama, I just want you to know, when the applications came in for the internship slots this year, your daughter's rose like a spray of perfume to the top of the heap. Your little Maya was number one plus. Not only an excellent student at the best schools with English as her native language, but also fluent in Hindi, not to mention Marathi, Gujarati, some Urdu, some Bengali, some Tamil—plus a very nice reference note from Charlotte aunty. So maybe she's a little on the young side for a westerner who matures more slowly, but it was a no-brainer, Mama."

"Also Hebrew," I said, who knows why, a mother's boast, or just for the sake of completeness.

"Yes, also Hebrew, for sure, *betakh*. So Mama, with all that under her belt, do you think we would waste such talent setting her to baking bloody matzahs all day? Of course not! Your daughter will be a teacher in Dharavi—a beloved, respected teacher of women and girls of all ages. She will teach English, computer skills, maybe another subject or two. After she's oriented, with her superior language gifts, she can also fill in sometimes for Sita or one of the other girls as an apprentice tour guide. You know, our tour business is very successful, Mama, one of our biggest moneymakers—slums by day, the red-light district and Falkland Road with the merchandise on display in cages by night, a huge tourist attraction—the Lonely Planet kids love it, it's a must-see, a tremendous draw, awesome. But of course, for such a respectable girl like your Maya, we would only put her on the slum tour detail, no trolling by night, no cages, don't worry your head about it for one minute."

Slum tours. It had been a proposal that had crossed my desk in connection with my own business, I now recalled, but I had quickly rejected it as prurient, disgusting, and above all too confusing for my clientele in their designer traveling gear seeking their spiritual center in accordance with their idea of India. Who would want to go on a tour of a slum anyway, with its filth and disease, its sick cows and goats, its squealing copulating rats and squealing defecating children squatting in the mud, its full-frontal exposure of every revolting insult life dishes out, from birth to death? Only mental cases, people with a screw loose, voyeurs, masochists, perverts, only nutjobs would want to slosh through the open cesspools, subject themselves to such an ordeal—it was a sick idea, obscene.

I could have gone on in this vein, but you stepped into the room in your jeans and orange T-shirt taking our breath away, the three of us earthbound there at that table were overcome as if struck by a vision. On top of everything else, she's also gorgeous—I could read that in their eyes.

As you were pulling on your knee-high rubbers and poncho, arming yourself to go out and face the elements, Sammy went on. "It's our hottest ticket, the slum tour. You should try it, mama, it's not only for the backpackers. We're always full up, first come, first served, always turning people away, but if you SMS me, I'll jump you in the queue as a special favor for our friends. It's very illuminating."

Yes, I'll register myself for this abomination right away, I decided the minute you left, no matter how distasteful I considered the whole idea morally and aesthetically. I would do it for you, Maya. It would be a way to get closer to you, to bond, mother and daughter.

For some reason though I kept putting off signing up for my slum tour. Already we were three weeks into July. I would rise up in the morning meaning to get the job done, but the rains hammered down against the windows and puckered the walls with mildew, wetness permeated everything. I pictured myself sloshing through the muck and contagion of the basti, and my good intentions washed away with the day. But what really was stopping me? Tourism after all was my business. If a particular destination however repugnant or contrived draws in the paying customers, who was I to object? I hadn't yet stooped to peddling sex tours, it is true, but certainly I knew very well how I myself took full advantage of the sad human longing for meaning in this life, for relief from suffering by delivering all of those spiritually needy souls to the feet of gurus such as Amma and other frauds. Truly, the entire India itself that I served up was a freak show—tourists flocked to gape as if at performing monkeys, they couldn't get enough of the grotesque novelty, the garish exotica, the nonstop street performance, within half a day after arriving they were all flying high in shawl and salwar kameez, and I was their enabler. I had no right to sit up there on my high horse declaiming about this pathetic minor manifestation of human prurience, these harmless sideshow tours of the slums with their landscapes of shit lakes and garbage mountains, and especially because in the end it seemed everyone left feeling good, everyone benefitted, spiritually or monetarily, and no one was harmed.

You didn't pressure me, you never even reminded me to sign up, which, to excuse myself for my procrastination, I interpreted as a sign of your dread of being embarrassed by having your mother show up at your place of work in front of all your friends, a totally normal adolescent reaction, I was not offended. It was your preference that I stay away, I decided, I was only doing what you wanted. Still, your friends were the ones who had invited me—that was a fact. I knew virtually nothing about what you did all day, even into the night. You were coming home later and later, always escorted by someone, you assured me, Sita, Samir, others I had not met, though they never came in to show their faces and say hi mama, they didn't want to disturb me, you said. There was so much to be done after the day's teaching, you said, paperwork, planning, meetings, but otherwise you revealed almost nothing. You were not silent though. You talked over the light supper I set before you. Whatever the hour you came home, I was always waiting up for you with a warm meal, lentil soup, biryani, vegetable curry. You talked with striking animation and heat in fact, but never about yourself, always in generalities, about social and political issues, your consciousness was being raised, in principle a good thing. I suppose in retrospect, though, I should have realized that this was your way of talking about yourself, you were trying to send me a message, I should have understood.

Your main topic, in essence your only topic when you talked on and on so passionately on those nights, was slums—not only Dharavi, but slums in general, the condition of slumdom. Everything else you touched upon seemed to flow from this theme as from an open drain. How could we allow ourselves to be bystanders while human beings lived like that—no toilets, no privacy, cardboard walls and rusted tin roofs, all of it lashed together with old electrical wires, bits of rope, tape. Yet even so, this was home, neighborhood, community, you declared. Why don't people get that? Why is everyone on the outside so clueless when slum dwellers hold out against fat-cat developers, even when they're bribed with lakhs of rupees and a brand new flat in a concrete block? They never asked to be relocated, they never petitioned for slum clearance—all they wanted is a working toilet of their own instead of being condemned to stand in the pouring rain in that humiliating loo queue every morning, for God's sake, you declaimed as I nodded now and then to prove I was listening, marveling to myself, and yes, also deeply moved at the wonder of youth pouring forth newly discovered knowledge with such ardor as if it were fresh wisdom on the face of the earth, never before thought or heard. And really they're such good people when you get to know them, you went on discharging your grand associative verbal torrent, such kind, generous neighbors, there's such a real sense of community in the basti, it's a village really, everyone helps each other, everyone looks after each other's kids, everyone gets along just fine until suddenly, some evil spirit blows in—politicians, gangsters, cops, big money, all the usual instigators and perpetrators, and the whole place explodes. Rioting, killings, mutilations, rape—the Hindu nationalist majority comes rampaging through the Muslim ghetto, which makes it by definition a pogrom—right? The Muslims are plotting to shoot off rockets from the slum aimed at the airport, they're screaming, get them out of here, it's ethnic-cleansing time, ship them all in cattle cars to Pakistan, they're all terrorists—exactly like what's happening now in the Middle East, in Gaza for example, which they call a refugee camp, but what's a refugee camp anyway? It's really just another word for slum. Gaza is one giant slum when you think about it, a filthy, disease-infested shantytown, the most populated strip of land on the planet. Nobody wants Gaza, not the Americans, not the Russians, not the Arabs, not the Zionist entity, nobody.

The Zionist entity? Where did that come from? If only your father, the Holy Beggar Shmiel Shapiro, either devoured by cannibals on the Andaman Islands or perched there on the lip of Reb Shlomo's grave in Jerusalem, strumming his guitar and warbling on about how the Nation of Israel lives, could hear you now—what would he say? Oy, this needs such a fixing, he would say. But as for me, I remained silent. I merely sat there admiring your precocity. Already you were ready for the Ivy League.

Night after night into July to the accompaniment of the drumroll of thunder and the beating of the rain, I sat there nodding in silence as you played variations on this theme, starting always from the rogue cell of slumdom and ending always in the scapegoating of Islam. I am your mother. Whatever you hand out, I take. I was simply grateful that at least you were talking to me. I no longer expected any classified personal information. Often I admit my brain would zone out, confident I could deliver an appropriate grunt if you ever addressed me directly. But then late into the month, you surprised me; you snuck in something almost personal, as if to catch me off guard, like some of my teachers would do when I was still in school to see if we were awake, if we were paying attention. As if in passing, as a sidebar, you let drop that Geeta had come to Dharavi that day, on a VIP tour.

"Geeta? How did she look?"—the first question that popped into my head, then right out of my mouth.

"Filmi. Like a movie star. She looked straight at me, but didn't recognize me."

I was stunned that you had volunteered this morsel—eye contact between you and Geeta, such an intimate detail. I had no idea when this window of opportunity would slam shut on me; I felt intense pressure to find out as much as possible while you were still ready to talk. "She was leading a delegation from the orphanage ministry or whatever," you said in response to my next question. "They're giving full scholarships to fifty slum girls under ten to come to Delhi to be educated. Their families will also get a lot of money. She was there to pick out the girls. She gave a little speech and promised to be like a mother to them."

"I hope you talked to someone high up," I said. "She would be a terrible mother."

But by then the well had dried up, you no longer were talking. You lowered your head. I was afraid you might start to cry. I understood what you were feeling. Quite apart from your own personal loss—a mother is a terrible thing to lose, even a terrible mother, and yes, let's face it, for better or worse, Geeta was also a mother to you. What would have happened had you gone up to the slum bosses with your pals trailing behind you, Sita, Samir, the whole gang, to warn against letting the girls go off with such a travesty of a mother as Geeta? They would invariably have inquired how you knew her, and at that point you would have been obliged to tell them that she had been married to your mother, that she had been your mother's wife. It was an impossible situation. They would not have believed you, they would not have understood it, such things do not happen in the world, they would have thought you were joking, they would have thought you were mocking them, they would have thought you were mad.

"It's okay, Maya," I sought to comfort you. "I understand. It's not your fault, whatever happens to those girls."

At the same time, though, I privately resolved to go on the slum tour as soon as possible. If Geeta your cold-hearted absentee parent could gaze upon you on planet slum where you passed your days, I certainly had earned the right to see you there too, I who had stuck it out.

I decided not to let you know when I would be coming. I wanted to spare you the state of living dread, or the obligation in such a traditional society to drop whatever you were doing and come forward to greet me, your honored mother. In any event, there were over a million people living in Dharavi. Chances were very small that we would run into each other. I could come and go, and you would never even know I had passed through, but anything I might learn would give me some insight into where your head was at now, and I could help you—helping you was my reason for staying alive. I was doing it for you, Maya, but it would not be an invasion of your privacy, like opening your mail or reading your journal. I had been invited, publicly and in your presence, fair and square, and now I was accepting the invitation as discreetly as I could to spare you. I would leave no footprint.

But who leaves a footprint on this earth anyway, and especially in a slum where life is so cheap, and most especially in a slum during the monsoons when every sign is washed away and erased? Trailing through the thickets of narrow congested lanes behind the backpackers, tuning in and out to the upbeat patter of our guide Sunil/Sunny, the first thought that hit me as we waded up to our knees in brown sludgy fluid floating with dead vermin and turds with personality, decomposing flesh and rotting garbage, was, did the Hindu princess Geeta really trek through this? The second thought was, maybe you had made up the story of Geeta's visit in order to finally get me up off my tukhes to go on this damn tour—a sweet thought only in that, contrary to every indication, its implication was that you might actually have wanted me to come, you were not ashamed of me after all as I had so foolishly imagined—but it was also a thought that I quickly scratched as fantasy since I knew that the memory of losing Geeta was still too fresh and painful for you to evoke, even for my sake.

Still, I simply could not picture Geeta wading through this sea of offal like other mortals. She must have been forearmed, she was probably wearing a pair of offensively expensive thigh-high custom-made designer boots cobbled by hand out of some high-tech water-repellent material, I decided, a monsoon fashion statement on the slum runway, or maybe she was borne aloft in a palanquin like the Maharini of Mumbai, and her feet never touched the ground, she never left dry land. Then I thought of you, Maya, I pictured your tall rubber boots caked with stinking brown gunk that you took off every night in the hallway outside the door, I pictured you sloshing through this filthy soup day after day, with more liquid pouring down from the low black clouds overhead, and again I thought, thank God your falling sickness days have passed—what if you slipped and fell into this swamp, infested with parasites and feces and disease, what then? The kids trudging ahead of me were soaked, but still they kept badgering Sunny, Where's the shit lake? Are we there yet? The open lake of raw sewage, it seemed, according to the yelps, was the highlight of the slum tour. They kept on nagging him until finally, even with the positive, gung-ho demeanor all Slum Power employees were required to maintain, he lost it. "The shit lake overflows in monsoon," he snapped. "You're walking in it right now."

It was still midafternoon, but the low cloud canopy brought on an early end-of-day darkness. The blue tarpaulins that were stretched across almost every rooftop in a pathetic effort to keep out the steadily falling rain gave off a dusky, twilight disorientation. In the cramped passageways, people moved about as if in an underworld, picking their way through the large objects bobbing in the water by the light of their cell phones. Water had risen into almost every shack, we could track it flowing in inexorably. Through the doors, open to catch the fading rays of daylight, the whites of eyes glowed out as if from the portholes of a doomed ship, the lower half of bodies were sunk in still, stagnant water like emerging life forms in evolutionary distress.

To demonstrate how ingeniously some citizens improvised and coped, Sunny led us into a comparatively larger hutment, constructed on a slight elevation of compacted trash and recycled junk. Even so, inside the water was at least ankle deep. We were clumped at the entrance, not wanting to invade as uninvited guests by venturing boldly into the interior, pointing the flashlights we had been instructed in advance to bring along as part of our slum tour gear, listening to the master of the house muttering, Welcome, welcome, observing him smiling genially and nodding his head as if in total agreement with every word spoken in a language he likely did not understand, while Sunny directed our attention to the shelves and ledges jutting out high up along the walls. Human figures were reclining on them, or engaging in some domestic task, a mother nursing a baby, an ancient grandma curled up snoring, flicking away in her sleep the drops of rain falling on her hollow cheek, children eating street food, samosas and bhel puri off torn sheets of newspaper since the contamination permeating everything made cooking at home a mortal threat, Sunny explained. In the most protected position, the place of honor, Sunny pointed, we could see the family's most treasured possessions wrapped in plastic, the television set above all else, though unfortunately it was impossible to switch on the electricity in the basti during the monsoon, not only because the power was on the blink almost full time as usual, but also because of the danger of shock due to the moisture saturating everything.

When Sunny concluded his spiel, an awkward silence descended, the meaning of which as a travel professional I instantly grasped. I seized the initiative, opened my purse and handed a nice pile of rupees to our host, which he accepted with a practiced gesture, placing the cash over his heart with both hands flat on top of it and bowing his head in gratitude. All the backpackers followed my lead and did the same, except for the kid outfitted head to toe in top-of-the-line travel wear, who inquired if they took credit cards. The master of the house reached up to one of the shelves and pulled down a plastic bag containing a portable credit card gizmo, and the transaction was completed.

The gratuity for the owner of the monsoon showhouse was on top of the price we had paid for the tour itself, amounting at the very least to what an upwardly mobile slum dweller might earn in a month. Now Sunny was warming us up for the biggest payout of all—I recognized this as a tourism insider—the contribution we would be asked to make at the end of our tour to his worthy nonprofit with an additional tip to him for his superior services. In anticipation, for the grand finale, he announced that we would now be taken around to view just a small sampling of some of Slum Power's cutting-edge, life-altering projects. All of it was contained in a very small space, he reassured us, so there would not be that much more walking on water to do; in any case, the basti itself with its one million inhabitants right in the heart of the frenetic metropolis of Mumbai hardly took up more than a square mile of land, he reminded us.

He failed to mention the climbing, however, up narrow, steep staircases, sometimes even ladders in near darkness to the factories where men and boys sat shoulder to shoulder, melting recycled plastic water bottles, firing clay pots, stitching garments, a rapturous smile lighting up every face, they looked as if any minute they might all burst out in song as in a socialist realism propaganda film. Most heartwarming of all was the happy leather workshop reeking of animal carcasses employing *Dalit* untouchables and Muslim outcasts. "Equal opportunity employment, nondiscrimination, that's our motto, the rejects of Indian society empowered by Slum Power," Sunny intoned. The previous week alone this factory had shipped out five thousand designer belts, he proudly announced, special order from a very famous chain of stores that we may have heard of, Sex Filth Avenue in the United States of America.

"But what about the other 50 percent?" a pretty blond feminist called out, right on cue. "Good question, Pipi." Sunny replied. Was I the only one not given a name tag? He flashed an irresistible smile, and promptly led the way to the women's workplaces set up by Slum Power—embroidery shops, children's nurseries, bakeries, and the like, as well as self-improvement programs ranging from basic literacy to computer literacy, women's healthcare and hygiene, and yes, even family planning, or more to the point, sex education. Slum Power had fought a mighty battle against the prevailing conservative mindset to get that sex-ed class up and running, Sunny told us, but the need was undeniable. The last stop on our tour would be a rare glimpse of the fruits of Slum Power's progressive victory in one of the most reactionary communities of all, though in deference to the sensitivity of the subject and the modesty of the young ladies, it would be only a very brief stop, yet even so, highly informative. Yes! One of the kids leading the way pumped his fist. Even better than the shit lake.

It was on the fringe of the basti, in what you had called the Muslim ghetto. We clustered in the doorway of the classroom, not quite entering, the women of our group in front and the men and boys screened behind us, craning their necks for a view over our heads. It was a traditional schoolroom setup—rows of student desks, blackboard, the teacher's desk in front facing the class and us. The students ranged in age from approximately nine to somewhere in their midteens, according to Sunny, the prime age for marriage, every head covered in a hijab. You sat at the teacher's desk, your face veiled in a niqab, only your eyes were visible. Spread out on the surface in front of you were packets of *Nirodhs* and a bunch of bananas. One of the Nirodhs had already been unrolled in a demonstration on a banana. In a Skype audio conversation we had had over the past year, one in which you had been a bit less guarded, you mentioned that the sex-ed instructor in your fancy girls school in Washington, DC, had also used bananas to demonstrate protection with a selection of pleasure-enhancement condoms—flavored, fluorescent, ribbed, and so on—to enlighten you at the same time on the joy of sex. Recalling this you had laughed so girlishly, it had been so sweet to hear your laugh. But the condoms you were demonstrating for your students were just ordinary, no-frills Nirodhs. "Condoms are permissible in special situations after marriage," you said, "such as during jihad, to prevent the birth of orphans. For even then, the excess energy of the faithful must find release in order to carry on the work of the shahid."

What? What? The people behind me couldn't hear what you were saying; you were speaking so softly in a mix of Hindi and Marathi, but mostly Urdu. They would not in any event have been able to understand you even if you had shouted in English; your words were incomprehensible, they made no sense. Your eyes were cast modestly down, no doubt because you were aware of the presence of one of your colleagues and his group, including male members. You did not raise your eyes for a second, even out of curiosity. You did not know I was there, I felt sure of that. You did not feel my presence, you did not see me turn and push my way through the group past Sunny's hand extended for a tip, out of the collapsing building into the dark lanes of the slum, churning up the brown water and sloshing it all over me as I ran, searching for my lost reality.

No taxi would stop for me after I had finally found my way out of the basti. I looked like an alien being emerging from the primordial soup, molded out of mud and clay like the first attempt at golem-making by a novice in a kabbalah workshop run by Madonna, still missing the divine spark that would give me a life. The autorickshaw driver who pulled up alongside me at last out of desperation for a fare first handed me a soggy *Mumbai Mirror* left by a previous passenger, and would not let me board until I had spread it to his satisfaction over the seat as well as every surface with which my befouled physical person might come into contact.

Skidding and bumping along on the slick, potholed and rutted streets in that *tuk-tuk*, my entire being wanted nothing more at that moment than to be cleansed of the slum filth, like a prisoner in a sealed cattle car dying for a shower. But the first priority was to save your life, Maya. Above all it was imperative to get you out of Mumbai, out of India, back to the rational side of the globe, far from the Hindustani soul trap. I needed to be in touch with Charlotte, she was responsible. She was the one who had engineered it all, who had snatched you away from me, who had sent you to a school that encouraged such a lethal internship, with such catastrophic consequences. It was her fault. Now it was her duty to repair the harm she had wrought—to pluck you out of the slums at once, call out the big guns if necessary, Amma herself and even loftier personages, not excluding the Obamas up the street, especially her best friend, Michelle, to fall down on her knees and supplicate Michelle during one of their naked hot-yoga sessions in her private home studio, to insist that Michelle get the Man to order the Green Berets or some other superhero special commando unit to evacuate you. Michelle needed to be made to understand that she must do for you exactly what she would have done for her own daughters had they too come home from Sidwell Friends School one day with their heads wrapped in hijabs, slated as brides for shahids, stepping out of one of the fleet of presidential limousines with the cameras flashing, had her girls too been seduced by the masochistic self-annihilating romance of Islamic fundamentalism, their souls taken into captivity, as I now understood yours to have been taken; it could happen to them too, they were not immune. This was an emergency situation, no possible remedy should be overlooked. You were in terrible danger, there was not a minute to waste.

Charlotte picked up right away. It was her private line, the access code available to only the chosen few. "What a coincidence, Meena darling!" There was a condescending edge to her tone, it pierced me instantly. "I just got off the phone with Maya. She said you'd be calling any minute. Ha ha. She mentioned you had dropped into her sex-ed class for Muslim brides-to-be today at Dharavi with one of those tour groups, but then suddenly you ran off without even saying hi or bye—maybe some business emergency you had to attend to, she thought. I hope everything is okay. I hope it wasn't the Mumbai version of Delhi belly—that would be a real bummer, everything is always a million times more intense in Bombay, maxed out to the limit. Frankly, I have no problem whatsoever with Maya teaching sex-ed, if that's your concern. It's very therapeutic, such a cathartic form of emotional self-healing, such a healthy channeling of all that bad stuff—you know what I mean? Anyway, she's feeling great—she was calling to tell me that. Her three *doshas* are all in correct balance. Her seven chakra centers are completely open and unblocked. Her self-esteem has come back like gangbusters. She's feeling so healed, she's decided not to return to DC after the summer but to stay on in Mumbai, go back to her old school, and continue doing volunteer work in the slum, which will look absolutely brilliant when she applies to university—don't you think? I'm totally in support of this plan. It's just so rewarding when one of my girls graduates from my program completely detoxed and ready to press the restart button. It's like an extreme makeover, it makes me feel like jumping on top of my seat and giving her a standing ovation."

Charlotte was flying high, nothing I said in response was registering. She simply brushed me off when I insisted that it was essential for you to go back to DC right away, that you had fallen in with a very negative crowd, there was a danger you might run off to some terminally misogynistic Middle Eastern country, not Israel, and marry a terrorist suicide-bomber wannabe and maybe blow yourself up too in the bargain, or turn into a sex slave, or get yourself honor killed, or stoned, or blinded with acid, or some other stock variation on the theme. You were being brainwashed, I informed Charlotte. I begged her to get Amma to force you to leave India and ship you to DC immediately, as she had done the previous year. "We didn't force her," Charlotte said coldly. "She wanted to go, it was her idea."

Could that really be true? But now was not the time to fact-check the past, you were in immediate existential crisis. I reminded her of how impressionable you were, how sensitive. I was practically weeping. I told her that you were under the influence of a Muslim fanatic; granted he was cute, terrorists can be super cute and super sexy, you were in love and therefore irrational. Had she been with me today and seen you in that classroom, she would have gotten the picture. You were talking about shahids, jihad, surrender, your face was covered with some kind of *schmatte*, all you needed was a pair of dark sunglasses, and not one inch of skin would have been visible, like wearing a burqa. I felt I was suffocating when I saw you in that classroom, I told Charlotte. I had to get out of there, I simply could not breathe.

"Ah, burqas," Charlotte mused. "I consider them the ultimate feminist fashion statement. It's like walking around in a room of your own." She had just hired a team to design and market variations on the burqa for the contemporary woman. Perfect for when you're feeling a little fat, or your face breaks out in zits, the burqa could become the mumu of the new millennium.

"Meena darling, relax. I do believe you are overreacting." Charlotte was focusing; she was making an effort. "Maybe Maya's going through a minor adolescent romantic Muslim stage, but it will pass.

If it makes you feel any better, the variety of Islamic religious experience she's involved with happens to be really quite liberal and gender-friendly from what I can tell. She's planning to go tonight with a group of friends to Haji Ali, she told me—you know, the Sufi saint, his tomb? Sufis are the good Muslims, everybody loves the Sufis—right? They're the Muslim hippies, the mystics, the poets, the cuddly Muslims. I mean, didn't you ever go through a Rumi phase? Anyway, she was telling me how it's really so fun to walk to Haji Ali at night during the monsoon singing a *malhar raga* with the waves crashing against the long concrete causeway leading to the mosque on its little island. But there's always the possibility of flooding, or high tide and the causeway getting submerged. So she wanted me to tell you when you called that there's a very good chance she might not be able to get back right away, she might have to stay there overnight or even longer, she doesn't want you to worry or call the Mumbai lost and found or the cops or the missing persons squad or something. But the real reason they're going to Haji Ali, you'll be so proud to hear, is not just for the scenic walk, or for the view of that lovely little white mosque in the middle of the Arabian Sea as if floating detached in mist. No, she and her friends are going for the express purpose of occupying Haji Ali, to protest the recent ban against women entering the inner sanctum of the saint's tomb. The Dargah trust likes to boast that they're open to all races, religions and creeds—so hey, what about gender? I am so proud of Maya! She and her pals are not just taking it—no. They're planning an action, speaking truth to power. They're going to walk right through the barricade blocking the women and stage a sit-in at the tomb, she told me, which is just so cool—Girls at the Grave. Now doesn't that make you feel better, Meena?"

I have no memory of hanging up and ending that conversation with Charlotte. I believe it continues to this day, all the things I should have said, every regret articulated. What I next recall is being startled into alertness by the constriction of my heart, a polluted gray dawn filtering in through the window, and I am still sitting in that chair at the kitchen table clutching my mobile, flakes of stinking slum excrement peeling off me and mounting in piles on the floor, continuing to shed as I make my way to your room to divine for signs of preparation for an extended absence. The same mess as always, untouched. Under the circumstances, I reasoned, it would not be a transgressive violation of your sacred privacy if I were to open your laptop to check for even a cryptic reference to plans for a demonstration at the mosque, but all of your devices were gone. Of course—you took them along with you to the slum every day in your backpack. I had failed to pay attention.

As the hours passed, my entire self continued to fall away in flakes of dry slum shit, exposing my vital organs to every insult. Compulsively, I was checking and rechecking on my own computer on every conceivable news source site, listening to the radio and TV for bulletins and alerts, every cell of my body susceptible to the slightest reference to a takeover at Haji Ali. Nothing, not a syllable. In India a mosque, a temple, is a tinderbox; set a spark to it and the fire spreads ravenously, the whole madhouse convulses for days and days and is ravaged. It was clear to me that the powers, police, politicians, all of the main players, were ruthlessly focused on keeping the incendiary news of the takeover from leaking, bent on negotiating covertly with the occupiers, to extricate them from the premises with stealth tactics so as not to trigger yet another riot of unforgiving dimensions.

By late afternoon the waste matter of the slum that had attached itself to me—whatever had not already seeped into my skin and permeated my inner core forever—finally washed off in the monsoon rains. I was standing soaked, holding up my wrecked umbrella, spoke-twisted and shredded, at the entrance to the causeway to Haji Ali. I could no longer bear the media silence—the state of not knowing what happened to my loved one, by all accounts so detrimental to achieving closure following a disaster according to the testimony of survivors. This situation became intolerable. In desperation I left my flat in spite of my fear that you might show up while I was gone and I would not be there to welcome you home, and came to the scene to find out for myself what was going on. My heart soared at the sight of the barricade at the causeway entrance, and the policemen hanging out under a nearby shelter, perhaps rather too casually it occurred to me, though I quickly censored the thought, and there were not as many as I would have expected or liked to see considering the provocation, nor any sign of the loved ones of the other kids demonstrating inside, a danger to themselves and others. I was the only parental figure present. Still, there was a barricade, there were armed guards with visible lathis barring access. I stood there letting myself be washed by the lashing rain, taking comfort in the thought that at least I knew where my child was tonight.

The cops occasionally aimed a glance my way, judging me to be harmless, inconsequential, female, possibly hysterical, possibly deranged, reluctant to venture out of their snug little clubhouse to deal with this nuisance. One was finally dispatched, however, a Sikh. He approached with a plastic grocery bag over his turban, annoyed, his beard dripping into another plastic bag, the handles looped over his ears. "Madam, move on, the mosque is closed today."

"My daughter's in there—you know, with the kids protesting the ban against women? I respect your need to keep this top secret because of the possibility of rioting and all that, but I had to come, I am a mother."

"There is no protest, madam. No one is in the mosque except the dead saint, and he is not causing any trouble at the moment. The causeway is closed due to flooding. It is underwater. Standard procedure in July and August during monsoon—unscheduled closings, weather related. You can return when the water recedes. Now madam, you must go—or I will be obliged to take action."

"What kind of action? Are you going to encounter me, or something? Go ahead, encounter me, I don't care."

Let him shoot me, let him eliminate me like a common thug and claim self-defense, dispense with justice and law, it was so much more efficient, but then I reminded myself that one of the privileges you give up when you become a mother is the right to commit suicide. This is a rule my own mother had violated—and I have never forgiven her. At the same moment it struck me with perfect clarity, as if I had been given an unobstructed view down the kilometer stretch of the causeway through the walls of the mosque complex now rendered transparent to me, that you were not in there. I did not know where you were. I had to get home. I had to wait for you. I had to be there when you came back, to open the door and let you in.

A bicycle rickshaw slowed down, then zoomed off at the sight of me dripping rainwater like endless tears, raising waves in its choppy wake that drenched me even more. I sloshed on through the filthy puddles, gesticulating with thumb pointed backward for anything that moved to stop, stop in the name of heaven, give me a lift, raise me up, take me away from all this. My throat was clamped by a pain-ful urgency—I needed to get back home at once, to be there for you. Ahead of me, the words Slum Power beckoned, glowing like a burn ing bush through the rain, I thought I might be dreaming. It came back to me then that the NGO's office was in Worli, close to the Haji Ali shrine; I recalled that now from having mined the website. This is where I would have been taken after the tour, to write a fat dona-tion check, had I not fled at the sickening sight of you shrouded in veils. Now it seemed to me a sign from heaven, reaching out to me with the promise of news of you. To ignore it, to pass it by even with the pressing mandate to be in my assigned spot at home when you returned would be an unforgivable sin of omission. I would have lost my chance.

Other than some filthy cows that had come inside to take shelter from the rain, only one employee was in the Slum Power office at this late hour of the day, a young woman festooned with silver piercings dangling from her eyebrows and lips, and a name tag—Maya. "My daughter is Maya, too," I informed her. "She's an intern here. Do you know her?" Interns come and go, she observed, she never bothered with them; for her they did not exist, Maya is illusion. She added this with an insider's smile. And even despite the tongue ring that snagged her speech, I could tell by the lilt of her studied English that she was Israeli—post-army road-trip decompression, she confirmed when I inquired in Hebrew to soften her up, tarrying in India beyond the finding-yourself grace period to the terminal distress of her parents, both of them professors of international affairs at Tel Aviv University with a specialty in Middle Eastern and Muslim studies, lingering in

Mumbai on account of her Indian boyfriend, Sunny, the night manager of a dance club in Bandra. But she knew all the full-time Slum Power employees, she conceded when I probed—so did she know a guy named Samir Khan? She boomed out a coarse snort resembling a laugh, startling me. Samir Khan? Wasn't he that idiot Pakistani American guy who got himself killed in Yemen? Deftly she did a quick Google search on the office computer. *Nakhon*—taken out two years ago by an American drone strike, along with another Muslim fundoo jihad propagandist, Anwar al-Awlaki, a really big prize—Good job, says Mr. Barack Hussein Obama insincerely. Anyway, *beineinu*, Slum Power never hires Muslims, even though it calls itself equal opportunity multi-culti, blah-blah. So no way any Samir Khan ever worked here, that's for sure. Besides, every other Muslim in Mumbai is Khan, and every other Khan is Samir. Sorry mama.

This namesake overdose was verified when a few days later Charlotte prevailed on me to leave my apartment where I had voluntarily confined myself to faithfully await your return, and to spend the morning at the police station viewing a lineup of Samir Khans rounded up from all over the city. Finally, Charlotte was getting up off her toned little overaged bum and swinging into action. She was panicking; her benefactions and patronage on which she so prided herself, and with which she manipulated and controlled so many of her vassals, had backfired. It was now an established fact—you were missing, gone. This was not some delusion on my part. At last she was convinced, and on some level I believe it also penetrated her thick wall of defenses that she was to blame. At first, though, I refused to leave the apartment to go to police headquarters, despite Charlotte's litany of persuasions, agreeing only after Manika was flown up by Krishnapuri in Amma's private jet from the ashram to Mumbai to take over watch duty from me in case you returned during my brief absence checking out the Samir Khans of Mumbai.

It was surely through Amma's interventions, too, with Charlotte oiling her strings, that I received such exemplary VIP treatment. An unmarked black Ambassador drew up at the door of my building, the driver darting out flapping two rubber mats, which he set down before me one in front of the other, bending over again and again after I stepped upon the first mat to reposition it ahead of the second, unrolling a dry pathway for me in this way to the car door so that for the first time in days I was spared wading through puddles of fetid water. Policemen unfolded from their slouches as I was escorted into the station, rising to greet me with a cordial dip of the head and a respectful, Namaste, madam. I was ushered to a plush seat as if in a theater in front of a one-way viewing window screen as the Samir Khans of Mumbai with numbers on their chests were rolled out one by one for my inspection, smacked under the chin to provide a full-face view, slapped hard into right profile, another hard slap to spin the head into left profile, all of these visuals to the background static of, Stand up straight, *maderchod*, open your *bhenchod* eyes, *gaandu*, or I'll cut off your *golis*—then dragged offscreen as if with a cane by the shirt collar like a bad act in a burlesque that the audience hisses and boos out of its sight as I shook my head, no, no. It felt as if hundreds of Samir Khans were passed in front of me, from slum urchins, to enraged teenagers, to the newly radicalized with full black pubic beards, to skullcapped merchants, to imams in white-robed splendor, to the aged with wiry beards hennaed bright orange. My eyes blurred over, all pity was leached out of me for these mothers' sons, each of whom surely had sinned in some fashion to deserve such treatment, I reasoned, but the sinner I was seeking was not among them—the Samir Khan who had stolen you from me.

Most apologetically for the failure of this exercise, with an exaggerated show of solicitousness, a senior official approached to suggest that under the circumstances, since I was already out of the house, I allow myself to be conveyed to the city morgue to view the remains of unidentified female missing persons—a painful experience, yes, but necessary, and one that he and his staff would do their very best to facilitate with utmost sensitivity. I allowed myself to be taken into the stone edifice of the morgue, through the autopsy chamber where naked bodies were laid out on the tables constructed of stone like altars, torsos split open into two flaps folded back as in an anatomy textbook, scalps lifted off like the stem of an aubergine, then onward to the cold room to view the corpses already processed but unclaimed. At the entrance I was offered a mask against the stench, which I rejected with a proud dismissive brush of my hand, exactly as I would refuse a blindfold on the road to my own execution.

Inside, we pushed against the density of the stink even in that purportedly subzero environment. The floor tiles were slick with body fluids and fat leaking out and liquefied chemicals. Racks of naked men were stacked against the wall. Across the room, as if on the other side of the partition in my father's synagogue, the naked bodies of the women were piled in a haphazard mound, a mass grave, reeking of atrocity, evoking the death camp imagery we would pore over when we were children, so horrifying and yet so pornographically gripping. Workers with long poles were already stationed there, untangling rigid limbs and flipping corpses to expose drained waxen faces for my inspection and deflated bodies stitched closed down the middle with coarse black thread. Thank God, thank God, I kept muttering to myself, you were not there, no child of mine would ever be found in such a place, in this obscene heap of the disposable and discarded.

After that I remained at home waiting for you, except for the occasional summons back to the morgue when a potential candidate was delivered, generally either an unidentified female accident victim or a foiled terrorist or suicide bomber loosely fitting your specs, and once even a sex-trafficked juvenile mutilated to the point that it was no longer possible to suppress my nausea, my gut heaved and I vomited on the floor, contributing to the laminate of bodily fluids. Manika stayed at the apartment the entire time, sacrificing her berth at Amma's ashram, giving up her grand call-center ambitions, just to be available for those periods when I might be whisked away for one of these grim viewings; otherwise there is no way I would have agreed to go and leave the house empty, I had no idea if you had the key. All day Manika squatted on her haunches in the corner, she could have been mistaken for a footstool, head lowered, the *pallu* of her sari drawn up across the lower portion of her face. Now and then she would get up to bring me a glass of chai, or a bowl of rice and lentils and some naan, or to urge me to lie down and get some sleep. Why do you do it? I once asked her. For Mama, she responded. Was she referring to Amma, or to my own late mama whom she had tended in her last days, or could she possibly have meant me? I too was a mama, wasn't I? Your mama. But I didn't have the energy to pursue it. What difference did it make? She stayed, that was all that mattered, she didn't budge from her mission, condemned in this life to be forever invisible and forever on call.

I sat at the kitchen table, my laptop open in front of me, my cell phone juiced within easy reach awaiting the call. Even now I cannot say how long I sat; I never inquired, and no one has come forward. The shades were drawn, there was no day, no night, no passage of the season. My tour business no longer interested me; I left it to die of mismanagement in the hands of my associates. I was entirely consumed with searching the internet for even the slightest reference to girls who had vanished into the black hole of the Muslim universe never to be heard from again except for the occasional rare smudge of their existence preserved in the ether like a bloodstain on a sheet, or who emerged for one final spectacular big bang of martyrdom, taking along with them the children of other mothers. Whether they were swallowed up out of love or conviction, or dragged away by the hair flailing and screaming, whether they went actively or were taken passively, whether they set forth as jihadi brides to anoint the fighters with the lubricant of their bodies, or as mujahid mothers or black widows bent on revenge, whether they drew their kitchen knives out from under their burqas to plunge into the flesh of strangers or implanted explosives in their breasts or bellies feigning pregnancy to expiate the violation of their honor perpetrated deliberately to turn them into living bombs, whether they detonated themselves by their own agency or were triggered by remote control in the hands of a man standing watch in the distance—all of this that had happened and was still happening, and so much more, I followed obsessively online, hoarding every possible detail about how a girl could throw herself away in that world until I felt that I had covered every inch of the territory.

I had exhausted all the possibilities and could not find you. Among such girls who had thrown themselves away there was no sign of you. Wherever you were, you were not there.

My cell phone connecting me to the world within easy reach faceup on the table had an app to alert me with bulletins of terrorist acts worldwide, zeroing in on those featuring Muslims in India and Pakistan either as perpetrators or victims. The alert sound was customized from a siren to something less heart-stopping since it went off so frequently as if malfunctioning, seeming to shudder in place like a spoiled child on the verge of a tantrum, demanding immediate attention. Most of the alerts were not relevant to your case, but now and then the deadly silence in the room where Manika and I sat waiting for you was broken by an alarm that conceivably could apply. Then, my heart pounding, I would call my friends at the police station to check out the situation if they had not already contacted me first, and more than once, with Manika on duty on the home front, the black Ambassador was dispatched to collect me for yet another gruesome viewing on the stone altars of the morgue—but the good angel always appeared right on cue, crying, Stop, let another living creature be sacrificed instead, this time it will not be you.

Except for contacting the cops on those occasions, I almost never used my mobile to call out. I did receive some calls, though, quite regularly from Charlotte, to assure me that she was here for me—I'm here for you, Meena darling, she said—stressing that she was speaking also on behalf of Ammachi, who had made special offerings to mother Kali to find you among her lost children. The rebbetzin Mindy also got in touch, expressing regret that she was unable to carry out the mitzvah of coming by in person to sit with me, taking for granted that I was already in mourning because you had run off with a goy, may the merciful one spare us. She was calling me from Antwerp, she said, where she had gone to help out with her two new grandchildren, born to Shmuly and to Malkie in the same week, they looked like twins, two boys no less, so handsome, the greatest blessing, grandchildren, she had gotten in touch with the *Ayin haRah* Lady to make sure that any evil eye cast upon these precious babies by the envious and the bitter whose children did not turn out so well and did not produce grandchildren in the normal course of events be rendered null and void at once. The Ayin haRah Lady cost an arm and a leg, by the way, but never mind, she delivered her money's worth. She poured the molten lead into a pot of cold water and chanted the powerful holy words as the bubbles swelled and burst, and now the babies are safe, 100 percent safe, thank God. Maybe someone had given you the evil eye, the rebbetzin speculated, maybe that was the explanation for your disappearance, and I had never bothered to spend some money on the Ayin haRah Lady to neutralize it. You were such an intelligent girl, with such a pretty face, the rebbetzin reminisced, if only you had kept to the path. You were making such good progress for a while under Malkie's influence, you were Malkie's personal special pet project. She recalled how Malkie had instructed and guided you with the visual aids of the paper dolls. But you were always falling, that was your problem, falling, falling, such a pity, and now you have truly fallen into the lowest depths, into the abyss, it shouldn't happen to us. What can you do? Blessed is the True Judge, the rebbetzin pronounced, May you be comforted among all the mourners of Zion and Jerusalem.

From Jerusalem your father Shmiel the Holy Beggar called— the last thing I needed at that moment. I hadn't heard from him in over five years, when I had bought off all his rights to you with an all-expenses-paid, five-star deluxe spiritual tour. I had assumed the cannibals of the Andean Islands had taken care of him for me, but apparently he was unpalatable even to them. Now he was calling to inform me that business was very bad at the gravesite of the Singing Rabbi, nobody came anymore—and why was that? Because word had spread that his daughter—his own daughter, the daughter of Shmiel the Holy Beggar no less—had run off with an Arab. According to the intelligence reports, there was a danger the couple might figure out a way to sneak into the country on her Israeli passport even though there was an all-points bulletin out blocking them, and make their way to the cemetery to blow themselves up at the grave of the Singing Rabbi while everyone was sitting around having such a nice kumsitz, and feeling *mamesh* so high, so openhearted, turning their pockets inside out and emptying every last *grush* into his guitar case. The whole cemetery was crawling now with military types with shaved heads and walkie-talkies, Mossad, Shabak, guys in suits and sunglasses and hearing aids, the security was so tight with X-rays and shmex-rays and body searches and pat downs and friskings and the whole shmear, nobody wanted to put themselves through all that garbage even for the Singing Rabbi, nobody was coming to the gravesite anymore, it was just too much of a pain in the you-know-what. His whole personal income, his livelihood, his bread and butter, his pita and hummus, all of his revenue was flushed down the toilet, down to minus zero—and why was that? Because bottom line, he claimed, I was too busy to do my job as a mother and watch over my own daughter in the proper way, I was too busy bowing down to elephants and monkeys, sinning and causing others to sin like Yerovam ben Nevat, with my idol-worshipping tour business, I was too busy chasing after other women like a "prevert," and so on and so forth.

I cut him off; I could not bear it any more. I did not deserve this, I was in pain. I was quite possibly a candidate for the title of *em shakulah*, for which there is no equivalent word in the English language, as if only a Jewish mother can be a mother who has lost a child in the tradition of our Mother Rachel weeping over her children, unreceptive to comfort of any sort, and here he was your own father thinking as per usual only about himself and where his next falafel would be coming from, it was inhuman.

Since he had the audacity to refer to Geeta, however, albeit indirectly of course, without of course uttering out loud the anathema of her unmentionable name, I should tell you in case you were wondering, that, yes, she did get in touch during this period—exactly once. I don't know who told her what was going on, maybe it was Manika who had a smartphone of her own, one of Amma's old models; Amma was always upgrading, the castoffs were encrypted and wiped clean of all data by the techie devotee and presented as a much prized trophy to a chosen follower. The entire communication from Geeta amounted to a tweet with the hashtag, #ItsNotMyFault: "She's not here, if that's what you're thinking. No clue where she is. Ready to offer help. Just ask nicely."

Not her fault? My head spun, I was barely holding myself together, and now it felt as if I might not be able to go on after all, I would just fall apart, collapse. Whose fault did she think it was if not hers? Did she imagine for one minute that it's a small thing to be abandoned by your mother? She was your mother exactly as I was, we had always regarded it that way, we had never discriminated between biological and adoptive or whatever, that was how we conducted our life together, yet she just picked herself up one day and walked off without looking back. You were traumatized, your self-esteem plummeted to ground zero, everything that happened to you happened after she walked out on us—your two sad little crushes, first on Shmuly, then on Samir, one and the same—hopeless, doomed monsoon crushes, which you fixated on subconsciously to court rejection, to confirm that you were essentially unlovable. After all, how could anyone ever love a girl whose own mother had abandoned her? The most basic human right, a mother's love, and even that you couldn't count on, even that had been withdrawn from you. How dare she claim it was not her fault? Of course it was her fault, she was entirely to blame for everything that had transpired after she walked out, including the smashed hopes and endless depression of the monsoons, and now your disappearance. There was no way I was going to stoop to ask for her help—nicely or otherwise, thank you very much. Fortunately, I did not need it. For cash and connections I had Charlotte and Amma, with resources in and out of India that sufficiently matched Geeta's to get the job done. And for the human touch, for tenderness and sympathy, I had my twin brother the guru, Shmelke, known worldwide as Reb Breslov Tabor, safe at last in the asylum of India, venerated now as Rebbie-ji, who somehow, I believe through his own rare mystical powers and the unbreakable connection formed between us in the pools of amniotic fluid in which we had floated side by side during our gestation, discovered what was going on and reached out to me.

Every day throughout my ordeal, Rebbie-ji found a few minutes in his busy schedule to call and check on me. How ya doin', Meena'le?

His intimately familiar voice wrapped me in the warmth of the Brooklyn of our innocence, it took everything in my power to keep myself from opening my mouth and howling. Not a single call passed without him urging me to come to his ashram in Mother Teresa's old hospice in Calcutta, near the big Kali temple, his House of Holy Healing, HHH, like Ha Ha Ha. He erupted in laughter. It would do you so much good, he declared. Come and stay for as long as you like, Meena'le. You are so, so welcome, not only are my doors open to you, but also my heart. I know you will come soon. Maybe next week you will come, maybe tomorrow you will come, any minute now I will see you, you are on your way, I feel you are near, ah, here you are.

The alert went off. A developing story was unfolding very close by in the packed women's compartment of a commuter train as it was coming into the Churchgate station during the evening rush hour. Details were still sketchy, but so far what was known was that two burqa-clad passengers had suddenly shouted, Allahu Akbar in the mosh pit of the ladies' car and thrust out their hands from under their black robes waving butcher knives. They proceeded to slash indiscriminately in every direction, according to eyewitness accounts, inflicting numerous injuries and drawing streams of blood until the heroic ladies in that car banded together and took matters into their own hands. With the full united force of their bodies, the ladies pushed the alleged perpetrators off the train through the open door of the compartment down onto the tracks. According to early unconfirmed reports, the two suspects were neutralized either from the fall itself, or crushed under the wheels of the train, which was still moving, or beaten to death by enraged citizens who happened to be in the vicinity.

I have no memory of summoning the black Ambassador, or of my ride through the choked traffic to the morgue. My first vivid memory was of incredible relief as I paused to gather strength at the now-familiar entrance to the autopsy room where the two bodies were laid out on top of the stone altars, side by side, naked, still awaiting the knife of the medical examiner, and I was struck by the unmistakable sign of maleness. It was a common tactic for men to disguise themselves in burqas and chadors, I reminded myself, assuming the roles of women, the perfect cover-up for all kinds of male mischief. As I drew nearer I could see that the bodies were severely battered and discolored and swollen, the noses smashed in, the limbs broken, they had been dumped from the train like trash. The maleness of the one nearest to me was confirmed as I stood beside him—Samir Khan, the one we had been seeking, surfaced at last. On the altar beside him was the girl, so young, so slight, so beaten, so abused, no one on the face of the earth would have recognized her except her mother.

Save your poor daughter, mother. See how they have tormented her.

O my daughter, Maya, would that it had been me in your place, my daughter, my daughter, Maya.

Her name is no longer Maya, mother says. It is Malala. Look, she lives. They tried to kill her in the Swat Valley but kind-hearted souls saved her and brought her back to life for the good work she was destined to do for the sake of the feminine gender. The perfect daughter, a mother's heart bursts with pride. Did you know that she has just won the Nobel Peace Prize, the youngest laureate ever? Rejoice. It will look awesome on her college application.

Meena

· I ·

IN THE MIDDLE of the journey of our life, having passed through the phases of studentship and householder, the first two of the four stages allotted to mortals on this earth according to the wisdom of the holy men of the East, I found myself in a black hole. Two more stages stretched ahead of me—renunciation and withdrawal—on the long road to liberation, but I felt myself unable to go on, craving death.

How I had arrived to this dark place I could barely say aloud, the memory was too bitter to form into words. But as I was falling into the abyss and succumbing at this halfway point, weary and lost, there appeared before me a holy man from my deepest beginnings, like an angel with white hair flowing down his back parted in the center into two flanks like sidelocks, long white beard, robed entirely in white linen, starched and flowing. He clutched me by the waist, reaching up with two mighty arms strengthened by years spinning the wheels of his throne taking him along his destined path, and he halted my descent. "Let me go, Rebbie-ji, have mercy," I cried. "Stay," he said. "Even in this place of death, my message to you is, choose life." His voice was my blood voice, my brother's voice calling to me as if from the ground. There was no place to hide.

For his sake, conditionally, I continued in life, but not by choice. Choice was his domain. He had chosen for his sins to be a fugitive and wanderer on the face of the earth, marked and set apart. I had rejected all that when I had chosen to no longer count myself among the chosen. But he needed me now, he had asked me to stay, he had asked me to do him a kindness, to say I am his sister, in this strange and dangerous place he had asked for my help, never an easy thing for him to do. I remembered his youthful sweetness. He had been such a dear boy, my soulmate. My innards ached for him. I pitied him and could not refuse.

In special circumstances it is permissible to skip over one or two of the four stages in life and head straight to renunciation well before the designated age of seventy-two, or to personalize and tweak the stages in some way, or even to invent a fusion of sorts. This was the option I was forced to accept for the interim, under pressure from my twin brother, Shmelke, revered and reviled worldwide as Reb Breslov Tabor, Rebbie-ji, who had beseeched me to stay. The time had not yet come when I could indulge the luxury of dying, or even of withdrawing to a hermitage in the forest for the third stage of retirement and meditation to prepare myself for the fourth and final act, sannyasa. I was obliged to remain at Rebbie-ji's ashram in the throbbing heart of Kolkata. My involvement was still mandated, I was still needed it seemed. I had not yet won liberation, a reprieve from my life sentence. I had not yet earned the privilege of setting out in search of moksha as a *sannyasini*, my face smeared with ash, my hair matted, nothing on my back but a garment made of grass chewed and regurgitated by a cow, nothing in my hands but a stick and a beggar's bowl, but with full conviction of my sanity, oblivious to the world that might think me out of my mind.

Still, until the blessed moment arrived of complete renunciation, I could improvise. I could practice austerities and carry out various forms of asceticism. The ultimate goal was to achieve a state of detachment as if I were already dead. I regarded myself as my own widow. My husband who had died was myself. Instead of throwing myself on my pyre as a sati, I gave up all of life's pleasures like a pious Hindu widow. I shaved my head, cast off all ornamentation, shrouded myself in a borderless white sari, fasted three days a week, and withdrew. I was dead in this world as if I had been reduced to ash.

I was doubly dead, since a sannyasi is considered to be dead too. Like a sadhu, I renounced all ambition, all striving and desire, except for the desire to be dead. During the day I collaborated at my brother's side, counseling and strategizing, but it was as if I were doing nothing at all. At night I slept in a primitive coffin, a stretcher bier, on the floor of the cell I shared with the cast-off girls whose care Rebbie-ji had entrusted to me in his House of Holy Healing, formerly Mother Teresa's Kalighat Home for the Dying Destitutes.

It was also during my time in Rebbie-ji's ashram that I took upon myself the task of setting down this memoir in the first person, though the first person no longer mattered or even existed. I was completely detached, indifferent, merely an observer—the omniscient third person observing myself, the nonexistent first person, a work of fiction. It was simply an exercise in overcoming the limitations of the first person in the narrative of remembrance—a way of carrying forth with the me-me-meena story even when she no longer is present, a way of negating the first person by validating my witness even though I was already dead. It was a laboratory experiment, and I was the rat.

Unconsoled and inconsolable, I nevertheless sat down with my twin brother, Shmelke, at a table in one of the two great halls of his ashram that once had been packed with rows and rows of narrow cots upon which Mother Teresa's lepers, tuberculars, malnourished, and other assorted terminally diseased had lain. This ward, which had housed the women in the days of the hard-hearted saint, now served as the common room of the House of Holy Healing—dining hall, synagogue, meeting place, the space in which my brother held audience when seized by the spirit. From hospice to hope, as Rebbie-ji liked to say—anguish to joy, mourning to holiday, like Purim, when all are obliged to turn themselves into clowns with Rebbie-ji banging his drum and gyrating in his wheelchair leading the way, like King David leaping and dancing half-naked, making a spectacle of himself as he brought home the ark of the Lord through the streets of Jerusalem.

In the second ward the men had undergone their death agonies, shards of their horned toenails hacked off by volunteer missionaries of charity still occasionally suctioned up by our bare feet as we moved about. Still visible on the walls all around us were the white numbers that had been painted over each cot once positioned there with a nameless dying body coiled up on it, sixty and more in each ward. Now the space had been converted into the ashram's dormitory, with ropes strung across the length and width like a chessboard over which madras cloths and worn saris and old sheets and other assorted rags and even drying laundry were hung to form tiny cubicles accommodating at least four seekers stretched out in sleeping bags and on straw mats or directly on the floor in each pod, the sexes rigidly separated by a thick clothesline draped with woolen prayer shawls only slightly moth eaten to form a *mekhitza* bisecting the room. This is where I slept too, alongside my damaged girls, in a pod of cubicles set aside for us.

Across from where Shmelke and I we were sitting in the great public room, high on the opposite wall, Ma's extra-large stained damask Sabbath tablecloth given to my brother upon his marriage in the expectation that he was destined to become a rabbinical eminence presiding at the head of a great *tisch* was draped over a wooden cross; we could make out its menacing cruciform skeleton underneath. In the dormitory ward, the cross was concealed by a soiled moth-eaten woolen prayer shawl, our father's wedding gift to his gifted son. Somehow, by a miracle, Shmelke had held on to these gifts throughout all his wanderings. Through the high windows pouring down beams of dust motes and malarial flies, the smell of burning flesh drifted in accompanied by the tortured screams of the goats sacrificed daily just up the road in the temple of Kali, most fabulous and savage of mothers.

Manika padded in silently and set down before us on the table two steaming glasses of tea in monkey-dish saucers, and a bowl of brown sugar cubes irregular like chunks of granite. Tea was always served in glasses at the ashram, the very same type of glasses that had been used in the home of our Brooklyn childhood—yahrzeit memorial glasses, imported from Israel and stocked at the ashram by the caseload, recycled for drinking purposes after the candle inside was consumed during the chronic power blackouts of Kali's cruel city. Without even thinking, operating on automatic as if in the private wombspace of our twindom, Shmelke and I each positioned a sugar cube between our upper and lower teeth, poured some of the hot tea from the glass into the monkey dish, lifted the dish in both hands with pincered thumb and forefinger and winged elbows to blow on the amber pool and cool it, then tipped it with a precise motion to send the tea streaming on its passage through the sugar cube, sweetening it thoroughly as it came into our mouths and glided along our taste buds. Nice tea, bliss, so good—and exactly as we used to do it at home in Brooklyn on a late Sabbath afternoon as the sun was setting and darkness descended. The comical synchronicity of our movements and the convergence of deep memory assaulted both of us at the same moment, and we burst out in wild and tragic laughter, sending our moist sugar cubes flying like a stone from a slingshot across the room in the direction of Ma's tablecloth to pierce it through the heart.

How did this happen? If such a story were told, it would not have been believed. How had this brother and sister, separately and apart, made this terrible journey from there to here, from *Bava Kama* to *Kama Sutra*, as if blindly burrowing like worms through the bowels of the globe, and come out blinking together now at this end, in this most alien of places?

Simultaneously and wordlessly we had asked this question of ourselves and each other over the tea and sugar, my brother and I. It had appeared like a cartoon bubble over each of our heads for the other to read, discernible only to our eyes. It was in essence the question I was already embarked upon answering in my first-person experiment at night in the cell I shared with my ruined girls, by the light of a yahrzeit candle, working on my laptop even during blackouts, tethered at those times to the cell phone system at megawatt cost, thanks to Charlotte's beneficence.

There was internet at the ashram; this was something Rebbie-ji insisted upon and would never tolerate foregoing. But in every other respect, he was rigorous about maintaining the monastic austerities as practiced in the days when Mother Teresa had ruled this space with such righteous severity. There was still no private electrical generator to kick in during the perpetual outages. There were no large institutional appliances, such as washing machines, dishwashers, and so on. We laundered our clothing by hand in tubs, slapped them against the stone walls, and hung them to dry on lines, just as the nuns in their white habits with the blue stripe (like the flag of the State of Israel, it had always struck me) had done in the days of the hospice. There was not even an elevator, though there was a shaft in which one could have been installed, and donors who had clamored to finance it. The saint had refused. Two slight nuns could carry an emaciated body up and down the steps, she had decreed, it was good for their spiritual development. But when Rebbie-ji needed to be moved from floor to floor, five muscled men known as the *Bulvans* were summoned, four to haul his person, since even on a vegan diet of beans and nuts and dates and tofu (which Rebbie-ji pronounced the original manna—white in color, and taking on all flavors and tastes) a human being can acquire superfluous padding amounting to many kilos, and the fifth ox to follow behind carrying the wheelchair in one hand. As a matter of principle Rebbie-ji had always refused a wheelchair upgrade to a top-of-the-line electric model, a wonder that could even bounce up and down the stairs. This self-denial was a personal form of austerity and soul affliction that he had taken upon himself, with a strictness akin to Mother Teresa's who forbade painkillers for her sufferers before baptizing them and dispatching them to their reward. My brother's lower body as a result continued to shrivel and waste away, its gross-ness appropriately nullified, while his upper body, arms and shoulders spinning the wheels that took him along his chosen path, grew more and more powerful like a god's. His head remained untouched, its celestial brilliance shining through, illuminated even more blindingly now by the glowing whiteness of hair, beard, sidelocks that framed his face so that many of his followers dared not lift their eyes to gaze upon him if they wanted to live.

But as for the internet, Rebbie-ji regarded it as indispensable to his mission of spiritual outreach. Like Ammachi, he was never without his smartphone, except of course on the Sabbath and holidays when it is not permitted. The smartphone had evolved into essential guru gear it seemed. In his notoriety, my twin brother often was lumped in the mind of the public with the whole gang of indistinguishable ultra-Orthodox fanatics, including those who railed against the internet on posters and fliers, their polemical texts delivered to the printers as attachments to emails, declaiming that the internet is the cause of drought, cancer, diseases of the base organs, and the next Holocaust—Shoah: The Sequel—and so on and so forth. But Rebbie-ji declared the internet to be a mighty-blessed force of creation, like the spirit of God hovering over the face of the waters, omnipresent, omniscient, a glimpse of the divine consciousness, containing within it for those who truly knew how to seek for it, the answer to every question.

Yet though I was toiling by night in the first person to extract the larger picture of the trajectory of the first two stages of my life's strange journey, with regard to the immediate question—how I got from that morgue in Mumbai to this hospice in Kolkata, as if risen from the dead—I simply had no recollection. It was a blank. I had blocked it out in classic trauma mode. Nor did I choose to inquire—a personal preference that those who surrounded me were considerate enough to respect. Manika was the first person I saw when I emerged from the blackest of pits to this false earthly reality. She was crouching like a tumor attached to the wall in a corner of a cell I was sharing at that initial phase in my brother's private suite. My roommate laid out on the other bed, I eventually learned, was an exceptionally venerated woman whose worshippers could not agree whether she was alive or dead, she seemed still to be mutating through the stages of life; her fate was to lie there unburied, skin flaking down to the bone. Where was I? In Kolkata, Manika told me, in the Christian Kali's hospice. Good, I thought, hospice means I'm certified dying. But then my brother rolled in and reminded me that he had taken over the site from that severe little Christian saint, asserting his squatter rights, as it was abandoned and vacant except for my roommate, who had been delivered just before his anticipated arrival and whom he allowed to remain because she reminded him of where he had come from and where he was going, and he had transformed it from a place of certain imminent death to a house of holy healing.

This was extremely disappointing news. I could only hope Shmelke would be kicked out of this squat as he had been from all of the others, and it would revert to a hospice so that I could continue with the dying process undisturbed. Charlotte arrived next with her entire girls band, Lakshmi and the Survivors, including her great reed player, Monica Lewinsky, blowing away. She was bursting with the fantastic news that her legal team was now closing a deal with the city thugs in Dalhousie Square and the Kali temple goondas up the road to buy this abandoned shelter for Rebbie-ji. It was looking very good, knock on wood, Charlotte said, tapping the air in the direction of the head of my narrow bed, over which a wooden cross was hanging covered by a bath-sized towel. We're almost home free, keep your fingers crossed, she declared. After scuttling like a bug from one miserable country to another without rest to escape extradition back to Israel on such false and absurd charges that would be beneath us to even enumerate, Rebbie-ji will soon have permanent headquarters right here in toler- ant live-and-let-live India, a nation that instinctively comprehends the duality of the spirit, the holy and the profane, the dark and the light. In this place he would at last have full protection and sanctuary from primitive Abrahamic vengeance and punishment.

From all of this I concluded that how I had gotten from Bombay to Calcutta had something to do with the interventions of Manika, Shmelke, and above all Charlotte, who now, having successfully redi- rected my past, was charging straight ahead to arrange my future. She invited me to join her in her private kabbalah tutorial with Rebbie-ji. They were working with clay to fashion a golem to defend all the per- secuted and pursued of the world. "Do you know how therapeutic it is to stick your hands into clay and just squeeze?" she asked. "Excuse my French, Rebbie-ji, but it's a privilege, like playing with your per- sonal caca—pure regressive pleasure." Such talk is permissible if you're paying, I reflected, even to such a holy figure as my brother. She also insisted that I attend a performance of her band that night in the great room—for women only, she added, since Rebbie-ji has taught that the voice of a woman is nakedness and therefore cannot be listened to by men who are always so prone to sexual arousal. Rebbie-ji of course will be there, however, Charlotte assured me, the only man allowed to watch the show since he is completely hopeless below the waist, totally harmless and nonthreatening no matter what his enemies say, all you need to do is take one look at him in his wheelchair for God's sake.

I am in mourning, I responded. For me, music is forbidden.

The wheelchair became Shmelke's defining accessory early in his career, by our late twenties. By that time he was also already recognized as a scholar and mystic of extraordinary charismatic gifts, appearing only once in a generation to recapture the lost light of creation and usher in the golden age. The event that put him in the chair took place in Israel, where he had gone for higher studies at the age of eighteen, immediately after his marriage to the daughter of rabbinical aristocracy. The wedding was attended by more than ten thousand invited guests, the ceremony held under the stars in the streets of Williamsburg, Brooklyn, closed off to traffic and encircled by ranks of New York's finest in their blue police uniforms stretched across formidable guts. It was rumored of my brother, and also confirmed by him in a lecture of tremendous esoteric profundity that could be interpreted only by those with exceptional powers of penetration, that he was the reincarnation of the great Hasidic master, Rabbi Nahman of Bratslav, who died in the year 1810 in the city of Uman in Ukraine with no male descendant to carry on the dynasty, leaving his disciples, thereafter known as the Dead Hasidim, leaderless, adrift, in perpetual mourning until his promised return. So great was the joy of my brother's followers when the good news was privately circulated that the master had come back at last after nearly two centuries of concealment that they renamed by brother Breslov, and he became known worldwide as Reb Breslov Tabor. Only Ma and I, and also his wife, Zlatte, who by the time of his confinement in the chair had already given birth to all nine of their children, all girls (almost a statistical impossibility, but nevertheless my brother's burden, like Rabbi Nahman's, to be left without an heir) continued to call him Shmelke.

Central to my brother's teaching was a mystical reinterpretation of the concept of tikkun, focusing on the personal obligation of each individual to repair the world, hugely corrupted and damaged when Adam ate of the fruit of the tree of knowledge. But as Shmelke conceived of it in esoteric kabbalistic terms, such tikkun often entailed sin and transgression at the behest of a holy man such as himself, a mandatory plunge into seemingly immoral behavior for the purpose of rescuing the divine light lost in the lowest depths during the fall of Adam from paradise, thereby restoring the world to its original state of illumination and bringing on the messianic age. This teaching, along with the ways in which so radical a form of tikkun was implemented, inspired intense controversy and also severe condemnation, including from the more mainstream Breslover Hasidim, who ultimately disavowed and excommunicated him. At the same time it also attracted a multitude of supporters, among them vastly wealthy donors, primarily American fundamentalist and evangelical Christians bent on hastening the rapture and the end of time, which pivoted on the ingathering of the Jews in the Holy Land; it was they who endowed his activities and financed his compound in the Muslim Quarter of the old city of Jerusalem. By his late twenties, my brother had also amassed thousands of followers and devotees, many of them ex-hippie returnees to the faith, but also countless souls discarded by society whom he had rescued, literally pulled them up from the depths, from the streets, the slums, the drug scene and the underworld, from prisons and lunatic asylums, exactly as he would descend to the lowest realms to pull up through acts of radical tikkun the hidden divine sparks trapped during the fall in the filth below, and restore the world to the purity of its original light as at the time of creation.

After the Yom Kippur War of 1973, which he prophesied was a herald of far worse future shock and disaster, a *forshpeis* of *hurban*, as he put it, his tikkun activities intensified, spilling out into the streets. It was imperative to descend to the depths to dredge up the divine sparks in order to forestall the coming annihilation, he believed, and to do so at once, without delay, with the greatest possible alacrity. Toward that end he instituted the tikkun of pursuit of the holy man, calling upon his followers to pursue him every night after midnight as he set out at top speed on his motorcycle from Jerusalem to the Galilee to pray and beseech for mercy at the graves of the righteous. Behind him rode his inner circle, heaven's angels, and in their train, scores of followers in all kinds of vehicles in a wild and raging caravan, including taxis and buses, and also some on horseback, donkeys and camels. They rode without helmets or seat belts or saddles, heedless of danger, which was beneath them spiritually to contemplate. They rode at top speed, two hundred kilometers an hour and more, defying all civic laws and regulations, never stopping for lights, flouting all road signs, cutting through traffic, jumping onto sidewalks and highway shoulders, leaping over dividers, zigzagging lanes, plowing through to the opposite side of the road wherever they spotted an opening, leaving the laggards far in the rear, leaving behind the fallen and casualties and smashed up as necessary sacrifices in pursuit of their rabbi as he headed at breakneck speed to the graves in the North, in Tiberias, Safed, Meron, of such luminaries as Rabbi Simeon son of Yohai, Rabbi Moses son of Maimon, Rabbi Meir Master of the Miracle, Honi the Circle Maker, Rabbi Hutzpit the Interpreter, and all the other lofty souls with power to intervene and prevent the looming catastrophe.

Every night on their wild ride in pursuit of my brother, the pursuers would be pursued in turn by the police with shrieking sirens and flashing lights, and even occasionally by the military, a veritable chase scene as if from the movies to electrify the heart and leave the viewer breathless, but at some point the authorities would inevitably fall away, their wallets fattened, or simply wander off on the strength of the conviction that the world will be a better place if all of these nutcases simply self-destruct of their own accord without official interference. On the occasions when the speeders were forced to halt by an uptight rules-and-regulations type, it would be patiently explained to this obsessive-compulsive that religious law required obedience to the rabbi, and the rabbi required pursuit. There was no higher mitzvah than chasing the rebbe; the officer was welcome to join in the pursuit if he liked. Nothing could be done to stop it; it was a decree from heaven. If the earthly powers had a problem with the free and unimpeded exercise of these religious rights, they were welcome to go take up the matter with the holy rabbi himself. There he is, up front—see him? And they pointed to the posse riding furiously ahead astride their motorcycles, every one of its members with exceptionally long black sidelocks and long black beards whipping in the wind, large white crocheted yarmulkes pulled low over their heads, long black kaftans draped over the seats of their motorbikes, and fluorescent crash goggles. Which one of these bikers was the holy rabbi? They all looked exactly alike, like creatures of another species from outer space, you couldn't tell them apart.

Yet despite this massive effort of pursuit and prayer, the cosmic forces remained in a state of agitation, the celestial sparks still lost in the putrid depths. In time, my brother, Reb Breslov, declared to his followers that the midnight rides as enacted were not sufficiently strong to avert the imminent disaster, much less restore the nobility of divine light. Greater risks and sacrifices were called for. Now under cover of darkness he raced into hostile territory—to the tomb of Mother Rachel in Bethlehem, the tomb of the patriarchs and matriarchs in Hebron, and potentially most powerful of all, Joseph's tomb in Nablus, also known as Shehem, in the shadow of the mountains of the blessing and the curse. His followers pursued him in long speeding convoys over the hills of Samaria, through Ishmaelite territory, ignoring military and police checkpoints, heedless of warning shots, crashing through barriers, until they arrived at Joseph's holy gravesite, desecrated and ransacked, where they fell to the ground kissing it passionately, and hugged the stone walls, praying and weeping.

Joseph's tomb became the destination to which my brother now led his flock in pursuit of him night after night. Who but Joseph—favored son in the light-suffused household of his father the patriarch Jacob, twice cast into the darkest depths, the pit and the dungeon, then rising again like a brilliant star to the heights as ruler of Egypt—who but this first court Jew, this first paradigm of spectacular Jewish success in the diaspora could be a more perfect embodiment of the fall from paradise and ultimate elevation? Every night they arrived in pursuit of their rebbe, my brother, under a hailstorm of rocks and rotten vegetables and old shoes hurled by the enemy. "Not even old shoes will we throw at you," one of the hooligans was quoted in the press. "Flip-flops we will throw at you—old stinking rubber flip-flops. You don't even deserve to be hit in the head by a shoe."

They worshipped and studied at the tomb and left before dawn, carrying away their casualties, but there were no fatalities. They were under the protection of the Israel Defense Forces in occupied territory, though they never gave the military advance notice when they would appear, as required. The site was their rightful heritage, it was their property as far as they were concerned. "You don't have to make an appointment to enter your own house that belongs to you," Reb Breslov, my brother, said. The fatality occurred the night the tomb was handed over by the Israelites to enemy jurisdiction—Joseph once again sold by his brothers to the Ishmaelites, as so many had noted. One disciple dead, shot in the head by thugs masquerading as the official Muslim police force armed with AK-47s, a second grievously wounded, condemned to spend the rest of his days on earth as a cauliflower, as my brother so sadly observed—and the biggest prize of all, my brother, whose back was broken but not his spirit when he emerged half a year later jubilantly clapping his hands over his head and singing at the top of his voice in his speeding wheelchair to the ecstatic celebration of his followers dancing in the streets along the entire route from the private rehabilitation center where he had been put up by his benefactors, back to his headquarters in his compound in the Muslim section of Jerusalem.

It is the fate of the righteous man of the generation to absorb the suffering of the world in order to save mankind, Rav Nahman taught. My brother, Reb Breslov, as his gilgul, now felt the truth of this observation even more keenly, weighed down as he was by the confinement of his wheelchair and the increasingly painful urgency of his prophetic vision—the inexorable approach of the next and final holocaust. Averting this calamity was a priority. No personal suffering inflicted upon him would be too much in the fulfillment of this mandate, but given his revised circumstances, the performance of tikkun through pursuit no longer seemed the best option. Rather, it was necessary to repair the world by retrieving the divine light through an act of extreme degradation—by crawling again and again down to the lowest depths of sin and transgression where so many of the holy sparks had fallen and were lost, crawling on his belly and eating the dust of the earth, like a snake.

The gematria of the Hebrew letters adding up to *snake* (*nakhash*) is exactly the same as the numerical value for *messiah* (*mashiakh*)—358. Together, they equal 716, the numerical value of the Hebrew word found in the second book of Kings, *le'hitrapeh*, to heal—holy healing! It was impossible to overestimate the significance of these confluences both in terms of my brother's personal physical circumstances and his overarching obligation to enact tikkun, which bottom line amounted to nothing other than ultimate healing; only an idiot would regard this convergence as coincidence. Now that my brother no longer was able to stand up and move about on his feet, the only way to perform the necessary healing act of tikkun, retrieving the hidden light that would bring on the messianic age, was to crawl, to turn himself into a snake, the most vulgar and naked of seducers.

According to a secret scroll, it was mandatory for the purpose of carrying out this tikkun that eighteen women be attached at all times to different parts of his body like tumors, like an affliction of elephantiasis, causing him excruciating pain and rendering him grotesque in the eyes of the world. Each would submit to him, but afterward she would despise him and tread on his head. The suffering he would absorb would be endless, but the sins he would be obliged to commit with these women would be essential to bringing about the redemption. Instead of being pursued as a holy figure, he would be pursued like the most base and repulsive of criminals. Yet through this suffering that he took upon himself, the imminent catastrophe would be averted, and the hour of reunification of the lost sparks with the infinite source of the mystical light would draw closer and closer, the radiance beckoning just over the horizon.

When a young woman would come to his chambers for a blessing, my brother, Reb Breslov, was able to take one look at her and recognize at once if she was potential material for one of the eighteen boils destined to be attached to him for tikkun purposes. If she was married and arrived with a husband, he would inquire when she had last immersed herself in the ritual bath. Depending on the answer and other mystical factors known only to him, he would command the couple to abstain from intimate relations for a specified period of time based on his calculations, after which they would receive a visitation in the form of a child. He would then request that the husband leave the room and wait outside while he sanctified the wife. He would ask the woman to sit on his lap in his wheelchair, drawing the prayer shawl he always wore up over his head and down over hers, thereby creating a sacred space of seclusion as after the breaking of the glass at a wedding. Within this talit tent he would insert his hands under her clothing to check every part of her body for as long as necessary to certify if she was one of the eighteen buboes chosen to be attached to him, soothing her the entire time during this procedure with such words as, Take comfort, daughter, you have entered the world of nobility. If she passed this test, he would request that she take off her clothing and stand before him naked as he licked her entire body with his tongue; it was important for the sake of salvation not to miss a spot. If he found her worthy, he would then order her to undress him as well and help him from his chair so that he could lie down beside her on the daybed in his chamber, the two of them naked.

Nor was it necessary for the woman to be newly married; she could also be even younger, a virgin. For the purpose of carrying out his work of purification and deliverance and of averting another holocaust, as he informed the candidates, the essential point was that there always be eighteen females attached to him, married or virgins, since as might be expected, some fell away for one reason or another over the course of time, like scabs, there was always natural attrition, and replacements might be required. It was with one of these younger unmarried girls that he was lying one afternoon, when he turned and saw the face of a disciple pressed against the half-open window. As if no one had told him he was naked, with the innocence of Adam before the fall in the Garden of Eden, he slithered off the daybed and crawled on his belly to the window to confront the disciple perched on a ladder. "You have merited to see your master in the midst of performing the act of tikkun," he said. He reached his powerful arm up from the floor and slammed the window shut, sending the ladder reeling backward as the disciple hung on to the ledge like a spider.

The disciple unfortunately was possessed of a limited understanding of what he had witnessed. In recounting all of this to me, my brother speculated that the boy likely had base designs on the girl, and for this reason alone, to protect the maiden, a few of his stronger followers were dispatched to teach him a lesson. Even so, within twenty-four hours, false and sensational accusations involving my brother leaked out, appearing in the press and all the media, and a warrant for his arrest was issued by the Israeli police. For his own safety and protection, his supporters had no choice but to spirit him immediately out of the country. The whole thing was completely ridiculous, Shmelke told me, reverting to the Brooklynese of our childhood, to our conversations in the womb. By that point, because of his regimen of fasting and the various forms of ascetic practice that he had taken upon himself to hasten the redemption, not to mention the obvious desiccation of his lower half as a result of his injury and his confinement to a wheelchair, his whole sex drive was a nonstarter; he would not have been able to get it up if you paid him, he confided to me. I was after all his twin sister, we had been naked together for forty weeks in the womb, we had played naked in the mud as children, his *baitzim* had shriveled to the size of two raisins, he confided to me. Nevertheless, and despite his disability, he was branded an abuser and offender, and forced to hit the road and take up again the extremely onerous tikkun of pursuit, but now he was pursued not only as a holy man by his disciples who chased him exuberantly into exile wherever he might lead them, but also by the authorities, who pursued him relentlessly like a common criminal.

For seven years, as his hair and beard turned a brilliant patriarchal white, my twin, Shmelke, was on the lam. In general the family had no idea of his whereabouts—and I least of all since I had so radically severed the ties not only because of my marriage to Geeta, a gentile, but especially after word reached them of the manner in which our mother's remains had been processed. I was cut off without hope of access, any reference to me inevitably followed by a sputtering execration as if I were already dead, May her name and memory be blotted out forever and ever, pooh pooh pooh. Nor did Shmelke contact me privately, through alternative underground channels, falling back instead on our extraordinary soul connection from prebirth, trusting that I would know, simply know, trusting that I would be his ally and never betray him. Except for a single extremely critical occasion that forced him to solicit my collusion, he never overtly thought of me, never reached out until finally he arrived in the lap of Mother India and found a haven there at last. During the greater portion of his years as a fugitive, I, like everyone else in our family and the public at large, was not briefed as to where he was in the world. Only when some mention of him and his merry band hit the news were we able to get a precious clue as to his location and stick a voodoo pin into the map, usually when he and his loyalists were kicked out of a place where they had found some temporary sanctuary, or when the Israeli government from which nothing is hidden, every hollow and cavity, blocked or ruptured, all of it exposed and revealed before its seat of glory—only when all-knowing Israel was inspired for some reason to insist yet again on extradition from the country in which he had taken refuge could we pick up his trail and follow it in the media as the case was fought in the courts by his armies of lawyers bankrolled by the exclusive secret society of his supporters and benefactors, independent thinkers one and all, including, thanks to me, the very influential and very rich Charlotte Harlow.

The tale of his wanderings as my brother, Rebbie-ji, recounted them to me in Kolkata at Mother Teresa's starter hospice, now reconsecrated as Rabbi Tabor's House of Holy Healing ashram—that tale as he laid it out before me to cheer me up with its happy ending, had by then already been sculpted and polished into lore—epic and myth. Whenever he and his flock, including women and children, arrived in their wanderings at a new place, Shmelke told me, their modus operandi was to take over an entire motel and camp there until, for one reason or another, they were forced to move on.

As he recalled those unsettled years, Shmelke shook his head as if in disbelief. The most amazing thing about it all, he said, was that just about wherever we went—and they had stopped at a multitude of out-of-the-way places, seriously off the beaten track on this lonely planet, he assured me, he would only mention some of the major power points—the motel they took over was always owned by an Indian named Patel. After a while, Shmelke would just roll up to the front desk upon arrival surrounded by his tight escort of the inner circle of his Hasidim secret service, his arm outstretched in readiness for a hearty handshake provided the clerk behind the counter was not a female, and he would boom out, "*Sholom aleikhem*, Mottel Patel. How's it going? *Vos makht a Yid?*" And indeed two of these Mottel Patels, big Mottel and little Mottel, eventually converted to Judaism thanks to my brother's charismatic influence and took the names Mottel Patel-Aleph, since he was the Patel from America, and Mottel Patel-Zayin from Zimbabwe. Now that these two freshly Jewish Mottel Patels were back home in India they rechanneled the skills acquired for survival in exile, bustling around the ashram in their glossy black beards and sidelocks, great bowled white yarmulkes fitting snugly on their heads setting off their dark skin, robed in long kaftans girded with a rope belt, in charge of overseeing the hospitality end of the operation.

He couldn't believe it had taken him so long to read the sign hurled directly in his face over and over again by the Master of the Universe, Shmelke told me—that his final destination was India. It could only have been the built-up tension and pressure from being cast adrift as a wanted man, forced to run in circles like a cockroach in the beam of a searchlight that blinded him to the obvious signification of all these Mottel Patels, he thought. My antennae were going bad, the wax was drying up, I wasn't picking up the vibes. I should have headed straight to Mother India—she was calling out to me, arms open, breasts bared, Come to me, my darling boy, suck, suck— how come I couldn't see what was right in front of my eyes? My own mother of blessed memory was in India, her earthly remains in the form of ashes, like so many of our holy martyrs scooped with a shovel from the ovens, and you were there too, my sister, my seeker, my twin, calling to me. What was wrong with my head? India and Israel—one and the same—both equally renowned for their formidable mothers and math-genius sons and over-the-top weddings and wildly successful diaspora communities of unstoppable ambition, number one in so many realms, not only motels. Coming to India was like coming home at last, returning to the true Zion, it was as if I were dreaming. From the spiritual angle, India and Israel, both the final destination of the holy seekers of the world, from the political angle, both spitting out their British oppressors, then brutally torn asunder, partitioned in the same blink of an eye 1947–48 in the universal timeline. It was a trauma from which neither has yet recovered and never will, a violent slashing that fired up the sons of Ishmael, wild asses of men, their hands mixing it up with everyone and everyone's hands mixing it up with them. Israel and India, together they will bring on the end of the world.

In addition to the Patels, my brother picked up other converts along the way, easily identifiable in his retinue and circulating through the ashram because, Let's face it, *didi*, as he put it—he had taken to addressing me by the Bengali term for older sister, which I was, by six minutes—even with the beard and *peyes* and the whole getup, they don't look Jewish, right? It was not that he sought them out like a missionary, God forbid. It was simply that coming from a place of extreme suffering and despair, the lowest depths, they were restored by Reb Breslov's potent cocktail of ecstatic release mixed with meditative, confessional solitude, and as if born again.

Most of the converts were collected in America, because it was in the heartland of America, in Postville, Iowa, that my brother and his Hasidim sojourned for the longest period of time during their wanderings in the wilderness; Postville, Iowa, was their Kadesh Barnea, their oasis. A Jewish infrastructure was already conveniently in place around the Chabad kosher slaughterhouse and meatpacking sweatshop located there, the town's main natural resource. And to ease the way for my brother, Shmelke (a vegetarian from his earliest years), there was the flat terrain, so friendly to the disabled in wheelchairs. Above all, he was born in the USA, he was a citizen, he had a US passport, he could even run for president. As an American citizen he could expect full rights and protection from his government. Even if an extradition treaty existed with Israel, he would not be handed over, his legal team assured him, without serious prior concessions from the Jewish State in territory, right of return for Arab refugees, and other nonstarters as part of the deal. Just keep the old lecher, he's all yours, we're not giving up anything, Israel would declare, and wash its hands of the whole business. And should his enemies persist out of sheer stupidity and stubbornness, committing the gravest of sins by turning into informers, chasing and pursuing him in exchange for nothing but the sadistic pleasure of the hunt, his lawyers would fight his extradition all the way to the Supreme Court, the fight would drag on for decades, plenty of time to pack up and move on in search of the elusive Promised Land.

As it happened, though, what caused my brother and his followers to decamp from Postville, Iowa, in the end was not the notorious event that took place there—the massive raid by immigration authorities on the Chabad-owned meatpacking plant and glatt kosher slaughter-house, the arrest and deportation of hundreds of illegal immigrants, the charges of child labor law violations, identity theft, social security manipulation, sexual harassment, fraud, money laundering, and so on and so forth, not to mention the ethical issues churned up when labor exploitation is linked with kosher certification, toxic work environments in which human beings are treated more cruelly than animals destined to be served up in a cholent stew for the Sabbath lunch. Rather, it was the ongoing war between the Chabadniks and the Breslovers over messianic issues—whose rabbi was really dead, whose would reappear quickly and in our time as the Messiah in white robes riding on the back of a white ass, and other matters of equal gravity and weight.

This war had, over the time of my brother's stay, played itself out mostly in petty, even childish, skirmishes—puncturing each other's tires, wrapping toilet paper around each other's trees, chalking each other's kaftans, fistfights, flicking spitballs, seltzer squirting, dumping slop from rooftops on passersby below, women from rival sects tearing off each other's wigs and kerchiefs, and so on. Then one day it burst out into a full-scale gang war rumble involving knives from the slaughterhouse and other weaponry. The immediate provocation was a disagreement over which of the two groups could take credit for having inspired the conversion of an exceptionally desirable candidate, a six-foot, six-inch former sheriff named Buck, who came complete with a six-pointed silver star badge. The rumble took place in nearby Waterloo, at the National Cattle Congress fairground not far from the sheep and swine pens, the very same *umschlagplatz* where the illegal Immigrants rounded up from the kosher slaughterhouse had been held, handcuffed and chained together in packs of ten like slaves on the block.

That very night, on the urgent advice of his lawyers and financial backers, my brother and all of his followers left town, and to play it super safe, they also bid farewell to the good old USA, his native land. Joining their ranks, in addition to the Mottel Patel of Postville, Iowa, and his entire extended family, was a mixed mob of leftover illegals who had managed somehow to hold on after the raid and deportations and become converts too, Mexican, Guatemalan, a Ukrainian, a Somali, a Micronesian, and also, as my brother, Reb Breslov, was so proud to inform me, the big prize, Buck himself (but this of course was public information, his figure so striking as he blissfully undercut the Bulvans at every opportunity to carry his beloved guru on his back around the ashram), who, upon his conversion, had taken a new name as if he were reborn. Thereafter he was known as Buki ben Yogli, cited as the leader of the Tribe of Dan in the book of Numbers, alluding in this fashion, for those paying attention, to that most famous Danite of all, the Jewish Hercules, our legendary strongman, Samson.

In consequence of that experience, Shmelke confided to me, he resolved that wherever in the world his wanderings would take him, under no circumstances whatsoever would he step foot on two continents—Antarctica or Australia. The reason for this was that the first was overrun by penguins and the second by Chabadniks, both in their black-and-white suits, an external physical manifestation that possessed deep negative mental and emotional associations for Shmelke, and even more negative inner spiritual signification, so far beneath his sacred mystical level in the aura of the divine. The five remaining continents were enough, he reasoned, in which ultimately to find a haven from his pursuers. On this point, he was immovable. He was going with his instincts, which since childhood had always been impeccable, empowering his survival and ultimate victory over his enemies, shaping him from Rabbi Shmelke Tabor into Reb Breslov Tabor—and ultimately, triumphantly, into Rebbie-ji, the world-famous guru whom the entire global congregation had come to recognize for his extraordinary spiritual access.

In all of the Americas, north, south and middle, Shmelke told me, his favorite stop was Cusco, the old Inca capital city in Peru. He and his followers settled into the Mottel Patel just beyond the astonishing stonewalled Inca ruins of Sacsayhuamán, on a hill overlooking the city. The setting inspired teachings about the temporal nature of human existence, a passing shadow, a fleeting dream, as well as about the rise and fall of empires and nations, and attempts throughout history by human predators to exterminate whole peoples—why some survive, such as we Jews, and others disappear, for instance, the Incas. It was also of course an occasion to reflect on walls—walls that protect, walls that divide, and so forth—Walls that are worshipped, Shmelke added pointedly, such as our own Western Wall in Jerusalem, a form of idolatry, didi. But even Herod the Great could not have constructed walls of such magnificence and perfection as the walls of the fortress or temple or whatever it was of Sacsayhuamán—giant, smooth boulders fitted together without mortar to perfection like a jigsaw puzzle so that even the thinnest blade of a knife could not be inserted between them. Who were the master masons that built these walls? The Spaniards believed it was the work of demons. Others are convinced it was extraterrestrial aliens transporting the giant stones in their spaceships from a faraway planet in a distant solar system, and setting them down on this hill, since such a creation is beyond human power.

But whoever was responsible, for us it was an almost ideal setting, my brother recalled: Walls behind which we could seek the privacy and seclusion in nature to meditate, to practice our *hitbodedut* and converse with God in solitude from the depths of our souls with such closeness and intimacy, as with a loving father; large open spaces within the walled compound in which my Hasidim could dance ecstatically in circles for hours as tour groups in identical logo hats came and went led by guides holding aloft an umbrella to show the way under the sun, stopping as they trudged back to their buses to drop coins and bills into the cups my boys held out. They were young, my wild boys, busting with energy and enthusiasm in their white, knitted *kippot* and striped, blue and-gold kapotes, their beards and *peyot* flying like birds. I don't hold them responsible for what happened, they were soaring on spiritual heights, on the condor wings of the one above. But in short order the Incas showed up as if risen from the dead, climbed up the hill in their bright woolen ponchos, blowing on their bamboo windpipes. Who knew they still even existed? We thought the Spanish had taken care of them all. We had no intention, God forbid, of poaching on their territory.

For a week or so, it is true, there was competitive dancing. They were a strange looking bunch, short and squat, stomping around in their striped blankets and vaudeville bowlers, men and women, some even cloaked in the full skin of a llama performing their Andean flash dances, but in the end we had to do the right thing, and cede the turf to them. They claimed to be the indigenous stock, the true Canaanites from time immemorial. I wasn't about to argue with them. Who is an Inca? Who is a Jew? If you say you're an Inca, fine by me, you're an Inca, as long as in return you respect my right to be whatever I decide I am, even the extraterrestrial who built these walls. Because up on that hill, there was no question that in their minds, we were the aliens come back to stake our claim on the rocks.

Still, there was no profit in fighting it. Under the circumstances, for practical reasons alone, it was obvious that in this instance we were the ones who must yield. I don't blame those so-called Incas, Shmelke said, everyone has to make a living, they just couldn't deal with the competition. I still regard Cusco as one of the best places we visited. I would recommend it with five stars if I were writing a guidebook, but

I was in flight, I had no time for such indulgences, I was not a tourist, I was running for my life, and so I mounted my steed, my trusty wheelchair, and I led my flock down the hill to our next station, whatever it might be, taking along as a convert their best panpipe player, renamed Yehuda Puma. Even now, didi, he is busking in the street outside Kali's temple, collecting rupees for our cause. The music penetrates my soul, my spirit, my anima, my *neshama*, you can feel within it the breath of life, struggling.

On the other hand, the worst place we stayed was our final stop in Africa—Western Sahara, not even a country, as far as I know, a territory ruled by Morocco, at least the part of it that our spaceship touched down on bearing our rocks. Thank God the good old reliable Mottel Patel stood out to receive us like a beacon even there, perched in the distance on those miles and miles of sand as far as the eye could see. Other than that, there was nothing there. Nothing! *Gurnischt mit gurnischt*, I'm telling you. Some tents, a few nomads shuffling around scratching their balls, Bedouins, Berbers—who knows what?—and camels. All the time my wheelchair was getting stuck in the camel hoo-ha. The only positive thing about the place, didi, was that it was like a frontier town in the old West from the cowboy shows, lawless. They never even heard the word extradition, they had no diplomatic relations with anyone, nobody bothered to even recognize them, there was no chance they would ever hand me over. But the place was so inhospitable to human habitation, like the landscape of that distant planet from which we Jews were said to have hauled down the stones of Sacsayhuamán, that at times I even considered turning myself in. Expatriate me, please, I'm begging you, turn me in, get me out of here. Anything is better than this. Think of all the treasure you can acquire from the Israelis to stuff into the carpet saddlebags of your camels in exchange for this old cripple with a long white beard stuck in an antiquated wheelchair. They didn't know much about the world, these tribals, but one thing they did know for a fact: flip a Jew upside down and shake him, and the coins pour out of every hole, enough to adorn all the wives of Arabia.

Luckily, just as I was about to give into this irrational urge and surrender to some boss man, the king of Morocco himself did me a favor and kicked me out—not in a deal with Israel, he just wanted me gone, he didn't care where in the world I went. He had heard the false rumors regarding the indecent charges leveled against me. It was not in the interest of the good name and image of his degenerate nation of debauchers to harbor even within the borders of this disputed territory such a reputed deviant and pervert as I so falsely was accused of being.

I regret to report, didi, that these trumped-up charges involving me reached the ears of the king from fellow Jews—for the slanderers let there be no hope, may they perish in an instant, may they be cut down, uprooted, smashed—Israeli Mafia and criminals of Moroccan descent given safe haven in Marrakech and Casablanca in exchange for baksheesh, bankrolling the realm. Murderers and extortionists and money launderers like themselves were one thing, the kingdom could handle that; but an alleged sex offender was intolerable, insupportable in terms of pubic relations. Harboring such a fugitive from the point of view of the officials could damage a country's good name, ruin its image in the eyes of the civilized world, yes, but even more important, the way our Jewish gangsters so cynically calculated, it could seriously jeopardize by racial association the asylum granted to them.

And I had been so good to these guys in Israel. I had done them so many favors, rescuing their sons and other low-life relatives from drugs, murder, gang warfare, crimes of rape and sex offenses, arms dealings, and so on and so forth, reaching out to their troubled youth, drawing them close, using my powers to rehabilitate their children, turning them into pious, religious Jews who prayed with such fervor three times a day. The transformation was breathtaking, everyone marveled, you can see my handiwork even today, these Sephardi and North African returnees to the faith dancing rapturously in circles and carrying out the good work of our ashram. And this is how they thanked me? Where was their gratitude? You may wonder, didi, how it is that I know they were the ones who squealed on me to the king. The answer is, one among them whose son I had saved from sure madness and death due to heroin addiction, plucking the kid right from the brink—that father still possessed a shred of decency, and he alerted me. I cannot mention his name, his life would not be worth a single dried-up turd of a constipated camel. But he gave me a heads-up, and moreover arranged for a private jet to transport us in the night over the waters and snowcapped mountains to Switzerland, another haven for criminals who could afford it. How it galled me to be regarded as a criminal, didi, I cannot even begin to tell you.

As my brother, Reb Breslov, formulated it, the unique attraction of Switzerland consists of two factors—money and sanitation. For him, the problem arose when these two values collided. From Lugano Airport they were conveyed in a fleet of limousines like dignitaries headed to the World Economic Forum, up over five thousand feet into the Swiss Alps to Davos, and settled into their magic mountain. On the face of it, this might be considered an obvious welcome change from the squalor of Western Sahara, but the problem was, it rained nonstop, through the summer and into the fall, so that even carrying out the daily practice of hitbodedut within the splendor of nature was a dispiriting, sodden affair. Most of the time they were stuck in the sanitarium of their Mottel Patel noshing chocolate, going stir-crazy staring at the cuckoo clock, Shmelke recalled.

It all fell apart in the month of October, when several thousand of his followers made a pilgrimage up the mountain from every corner of the globe with their families and other assorted relations to join him in celebrating the holiday of Sukkot, to partake with their rebbe in the Feast of Tabernacles, sit at his holy table and grab the blessed leftover crumbs from his plate. They put up their personal huts all along the promenade in the center of posh, immaculate Davos, constructing them out of cardboard and plastic and whatever salvageable materials they could find from the hidden trash dumps of this elite burg, reinforcing them with their own garbage, which they generated continuously, including soiled paper diapers and other toxic wastes, covering them with roofs of straw and twigs and a fantastic collection of material culture and junk.

There they lived in those flimsy booths for eight days oblivious in their ecstatic state to the rain as it continued to pound down, eating, sleeping, praying, singing, dancing rapturously in their ethnic costumes, which became less and less interesting as the days passed, drenched through and through. When the luxury hotels and shops lining the avenue refused to allow them in to use the facilities, they made do in the street beside their booths and behind municipal buildings, or squatted along the river, the men separated from the women of course. "What? Do you think this is India?" the town bosses demanded of my brother when they barged one day into the super-sukkah that had been erected for him in his Mottel Patel parking lot to accommodate his *tisch*. They went on to remind him that Switzerland had an extradition agreement with the State of Israel. Within twenty-four hours, if this eyesore weren't removed and the freaks weren't gone, he would be handed over to the Mossad or Shabak or whoever the appropriate Jewish authorities were. They had done the math. No amount of cash was worth turning their exclusive paradise into an Indian slum.

India! Why hadn't he thought of India before? Why did he keep missing the signs? Despite the personal and racial insults and innuendoes heaped upon him by the fat town burghers, as Shmelke recounted it to me, he would always be grateful to these Swiss anti-Semites for pointing him in the right direction, sparking the idea, telling him where to go. Now he could hear me at last, calling out to him from Mother India across the vast distance, he said, faintly at first, but then with increasing urgency and distress. There are times when your ears can be opened even by the most despicable of wretches, he said. I hear you, sister. You are pulling my umbilical cord as you were wont to do so playfully in our mother's womb, how well I remember it. I'm coming, didi, I'm on my way.

Over the seven years of my brother's flight, stopping at many more spiritual stations than I have strength to record, until he arrived in the earthly India for my sake, he said, and found physical refuge at last (but too late, too late for me—and you), he reached out to me once only. I recognized his voice on the phone instantly, it was my own blood voice calling to me, resonating from our shared gestational chamber, though he never identified himself by name, it was not necessary. "I am now going to the most dangerous and symbolic of places. If you are contacted, say, please, that you are my sister, so that things will go well for me, and my soul will live because of you."

And I was contacted, relentlessly, within the limited brackets of the attention span of the public. It was one of those times during my brother's journey that his movements surfaced in the media. It was also the exceptional occasion when he did not opt to stay in a Mottel Patel, but instead took up residence with his closest followers in Block 5 at the Auschwitz death camp. He chose Block 5 because of its museum display of mounds of prosthetic limbs, crutches, and similar artifacts confiscated from inmates, to which he ceremoniously added his own wheelchair. For the interim, he was transported on the back of the sheriff, Buki ben Yogli.

The action was titled, Occupy Auschwitz. Every attempt by the Polish officials who ran the complex and museum to eject him and his band of loyalists was fearlessly resisted, dismissed, derided. My brother would not even look at them, or speak to them directly. Astride the shoulders of Buki ben Yogli, framed by the dark opening of Block 5, he would address the mass of his Hasidim gathered outside. He would address them in the softest of voices, and they would repeat what he had just said word for word, clause by clause, in unison, booming it out. Exceedingly quietly my brother said, "The motherfuckers locked us up in this shithole against our will. Now that we voluntarily demand to be here, the motherfuckers are kicking us out. Fuck them!"—and his boys in turn shouted it out. This was an occasion when such language was permissible, my brother ruled, even necessary in the name of heaven for the sake of capturing the attention of the world, unfortunately sick and tired of Jews still kvetching about their Holocaust; a shock to the system was needed to get them to focus. From the perspective of the authorities, the only way to shut them up would be to drag the crippled rabbi out along with his groupies, or turn them over to the Israeli *kapos*. Either way, it would not be pretty for Polish–Jewish relations.

"I am a child Holocaust survivor," my brother practically whispered from his Buki ben Yogli heights.

"I am a child Holocaust survivor," his Hasidim screamed on cue.

He pointed to the dark interior, to three protruding ledges of planks behind him lining the wall in the barrack. "That's where I slept, on the bottom level of that triple-decker, squeezed in the middle, between ten grown men, the diarrhea from the prisoners above us dripping down through the slats all night long, like leaking toilets, covering us with shit." His words were repeated, amplified. Who needed microphones?

Within hours a well-fed bureaucrat was produced, affiliated with the august Holocaust museum in Washington, DC, who delivered a passionate speech about the dangers of abusing Holocaust memory—providing fodder to deniers, anti-Semites, and so on. Moreover, he said, they had certified records to prove that my brother was born well after the war, in Brooklyn, New York.

"I am a child Holocaust survivor, asshole," my brother reiterated calmly and evenly, and the chorus echoed this again, syllable by syllable emphatically at the top of its lungs. "My twin sister, Meena, is also a child Holocaust survivor. She was used as a child prostitute, a sex slave. It screwed her up for life, which is why she now lives in India. You can check out our fucking Holocaust creds with my sister, motherfucker"—and every word he had uttered so softly, so wisely and deeply for those with the gift of understanding, was repeated by his boys at top decibel at the rest stop of each designated clause, including my telephone number, which was the last thing he gave them, digits like a tattoo branded on a forearm, and after that, silence.

When the call came, I provided confirmation. Yes, he is my brother. Yes, we are survivors, my brother and I. After Auschwitz, we are all guilty of surviving.

After Auschwitz, your existence is illusion, as you were marked for death and only by chance were you spared. After Auschwitz, including the arrival of my brother and his merry band to India, wherever they stopped on their journey, chimerical places, mirages, too many to recall here, it is all Maya. Their penultimate station was Uman, in Ukraine, in a final attempt to carry out the tikkun of pursuit of the righteous, the resting place of Rabbi Nahman of Bratslav, the most seductive, most healing guru of them all.

They tried to talk my brother out of making this pilgrimage, his apostles and those who loved him. Way too dangerous, they declared, especially now on Rosh Hashanah when tens of thousands of Hasidim, men only, from all around the world flock to Uman to chant the *Tikkun HaKlali* beseeching the holy Rabbi Nahman for his intervention in granting a blessed New Year, and also to prophylactically vaccinate their young sons, dragged along for the festivities, from the pollution of wet dreams. It was the Jewish version of the annual Muslim hajj, the Hindu Kumbh Mela, Woodstock, they would be stampeded to death by the herds. The Ukrainian high-rises, slapped together by alcoholics from the cheapest junk, which had been vacated by the locals so that they could rent their apartments to the Jews for extortionate sums, these excuses for housing would crumble and collapse thanks to the pounding and stomping of the Hasidim dancing twenty-four hours a day in ecstatic circles. He would be crushed to death for sure along with the rest of them because, due to the fact that he was crippled in body though not, God forbid, in soul, his apartment would be located on the ground-zero floor, anything higher was not feasible, the elevator, if one existed, chronically out of order, the Sabbath elevator, programmed to stop automatically on each floor on days when it is forbidden to summon it electrically, lost in limbo, the whole pile of schlock would come smashing down upon his head, his precious body parts would be buried in the rubble, their sacred sparks growing more and more feeble. The town would be crawling with drug dealers and bootleggers and prostitutes from end to end, converging on Uman from Kiev and the far corners of the cursed land, Baba Yagas from the black hole of Babi Yar, descending on the Rabbi Nahman mosh pit during this holiday season to service the Hasidim who were soaring on the heights, all their senses ravenous and aroused. Under the circumstances, it was not in his interest to add fuel to the fire by letting himself be seen and recognized in such an environment, considering the nature of the false charges that had been leveled against him, which had launched him into such a mercilessly grueling flight. He would be obliged to go around in public wearing a heavy modesty veil attached to his black hat draped over his face to hide his identity, but above all to conceal such offensive sights from his eyes, to prevent himself from unwittingly catching a glimpse of the short, tight skirts packaging buttocks like two rising challahs, the high heels like a dagger to the prostate, the overflowing milky breasts, the meaty lips, bright, moist red. Above all, his disciples pleaded with him, Uman was now infested with Israeli official types, ruthless enforcers, Mossad, Shin Bet, cops, many of them disguised as fellow Hasidim so that you couldn't tell who was what. Ukraine had a very strict extradition treaty with Israel, it welcomed these *judenrats* with open arms, let them do the dirty work. As far as they were concerned, he could be their very own Son of God, JC himself (not to compare, God forbid, to separate by thousands upon thousands of separations), it would not stop them from snatching him in a flash and turning him in for thirty silver shekels, disappearing him, handing him over to the Pharisees, they were shameless, without scruples. No one would ever see him again, except maybe in a glass booth Israeli-style like a freak in a circus, or an iron cage Russian-style like an animal in a zoo before he is dumped into the sea and finds his resting place at last in the belly of the big fish.

God will help, my brother, Rebbie-ji, is reported to have responded with angelic calm. A Mottel Patel will appear to give me shelter. Those girls don't turn me on, he was immune to that type. Anyway, with all his tzores over the last seven years, his yetzer harah had dried up and shriveled to the size of a raisin, as he liked to remind his tormentors. If ever he had lusted, he lusted no more. Besides, just for their information, the State of Israel had no jurisdiction over him whatsoever. This is because the crimes he is alleged to have committed were not committed in Israel but in the Muslim Quarter of Jerusalem, internationally contested no-man's land; setting aside the fact that there was no crime, no one disputes the scene of the noncrime. Any charges brought against him by Israel would never stand, even in an Israeli court of law. Don't worry so much, brothers, Rebbie-ji said. As Moses cried out when he laid eyes on the golden calf, and also Matathias the Maccabee echoing him down through the generations more than a thousand years later in the days of the idol-worshipping Hellenizers, Whoever is with Hashem, come with me! And by Hashem I mean God Almighty ruler of heaven and earth, not some Arab kid named Hashem picking his nose and flicking the snot into your hummus.

Stirred by my brother Shmelke's words, they followed him into the breach to Uman, their hearts overflowing with pure joy. As the buildings all around them shuddered and quaked from the marathon dancing of the pilgrims, they too danced, but in the streets, around the plastic rubbish bins they set on fire, tossing in all the Israeli flags they could lay their hands on, cremating them. When no more could be found, they improvised with blue paint on white linen or underwear, oblivious to the yellow and brown stains, and on paper, two stripes, a Star of David, a simple design, child's play, dumping these into the auto-da-fé as well, dancing rapturously in circles as the flames shot up toward the heavens, higher and higher. Reb Breslov, meanwhile, disguised as a Ukrainian peasant, in an embroidered shirt, homespun trousers tucked into his felt boots, and a sheepskin *chapka*, so as not, God forbid, to go bareheaded, was pushed in a wooden cart by Sheriff Buki ben Yogli, honored for the occasion to serve as my brother's *ba'al agalah*, right up to the holy grave of Rabbi Nahman of Bratslav. For the sake of good diplomatic relations with the host nation, the boss Hasidim in charge of the site for the holiday gave way, standing back alert, waiting to see what this goy would do, watching with eagle eyes for what would happen, their security squad ready to pounce.

Tears streaming down his face, Reb Breslov, my brother, raised his voice and cried out in English, in an all-purpose Russian accent picked up from so many of his disciples rescued from heroin dens and jail cells. "On kholiday of repentance, I make long journey to ask forgiveness for sins against your people." He named names, pounding his chest mightily with his fist with each recitation: Bogdan Khmelnytzki. Symon Petilura. Ivan Demjanjuk. "Remember Babi Yar!" he suddenly bellowed. "For sins we commit against Jewish people, let khassids waste Uman, please, trash khole place, it is okeydokey, we deserve, khave fun boys, welcome, welcome, khappy New Year!"

A righteous gentile. The establishment overseers were satisfied, they relaxed.

He pressed his forehead against the side of the holy tomb, my brother, my twin, brushed his hand over the faint remains of graffiti, Jew-hating slurs not fully wiped away, and wept, his shoulders pumping. "Tatte, Tatte," he cried in muffled Yiddish, "I have suffered so much, I have no home, there is no place in the world for me to go. They pursue me for no reason, like a dog, they surround me all around, yet in God's name I will cut them off, for from your commandments I have never swerved."

As he departed the holy gravesite with no discernible provocation or incident to mar the visit, but with agonizing regret, never knowing if he would ever again see his holy father in this life, a building to his right crumbled almost silently to the ground. To his left, a tongue of flame leapt up. Word had passed to his Hasidim as they formed a train behind him, that the holy Rabbi Nahman of Bratslav had appeared to his gilgul Reb Breslov in a vision. "Shmelke, Shmelke," Rabbi Nahman had called out to him from the depths of his tomb. "Here I am," my brother had replied. Rabbi Nahman spoke: "Wherever I would go during my brief span on earth, I was always going to the land of Israel. The heavenly land of Israel. Follow in my footsteps, my son. India is now the earthly Israel. Go to India. Seek there and seek there, because for now, until my return, all that there is, is there."

They processed away from the site, my brother and his Hasidim, past buildings collapsing on one side, on the other side, everything burning, directly to Sofia Park, where a helicopter awaited them on a clearing. Within minutes they were swooped up and carried away, "As if on eagle's wings, like the chariot of Eliyahu the prophet," Shmelke was telling me when I opened my eyes to find myself in Kolkata, in his House of Holy Healing—when finally I was ready to let it be known that I had emerged from the depths of self and had begun tentatively to take in the other. "As you know, didi, our sages teach that danger to life trumps the Sabbath. Also here in this country of my refuge, saving a life is considered the supreme dharma according to the Vedas and the teachings of the most learned Brahmins. I was in mortal danger. My cover was blown. The Israeli collaborators were on to me, also the Ukrainian perpetrators, also the Hasidim bystanders from other sects. Under those circumstances it was permissible to violate the prohibition against travel on the holiday. This was confirmed by the mystical appearance of the chopper on that pad. It was literally a sign from heaven, ignoring it would have been the gravest of sins, it was a positive commandment from the One Above that could not be refused, it was my duty to save my life and let myself be borne aloft, higher and higher."

He had taken to visiting me once a day for the relief of unburdening to his sister, his twin, all that had happened to him during the years of our separation and his wanderings, even though in his heart he believed I must already know everything without needing to be told, just as, when we were children, I could always tell him, in case he had forgotten, what he had dreamed in the night by virtue of having shared a womb for forty weeks, and he too knew everything about me without requiring further elaboration. He would roll up in his wheelchair at unspecified times when the spirit seized him, into the room in his private suite in the House of Holy Healing that I shared in those first weeks with the old woman on the bed across from me who gave off a warm, faint fragrance like chicken soup with matzah balls, filling us both with such sweetly painful nostalgia. I had been as motionless and as uncommunicative as my roommate laid out over there when he had started coming by, he told me. But it was not the same, Shmelke insisted. I was his wombmate. Let them all think I wasn't registering a word he was saying as he went on and on at my bedside about his ordeal of wanderings. He had no doubt I was taking it all in, not missing a single thing, I was absorbing and understanding every syllable. Besides—he flashed me with his wicked grin—there were definite advantages to talking to a woman with no chance of being interrupted, no chance she'd butt in to demand equal time to disgorge her own problems or to contradict or to argue, it is an ideal situation for good conversation.

The old lady on the twin bed across the room had been shipped to him special delivery from Varanasi via Mumbai coinciding almost exactly with his arrival in Kolkata. She was his one-woman welcoming committee to this former hospice. It was believed she was a Jewess, a Hebrew holy woman, and therefore his department. This conclusion was reached after she was removed from her funeral pyre on the cremation ground of Manikarnika Ghat, when she sat up, opened her eyes with their singed lashes, and inquired if she was dead yet. Eventually it was determined that she must be Jewish as history and experience have shown that Jews are not flammable, like cockroaches they cannot be entirely exterminated, they stubbornly survive in some form as an entity to haunt you, to remind you for eternity of how you tried to stamp them out. She was passed off to the Jewish team at Assi Ghat because she could no longer remain among the living; she had been contaminated by death, it was mandatory that she be isolated from human society. From Benares she was dispatched to the Bombay emissaries, and now here she was where the powers decreed she belonged—with my fugitive brother in a former hospice for the dying right next door to the temple of Kali, the great mother goddess who fornicated among the dead on the cremation grounds, Shmelke said.

He didn't mind. She was no trouble at all, especially now with Manika attending to her with, if anything, a tenderness even more exemplary than she poured out on me, if that was possible—dribbling hydration into her mouth, washing and changing her, sticking a tissue down her throat to draw out the thick green gelatinous globs of slime blocking her passage. She could stay on as long as she liked as far as Shmelke was concerned, until there was agreement on her status, whether she could be counted among the living or the dead— "A far more complicated determination than you might imagine," he observed.

He would give me an example from his own personal experience. Had I ever wondered about the ready acceptance that he, a proud, openly Jewish man, had enjoyed and continued to enjoy here in

Kolkata, in a former Christian hospice, abutting such a volatile major Hindu temple? It would be a mistake to attribute this to Indian tolerance, which, in any case, did not exist, it was a total myth, or to the cash Charlotte and some other fat cats forked over, or to anything else of that sort. No. It was that the local Bengalis, when they had laid eyes on him with his long white beard and long white hair and long flowing white robe, were gripped with overwhelming joy that their divine poet, their Nobel laureate Rabindranath Tagore, whom they had mourned with such a massive outpouring of grief, had returned. He had come back to them, he was not dead after all, here he was, yes, it is true, confined to a wheelchair now, crippled unfortunately, but still dazzling with his white mane in his white robes as if packaged by central casting—their beloved poet possessed of such fine lofty sentiments, their prophet, their Oriental mystic, known familiarly as Rabi Thakur, Shmelke recounted, relishing the memory. And when word spread that my brother's name was Rabbi Tabor, all doubts vanished. Thousands mobbed the House of Holy Healing to celebrate the return of Rabi Thakur, lining up to perform *pranam* due the elderly, and especially an honored sage of such renown and distinction, waiting patiently for the privilege of bending down to reverently touch his feet with their hands as he in turn reached out to touch their heads in blessing. He sat there in his wheelchair for a week, my brother, Shmelke, receiving pranam and giving blessings, it almost completely wiped him out, his arms felt as heavy as stones, two of his Hasidim were required to hold them up, like Aaron and Hur held up Moses's hands so that Joshua could triumph in his battle against the Amalekites in the field below. In just this way, with his raised hands, my brother, Shmelke, defeated his Israeli pursuers and tormentors of the innocent. There was no chance they would dare try to grab him and spirit him away now. It would start a world-class riot for sure in a fiery nation possessed of nuclear capacity. He was home safe.

What terrible sin had Rabi Thakur committed, and the old lady in that bed across the room, that prevented them from being set free? And I, what terrible sin had I committed in a past life to be stricken with such suffering? Cut me loose from the wheel of life, I cried.

Where is my liberation? I have lost everything. I have nothing, like a *sannyasi* who is regarded as dead. Let me set out then like a sannyasi with nothing in my hands but a stick and a bowl to find my moksha.

Not yet, sister, Shmelke responded.

He needed me now. There was no one else he could trust as he could trust me, for my loyalty, my advice, my discretion. He was a wanted man, wanted in both senses, negative and positive, by enemy and devotee, all of it a burden too heavy to bear alone. He needed my help. If I loved him, I would stay. If I felt an uncontrollable need at this time to cycle into ascetic mode without delay, I could begin my austerities here in the House of Holy Healing even as I carried out my duties as his counselor and confidante—let my hair grow wild and matted, abstain from food and drink three times a week, clothe myself in rags, carry a skull for a drinking cup, sleep on a stretcher bier on the cold ground, detach myself from all comforts and pleasures, surrender desire, cease wanting. If I felt I had sinned in another life, I could undertake tikkun now through selfless service. As it happened, right at this very moment, there was an urgent need here at the House of Holy Healing for a woman to oversee the prepubescents, my brother said. He would have me moved tonight from this room in his suite to the prepubescent pod in the great ward. He would put me in charge of them, the girls they had rescued who had been sold by their mothers.

· 2 ·

THERE WERE FOUR PREPUBESCENTS when I took over the pod in the great ward that night, ranging in age from five years old to thirteen. Two of these girls were from the very lowest of castes, from desperately impoverished families in villages in the north. They were sold by their mothers in straightforward deals for a few hundred rupees to sex traffickers specializing in servicing locals and tourists who happened to prefer pedophilia. After many sordid encounters, they were ultimately delivered, battered and sick, from Kamathipura, the red-light district in Mumbai, to Rebbie-ji's House of Holy Healing in Kolkata, rescued by the sheriff, Buki ben Yogli.

Buki also rescued the other two, sisters from Karnataka in the south, whose mother had unloaded each in turn at the age of five by dedicating them to the goddess Yellamma. In this way, they became temple girls or devadasis. They still wore their devadasi necklaces of red and white beads on a saffron-colored string when I met them. The older girl, Devamayi, was thirteen. She had already undergone her puberty ceremony consummating her marriage with Yellamma, following which her virginity was put up for auction to prospective patrons. From the aspect of the House of Holy Healing, therefore, she did not strictly fall into the prepubescent category. Nevertheless, a decision was made to let her stay in the pod in the spirit of family togetherness along with her eight-year-old sibling, Mahamaya. Shmelke felt very close to the sisters, he confided to me, a deep inner personal connection, he said, and not only to these two but to the whole universe of devadasis in general. When the story of my life ended three years later and I departed the shell of the House of Holy Healing, there were eighteen girls in the pod, all of them devadasis.

Rescuing devadasis became a major element integrally tied into Rebbie-ji's overall master plan at the House of Holy Healing. He regarded himself to be a male incarnation of a devadasi. *Ich bin ein devadasi*, he would introduce himself to jubilant ovations. Of course, I understood. He too had been sold to the temple, like his namesake, the prophet Samuel, who had been offered by his barren mother, Hannah, to the Lord in a deal in exchange for a child, delivered as promised to the high priest Eli in the tabernacle at Shiloh after he was weaned as part of a sacrifice package that also included three bullocks, an ephah of meal, and a bottle of wine. "I never had a choice," Shmelke said to me, in full awareness that I of all people would get it and feel his pain. "I never was allowed to find out what else was out there in the world. You think I was handicapped by an accident as an adult? I was handicapped from before I was even born. What else could I do when I grew up but become a rabbi?"

Devamayi and Mahamaya were the House of Holy Healing's first devadasis. They were dedicated to Yellamma by their mother in the hope that the fertility goddess would intervene on her behalf and give her a son who would take care of her in her old age, unlike daughters who were nothing but a burden. From then on, the two girls were considered to be married to the goddess (as I was married to the goddess Geeta, a sacred gay marriage), and therefore forbidden to marry any mortal man as long as they lived. This insider connection with the goddess was a devadasi's greatest asset even after her patron tired of her and dumped her in a brothel; it was a badge of pride and honor even in the pecking order of whores. A devadasi was not a sex slave, she was God's slave. Yet despite these benefits, there is no question in my mind that the sisters were better off to have been evacuated from the squalor and degradation and abuse of that life. Neither girl remembered much from her initiation ceremony except having the pretty string of beads tied around her neck. Their duties during their novitiate included sweeping the temple, they recalled, among other chores. Sometimes they would perform ritual dances and sing traditional songs along with the other temple girls. They also would serve the priests, whenever they were summoned, day or night.

"Serve the priests?" Charlotte's eyebrow arched into the punctuation of an exclamation point.

Charlotte, too, like my brother, had taken a serious interest in the sisters and in all devadasis, an estimated quarter million of them still operating in Mother India, even though the practice had been declared illegal, like sati, according to data gathered for her by one of her flunkies sent out on a fact-finding mission. She was already talking about bringing them all to the States and educating them properly. Clearly they were under threat of persecution, which definitely would qualify them for refugee status. She would pitch this idea to Michelle next time they met for hot yoga. Every one of the devadasis would become a member of her all-girls band, Lakshmi and the Survivors, along with its fabulous virtuoso wind player, Monica Lewinsky; they were already in show business, after all, trained as temple performers. It would be awesome, the world's largest multicultural, diverse, all-female band, definitely a *Guinness Book of Records* contender.

After Buki enacted the first daring rescues not only of Devamayi and Mahamaya, but also of the two other little girls, Charlotte took on the cause, charging ahead with the full thrust of her formidable energy and resources. She put Buki at the head of the operation, ordering him to focus for the time being on the devadasis rather than the other sex workers, even the littlest girls, practically babies, no matter how pitiful and subhuman their plight, since the devadasis and everything they signified meant so much personally to Rebbie-ji and were so tied into his present mystical studies and teachings.

Buki was the one who introduced my brother to the institution of devadasis. He first learned about them when Rebbie-ji dispatched him to Mumbai to check out the place with regard to the Jewish scene there, in particular the Chabad center newly restored and up and running at last following the terrorist attack and all the subsequent sordid financial fallout. It was a secret mission. Despite his physical conspicuousness due to his height and Hasidic finery, he was still the perfect spy for this assignment thanks to his familiarity with the Chabadnik modus operandi from his time as sheriff in Postville, Iowa, keeping a watchful eye on their slaughterhouses, their meatpacking sweatshops, and all their businesses, on the table and under the table.

Nevertheless, he concluded it would be preferable not to pay an official call on the emissaries, Rabbi Mendy and his rebbetzin Mindy, due to the longstanding rivalry between the followers of the two dead rabbis, the rabbi of Chabad and the rabbi of Bratslav, and in particular the violent feud as to which of the two would rise up from conceal-ment one day and return as the Messiah. On top of that there was his well-known close affiliation with my brother, regarded as an out-cast and fugitive smeared with particularly unsavory false accusations, about which the Chabad boys, so media savvy, did everything in their power to keep the world up to date with timely reminders and bul-letins. And from Buki's own perspective, there was also the painful memory of the rumble between the two sects at the National Cattle Congress fairground in Waterloo, Iowa, over which of them could take the credit for his conversion and claim him as their own, as if he were a prime blue-ribbon bull. Then, to cap it all off, in an obvious ploy to humiliate my brother, Shmelke, to reduce him to the level of the dumping ground for all Jewish castoffs and undesirables, the Mumbai Chabad had passed on to him the old lady who smelled of chicken soup, or maybe it was stale urine, about whom no one could say who she was or what she was or whether she was dead or alive, and all the aggravation and guilt that leaked out from that toxic case.

So although it had been customary over the centuries for wander-ing Jews traveling in strange and hostile places to count on hospital-ity from fellow Jews, in this particular situation it was impossible. In Mumbai, Buki had to make do with the Taj Mahal hotel, with Char-lotte footing the bill, five-star luxury accommodation it is true, but no kosher food, and a truly goyish, even heathen atmosphere. Forgive me, Shmelke, for bringing this up here, you know how much I love you, my brother, my twin. But when you sent Buki to Mumbai to spy out the land, why did you not send him to me? I would have been thrilled to receive him, with open arms. I would have rejoiced to be his Rahab. Why didn't you order him to check on me too? Am I not also a Jew, brother? I needed him to save my life.

He went everywhere in the city, but he did not come to me. Had he come, maybe he could have intervened, as he intervened for strangers, the devadasis and the trafficked little girls. Maybe things could have been different. He visited all the slums, including Dharavi, but he never noticed her in her Muslim camouflage. He rode the trains, but he was not there to catch her in his arms when she was pushed out as if she were a lower form of life, trash, of no account at all, as if she were unloved, as if she were motherless, as if she did not matter to anyone on this earth.

He must have made a striking figure on the streets of Mumbai, six feet, six inches tall, solid muscle, with his long blonde beard and flowing blonde sidelocks, his best kaftan, satin, gold-and-blue striped, with its prominently displayed sheriff's badge, a silver, six-pointed star on which he had proudly printed in indelible ink the word *Jude*, a silken tasseled rope belt girding his waist, or perhaps, as many who had seen him maintained, it was a leather holster bulging with two pistols, his black felt Borsalino hat with its extra-wide brim rakishly angled like a Stetson, and the personal touch of his impenetrable mirrored sunglasses, like the Lone Ranger's black mask. Who was that masked man? Everyone wondered as he rode off, fighting for truth and justice. Passersby pulled out their cell phones and snapped, his image sluiced through the pipelines of social media. He looked like a supporting cast member from the thrilling days of yesteryear who had gotten lost, wandered off one of the Bollywood sets, like a Gary Cooper knockoff striding into the wrong ghost town too late, too late, long past high noon.

He made his way, bowlegged from having spent too long in the saddle, through the lanes of the Kamathipura red-light district as if tracking down the bad guys. What he was actually searching for though, like a vigilante, was any Jewish girl who might have been trafficked, or one way or another had taken the wrong turn and gotten herself caught in this shameful place—a post-army Israeli backpacker, for example, or a zoned-out, spoiled American kid from New York stricken with swami syndrome who had fallen down this black rabbit's hole. As Rebbie-ji always said, "The kids are out there seeking,

seeking—so why is it that they are finding them and not us? Oy, we have such a big job to do." Whatever foul mess she had gotten herself into, if she was Jewish, Buki wanted her. It was his responsibility to free her in fulfillment of the exceedingly crucial mitzvah to redeem Jewish captives. And even if there was disagreement as to whether this mandate applied to women captives as well, Buki felt very strongly that it just was not nice for a Jewish girl to be seen in such a place.

Whores, pimps, madams converged on him gesticulating lewdly, trying to pull him into their web, enticing him with samplings of their wares, but he shook his head and swatted them off, muttering in a deep drawl that the only thing he's out here shopping for in this decrepit mall of India is a nice Jewish girl, did they happen to have one by any chance? He would settle for nothing less, he was not in the market for anything else. Nobody could understand what he was after. The workers who had picked up some functional English to service the foreign tourists couldn't figure out what he was babbling about, no one had ever heard this word *Jewish*, this was the first time in their memory that any prospective client had requested such an item, it was obviously an extremely rarefied fetish or perversion, probably the latest new invention from America, blank looks came over their faces like window shades drawn down with a snap, and they shook their heads yes in the Indian way, which meant no.

He did his best to convey a sense of what is generally meant by *Jewish* using a kind of sign language. He rotated thumbs against forefingers to indicate avarice, rubbed his hands together and leered to signal lasciviousness, folded downward the tip of his nose, which in its normal state was splendidly snubbed. It was turning into a game, charades, a mockery in such a setting, yet they all participated eagerly, it was a welcome diversion, they threw out their guesses enthusiastically, but to everything they produced Buki just shook his head, deflated. He was considering showing them his member of which he was justifiably proud, circumcised in its maturity in Postville, Iowa, by a slaughterer who doubled as a mohel, but restrained himself when he realized they would only conclude he was a Muslim and lead him to a whore naked under her burqa. He angled his two hands together in front of his face like an open book, and began swaying as if in prayer, but they only shrugged. Their excitement was waning, they were losing interest, a few were already turning to go. Whatever it was he wanted, it no longer was worth their time, it was obviously a very particular commodity not in general demand and therefore not worth stocking. In desperation, to keep them tuned in just a little longer, he leapt into the air and began to dance ecstatically, whirling with arms uplifted, a Hasid transported to divine heights.

Devadasi! a voice from heaven cried out.

Buki stalled, then nodded his head heartily—Yes ma'am, that's it, a doxy, thank God!

He had come here searching for a nice Jewish girl; he had never expected to find an Orthodox one. That was a huge bonus. It was his lucky day. Rebbie-ji would be very impressed when he came home with a doxy. It was a tremendous relief all around. They had solved the puzzle, customer satisfaction—a temple dancing girl, that was his thing. Every man had his thing, you just had to probe patiently to figure out what it was. They knew now exactly where to deposit him.

Buki had complete faith in his own physical strength in just about any situation, and he also had faith in God. It struck him that now he might need to put himself in God's hands to find his way back out again through the maze of constricting lanes and alleyways, court-yards within courtyards overflowing with trash, reeking with sewage, to wherever he was being taken. Buried somewhere in the net of this serpentine world there was a tiny dark room that he was forced to stoop to enter. Without stepping inside, his escort pointed to the narrow bed against the wall across from the entrance, and motioned for him to sit down. Then he closed the door and walked away. Buki heard the key turn in the lock.

He sat there with his long legs spread wide, his elbows on his knees, his head lowered in the sling of his palms, waiting. A rat shuffled across the cement floor. There was a basin and a pitcher against the wall, a rag of a towel on the stub of a peg. The room was lit by one small yellow bulb hanging by a wire from the ceiling with a pull spotted with dead black flies. He made out a small shrine in the corner with a glossy picture cut out from a calendar of the goddess Yellamma. Squatting beside it was a girl, a child almost, plump as if she had only recently been fattened in order to be eaten. Her face was far too heavily made up for such a young human specimen, and she was wearing a sari made of synthetic cloth with a bright pattern of Santa Claus faces on it with a white beard like Rebbe-ji's, which she was beginning to unwind. Buki raised one large hand, palm outward, pushing it forward like a traffic cop to compel her to stop. She was very dark skinned, so black she was almost blue. Maybe she was a Bnei Israel or a Bnei Menashe or something like that, Buki speculated—one of those ten lost tribes of Israel who had wandered to the subcontinent and gotten lost in this whorehouse. "You sure don't look Jewish," he suddenly heard himself blurt out.

She was not a Jewish, but the Jewish will be the winners in the end of days, that is what Muhammad always says, you just have to face it, nothing you can do about it, the Jewish are the children of apes and pigs but they will rule the whole world in the end, she would like to be a Jewish if he would be so kind. She went on in this way for a while until it suddenly dawned on Buki that she was speaking English. Where had she learned? From Muhammad's TV, she replied. Muhammad was her patron, the man who bought her virginity. He sent one of his Hindus to her town, Saundatti, to buy him a new devadasi virgin every year. A devadasi is very holy, they don't sell us to Muslims. He is very rich man, Muhammad, main man in Mumbai for Gulf States for buying and selling Indian slaves, Dalit men and women, boys and girls, but never devadasis. Devadasis he keeps for himself, private, until he stuffs them so full they are too fat to dance any more. Then byebye, finished with you, he dumps us here on Red Street, in Kamathipura. He is also very fat, Muhammad, more than one hundred kilos. When he is on top of you, you cannot breathe, all the air is coming out of your balloon. Sometimes he cuts with a razor blade, sometimes he burns with fire, sometimes he hits with a strap. There are marks on her body in places you could not see, she would show him for extra price. Soon I am going to buy your sister, Maha—Muhammad says this to her, many many times—I will buy her after her first period when they put her on sale, Mahahaha. If the priest got his dirty hands on her first I will return her, damaged goods, not like advertised. My name is Deva, if you wanted to know, my sister is Maha. I will tell you something big. They are going to steal everything you have, your hat, your coat, cut off your beard halfway and half the hair on your head and your two thumbs and your two big toes and strip you naked, they are going to beat you up and poke out your eyes and maybe kill you Mister Giant if you do not hurry, get out of here soon, soon, fast, very fast. But how will you get out of here? You do not know the way out. You need the help of the goddess. She would show him how to get out if he took her along, she would be his guide, but he must also swear—swear by Yellamma Renuka and also your Jewish God, Elohim, and also Allah—to take her to Saundatti in Karnataka after they escape and together they will kidnap her sister Maha from the temple. She will save his life today if he will pledge to save her sister tomorrow. Then they will all go together to where the Jewish are, and they will all be Jewishes together.

"But I came here to get me a Jewish girl to bring home to my guru. It's okay if she's not religious." Buki still could not let go, he did not like to fail.

"There is a madam," the girl finally offered. "The most mean, fat like an elephant. She is a Jewish, they say." Buki considered this option briefly. Rebbie-ji welcomed Jewish victims of all sizes and shapes and life experience to the House of Holy Healing, nobody was considered unworthy or a lost cause, in some select cases you didn't even have to be Jewish. Still, it might be too dangerous to tackle this one at this time. They could come back to get her later, with a battle plan, maybe a few men, take her out with a truck. The girl pulled the end of her sari over her face, and lowered her head.

"Are you telling me now there's not one single Jewish whore in this whole damn whorehouse?"

There was a long pause, and she lifted her head sharply. She had just remembered. Yes, two girls, very small, only four and five years old maybe, in cages, their virginity sold already many times, worth many lakhs of rupees, she had heard they were Jewishes, it would be very hard to save them, not possible.

"Let's go git 'em, girl. It's a major mitzvah."

Buki stood up in a flash, his head ramming against the ceiling, pancaking his Borsalino. He followed the girl's glance. She was staring forlornly at the door, locked from outside. "No problem, sister." One pull with his mighty hand, and it opened like a can of beer.

It was surprisingly easy to carry out this rescue, Buki commented to me soon after I had taken over the prepubescent pod, when he recounted the whole story as part of my orientation. At first their hearts were pounding, the girl's and his too he admitted. They would run a short distance, press themselves against a wall and take cover, poke their heads out cautiously to check if the coast was clear, then dart out again. Soon though, they realized nobody was around, it was midafternoon in India, the unforgiving heat of the day flattening everyone, they were all sleeping, recharging for a long night's work ahead. The few who were awake and might have noticed them must have concluded that it was nothing out of the ordinary—just another newly inducted devadasi whore following orders, leading an overgrown transgender or cross-dresser or other hormonally challenged type, maybe even a hijra eunuch, to whatever he was paying for.

Everyone was also fast asleep in the segregated area where they kept the youngest girls and babies in their cages, including the two little targets of their raid, as if a spell had been cast over the whole castle. Buki simply lifted them up and carried them off, careful not to disturb their sleep and startle them; they were almost two-dimensional, the only material weight was that of their wooden cages. They were wearing flounced synthetic chiffon-and-netting dresses in pinks and lavenders, tinseled ribbons in their hair, smears of glossy red lipstick, black kohl on their closed eyelids, gold-colored rings in their ears. Curled up in their cages they looked like tropical birds of many colors captured in the jungle.

The devadasi led him easily through the labyrinth of Kamathipura, following directions whispered into her ear by her inner goddess

GPS. They came out into the street where a black-and-yellow taxicab awaited them, as if hailed in advance by the good fairy. He did not even go back to the hotel to collect his things, including his precious sable *streimel* that added five inches to his height when he wore it on the Sabbath, and his cherished velvet bag containing his prayer shawl and phylacteries, trusting that a premium operation like the Taj would overnight it all exquisitely bubbled and bowed back to him in Kolkata. He ordered the driver to take them directly to the airport where he bought two first-class tickets from Mumbai to Kolkata, flying with the girl beside him in the window seat gazing out, marveling at the bed of clouds while gorging on peanuts and Coca Cola, and the two other little girls as his hand luggage stowed at his feet, their cages blanketed with his striped satin kaftan, the silver sheriff's badge prominently displayed.

"I'm sorry, but they don't look Jewish to me," Rebbie-ji concluded after a long silence, when Buki set them down still in their cages at his master's feet.

Nevertheless, he gave his permission for the two little girls to stay on for the interim at the House of Holy Healing until a suitable home could be found for them through Charlotte's benevolent intervention. It was an act of hessed; loving-kindness is not an exclusive commodity to be dispensed only to other Jews. He would call them Bilha and Zilpah, like the concubines of Jacob, and maybe when they got a little stronger they could help out around the ashram until their case was settled. In general, however, it would be preferable not to bring any more such unfortunates into the sanctuary of the House of Holy Healing, if Buki didn't mind, he should not take this as a criticism.

The devadasis, on the other hand, were another matter. True, they too were not Jewish, but they represented a feminine model for union with the divine so sorely missing in Jewish practice. We need our nuns, which is why it is permissible for us to squat here in the strict Mother's old convent still creaking with the agonies of the tortured Christian God, and we also need our devadasis. There was a great deal to be learned about divine female power from the devadasis through dance and other physical forms of worship. They are artists of spirituality.

Rebbie-ji charged Buki with the task of organizing a team to buy up as many devadasis as possible. Buki would have access to unlimited funds to purchase them when their virginity went up for sale, and bring them back to the House of Holy Healing. In the meantime, Rebbie-ji gave Buki his blessings as he set out the next morning to Karnataka to keep his word and rescue the sister of the devadasi who had saved his life, like Rahab the harlot.

It was an arduous journey from Kolkata to Saundatti the next day, Buki recalled, requiring two flights each way, and the exclusive full-time service of a taxi to bring them to their destination, and to wait for them in a designated spot for a quick turnaround and getaway. But that was the least of it. It was above all the emotional wear and tear. And the truth is, it would have been far more difficult, on the face of it, almost impossible, to execute this rescue without the help of the girl, the big sister, not only because she spoke Kannada, one of the babel of languages in the Indian loony bin, but also because this was a very inside job, and she was a supreme insider, she knew the territory, its map was scored with a blade on her brain. In the future, Buki assured me, acquiring more devadasis for Rebbie-ji will be a much more routine affair. He would take along one of their Indians, Mottel Patel-Aleph or Mottel Patel-Zayin, suitably costumed for the occasion, and simply buy a devadasi when a good one went on the market in the normal course of events. Price was no object, and it made no difference to them whatsoever if the priests had fooled around with her beforehand. She only had to meet Rebbie-ji's specifications for female spirituality insofar as they could determine this endowment from her outward appearance—and the Patel boys were true connoisseurs from their years in the motel business, sizing people up in a blink. If they found out later she wasn't a virgin, no big deal. They would not consider themselves to have been ripped off. Even the Virgin Mary wasn't a virgin, yet she still was good enough for the holy ghost.

When they arrived in Saundatti toward evening, the girl instructed the driver in their language to go directly to the Yellamma temple on a hill a few kilometers outside of town. Buki had offered her the opportunity to make a quick detour to say hi to her mom, but she shook off the suggestion with a shudder, as if it were a spider. It was already dark, but they could tell from a distance that some sort of ceremony was underway at the temple. Fires were burning and drums beating.

They made their way up the hill on foot. Beggars with stumps for limbs crawled around them on their bellies like worms. Women clutching naked babies turned their faces up to him, jabbing a finger into their mouths, miming hunger. Peddlers lined the path, hawking glass bangles, brass images of the goddess, peacock feathers, flower and food offerings. Every eye noted then dismissed them—a devadasi serving the goddess, leading by the hand a giant in a bizarre costume, an eccentric rich patron perhaps, or a pilgrim of no recognizable gender in a woman's long robe afflicted with a rare disorder, coming to petition the goddess for a cure. The air was ripe with the smell of turmeric and incense. As they entered the open courtyard of the temple where the rites were being enacted by the light of the fires, to the sounds of drums and bells and conches, a creature leapt out of the dark and emptied a pail of yellow powder on them. "Hey, watch it buddy!" Buki shot out as he attempted to wipe the stuff off his best kaftan and hat, but the girl dragged him away before he could teach the perpetrator some respect.

The same yellow powder completely coated the women dancing in the center of the courtyard as if they had been rolled in it—their hair, their faces, their arms, their saris. They were dancing in a frenzied state of total abandon and ecstasy, their arms grasping upward, their eyes sealed. They reminded Buki of Hasidim in rapturous bliss, blocking out from their consciousness the whole earthly scene, soaring as if in a trance, but he had never seen women in this state, he had believed they were not capable of it. They were channeling Yellamma, letting themselves be filled up by the goddess, their lover, their bridegroom, their husband. Devotees ran up to the bewitched dancers, tugging at their saris, dusted with yellow powder, urgently petitioning, supplicating desperately for the intervention of the goddess, then stuffing something in a hand that lowered from its exaltation to snatch the baksheesh. All around them children and young teenagers, mostly girls, danced completely naked or adorned here and there with the green leaves of a neem tree, and a sprig of neem in their mouths.

She spotted her sister instantly among these children, a lithe, heartbreaking fawn with dark eyes that seemed to have puddled over most of her face. You could see the resemblance, she too might have looked something like that before she had been sold and bought, though the child was blessed with a much fairer complexion, mocha latte—a different father for sure. She charged forward, scooped up her little sister, and hauled her back toward Buki so that they could make their escape, but the child managed to slither out of her arms and ran to one of the dancing women in the center of the ring, clutching her sari from which the yellow powder rained down over her velvety bare skin, crying, Ma, Ma, Ma. "Seems our girls come from a long line of devadasis, a very *yikhusdik* family, distinguished lineage, a dynasty like some of our top Chabad rabbis," Buki gave himself permission to interject; I chose not to respond. By then he was hovering over the family reunion, the huddle of devadasis, the mother devadasi and her two devadasi daughters, casting his large shadow over them, listening to their exchange though not understanding a word. The mother was raging that she no longer was receiving any money from her working-girl daughter, Buki learned afterward. The daughter announced that she had come to take the sister before the mother sold her too—or before the priests got their dirty hands on her. The mother let out a cackle, universal language that Buki comprehended, and spat out, Too late, ha ha. Her eye scanned Buki from head to toe, appraising his worth. She expected twice as much money now every month as it looked like her girls had snagged themselves a rajah, she screeched as she spread her wings and transported herself in a puff of mustard-colored smoke back into the inner circle of the goddess's handmaids, sorceresses, and oracles.

They left the temple precincts with the little girl carried by her big sister, tucked inside her sari like a baby marsupial, crying, Ma, Ma the whole way down the hill. She cried in the taxi on the long trip to the airport, and through both plane rides, all the way to Kolkata. She has been crying for her mother every day and night, Buki informed me. She misses the mother she has; you can't argue with that. They had gotten used to her crying, crying was the white noise in the House of Holy Healing, muting the screams of the slaughtered goats sacrificed instead of children in the temple of Mother Kali next door. Only recently they had noticed that the crying had died down, maybe even stopped, Buki said. They figured she simply had worn herself out and had given up. But then they made the connection that the change had coincided with my arrival in the pod. I had become her new maternal figure, bestowed on her by Rebbie-ji in his wisdom. I was Mother, the darkness of the all-encompassing and all-accepting embrace, and she was comforted.

Of all the devadasis who came and went over the next three years, leaving eighteen at the end like buboes on the wasted body of Rebbie-ji in his punishing pursuit of tikkun, the first two, Devamayi and Mahamaya, remained our favorites, our most beloved, my own and my brother's. He called them Shakti and Shekhina, drawing on his power to encapsulate in a name the essence of the soul. Thereafter, everyone in the House of Holy Healing was expected to refer to them by their true names, which Rebbie-ji had uncovered—Shakti for the creative female cosmic energy force of the goddess in Hinduism, Shekhina for the feminine aspect of the divine presence on earth as elaborated in the Jewish mystical texts. Rebbie-ji struggled every day for world repair not only through the male–female union of the divine feminine with the masculine godhead, but also through the universal sisterhood of those sacred attributes of feminine power in the teachings of both faiths.

He would summon the two girls to his suite, or stop by the pod, simply to delight in seeing them. He would stroke their silken black hair, ask them to perform a ritual dance or song for him, then as a reward draw the younger one up onto his lap as the older one was invited to push them in his wheelchair racing at top speed all around the ashram, all three of them shrieking hilariously as if they were riding the cyclone at a carnival. It was an immense privilege to see my brother Rebbie-ji playing again as we had played when we were children, to witness him setting down even for such a brief interval the heavy burdens he bore day and night for all of us. He deserved this small pleasure, no less than Gandhi-ji who had also sacrificed his health with all that marathon fasting and walking and so much more, and who had also enjoyed the company of young girls nearby to minister to his personal care before he was assassinated, and no one begrudged him either. The girls were a great comfort to Shmelke, he told me. They reminded him of his daughters whom he had not seen for so long, over the many years of his exile and flight, his nine daughters, my nieces, several of them, so far as I knew, already proper grandmothers.

Let us not invoke daughters. I implore you, Shmelke.

For my part, though, these two, our first best beloved devadasis, would always remain Devamayi and Mahamaya, and, whenever possible (preferably out of the hearing of others so as not to give the appearance of flouting my brother's ukase), I would call them by their true names—Devamayi, Mahamaya—in order not to traumatize them even more by cutting them off so radically from their roots, discarding even ownership of their given names.

But the truth is, my daily involvement with them and the pod was limited, my responsibilities did not permit me to interact with the devadasis full time or to keep on top of every detail of their lives. Sleeping in the pod was not for me a caregiving assignment. It was in reality another aspect of the austerities along with fasting, chanting, meditation and additional practices that I had taken upon myself in anticipation of the day when my brother no longer would need me and I could be released to set out as a sannyasini, emptying my life totally. My main duties were above all as Rebbie-ji's counselor and confidante, his chief of staff as it were. There was no one on earth he could trust more than me, his sister, his twin, his didi—his feminine emanation.

With regard to the prepubescent pod, I along with Rebbie-ji were of course the two major players in the making of the big decisions but not hands on in implementing them. That was left to Manika, she was the one who made things happen. It was she who managed its day-to-day operations, with the assistance of other low-caste Indians to carry out the menial work, sorely needed since the devadasi population at HHH was not only growing exponentially thanks to Buki's shopping sprees, but also turning over constantly. New girls were arriving all the time, old ones disappearing. One even gave birth at the ashram not long after she had been purchased, an eleven year old, though within a few weeks the baby swelled up, stopped feeding, and died. Three of the devadasis also sickened and died during the first year alone soon after they arrived, an unfortunate event that at the time some of us attributed to the occasional gifts of surplus prepackaged frozen kosher meals in compartmentalized aluminum foil trays shipped to us in trucks from the Goa Chabad.

It also became obvious as the pod took shape that the term *prepubescent* had become a misnomer, applicable in reality only to the divine nymph Mahamaya, whom Rebbie-ji called Shekhina. All the other girls were acquired post the curse of their first period, which is what put them on the block in the first place where they caught Buki's eye—and all without exception were illiterate. Manika came to us one day to make the case that the girls be taught how to read without delay, while the window of opportunity was still open, when the mind is still malleable and can still absorb new skills. It did not escape me that she was flattering herself while petitioning us, as she had picked up her reading skills in several languages in no time even at an advanced age. She threw me a complicit glance as she bent down to touch Shmelke's feet, muttering that the reading lessons I had arranged for her were the best gift she had ever received, there was no way she could ever repay me. "And your mouth is full of teeth," Rebbie-ji in his wisdom pronounced cryptically, in this way reminding her of another gift I had given her and what else she owed me while at the same time gently indicating that he appreciated the fox-like cunning of her manipulations since they were clearly meant to benefit the girls—and promptly he put her in charge of organizing the reading program.

She set to work at once, recruiting as teachers foreign volunteers, mostly women seekers passing through for longer or shorter stays.

A gratifying number of these souls were soon caught up in Rebbie-ji's irresistibly powerful mystical aura, some returning to the faith if they were already Jewish, others going to even greater extremes and converting if they were not, after which they were quickly married off to one of his eligible detoxed Hasidim, horrifying their families back home who were convinced they had been brainwashed by a cult. Yet others, Jews and non-Jews, used their community service and internships as reading tutors to the devadasis as the topic of their college admission essays or for other applications, with nearly universal acceptance even to the most competitive schools and programs. Not a single one of them emerged unchanged in some way, inwardly or externally, from their exposure to my brother, Shmelke.

English, naturally, was the chosen tongue for the reading lessons. It was in any case the lingua franca of most of the travelers and even as it happened of many of the devadasis, who came to us already possessing a selective English vocabulary, limited mostly to sex and prices for services. Whatever the language, though, knowing how to read could only benefit our devadasis in the long term, Shmelke and I concluded. Even if they chose ultimately to return to a career in prostitution, which we accepted as their inalienable right, at the very least they could parlay their literacy to become effective spokespersons for the rights of sex workers.

Our gem, our Manika, as I knew so well from my own personal experience, was simply a natural born manager, a quality that Shmelke had also very quickly picked up on even before I awoke to find myself in the House of Holy Healing crying out from the depths, despairing beyond words that I was still in this world. Within a few weeks she was supervising the entire HHH infrastructure, not only the care of the devadasis and their literacy program, but also the kitchen and all the services, including the hospitality end, accommodations for seekers and pilgrims and so on, and overseeing the dark-skinned workers, Bengalis, as well as Bangladeshi and Tibetan and Nepali refugees, along with the fair-skinned wives of Rebbie-ji's Hasidim who were responsible for the cooking and meal preparation to guarantee the kashrut level. Even they set aside their pride and sense of entitlement, and deferred to Manika's executive authority. She was in charge of the laundry and cleaning staff, the maintenance of the entire macro-enterprise, heat and light, but under no circumstances did she neglect the micro side either. With exceptional tenderness, she looked after the old lady shriveling up in the bed in Rebbie-ji's suite, neither living or dead, flipping her over like a latke several times a day to prevent bedsores, dribbling sugar water into her ulcerated mouth with a tea-spoon, extracting long green strings of gunk from her throat. She also took exemplary care of my brother and me, if for no other reason than to honor our mother, whom she loved beyond measure, and whose picture she kept in her room, the centerpiece of a small altar shrine decorated with garlands of marigolds and votive candles, doing puja there every day with offerings of flowers and the sweets so hard to find in India that she knew Ma could never resist, chocolate kisses and licorice twists.

The suffering of my soul had spread to my body. The fasting I had taken on three days a week as a form of ascetic practice was eating me up. My appetite for nourishment as for everything else in this life for-sook me. Finally I was as skinny as I had ached to be all my years, but there was no satisfaction in it now. My stomach twisted in pain, I sat on the toilet and poured out my guts like water against the face of the Lord before whose seat of glory every orifice is open. Manika herself administered ayurvedic *panchakarma* therapy to detoxify and purify me, massaging, oiling, brewing, cleansing with herbal remedies, nag-ging me until I submitted. I had not properly metabolized my sorrow and sadness, she said, it had spread to my entire system and poisoned it, I was completely out of balance, body and soul.

Manika also saw to it that my brother, Shmelke, was properly cared for, especially in matters of personal hygiene pertaining to his paralyzed lower body, which he could not attend to himself but which was so crucial in preventing infection in that vulnerable area so prone to contamination, and ensuring overall health and a long life. Toward that end, and in line with her conviction that the devadasis should not be lounging around all day in idleness except for their reading lessons, she received permission to create and strictly enforce a schedule—two girls in the morning, two in the evening dispatched to Rebbie-ji to perform the needed tasks gently, respectfully, with dignity. Only the pretty ones, please, Shmelke had said with such an endearingly innocent smile. But whoever showed up, he wasn't complaining, though he did put in a request for Shakti and Shekhina as often as possible, they were his preferred personal handlers.

Until then this intimate service had been carried out cheerfully and competently by a Filipino convert named Jerry, short for Jericho, who had been working in Israel as a *metapel*, taking care of a senior citizen rabbi in Jerusalem. He had come under my brother's influence after having had the good fortune to be in the path of Shmelke's inner circle racing in the night to the graves of the righteous, and as if struck by the hand of God instead of a motorcycle, had become a Hasid himself after he recovered, following my brother into exile.

The truth is, Jerry was not only stronger, but also far more adept and efficient than the devadasis in doing what was needed for Shmelke's personal physical maintenance, but the aging of his own parents required his return to Manila in compliance with the fifth commandment of the Torah, to honor your father and mother, whose suffering I had heard was mercifully cut short when they expired soon after Jerry's arrival, most likely from shock the instant they laid eyes on their son again after so many years in his beard and sidelocks and full Hasidic regalia. My poor afflicted brother did not seem to mind the changing of the guard however. He looked forward to the girls' ministrations however clumsy, he tolerated with good humor their fumbling and ineptness, he gave himself permission to relax and enjoy. The girls, even the not so pretty ones, were still so young and fresh, they smelled so sweet, their hands were so soft.

Manika is also the genius who deserves the credit for coming up with the idea of a devadasi dance program that for a period of time turned the House of Holy Healing into the go-to place on the entire subcontinent for female empowerment through movement. The girls were always practicing their intricate dance steps in the pod, and naturally

Manika, who missed nothing, took note of this. In typical fashion, never wasting a thing, not a single grain of rice, not a rag, not a clump of dung, the righteous Western innovations of recycling and sustainability coded into her Indian DNA from prehistory, she pondered how to make the best and most constructive use of these unique and in truth dying skills in the interest of the community at large.

She called me over one day to watch as a few of the girls were engaging in one of their favorite pastimes—a contest of nonstop rhythmic foot movements of infinitely subtle refinement. The winner was the one who could make the fewest jingling sounds with her anklets studded with bells. She proposed that I broach the idea with my brother of opening a dance studio at the House of Holy Healing for the sake of bringing in some income independent of donors, and not least, raising the self-esteem of the girls who would serve as the instructors, giving them a sense of pride and purpose, compensating them through this public appreciation of their gift and skills for all the ways in which they had been humiliated and discarded. The idea reminded her of the compost toilets she had emptied during her time at Ammachi's ashram, Manika remarked—taking a thing that stinks to high heaven and turning it into something that makes the flowers bloom under the sun.

Shmelke was receptive to the suggestion. We had several intense discussions on the matter. The biggest stumbling block for him was that most of the classic dance routines as far as he could ascertain included devotional worship of the idols, Kali, Shiva, Ganesha, Yellamma, the whole wild polytheistic gang of divine thuggees and goondas and dacoits. At first he rationalized that it was only art anyway, so it didn't really matter. Still, it was a problem. In the end, he ruled that this glut of Hindu deities were in reality aspects of one God, like the ten kabbalistic emanations of the *sefirot* comprising the single God of the Jewish people. Faiths evolved, they bled into each other, they dialogued with each other, they impacted each other, they took from each other whether they realized it or not, to the enrichment of all. And as a bonus, from the practical side, the wives of his Hasidim who would also be learning these movements in the dance classes could then bring them home to their bedrooms. This could only contribute to peace on the home front, Rebbie-ji pointed out. Anything that contributed to *shalom bayit* may be considered to be the highest form of mitzvah.

This was Rebbie-ji's reasoning, his responsum, and he put his stamp of approval on the dance studio, provided it be limited to women only. He called it Devadasi Yoga, and in a stunningly brief period of time it became a legendary success with a huge following, not only among the wives and daughters and occasional mothers and grandmothers of my brother's Hasidim, but also the expat community, travelers and seekers coming through, as well as the upscale and wealthy local Bengalis, of whom there were still surprisingly quite a number, notwithstanding the general decline of the city and the tourist attraction eyesore of the wreckage of humanity sleeping and defecating in the streets. The demand was tremendous. More and more classes had to be added to accommodate applicants, everyone was clamoring to get a spot in the program, it was the hottest new thing in town. Devadasi jewelry and ornamentation became the rage, headdresses, belts, earrings, bangles and bell anklets ecumenically decorated with little gold encrusted Indian swastikas and Stars of David.

Men were not only banned from participating in the classes, they were also forbidden to observe. This restriction did not apply to my brother, however, who was, after all, not only a rabbi, which is something like a doctor, a trained professional licensed to see it all, but he was also a martyr and saint who carried the sins of all humankind in his desiccated, out-of-commission lower quarters. As master of the domain, he asserted his rights and came out often, several times a day, to sit and watch with full entitlement. It was for me one of my most personal delights to crouch in a corner, doing my utmost to render myself invisible, and watch my brother watching. He radiated ultimate pleasure, swept up by the pure grace of the complex ritual gestures of hands and feet, the sinuous flow of the body defined by the waist like a vessel that could be grasped for pouring, the artful poses of the head, the flirtatious side-glances of the eyes. They were meant to be dancing for the gods, the devadasis, but I knew very well that Shmelke believed they were dancing for him alone. I watched him nodding his head to the beat of a small band of drummers and bamboo flute players or the a cappella of an impromptu group of devadasi singers, or to music streaming from a computer, stiffening sympathetically with the dancers as they froze into a statuesque posture, becoming once again the little boy I had grown up with as he breathlessly followed a story unfolding through dance, always a sad tale, a tale of heartache, love spurned, love forbidden, love lost, and more than once I saw tears slipping down his cheeks into his white beard.

I looked at my brother, Shmelke, and saw the florid rash near his mouth showing through under his beard where the tears had landed. His beard, once so rich, so patriarchal, had grown sparse—when did this creep up on him? He had been put through so much, more than any single human being had ever been meant to endure, it was no wonder he was in such a weakened and vulnerable state, so susceptible to the invisible pathogens lurking in the atmosphere. He had become so thin, taking up so much less space in his wheelchair. Every few minutes he was clearing his throat of a thick mucus, or covering his mouth, trying to suppress a cough, and I could see the sores on the back of his hand. I pleaded with him to let me bring in a doctor, but he refused with unrestrained fury, so uncharacteristic in his dealings with me. This is the House of Holy Healing, he reminded me—and if there's no healing, then we can always go back to hospice mode.

A hospice for the dying, of course, that's what this place was and that's what in the end it would always be, contaminated by that grim reaper Mother Teresa and her lepers—it explained everything. Our living quarters were infested with plague and disease. It was Charlotte's fault completely. So efficient, so famously in control, and yet she had never taken the obvious precautions, never bothered to have the premises checked out, fumigated, disinfected, sterilized, as if our kind were not worth the extra expenditure of mental or material resources. The great gift she had bestowed upon my brother with such fanfare and noblesse oblige was nothing but a sick building, sickening everyone who dwelt within its confines. I too was feeling unwell, contorted with bowel pain, canker sores in my mouth, my ankles swollen. Until my brother with his divine insight connected it all for me to the hospice, Charlotte's gift, I had attributed my own physical symptoms to my unspeakable losses, aggravated by my ascetic practice.

Others too who spent time in this former hospice were showing signs of illness, including some of Rebbe-ji's followers from his inner circle, which they then went home to spread to their wives. The devadasis were also presenting with all kinds of physical complaints, to lesser or greater degrees, among them a new girl who was found dead one morning on her soaked sheet. Even Buki, a giant of a man, seemed diminished—fading, shrinking, his face puffy and blotched, his eyes red and swollen, his swagger lost. We assumed these changes were due to exhaustion from his nonstop travels, his constant grueling trips across the breast of Mother India from Kolkata to Maharashtra and Karnataka and back to save devadasis, taking along with him the Patels, Aleph and Zayin, along with Devamayi/Shakti after all, because of her indispensable insider's knowledge of the workings of the temples and the brothels, and her cleverness and boldness in negotiating them. Devamayi too we noticed was coughing continuously, she seemed unable to shake a flu of some sort, though her little sister, Mahamaya, whom Rebbie-ji called Shekhina, appeared blessedly immune to the toxins that seeped through the walls of our building, she floated like an angel above us all in pure air, possessed of a kind of divine exceptionalism. If ever she had been gripped by whatever this affliction was, she had gotten rid of it through the act of giving it to someone else, which made complete sense. Manika also was largely untouched, seamlessly adding to her daily labors the care of the sick and the sweeping up of the rats that staggered out of the walls, turned belly up on the open floor, and expired.

Why should all this sickness surprise you? Shmelke demanded to know. Was he not the gilgul of Rabbi Nahman of Bratslav, and did not Rabbi Nahman also have to deal with so many health issues in his lifetime, such a weight of mortality—the death in infancy of two daughters, the death in their first years of life of his only two sons leaving him no male heir to carry on the dynasty, his first wife's death from tuberculosis, and then his own death, also from tuberculosis, at the age of thirty-eight? Rabbi Nahman lived in a house of death too, his home was a hospice that he transformed into a house of holy healing with his divine powers, through stories and music and dance, deploying his spiritual art to erase the tears from every face.

During this period, the darshan that Rebbie-ji gave daily to his followers seated on the floor before him in the great common ward always began with this focus on himself in his prior incarnation as Rabbi Nahman of Bratslav. For that reason alone it was explosively heretical, but what he revealed about himself in his former embodiment made it even more so. I was the only woman present to hear his darshan (this is how he referred to his appearances in deference to his status among the gurus of his host country), curled up in the fetal position behind a screen, I who had spent nine months alone with him naked in the same womb, which is why I am able to transcribe his words as Rabbi Nosson of Nemirov transcribed the teachings of the original Rabbi Nahman.

Rebbie-ji admitted that even then, more than two hundred years ago in the personification of Rabbi Nahman, he had already been a universalist, borrowing from other traditions and faiths, advocating openness and inclusiveness. His signature concepts of seeking out solitude and immersion in nature—these he had inhaled like a drug from the Romantic movement in the arts bouncing on the airwaves across Europe and Asia, from Byron to Pushkin, then down to him in the pits of Ukraine. Confession, needless to say, he stole from the Christians.

Even more shockingly, he confirmed certain rumors about himself in his previous life as Rabbi Nahman that had been circulating for over two centuries but had never before been definitively verified. It is true, he admitted, that in his travels as Rabbi Nahman, when he had stopped in Istanbul, he had shaved off his beard and sidelocks with a razor, and yes, even removed his yarmulke and gone around bareheaded, yes, even without a head covering he had frequented the opium dens and the Turkish bordellos, where they specialized in a very rare form of sadism from which he still shamefully carried the scars, like a tattoo carved into his flesh, an ineradicable reminder of his erotic debasement. At home in Uman he would also on occasion in those days as Rabbi Nahman set out in disguise to the underworld of sin and pollution and immerse himself in the forbidden as in a ritual bath filled with black water in which the divine sparks scattered during the fall from paradise had sunk. This is why, in case any of his followers had ever wondered, he has never, as Rebbie-ji, condemned those pilgrims to his gravesite on Rosh Hashanah who may be emulating him even without full awareness, by seeking redemption through transgression. Over two centuries ago in his incarnation as Rabbi Nahman and now in the new millennium first as Reb Breslov and then as Rebbie-ji, in Israel and in exile, he had sacrificed himself, the health of his body and soul, in the performance of tikkun to bring about the messianic age by plunging to the lowest depths to retrieve the lost light of creation. But by no means were his followers to conflate his acts of sacred depravity with the corruption of such false messiahs as Shabbtai Tzvi and Jacob Frank, who were nothing but dissolute con-men and degenerate seducers, Rebbie-ji cautioned severely. "I am *not* the *false* messiah," my brother, Shmelke, enunciated, vocally italicizing the key words. His Hasidim instantly got it, and were awestricken. From behind the screen I too was shaken, torn loose.

As if all of this were not mind-blowing enough, my brother, Rebbie-ji, then proceeded to come out with perhaps an even more stunning revelation. Between his incarnation as Rabbi Nahman of Bratslav and his present embodiment as Rebbie-ji, he informed us, he had also appeared for fifty years on this earth as the Bengali Brahmin mystic Sri Ramakrishna Paramahamsa of India. He was not only Nahman's gilgul, he was also Ramakrishna's gilgul. This revelation illuminated many hitherto hidden mysteries, including why Rebbie-ji's feet, so to speak, led him back to Kolkata as if on their own, without regard to his personal free will. Everything now became clear. And as in the days when he had walked the earth as Ramakrishna, now as Rebbie-ji he was again following the painfully difficult path of left-handed tantric teachings, breaking down all the barriers between the sacred and the profane in every realm, including forbidden carnal temptations, food, drink, sex, all of the base appetites in order to transcend them, to see the face of the goddess in all things and realize the exaltation of the cosmic mother. Just as in his Ramakrishna incarnation he had embraced Shakti, the primal female energy source, the active principle, the root of all creation and creativity, now as Rebbie-ji he opened his arms even wider to also include in his embrace Shekhina, the feminine aspect of the divine presence on earth, as a child embraces his mother. His openness as Rebbie-ji to the wisdom and sacredness of all faiths was no different now than in the days when as Ramakrishna he had made his devotions not only as a Hindu, but also as a Buddhist, a Muslim, a Christian, with the difference that as Rebbie-ji, he also worshipped as a Jew.

When I walked the earth as Sri Ramakrishna, I had lost contact with my prior life, my roots as the Jew Rabbi Nahman, Rebbie-ji revealed. As Ramakrishna I would perform the tantra discipline of sitting for hours meditating on Mother Kali, the chant, *Om Kali Ma*, fusing with my breathing. I would sit in the cremation grounds and see her ferocious image with tongue lolling down and her bloody garland of fifty severed heads. I would sit on the banks of the Ganges and see her emerge from the river, open her legs and give birth to me, lift me in her arms and nurse me so tenderly at her blue-black breast. Then she opened her mouth and ate me. Brokenhearted and weeping, plunged into darkness, I despaired that I would never see the face of my mother again. Only then, when I had reached the lowest depths, did she take pity on me and spit me out. Mother, I cried, my good mother—stay. She was the divine mother, absolute consciousness. I knew only joy then, I did not know from Jews. How delicious it was to be rid of this Jewish burden for just one lifetime, a reprieve, but it could not last forever, something would rise up from the depths to engulf me or drop down on my head from the heights to crush me, and I would be forced back again to my place in the world.

Now as Rebbie-ji, his journey had taken him back Kolkata, to the territory of his past life as Ramakrishna, to this former Christian hospice of the saint Mother Teresa alongside the Hindu temple of the goddess Mother Kali (the two witches, as he called them, but privately, for my ears only). It was all for a purpose: to restore the Jew into the mix where we rightfully belong. Our numbers may not be many, but our voices are loud, we give the impression that there are a lot more of us than actually swarm on the earth. We Jews are the kundalini of faiths, coiled up at the root like a snake waiting for the awakening of all the chakra centers, when all will bow down and acknowledge us as the source. Thanks to our ministrations, our devadasi dancers within these walls have now absorbed all religions, Rebbie-ji declared, our devadasis are the fusion of faiths—Hindu girls sold to Muslims rescued by Jews sheltered in a former Christian hospice, and so on, with other assorted pluralistic variations on the theme flowing from their diverse individual stories.

For these reasons, Rebbie-ji announced, as a teaching in universalism, and to honor the divine cosmic mother, and as a way of showing his gratitude to Mother India for taking him in, for extending sanctuary and hospitality to him in his hour of need, he intended to bring the devadasis out of the closet, out of the House of Holy Healing to the temple of Kali Ma, creator, preserver, destroyer—not as human sacrifices, God forbid, but as a gesture of inclusion and goodwill, a form of outreach even to the heart of idolatry, a model of tolerance and interfaith dialogue. And just in case any of us was concerned, he was here to inform us that there was no danger at all in introducing these quasi-Judeo/Christian/Muslim/Hindu girls onto the incendiary temple grounds. No one would be offended. Everything has been arranged. He had already spoken to Charlotte, who has worked it all out with the chief rabbis of the property, the noble Haldar clan, the owners and priests of the compound for generations. Opening up their precious venue for a harmless little dance recital by our girls will be well worth their while, Rebbie-ji assured us. Charlotte absolutely loved the idea, she was wildly enthusiastic, she proudly claimed it had been inspired by the success of her own band, Lakshmi and the Survivors, she considered it a compliment, a personal tribute, she took full credit, backing it 100 percent and opening wide her purse, cost was no object. A protected space would be cleared in the temple courtyard in which the girls would dance, it was all under control, Rebbie-ji assured us. Our devadasis would no longer be hidden away from the eyes of men or anyone else, they had too much to contribute to the spiritual enlightenment of humankind.

Rebbie-ji thereupon gave the order to ready a troupe of devadasi dancers and musicians, our best and our brightest, to be brought out to perform in the Kalighat Kali temple the next day, raising his voice and pitching it in my direction where I was uncurling behind the partition no longer alone, Manika had slipped in as smoothly as a midwife.

There were eighteen devadasis in the pod that night, including Mahamaya, who over the course of those three years had always remained the youngest, the pampered darling, the pet. Every one of them felt the momentousness of the occasion. They swelled with a sense of purpose and importance, setting aside all other concerns, overcoming simple weariness to prepare for the coming day. The light in the pod burned through the night, we were under such pressure; it was only by a miracle that we were spared a blackout on this night of all nights. No one slept. The girls spent the hours working out the program entirely on their own in a heartwarming spirit of cooperation and generosity, forming smaller and larger troupes and ensembles of dancers and musicians, distributing parts to everyone according to their gifts, no one was excluded, choosing soloists for their skill and also their stamina and stage presence, making the arrangements with open hearts, for the good of all, untainted by pettiness or envy.

The goddess Yellamma, the kindly mother who blesses the faithful and to whom they had been dedicated for life was an aspect of Kali, yet not a single one of them had ever stepped into the temple next door to do puja. They seldom left the House of Holy Healing, and certainly never unescorted, it was against the rules as set down by Rebbie-ji. A few remained too weak or sickly throughout their stay at the ashram, rising from their beds with difficulty, and the schedules of the stronger ones were packed with dance classes to be taught, reading lessons, and other constructive self-improvement activities leaving little time in the daylight hours for anything else. Outside the walls of the hospice the frenzy of the city and of that neighborhood in particular was alarming even for the bravest of these village girls, and the shrill screams of the beasts being butchered next door filled them with dread, but now they would set out under protection to display their art, to honor Yellamma, to bring recognition to Shakti and Shekhina as well, as their guru, Rebbie-ji, had taught them, and they were throbbing with excitement.

Manika and I spent the night sorting out their costumes. There was general consensus not to go forth in the classic devadasi outfits, which we all agreed might be too provocative for the setting and the occasion; the girls would look like belly dancers to ignorant eyes, like prostitutes to dirty minds. We approved all their devadasi ornaments and cosmetics, however, after a delegation led by Devamayi came forward to make the case to us that these were necessary, the bells and the bangles, the kohl and the vermillion, it would be impossible to go on before an audience without them, they were the tools of their trade. Devamayi was the oldest of the devadasis, recognized as their natural leader and spokesperson, and we trusted her judgment.

But following Rebbie-ji's mandate, it seemed to us that the costumes should in some way combine visual elements of several faiths, a delicate harmony very difficult to achieve in any sphere including fashion. The Hindu side was now covered with the trinkets and the paint, we decided. Devamayi then produced from somewhere in the former Christian hospice a stash of white saris with a blue border stripe, leftover habits of Mother Teresa and her nuns. It would be far from easy to dance in these shrouds, they were by no stretch garments meant for dancing, it would be almost impossible to see, let alone appreciate the complex artistic movements of the feet, the legs, the torso, but in the end we decided this form of dress was appropriately modest and sufficiently effective in delivering the ecumenical message, it would do the job. A devadasi was a kind of nun, after all, or put another way, a nun was a variation on a devadasi: each was married to a god or a goddess, depending on sexual preference and orientation; each had taken herself out of circulation and been declared off-limits to mortal men;

each was a form of erotic expression, which seemed to be the only career path fantasy would permit for women in religion, yet both, as Rebbie-ji liked to point out, represented in the end a noble and generous attempt, however mean and constrained, to provide women with a spiritual outlet, so flagrantly and totally lacking in Judaism. There was much to be learned from this, Rebbie-ji said, it would not hurt us to look beyond the chosenness of our big Jewish noses and pay attention.

That took care of the Christian side, leaving the other two main contenders still to be dealt with, the Muslims and the Jews. My suggestion of a hijab was instantly rejected. First of all, it definitely wouldn't go with the saris, which could in any case be extended by the pallu into its own built-in head covering. But above all, it was entirely in conflict with the entire aesthetic of the dance, it would confine the head and restrict its movements as if it were mummified in a bandage, it would ruin the whole effect, Devamayi sensibly noted. It was decided then to omit any direct reference to Islam, since either way, inclusion or exclusion, the Muslims would not be satisfied, they would take offense, fly into a rage, anything was possible, including a full-scale riot or massacre. As for the Jewish component, we determined that it would be sufficiently represented by our escorts to the temple grounds, Rebbie-ji and a band of his followers in their stereotypical Semitic garb. In any event, Jews do not believe in images, either to project or to worship. We reject any help we can get to reach the level of faith. It is a crutch, we spurn it.

As it happened, though, Rebbie-ji was unable to join us at the temple the next day, he was shaking with fever. He remained in his suite with Devamayi/Shakti to keep him warm. Buki, his chief minister, who was also ailing, stayed back as well, looking after them both. My brother, Shmelke, had requested at first that Mahamaya/Shekhina remain with him, but the child pleaded desperately to be allowed to come along with us for the show, her beautiful big eyes glistening with tears, she was wild with excitement, and in the end my brother who could refuse her nothing allowed her to go, settling meanwhile for the older and darker sister.

With a band of Rebbie-ji's Hasidim in our train keeping a proper distance behind us, Manika and I led the devadasis in their Mother Teresa nun habits, their jewels and makeup, on the short walk from the House of Holy Healing to the Kali temple. The moment we stepped outside it was as if a curtain lifted on another planet, swirling with color, pulsing with movement and noise. Along the way hustlers were planting themselves in the paths of tourists, pressing to serve as guides into the sacred precincts, fake priests demanded a nonexistent price of admission, beggars and pickpockets pushed against the mass of bodies, hawkers touted all kinds of supplies for the goddess, wreaths of red hibiscus, offerings of sweets and incense.

The girls made their way slowly, dragging their feet, wide eyed, especially transfixed by images of Kali Ma made up of strips of plastic that they could angle to morph into the image of Mother Teresa, pausing at these displays to jiggle them endlessly. They could have played with these novelties all day long, flicking them back and forth between the faces of the two weird sisters, ultimately one and the same, made out of the same stuff, until it became necessary for Manika and me to assert our authority to get the show on the road. Yet even in the midst of all this turmoil, with all of its stops and distractions, a path almost magically was cleared for us as we proceeded. We moved ahead unimpeded like guests of honor before whom a red carpet was unfurling. I don't know how Charlotte accomplished it, but it could not have been cheap.

A space had also been cleared for us in the central courtyard inside the temple grounds. It was late morning when we arrived, the optimal time as we had been advised by our high-level temple contacts—not yet in the heat of the day and therefore the audience would be sizable, but above all before two in the afternoon when the Kali Ma viewing area would be closed and the compound would empty out so that the goddess could have a chance to eat her lunch of freshly killed goat meat in peace, followed by a pleasant, well-deserved afternoon nap on a full stomach. Our devadasis were immediately directed to the center of the courtyard. They began to dance almost at once, like true professionals, to the accompaniment of their own singers joined by two men, naked except for their blood-spattered lungis, who had stepped out of the animal sacrifice quarter with their instruments to jam with our musicians, having finished their morning's work of banging out a drumroll each time a goat was beheaded with a single stroke of a sword.

We stationed ourselves on opposite sides of our dancers, Manika and I, in order to keep a close watch on them and alert officials if we happened to observe anything unusual or threatening. The program was proceeding exactly as rehearsed, Mahamaya's solo was especially enchanting, and the large audience that had gathered was clapping rhythmically, their faces ridiculously stretched into smiles even unbeknownst to themselves. There were some occasional murmurings, some questioning could be heard as to who we were and whether this dancing was a sacrilege or a mockery of some sort, an alien form of worship impermissible on these holy grounds, whether it represented an attempt to take over the temple by some menacing rival religion, but any sudden or untoward movement was swiftly detected and squelched by the alert guards.

I could see that matters were under control. I felt I could allow myself to relax for a minute, give myself permission to turn my head and look toward the sanctum sanctorum where the Kali idol sat on her throne in splendor across the pavilion directly opposite from where I was positioned. I had a clear view of her black stone face, her three eyes, her four arms, her long tongue hanging down wrought from gold, I could see the crowd of worshippers performing their puja, circling her bearing gifts along the pathway of the viewing area, human traffic propelled expertly in the desired direction, a commendable and sophisticated example of crowd control devised well before it had become a science. On the perimeter of the courtyard, away from our circle of dancers, devotees were sitting cross-legged on the floor in meditation, chanting mantras. Fire rituals were being enacted against the walls. A naked *tantrika* smeared with ash jerked toward me, moving in too close, holding a skull filled with blood, tipping it toward my lips, drink, drink, he was urging me to drink.

A spell of dizziness swept over me, I felt as if I were reeling, I was overcome with nausea, I thought I might collapse, so that for a bracketed space of time I must have lost my bearings and could not precisely follow the swift unfolding of events. It was as if I were a young girl again in Brooklyn at a wedding or holiday celebration, dancing sedately in a circle with the women when a mass of men charged forward to lay claim to our floor space, forcing us to retreat, to scurry to the sidelines, pushing us against the wall as they took control of the center.

Rebbie-ji's Hasidim had displaced our devadasis. They were circling ecstatically in the center of the courtyard, stamping their feet, crying out at the top of their voices in rhythmic song their longing for Nah-Nah-Nahman from Uman, rapturously extolling the great mitzvah of remaining perpetually in a blissed-out state. They succeeded in carrying on their wild dance unmolested far longer than anyone other than persons maddened with faith would have anticipated possible, while officials, in uniform and plain clothes, huddled all around trying to figure out if this was part of the program too, if this trancelike whirling was also something that the stupendously rich memsahib had paid for. It took a single cry from a voice in the crowd—Musalmans!— and everything became electrified, as if a fire had broken out in the theater and lit it up, unleashing the panic coiled up in wait just below the surface. For what else could these strange extreme creatures be spinning fanatically but another species of Muslim dervishes desecrating their Hindu place of worship yet again, attempting once again to blow up their gods and take over their temple mount? The gates to the Kali viewing area slammed shut. Loose objects began to fly—stones, shoes, coconuts, candles, animal entrails, balls of congealed blood mixed with incense and excrement from the goat pen, people were running frantically in every direction, some struggling to escape, others falling murderously upon each other, guards were swinging their lathis, there was screaming, crying, human and animal, I cast my eyes over the chaos searching for my devadasis, but could make nothing out in the masses writhing like worms under a canopy of white smoke.

The surging throng pushed me out of its path, to a corner near the opening to the chamber where the goats were sacrificed. Someone ran past me with Mahamaya under one arm, he was kidnapping her. Her legs were flailing, her arms fluttering, she was howling. He entered the sacrificial space, set the girl down between the two posts planted in the ground where the goats were positioned, and clamped her head in place. Laughing hideously, he raised a sword to bring it down in a single stroke on her outstretched neck—loosening everything inside me. I was spurting out vomit in great painful heaves. Emptied, hollowed—and then I must have passed out.

When I opened my eyes again in a strange white cell, I did not know how many hours or days or years later, Manika was sitting on her haunches against the wall opposite my bed, her chin propped on her knees, the end of her sari drawn forward over her head like a cowl. Geeta saved her, she said. Geeta came down from Delhi to take the child away to her exclusive orphanage.

I did not probe. She had contacted Geeta, she had sold her again.

I inspected my body. There were needles in my arm attached to plastic tubes hanging from a metal pole on wheels. From between my legs a tube extended, ending in a clear plastic bag filled with yellow liquid. Another plastic bag ballooning with what looked like a thick brown lentil soup was lying on the floor nearly bursting, attached to a tube that came out of a hole slightly northwest of my umbilicus that had once attached me to my mother.

It is an autoimmune disease, a medical attendant in a white sari with a blue stripe informed me, inflammatory bowel, Cohn's disease, a notably Jewish affliction, she added, looking at me meaningfully, Ashkenazi Jewish, like my mother's gefilte-fish cancer. My intestines were destroyed, nonfunctional, rotted away. That is why I was vomiting—my mouth was my only outlet. They had been forced to perform emergency surgery on me to create a bypass. Henceforth my waste matter will be detoured through the hole they had created at my midriff, it will come out of the tail of my small intestine now sticking out of that hole with lips hardening into an alternative anus and collect in a bag that will fit very neatly in the space under my sari blouse.

Ma, see what you have done to me!

So that is what has been going around in the House of Holy Healing. Everything was clarified—a plumbing backup, sickening everyone.

No, she said, those patients have been infected with something else. Your punishment is autoimmune, you did it to yourself, it is your own fault entirely, you have been peeling off the lining of your own gut and squeezing it out into the toilet, you have been eating yourself up alive. The other inmates at the hospice for the dying have a different disease, contracted from mixing their fluids with the libations of the temple girls, the devadasis are all positive.

Positive? Positive is good, positive is—positive.

No, she said, positive in the House of Holy Healing is negative—it is lethal, a virus, plague. They are all terminal.

Rebbie-ji, my brother, made his final darshan on the night of the fire. He was curled up in a corner of his wheelchair, pitifully frail, skeletal, swaddled in blankets and shawls pulled over his head like the angel of death to conceal as much as possible the purple blotches that had erupted on his skin. Buki ben Yogli, slumping over the handlebars of the chair, had pushed him out of his private quarters into the great communal ward packed with his followers, among them also the wounded warriors, survivors and heroes of the anti-Semitic riot at the Kali temple with bandaged heads, arms in slings, on crutches, some also in wheelchairs like their master himself. Women also came out that night, sensing the weight of the occasion, willingly taking their places behind the partition, desiring to pay homage to the holy man their guru who had endured such agonies on their behalf and whom they sensed was now being recalled from this mortal travail to enter a phase of concealment in advance of coming out of the closet as the one we all await. A special alcove completely enclosed was set aside for me due to the impurity I now was carrying in a bag attached to the outside of my body, instead of hidden internally packed away in my bowels like everyone else. Manika and the devadasis, and every other outcast untouchable disease carrier, were also invited to join me in my quarantine isolation booth.

The electrical power had failed again, and the entire ward was illuminated with flickering lights from the memorial candles set out that we always bought in bulk. The weight of parting pressed down on everyone assembled there that night, yet Rebbie-ji, my brother, when he spoke briefly, as if for himself alone, in a voice so quietly intimate but nevertheless audible aimed at our most vital inner cells, alluded to nothing about farewell. He chose to talk about Shakti and Shekhina. Where do they reside, these two essential cosmic female energy forces, these two goddesses, the Hindu Shakti and the Jewish Shekhina? That was the question he was asking. He had searched for them everywhere—he had sought them but he could not find them.

He was speaking discursively, my brother, with no plan, giving voice to his thoughts as they came into his head. He made reference to the complex rite of intense preparations for the entry of the high priest into the holy of holies of the holy temple in Jerusalem once a year on Yom Kippur day—and how the congregation was filled with such elation when he made it out, alive and in one piece, with a glowing countenance, unscathed by divine wrath. If the holy temple is where the Shekhina, the feminine aspect of God's presence, dwells on earth, Rebbie-ji asked, where then is its holy of holies? He paused, then answered his own question, using the Sanskrit word. It is inside the Shekhina's yoni, of course. It has been my burden in this life to serve as the high priest sent in to penetrate the sublimely dangerous territory of the Shekhina's yoni, her holy of holies, every day and night for the sake of carrying out tikkun, healing the holy congregation of Israel, he began by saying—but he did not utter out loud the remainder of his thought. Instead, in the most expressive of gestures, his hand moved up, opening toward his ravaged face as if to say, Behold how I have fared, there will be no rejoicing. Then he pulled his hooded blanket down over his sacred countenance, masking its lesions and sores.

No one doubted that the fire that broke out that night in the House of Holy Healing was started by a memorial candle, though many commented later that it was a miracle that such an accident had never occurred before. It was not a subject I cared to discuss, but I knew for certain that it was far from an accident. When plague broke out in the villages of India, I had once told my brother when we were children, they cremated the dead in their hovels, burning everything to the ground along with the bodies inside. I did not know if this was true, I had only read it in a book about India, I had been fixated on India from a very early age, it was the place on my inner map filled with all the starving children I could have saved with the piece of potato kugel I was leaving uneaten on my plate. But Shmelke remembered this tale, he made reference to it over the years. Lying in his bed after his darshan that night, I could envision him flinging out his arms with clear intention—even in the womb I already bore the scars from his habit of deliberately thinking and dreaming with his hands—knocking over the candles and shattering their glass.

The flames were confined to Rebbie-ji's suite, but the entire hospice filled with black smoke. The devadasis and whoever else was in the building were herded out by Manika. I could hear her calling my name frantically, but I stayed hidden in my corner curled up around my bag of shit and these pages that I had been writing every night by the light of a memorial candle, which I had grabbed instinctively, to fuel the fire. Now let the whole house burn down with us its dead inside, I prayed in my corner. I prayed for liberation, there was nothing I desired more than for my story to come to an end.

Let me go to Shmelke to die together with him as I was born with him, I told myself, but I was vanquished by my own weakness and did not venture out of my cave to cut through the smoke like a thick web and make my way to my brother's side. Instead, I lay there through the night as my bag continued to fill with the story of my life. When they found Rebbie-ji the next morning he was black and charred like a piece of wood consumed in a furnace where the martyrs are cast. Buki ben Yogli and the temple girl Devamayi were found on the floor melted together in an embrace from which they could not be prized apart. The status of the old lady on the bed in the next room remained the same, perhaps somewhat more withered and shrunken to the discerning eye, but still no final determination could be made whether she was dead or alive. The devadasis along with everyone else who had inhabited the House of Holy Healing, except Manika, had fled forever. It was a demonic place, cursed and desecrated from the days of Mother Teresa and the lepers from whom she had contracted her sainthood. It could never be cleansed.

From behind a partition I addressed my brother's Hasidim, commanding them in Rebbie-ji's name to contact the Israel government to set in motion their master's extradition. They had wanted him so badly, the Israelis, now they could have him, with our blessings. They were experienced professionals well versed in handling the ashes of dead Jews. Come and get him. Let them do with him as they saw fit. Wear gloves and a mask, I advised. Should they require some DNA for identification purposes, here it is. And I tossed over the partition a grotesque clump of my own hair that I had broken off—dry as straw, matted and twisted into ropes, gray like soot. I had considered offering them the gift of a bag of my excrement, now already prepackaged, since I had read somewhere in a magazine that hunted terrorists were traced by the DNA in their droppings deposited along their flight paths. But to avert the possibility of making a mockery of my brother's memory, I opted for my hair instead, which I had let grow out in anticipation of this very hour, when no one would need me anymore and I would be free to renounce everything, close my book of life, and set out as a sannyasini.

As a sannyasini, I was as if dead. The first person no longer was present to continue my tale, and this brought it to an end. All that remained for me now was to enact my own funeral to achieve liberation. I set out walking on the Grand Trunk Road from Kolkata to make my way on foot to Varanasi. Moksha awaited me there in the lap of Mother Ganga. My only garment was an ochre-colored robe. In my right hand I carried a single staff, a sign of my penance, for surely I had sinned in the confusion of my heart.

I ask you to forgive me.

In my left hand I carried a pot with a handle that contained a cup for water, and also my bag of excrement filling constantly, proof that

I was still alive, tethered to the nipple of the new stoma in my body by a long translucent tube passing through a slit in my robe. I had cut off all my ties to the world, detached myself from everything in this life, except my excrement. This I would carry with me in a bag in my pot every step of the way as I walked along the Grand Trunk Road. The pot also held a little bell that I would take out to ring like a leper, like an untouchable, whenever I saw someone approaching, to warn of oncoming defilement and pollution.

I intended to walk on the Grand Trunk Road alone and unaccompanied to the river of life and find enlightenment and liberation at last, but already at Howrah I could feel the breathing behind me, something grazing my heels, casting a black shadow, a stagnant pool into which I was sinking with every step. Had I been armed with the necessary discipline at that stage, I would not have turned around and congealed into a pillar of salt. Behind me walked Manika pushing the old lady in an ancient pram she must have found while rummaging in the black hole of Calcutta, left by the British when they absconded. Without a word I turned my back and continued walking as if I were alone.

If by the time I reached Varanasi the old lady had not yet coughed up the last of the scum blocking her liberation from the wheel of life, I would walk on to Lahore. If still she held on, I would continue walking to Peshawar. If she still refused to let go, I would walk onward over the Khyber Pass all the way to Kabul, the end of the road. There I would sit down in the midst of the dust and carnage, pry open her mouth, and root in the sludge to release her soul and deliver it in a long albuminous cord and set us free.

Tova Reich is the author of the novels *One Hundred Philistine Foreskins*, *My Holocaust*, *The Jewish War*, *Master of the Return*, and *Mara*. Her stories have appeared in the *Atlantic*, *Harper's*, *AGNI*, *Ploughshares*, and elsewhere. She is the recipient of the National Magazine Award for Fiction, the Edward Lewis Wallant Book Award, as well as other prizes. She lives on the fringe of Washington, DC.